A SOUTHERN ENCHANTRESS

A NOVEL

DEBORAH TRAHAN

atmosphere press

© 2023 Deborah Trahan

Published by Atmosphere Press

Cover design by Matthew Fielder

No part of this book may be reproduced without permission from the author except in brief quotations and in reviews. This is a work of fiction, and any resemblance to real places, persons, or events is entirely coincidental.

Atmospherepress.com

1

Suzanne

Gulf Coast, August 2013

Suzanne welcomes the hushed sound of stillness. The beach house nestled on the bluff in Pass Christian, Mississippi, drips in silence, the air thick and balmy. Her golden retriever, Bimini, rises from his sprawl at the foot of the king bed and starts pacing. An icicle chill rushes through her ribcage, then creeps up her spine, only to linger along her neckline. It is rare for a trapped ghost—even a wayward spirit—to reach for Suzanne at dawn. Until and unless its desperation overrides protocol.

She holds her breath, then exhales slowly for all that has passed and is still yet to come.

Papers shuffle in Max's office down the hallway. Then, as quickly as the rustling begins, it abruptly stops. Starts. Stops. Suzanne's hand glides smoothly across the silky aqua sheet, searching for her talisman, a wooden cross choker blessed by a beloved priest decades ago. Panic rises when she realizes it's missing, for Suzanne never sleeps without Madelaine's necklace tightly wound around her left hand for protection, leaving her right hand free to react.

Peering across the room's cedar flooring from the bed's edge, Suzanne keeps a firm grip on her down-filled duvet, eyeing where the choker may have landed. It wouldn't be the first time a spirit tossed a precious possession aside. Wherever the cross necklace is, it's nowhere that Suzanne can see. She soothes herself into a near-meditative state, commanding a blanket of calm to envelop her.

And listens for the unspoken plea of a trapped ghost.

Who's here?

Alert to errant spirits, Bimini, wise beyond his dog years, plants himself at the threshold of the bedroom door. He gauges Suzanne's movements and begins a low throaty growl as the white-blond hair on his neck stands at full attention.

"Max?" she calls out. Then, her voice filters into a whisper. "That you? Didn't expect you back tonight."

No response.

The bits of nightshade berries blended with your evening bourbon—are working.

Anticipating another confrontation with her stranded phantom, Suzanne eases out of bed. A twisted burst of light suddenly flashes across the four corners of the bedroom. Then another shot of radiance darts through a blinding prism that bears a floating orb of blue and purple: a signal. When an icy sensation spreads across Suzanne's shoulder blades and travels to her core center, her temples pulsate with a familiar rhythm. The high-pitched ringing in her right ear grows louder. Though the thermostat is set at sixty-six degrees, the room continues to chill as a patchouli scent, tinged in musk and May rose, slams into the room—a beguiling scent born decades ago.

Draped in Mademoiselle Chanel No. 1, Suzanne's phantom joins her. And it is no stranger.

Be still.

Suzanne whispers, "So—you again?"

Bimini barks at the specter's trail of wet footprints—then tracks the phantom's scent into the great room.

It's pointless to rush the process, so Suzanne lingers at the door to her husband's study. But when she spots an unfamiliar stack of spreadsheets piled on Max's desk and reaches to turn on a desk lamp, its single lightbulb explodes. As Suzanne jumps back from the shattered glass, her mind's eye captures the white wisp of a woman's figure, barely perceptible, dancing past her. A frosty breeze traces the swirl of the spirit's dress as it hums a sad Sinatra tune from the 1940s.

Once she enters the great room, Suzanne loses the phantom in the lingering rays of full moonlight. The remaining footprints left untouched by Bimini's paws reflect diamond-like sparkles, so piercing that Suzanne struggles to keep her eyes open.

Please, phantom. Reveal yourself.

"What do you want from me?" Suzanne asks, slowly twirling 360 degrees with her arms outstretched. Then, offering reassurance, Suzanne whispers, "Can you? Show me?"

Please tell me who you are. Sorry . . . who you were. Because I do not know you.

Bimini reacts to the pulsating energy in the room and runs circles around Suzanne, barking relentlessly.

After she releases the Bahama shutters on the front windows and opens the French doors facing the Gulf of Mexico's expanse, Suzanne entices her golden with a treat, so he'll join her atop an oversized ottoman in the middle of the room. She hugs his neck affectionately. He licks her face. Together, they drink in the ocean breeze. And wait.

Pushing past the remains of a moscato fog, Suzanne attempts to piece together last night's screaming match with Max. *How much of that nightshade did I add to your bourbon?* She remembers Calpurnia's counsel against misjudging poisonous portions and misusing incantations.

It's back.

She spies the phantom's movement in her peripheral vision. She watches it brush through the French doors as it billows in the breeze, then scatters onto the screened porch, where it dissipates.

"Might be easier to communicate if you stayed in one place," Suzanne says, stepping onto the grooved planks of the front porch. She hears the waves intensify as a pre-dawn thunderstorm approaches.

Stop chattering . . . be still. Listen. Indeed, I know this by now.

Bimini scampers to the east side of the porch and sits majestically next to a white wicker rocker that starts moving. When the rocker sets a slow rhythm, Suzanne approaches with caution. The faint outline of a woman's profile from another era appears. Suzanne memorizes this moment, grateful for the subdued background of the waning night.

Colors are bold, but fleeting. Wearing a red and white polka-dot dress, the elusive figure taps the cedar porch floor with her highly polished red pumps, humming that sad Sinatra tune. Is it "Time After Time?" A fashionable red hat sporting a black feather and white netting sits properly askew atop the ghost's head. When it turns slightly to the left and dips to meet Bimini's adoring gaze, Suzanne watches a smile deepen across the phantom's ruby-red lips. Her dark, luxurious hair cascades down her right shoulder.

Suzanne sits stone-cold still, barely daring to breathe.

"*Be very careful, dear. Our time is near.*"

The warning resounds in Suzanne's mind with an echo she cannot shake. "*Very careful, dear,*" cycles repeatedly in her mind. Careful about what—about Max? As tears stream along Suzanne's cheek, Bimini whimpers. When Suzanne reaches out, the wispy woman disappears. And a myriad of questions whisks away with the wind.

An apparition delivers a warning with no further instructions. No timetable.

Near might mean next week—or six months from now. Neither ghosts nor spirits share Suzanne's mortal agenda. Things will likely worsen long before improving. If only another enchantress—perhaps her mother, Madelaine—could offer guidance. If only Madelaine still clung to *her* life.

I know you, my dearest ghost. I know your heart. I feel your love.

An intense weakness seeps deep into Suzanne's arms, then her legs, an unavoidable consequence of sharing energy with an entity that has lived, died, and remains stranded on Earth. She stretches her tensed muscles, then sinks into the soft cushions of the white leather sofa facing the open doors to the Mississippi Sound. Unscathed by the early-morning visitor, Bimini locates his leash tossed behind one of the porch rockers, but Suzanne's asleep by the time he returns. Four hours later, compliments of the blinding light from the morning's sunrise, Suzanne awakes to Bimini's paw on her arms, still gripping his leash between his teeth.

"Need my coffee first, love," she says, caressing the dog's sweet spot under his neck.

A moscato morning fog isn't helping Suzanne gather her thoughts. As the coffee maker bleats loudly, Suzanne pours herself a mug and mulls over last night's argument with her husband before Max lost consciousness. Before Remé called 911. Before the ghost from the 1940s manifested.

"You can't play the market like a gambler, Suzy. Stop investing with emotion. Do some research, woman," Max said, shaking his head, covered in silky black curls, at Suzanne's risk-taking routines.

She remembers yelling, "Quit saying I can't handle money, Max!" Then, she recalls defending a decision to invest heavily in a pharmaceutical company whose stock plummeted within days of her purchase. "The hit's temporary. Earnings will pick up."

"Spoken like a gambler," Max said quietly. "You've lost tens of thousands of dollars because you refuse to take advice from seasoned brokers."

"I'll earn back my losses," Suzanne promised. "What do you care, anyway? It's my investment account. *Not* yours."

"Seriously? We're in this together, so the investment account *is* essentially ours. Since you rely upon me to keep funding it." Max flung back another shot of whiskey and gathered gusto for his threat. "Stop investing so recklessly. If not, I'll no longer cover the deficits."

Suzanne held her breath, uncertain of his reaction to the extra granules of nightshade. She instinctively drew back when Max lunged toward her, his face reddened, his expression contorted. In a familiar place. Again, the recipient of yet another man's pent-up anger and frustration. But this time, she was prepared, for tarot revealed what to expect. And hoodoo provided protection.

"I'm sorry, Max."

"Goddamn it, Suzanne, I work hard. You know how insane it is to develop real estate here on the Coast. Marketing devastated properties after Hurricane Katrina has been challenging," Max said, sweat pouring from his brow. "Please . . . I don't need you draining any more cash."

Suzanne remembered cocking her head slightly to the right and adding a smirk despite her apology, pushing him further.

"I'll set up a separate account for you, which I think is fair," Max continued. "And make regular deposits. For now. But the crazy investing stops." Max hit the bedroom wall with his fist. "I don't know what else to do. Either be fiscally responsible. Or return to work."

"Most of the money in that brokerage account is from my divorce settlement. Please explain why *you* get to manage it." She regrets the sound of her hollow words in the light of early Friday morning.

"Don't even start, Suzanne. Just because you've *had* money doesn't mean you can *manage* it. I'm struggling to hold onto my business, everything I've worked my whole life for, to stay profitable," he yelled.

"Whatever, Max." She wonders what he meant, since most of his recent business deals have proved highly lucrative.

"You know what? I'm sleeping in the study," he said last night, slamming the bedroom door hard enough to unsettle their wedding photos, now hanging askew along a hallway designed as a mini art gallery. Then, throwing the door open, he asked, "What's up with my upset stomach? Know anything about that, Suzy?"

Another slam of the door. Then it was finally quiet for the night.

Suzanne regrets grinding more of the green potato stalk than recommended. Regrets ignoring Calpurnia's advice to become familiar with roots before experimenting on anyone, especially her husband.

Nightshade is toxic.

Torn between adhering to her spiritual advisor's guidance and abiding by previous demands to deal swiftly and promptly with Max—now issued by more than one phantom—Suzanne sips her coffee and watches the shrimp trawlers linger near the coastline. It's a view worth killing for: this stretch of untouched sugar-white beach dotted with sea oats, palm trees, and diamond-like sparkles that skip across the Sound's placid waters.

She rests her head against a porch post and recalls how Max surprised her with this house. A wedding gift after returning from their honeymoon in Isla Mujeres, Mexico. A dream house that promised permanency. And a far cry from the tiny retro-rental supplied by Max's real estate company on Davis Avenue, where they'd first lived together in the Pass.

We were happy, weren't we?

Suzanne closes her eyes and shivers, remembering how Max reached for the small of her back. Slowly ran his forefinger along the length of her spine, into the crevice below her waist, and turned her chin toward him. And how she tilted her face, met his kiss, and explored his tongue.

If only everything else had remained in the background. *If only so much had not been asked of me.*

Bimini allows no further musings and hustles down the stairs to the white sand. They cross Beach Boulevard and walk along Pass Christian's seawall, which dates back decades, designed to protect the fishing community from the caustic water surges of hurricanes. When her retriever isn't chasing the seagulls that dip near the dunes, he makes a game of scampering up the concrete steps and back down to the sand. Strolling the coastline on this summer day perfectly cast for the area's anglers, Suzanne could extoll the wonders of living in paradise with a man she once deeply loved.

But now fears.

She considers her date with destiny—the mandate from the phantom to fulfill her legacy. Yesterday, today, and tomorrow were already foretold—charted long ago. Suzanne will manage Max until her ghost reveals further instructions. His sins of the past now have them both buried beneath secrets.

2

Max

Gulf Coast, August 2013

Nothing is ever good enough for damn Suzanne. No matter what I do.

Max slams his study door Thursday night but doesn't stop there. He slams it again. Then, he hits a wall. After grabbing his truck keys and wallet off the white-washed desktop, he turns his baseball cap backward and slips out from the side entrance of his home office. He and his leather boots clamber down the back wooden staircase of the beach house built thirty feet above the sand. When Max loses his footing on the final landing, he skids down the remaining twenty steps, his backside thudding against the railing, all the way to the crushed oyster shells at the bottom.

Max knows he doesn't trip. And he knows the surface isn't slick, for there has been no rain for days.

Daring to glare back over his right shoulder to the top of the stairs, he sees nothing. But he *knows*. An entity lingers, one that should have left Earth long ago. He has known Suzanne long enough to recognize shifts in her behavior and understand what they portend. And to identify atmospheric changes like when cold spots inexplicably flood a room on a beastly hot summer's day.

Still, Max fails to *see* beyond the surface, beyond the night's darkness. Nearly eighteen months into this relationship, he has yet to glimpse one trapped ghost or drifting spirit, though their presence has undoubtedly impacted him.

Tonight, he's convinced one of Suzanne's specters is up to some trickery. Yes, she collects them at the speed of Facebook likes. And at his expense. Because this one ain't playing friendly.

"You gotta be kidding," he yells, glaring at the stair's top landing from the gravel below. "If you knew . . . what I've gotten away with . . . you wouldn't mess with me." Max fails to grasp the concept of ghosts, for they lack consciousness and reason. And because he doesn't speak the language of the dead, there'll be no vocal response to his threats. With courage fueled by alcohol, Max adds, "Go on, now. Mission accomplished. Bring it on."

Never, ever taunt a dark ghost. Max remembers this warning, proclaimed by one of Suzanne's spiritual advisors, intent on keeping *her* safe from malevolent hauntings. Tonight, Max refuses to follow advice. Though he knows better, he cannot resist challenging the boundaries of common sense. It hadn't been long since he stumbled upon Suzanne smudging every square foot of their rented cottage in the historical district of Pass Christian: burning sage in an antique pottery dish, commanding a particularly ornery dark one to leave.

It didn't.

Yeah, and that damned ornery ghost will likely be the one to escort me to Hell.

Max isn't surprised when he hears the latch click on the French doors above him. It's either Suzanne pretending *not* to check on him or the ghost locking him out. Max pulls himself up and reaches for his keys, hanging from a palmetto palm that flanks the stairway. He hobbles to his truck parked under the house and wonders if his hip requires an x-ray. Managing to hoist himself into the front seat, Max flings his head against the steering wheel and mulls over his situation.

His financial scheme hatched upon meeting Suzanne is now in jeopardy.

When Max opened the Gulf Coast location of his New Orleans-based real estate firm in 2008, he and his partner, Remé, planned to capitalize on redevelopments after Hurricane Katrina devastated coastal Mississippi in 2005. As their plan emerged, Max required more funding than he'd imagined. Millions more. Placing his pride on a shelf, he had no difficulty blurring the financial boundaries between friends. And lovers.

Now, close friends and business associates no longer warn Max about mixing funds with Suzanne, though Remé's words still loop in his mind: "Dude, you need to protect our investments. If word gets out that your wife has access to even one of our business accounts, no matter how wealthy she is, we're finished here."

If they only knew . . . I'm so close to getting away with everything. Every. Last. Dime of it.

Max turns on the ignition and cranks up the air conditioning. He leans back against the rich black leather. After several shots of bourbon, it's hard to piece the day together. He remembers undressing Suzanne in his mind on the drive home, looking forward to a quiet dinner on the screened porch, then leading her into the master bedroom suite with a sea breeze at their backs. Maybe making it to the four-poster California king, maybe not.

Shrimp étouffée with a pile of peach cobbler for dessert. He worked on another bourbon while Suzanne stayed loyal to her moscato. When the time seemed right, Max moved his chair closer to hers, turned hers to face him, then glided his fingertips along Suzanne's inner thighs. Within seconds, her legs slid over his as she straddled him. When he grasped

Suzanne's long, wavy, highlighted auburn hair in his fist and pulled her in for a deep kiss, she whispered, "The Dow's down this week, baby. Spot me a couple of grand?"

Does this woman ever learn?

"Are you freakin' kidding me, Suzy?" he yelled, loud enough to spark a barking battle between Bimini and the Yorkie next door. When Max reared back from the table, Suzanne was thrown off-balance and landed awkwardly on the porch floor. She hesitated to move.

Bitch doesn't miss a beat.

"I'm in a bind, Max. You can cover for me. I know you can." She drew her legs together and leaned to one side, making no move to stand. When Max bent down so the two were face-to-face, Suzanne's glare met his anger. She's a fighter, always prepared to dish back as quickly as she receives.

"No," he said, pointing his finger, nearly touching her nose. "Do you hear me, Suzy? I should've said no, before, but I'm screaming *no* now."

In that unguarded moment amidst a flame of contention, Max forgot that their investment game was part of a much larger plan: a ruse—a means to an end. A solution that he envisioned and hatched, no less. Because Max cannot counter Suzanne's clairsentience and witchy ways, he weaponizes his tongue, never hesitating to charge her with reckless, irresponsible behavior. And truly believes that his derogatory words can control her.

Why can't she use her clairsentience for something productive? Like trading stocks?

Now, Max sits in his truck. Too drunk to drive. His cell vibrates. When he squints, he sees two missed calls: one from Remé, the other from his son, Jacob. He returns neither one.

How did we get here?

He recalls the New Orleans' Garden District party, where he met Suzanne. Though she caught his attention from behind, Max instantly recognized her beauty. He remembers watching her twirl around in his direction, recalls her slow-warming smile, even before noticing her low-hanging turquoise necklace dangling—inviting.

Such a dramatic contrast with his other wives, Suzanne is an intelligent, sassy, independent woman. Very different compared to Farrah, who smothered him with neediness and chattered about having babies. And Lily, who trapped him with a pregnancy. Things were good between him and Suzy for more than a year. At least that's what he thought until she got fired and allowed ghosts to take over her life.

That's when crazy moved in.

Max passes out, then jolts awake when his head hits the top of the steering wheel. His stomach burns with a churn he recognizes. And he immediately regrets the last shot of his tried-and-true bourbon, for here comes that all-too-familiar feeling. Max gets out of the truck, gagging, and struggles to the sand's edge before throwing up. Laying on his back, nestled in the sand, Max feels immediate pressure on his chest.

He fights to breathe and focuses on his foggy vision. A massive black opaque entity suspends above him and presses against his rib cage. He struggles to catch his breath. He can't fight back. When Max feels a black-blue chill begin on his forehead, race through his body, and settle into his toes, he loses feeling in his legs. Then his arms go numb.

"*You're surely damned now, lover boy*," the angry ghost hisses in his right ear. If Max could paint a picture of the sound this unearthly clatter produces, it would resemble stones and gravel crumbling over steel, filling the atmosphere.

Max weaves in and out of consciousness for nearly an hour before attempting to move his legs. At least I'm not dead, he thinks upon regaining awareness of his surroundings.

Touching his throat, he tries to swallow against the pain, believing a nasty bruise now sits there. Dripping in sweat, he sits up and reaches for his phone, hoping to illuminate the entire area beneath the house, anchored with pilings. It's dark, way past sunset. He sees no shadows—nothing to prove his encounter. Suzanne's probably the only person who might believe him since she trafficks with these sorts.

The phone rings. It's Remé.

"What?"

"Dude, you sound horrible. You down at Logan's?"

"I'm in Hell."

"More drama between you and Suzanne? How many drinks tonight?"

"Too many to count. I'm serious, bro. Some scary shit's going down." Max props himself against one of the concrete pilings. He focuses on Remé's voice. "What d'ya want?" he asks, his voice slurred.

"The property on St. Louis Street needs an inspection early tomorrow before closing. Care whom I send?"

"Don't use the idiot who works out of Long Beach. He doesn't know what he's doing."

"Got it." Remé continues: "Crash at my place tonight. It's stupid for you to stay there with Suzanne. I'm around the corner. Can be there in less than five."

"Might not be a bad plan," Max agrees.

"It *is* the plan. You can't manage another Farrah fiasco. And neither can I, Max. I've got limits, and so do you." Remé, his best friend since high school, his business partner . . . hell, his blood brother, stops before saying something he can't take back. "I can only manage one cover-up during a lifetime."

"Thanks, man."

Naturally, Remé still references Farrah: Max's *one* nightmare he'll never put behind him. Each time his friend mentions her name, Max revisits Mammoth Cave and the day his second wife tumbled from his life forever—the absolute worst day of his life.

Overcome with nausea, Max falls on all fours and vomits what's left of his guts with a vengeance, leaving him so sweaty and weak that he's immobile. He passes out in the sand before

Suzanne slowly creeps down the back staircase. Does she notice Remé getting out of his truck?

"I get a call from my partner here, drunk as a sailor, rambling about being in Hell, making no sense," Remé says. "What's going on, Suzanne?"

"Don't know what you're talking about," she counters. "I've been asleep. Just now realized Max hadn't come up to bed."

"Lame, even for you."

Remé finds Max curled up in a fetal position near the steps.

"Hey," Remé yells, racing to help his friend. He bends down and leans over. Checks to see if Max is breathing. The scent of vomit nearly overwhelms him—his appeals for Suzanne's assistance fall flat.

"Come, help me sit him up," Remé says.

Suzanne stands motionless.

When Remé reaches to find a pulse, he panics.

"Goddamn it, call 911!"

"My phone's upstairs," Suzanne says. "I'll be right back."

"Don't bother." Remé slips his phone from a shirt pocket while balancing a listless Max at his shoulder and taps three digits.

He kneels in the sand and listens to the operator's instructions for performing CPR. Then, as he starts chest compressions, he quickly turns back toward Suzanne and says, "If you've killed my best friend, I'll *fucking* destroy you. I can promise you that."

Suzanne sits on the staircase's first landing steps, shaking uncontrollably.

3

Addy (Adelaide)

Gulf Coast, Summer 1947

Adelaide Lafountain Lamar quickened her high-heeled steps along Market Street and walked toward Pass Harbor on Monday afternoon. Sunshine ricocheted from the brick building fronts in Pass Christian's downtown district, trapping a pool of heat that had no escape.

Bustling with energy and commerce, the town had oozed with the promise of new opportunities since the end of World War II. When she hustled past the temporary storefront of the Tarpon-Beacon, the coastal town's newspaper, Adelaide admired her reflection. She wondered what might be printed in the paper's daily edition now that young men had stopped enlisting in the service and women were less anxious to marry them. Death notices and engagement announcements had previously filled the paper. Would stories about debutante balls be tucked underneath updates about new businesses?

The silky black-haired beauty double-stepped past the White

Elephant, a local boarding house for transient oystermen and their families. Though old-monied residents labeled the nineteenth-century former hotel an eyesore, it served its purpose by providing housing for shuckers and fishermen anxious to trawl the Sound for shrimp and oysters. The structure held its own in the foreground of statuesque mansions perched on the bluff facing the Sound's entry to the Gulf of Mexico.

Adelaide knew better than to walk by the White Elephant with her nose in the air. Her husband, Cash, co-owned and managed the family-owned seafood cannery, Lafountain's, where most of White Elephant's residents worked. Cash's fleet now boasted twenty-plus schooners that harvested the oyster reefs buffeting the Pass's coastline. And the cannery's trawlers were legendary for catching loads of succulent brown shrimp netted farther out in the Gulf's waters.

When she reached the corner of Market and East Beach Boulevard, Adelaide glanced up at the second story of the Merchants Bank and Trust—did the windows beckon with a wink? She imagined opening her designer dress boutique right here. She'd talked about her life-long dream to anyone willing to listen and all who were tired of hearing about it. Adelaide's friends knew that when Addy—a nickname coined by her grandmother, Mimi Jeanne—set her sights on a goal, she was one step shy of achieving it.

Addy had postponed her dream while Cash fought in Northern Europe. As he co-piloted B-24s, she sketched designs during sluggish times at Madison's Boutique, a dress shop in nearby Gulfport. Then, one evening, a wealthy customer noticed Addy's sketchbook while she was kneeling to mark the woman's hemline. The next day, the woman called the shop and demanded a private booking with her. Begrudgingly, Miss Emily allowed Addy to create originals for her best patrons.

This small victory only whetted Addy's appetite for entrepreneurship: a career in designing high fashion. Addy dreamt of influential women riding the L&N train lines from New Orleans, Mobile, and even Nashville, to meet her in the Pass and be measured for an haute couture gown. She dreamt of Mardi Gras ballrooms filled with gorgeously-attired women—swirling around the dance floor, parading her designs in silks and satins, adorned with every embellishment imaginable.

I cannot wait one more minute. If Papa refuses to make good on his promise, then Cash best be ready to deliver.

"Addy, have the shrimp trawlers come back in yet? I need to get home before Eddy finishes at the harbor."

Jarred from her daydream, Addy spun around to face her friend, Marie. "I don't know, sweetie. Lost in my thoughts."

"You've missed the traffic light changing three times, honey. I only thought you might've looked over at the front dock and noticed." Marie caught up to her, balancing several shopping bags. "What exactly are you doing?" She tapped her right foot, waiting for the light to change again.

"I'm off to the pier. You caught me dreamy, that's all."

Marie's perplexed reaction to Addy's behavior failed to affect her. "I'd hoped Eddy might bring some shrimp home," Marie added. "My morning's spent volunteering at the Episcopal church. And shopping. I didn't put anything out for dinner."

Addy narrowed her eyes, cocked her head, and slowly smiled, knowing it would further annoy Marie.

"Addy, are you listening to me? If you run into my husband, tell him to bring some shrimp home."

"Of course, Marie. I'll ask if I see him." She made no move to step into the crosswalk.

"I don't understand why you keep staring at the Merchants building. Isn't that your grandfather's bank?"

"Now, Marie, you know damn well that's Papa's bank," Addy said. She opened her pocketbook to double-check that she'd tucked a few dollar bills inside to stop by the corner market on the way back. Dropping her gaze from Marie's prying eyes didn't hurt, either. "Okay, I'll admit it. I got lost in my dreams—designing my dress shop."

"You ought to concern yourself with giving Cash that baby

he so desperately wants instead of wasting your time whipping up expensive gowns for 'dem ladies up on Scenic Drive," Marie said. "It's not like you need the money, what with your family being rich and everything."

Her friend's judgmental words upended Addy's daydreams.

Why couldn't folks in this town mind their own business?

Only three people knew the truth besides Addy. And Cash wasn't one of them. Married for three years, and still, no pregnancy. Yes, the war had separated Addy and Cash for nearly two years. Family members said good things come to those who wait, or something similarly useless.

Addy ignored their aphorisms while Cash held onto every ounce of hope.

"Mind your beeswax, Marie. There'll be a baby when it's the right time," Addy fired back, ashamed for stooping to her friend's level. "I'm walking down to the fishing wharf to find Cash. I'll see you later." As Addy stomped off, Marie stooped to grab the apples and radishes that had slipped through a flimsy grocery sack and threatened to roll into the street.

Addy walked the length of the pier leading to the west wharf, avoiding several crevices that could have destroyed her heels. She made a mental note to tell Cash about the rotting planks, then waved at one of Lafountain's older shrimpers, slowly motoring back. "Did you fill your nets this morning?" she yelled.

"Yes, ma'am!"

Good. It would be a godsend if Cash came home on a Monday night in a pleasant mood. Maybe he'd be receptive to discussing the dress shop. When Addy didn't see Cash perched on his stool in his office, she ventured farther along another pier. Eddy, her husband's best friend since enlisting, saw Addy and called out to her: "Cash isn't here, babe. He's running an errand. But he wrapped a bag of shrimp for you to take home for dinner. It's in the front packing office."

"Thanks, Eddy," Addy said. "Oh, I just saw Marie up on Market. She wants shrimp tonight, too."

"Already wrapped," he answered.

Wondering how she'd missed Cash after walking through the town center, Addy grabbed her package from the bin and started home, remembering to stop at Sperier's for tomatoes, green peppers, and onions. This evening, Creole-style shrimp étouffée was on her menu because Cash loved the dish and always asked for seconds.

Having lived in Pass Christian since the summer of '44, Addy still cherished a walk through the town's streets to greet people, talk to folks, and browse unique shops. Addy glanced over her right shoulder as she opened the screen door to Sperier's—which doubled as a saloon and occasional produce market. Then thought she glimpsed her younger sister, Esty, walking back toward the harbor with Cash.

That's odd. Why's Esty with Cash? Her sister was supposed to be home in New Orleans. But when Addy did a double take, there was no sign of her husband or Esty. She shrugged, giving her over-active imagination credit for the sighting.

With a paper bag filled with vegetables, Addy headed toward their home on Davis Avenue, always excited to walk past the town's Railroad Depot, nearly filling the block between Davis and Fleutas avenues. She was no stranger to watching the L&N pull into the depot from New Orleans promptly at seven each night—she loved watching elegant women step down onto the platform to greet friends or relatives on the Coast.

Deep in her thoughts, Addy didn't notice an older woman wearing a colorful cape abruptly step from behind one of the timber columns supporting the depot's overhang. Until the woman spoke. "Hello, Bess. Your name is Bess, right?" The woman's raspy voice and fierce countenance utterly startled Addy.

"No, ma'am, you've mistaken me for someone else," Addy said, stepping back.

"I haven't," the old crone snarled. "I don't make mistakes. Not likely this time, either."

Her voice trembling, Addy said, "Well, you have. My Christian name is Adelaide." Being addressed as Bess jolted Addy back to a disquieting memory. One she still struggled to manage.

"Matters little what you're calling yourself these days, for I surely know you."

"Highly unlikely since I don't recognize you, old woman," Addy countered.

"Oh, I know you, miss. And . . . I *know* what you've done."

Addy's heartbeat pounded against her chest. Despite her attempts to swallow her fear, Addy's throat tightened. Less than a handful of folks knew what Addy had sacrificed.

Bristling at the woman's charge, Addy stood firm and said, "I've no idea what you're talking about." Then, she reconsidered her rudeness. "But, if you're in trouble, my grandfather, Mr. James Lafountain, is president of Merchants Bank. The one at the corner of Market and East Beach Boulevard. Say that Addy sent you."

"No need, miss. I'm not the *one* to suffer," the woman said. "Hear my words clear. I bring a warning. Plenty trouble coming your way."

"I'm sure you've mistaken me for someone else." Addy stood firmly, despite the woman's stony glare. Addy knew an old crone when she saw one.

"Look over your back, dearie. Others are watching."

"You've made your point," Addy said. She turned from the depot and toward home. "Do not follow me. *Never* approach me again."

Then she heard, "He doesn't know, does he?"

When Addy whirled around, expecting a confrontation, the busybody with weathered skin and tattered clothing had disappeared. In her place, the backside of a well-dressed man in a dark blue suit appeared from nowhere. The figure turned slightly and tipped his fedora as if to say, *I'll handle this.*

Addy hurried to their salmon-colored stucco cottage on Davis Avenue, looking forward to starting dinner to help calm her nerves. There was no reason to alert Papa. She already knew the witchy woman wouldn't approach the bank. Even if that happened, her visage wouldn't be visible to others.

The scent of sautéed vegetables and shrimp soon filled the cottage.

"Smells great, baby," Cash yelled when he opened the front door, leaving his smelly work boots by the garden's gate. He grabbed Addy tightly around her waist and hugged her while she flipped the vegetables in a pan sizzling with olive oil. "Thanks for making my favorite." He kissed the sweet spot on her neck and told her how wonderful she smelled.

Once seated for dinner, Cash lifted his plate and asked for seconds, then thirds. Addy kept a cold Jax coming, one after another, before broaching a conversation that should have been tabled.

"Cash, Marie asked me today why I'm not pregnant yet. Why would she do that?"

"I've no idea." Cash pushed his chair back from the table, feigning ignorance. But Addy didn't buy it. Cash looked down, refusing to meet her eyes.

"Do you and Eddy talk about me *not* getting pregnant?" she pressed. "Simple question, Cash." Though she knew better than to stoke this flame, she couldn't stop herself.

"I might have asked him a couple of questions, Addy." Cash scooped the roux off the plate with his last piece of French bread, picked up his dishes, and carried them to the sink.

"Great. So now everyone in Pass Christian knows how disappointed you are? Since you're not a daddy yet?"

"No, woman." He whirled around to face her. "Eddy's my best friend. We talk. I've been thinking it's me . . . like maybe something happened in Germany that's keeping me from getting you pregnant."

Addy's heart sank. She'd never considered that Cash would harbor any responsibility for them not conceiving. "You can talk to me," she whispered.

"Don't feel like I can, baby doll, not about this." Cash stacked the plates on the sideboard. Then, when ready to speak, he crossed his arms and turned to face her. "It doesn't make sense—seems like we make love enough times, 'least since I've been back, for you to turn up pregnant."

"So, it's my fault." Addy immediately regretted igniting the conversation. She had wanted to discuss leasing space for her dress business, not revisit this mess. Addy despised everyone's noses ending up in everyone else's business in this tiny town.

Times like this, I miss the anonymous hustle of New Orleans.

"That's not what I said, Addy." Cash lowered his head. "Do you think this has anything to do with what happened *before* I left for Germany?" He sat beside her, sipped his beer, and reached for her hand. "Like you'd been hurt, you know, when—" Cash left his sentence to extinguish itself.

Her fingertips barely brushed his. "I said I'd never talk about what happened that night, so I'm not going to start now." She gazed through the small window over the kitchen sink and willed her husband's interrogation to end. "I'll get pregnant when it's the right time for us to have a baby."

Cash sighed as he rubbed a small scar on his right cheekbone. "I'm gonna stretch out in the living room." But before he left the kitchen, Cash said, "The next time you have a doctor's appointment, Addy, I'm coming with you."

"No, you're not. Only Mimi comes to my doctor's appointments. That's been my routine since the summer of '44, and it's not changing."

"That's not right, babe. Not right at all."

She thought of the miniature calendar neatly tucked in the drawer of her bedside table, where she charted her monthly cycle. Addy knew the dangerous days and circled them in red. She smiled, thinking of her hidden diaphragm case, tucked away with a small tube of spermicide at the back of the bottom right drawer in their pink-tiled bathroom—her secret weapon.

After washing and drying the dishes, Addy sat at the Formica tabletop and reached for her sketch pad and charcoal pencil. Her pencil hovered over the flowing lines of an evening gown. Addy paused and carefully considered her next stroke. Then she smiled when her fingers scooped up the African amethyst bracelet from her apron's front pocket, which Mimi had given her on her wedding day. She remembered her grandmother describing the protective powers of amethyst—a precious family heirloom passed through generations of Lafountain enchantresses who knew the power of crystals and words of incantations.

She clasped the bracelet in her left palm as she sketched with her right hand, wishing she'd worn it earlier. Maybe the old crone would have left her alone.

When Cash appeared at the kitchen's entrance, she jumped when he yelled, "Explain this!"

Startled, Addy dropped her bracelet and charcoal pencil onto the black and white linoleum floor. Cash dangled the treasured bracelet he'd scooped off the floor in one hand and the diaphragm case he'd found in the bathroom—in the other.

Widening her deep violet eyes, Addy struggled to feign innocence. "The diaphragm? Or my bracelet?"

4

Suzanne

New Orleans, Winter 2011

Scheduled to sign her final divorce documents, Suzanne rushes to arrive at her attorney's office building before the doors automatically lock. Despite running behind schedule, she carved out a few minutes to steady the nerves of a senior student-athlete as she exited the school's main entrance. He's desperate to pass English this semester and begged for an extra holiday assignment to make his request a reality.

Suzanne obliged. After all, it is Christmas.

Once seated in the law firm's conference room, Suzanne reviews the instructions listed by a paralegal who left early to pick up her child. Then, considers the finality of her role as Mrs. Nottingham. Slowly, her gaze follows a wall overly decorated with antebellum plantation paintings, an uncomfortable nod to Louisiana's deplorable history of sugar planters enslaving others for their benefit and profit. Silently she recounts the leatherbound Louisiana Civil Codes lining the bookshelves—a self-calming habit she adopted as a child when uninvited spirits visited her at night and held her hostage with fear and unease until dawn.

Once she signs her name on the thin black lines peppered throughout the multi-page document, her divorce papers will be judicially filed, with an anticipated judgment issued in roughly thirty days.

Then, freedom from navigating Mr. Carson Nottingham's daily minefields. That endless exercise of sorting fact from fiction to determine which claims are fabricated and which may be trusted as truth. Yes, free of his belittling nature and odd obsession with taunting her clairsentient nature, a desirous trait others could only covet.

Suzanne reads the directives and follows the neon-blazed Post-it notes that dot the divorce lawsuit: Nottingham vs Nottingham. Picking up a weighty Mont Blanc, she signs away her former life. Then she discovers a last-minute addendum that relinquishes their house without a fight. Carson's gesture signifies everything, for he no longer cares.

At last, Suzanne takes a deep breath and scribbles her name at the bottom of the final page. She glances at her soon-to-be-ex's ostentatious signature at left and thinks of John Hancock's mark upon the Declaration of Independence. Suzanne shakes her head. Yes, she allowed it to happen, so she has no one to blame but herself. Nearly her whole adult life centered on her man, from their humble law school beginnings to their filthy-rich bitter end.

She places the pen on the table, ignoring the paralegal's note to accept it as a parting gift. Then, when the conference room lights begin to dim automatically, Suzanne leans back in her chair and closes her bright violet eyes. She allows relief to flood inward, linger, then scurry away like the ebb and flow of a morning's first tide.

A fast-forwarded video summarizing her relationship with Carson splashes across her mind in reverse order: the e-mail she received a year ago revealing his most recent infidelity;

that extended anniversary/guilt trip to Paris; a failed sailing hobby; the moment she stumbled upon his second affair; the twins' miraculous birth; the original home they built; that first heartbreaking moment she realized he'd been unfaithful. *For the first time.*

Suzanne exhales, glances around, and wonders where the liquor decanters are hidden, because she could surely use a stiff drink. Remembering these momentous events is one thing, but dredging up her ex's often public scenes ridiculing her conversations with spirits and encounters with specters is entirely different. Shoving the condescension deep down, setting his mimicry aside, Suzanne will not miss Mr. Nottingham's emotional abuse.

Before pushing her chair back from the table, Suzanne adjusts her posture and arranges her loose hair into a messy bun with an elastic band. She removes her wedding ring and tosses it into her handbag. Well, then, that's done with, she thinks.

It's going to take nothing short of a miracle for me to slip another one of those on my ring finger.

Suzanne follows the law office's maze of a hallway back to the entrance, pleased with being trusted as the last person to leave for the night. She's grateful for signing her papers privately, without the annoyance of nervous chitchat offered by a lingering office employee. But as she makes the last turn in the hallway nearest the exit, Suzanne senses a sudden shift in the area's energy. Her temples pound as the dimmed hallway lights suddenly glow brightly, and the temperature drops dramatically within seconds. Pausing for a moment, Suzanne stands still and waits.

"I'm not going to pretend that this isn't the worst time for you to appear. Whomever you are," Suzanne says, more annoyed than anything regarding an interruption in her evening. Suzanne can often dismiss a spirit along its way when she's forceful, steadfast, and confident if there's little urgency in its bidding.

But today is not that day, because she's bruised. And fragile. And vulnerable to a spirit breaking through her consciousness and delivering a demand.

Suzanne counts one, two, three . . . fifty-nine, sixty.

When she senses the surrounding forcefield dissipate, Suzanne walks to the entryway, closes the door, and steps into December's dense fog. She welcomes the symmetry of the mist as she enters the unknown. But when shadows beyond the thickening night vapors threaten to step forward, Suzanne flinches as a waft of a balsamic woody scent crosses her path. It is a haunting scent she's unprepared to confront.

Suzanne slowly exits the parking lot after her texts to twins Kyle and Beau go ignored. When her cell phone rings, it's Margie.

"Time to celebrate, honey," Margie says. "Meet at Wallaby's?"

"I'm on my way. Anyone else joining us?"

"Just the two of us," she answers. Wallaby's neighborhood pub in Mid-City had served as the women's favorite watering hole over the years, their headquarters for surviving life's passages.

Then Franny, Suzanne's spiritual advisor, phones.

"Where you at? Girl, you missed your tarot reading this afternoon."

"Join us," Suzanne suggests after apologizing for skipping their appointment. "You know the spot." Since Margie, her dearest friend, accepts Suzanne's reliance upon the tarot, there should be no discomfort with Franny joining them. Anyone acquainted with Madelaine remembers the enchantress never made a decision of merit without reaching for her favorite deck of Aquarian cards. Though less dependent on divination, Suzanne cannot resist a tarot reading.

When she enters Wallaby's, Suzanne waves to Margie, seated at an unnecessarily large cedar table near the bar where Franny's already holding court.

"What's going on? When did you two decide to get a head start?" Suzanne laughs, slipping into a chair between the two women. She appreciates Franny's restraint this time, for it appears her spiritual guide has yet to spread an audacious card arc across the table, designed to impress and intimidate.

"We knew you'd be ready to celebrate, so we ordered your favorite bottle of wine," Margie says, hugging Suzanne tightly. "It's on its way."

"Thanks."

"Was it painless?" Margie asks. "Or shouldn't I ask?"

A predictable question that suggests no easy answer. Suzanne considers before answering. "I felt sad when I flipped to the page about the house. I wasn't expecting that. But there's no way to predict what ten or twenty years will reveal about anyone. Even your spouse." She nods to the waitress waiting to pour the first glass of wine, and half-heartedly smiles, adding, "In the end, one wins our nearly-empty house, and the other never returns."

"But you can get over that real quick, honey," Margie says. "I'm assuming you received one *helluva* settlement. So that should remove a bit of the sting."

Wine glasses clink. Laughter rises and plummets until an awkward silence threatens a tremor in Suzanne's throat. "Time to reset and begin again," Suzanne whispers.

After Margie says goodnight, Franny suggests slipping into one of the booths in the back. She pushes her Bloody Mary aside before unwinding a black satin ribbon, holding the cards together. Franny grasps Suzanne's forearm and stares intently into her friend's now-darkened violet eyes. "You may fool Margie, lovey, but not me."

"I'm doing the best I can," Suzanne snaps back, pulling away from Franny's grip.

"Stop pushing your pain down so deep, Suzanne."

"What choice do I have?" Franny holds her breath and watches Suzanne move her wine glass in circles until a spill threatens. With her right hand, the one yet to unleash its energy. "I've got to be strong for the twins."

"It wouldn't kill them to see you're emotionally wounded." Franny hands the deck to Suzanne, reminding her to clasp the cards with both hands and meditate for a few moments. "Do you want to open the reading with a scripture verse? Something in Psalms?"

Though they're tucked in the back of Wallaby's, Suzanne glances around to see if she recognizes anyone. It's going to take a while for her to adjust. It seems Mr. Nottingham had spies in all sorts of places.

"Good Lord, no, let's get to it."

Franny nods and cuts the deck, shuffling several times before splitting the cards into three separate piles. "Transfer your energy, Suzanne. Envision your intentions. Inhale, exhale. And again." She sips her drink and waits for Suzanne to calm her spirit. "Identify your intention."

"It's simple. What's next?" Suzanne asks.

"We're set for a three-card spread . . . okay?"

"No, something different." Suzanne's confident response draws a smile from Franny. "I easily handle past, present, and future readings—myself. How about the pentagram?"

"How appropriate."

Franny gathers the cards and reshuffles the deck. Then places the top card face-up, slightly to the left, revealing the Page of Cups. The card displays a self-assured court page, holding a golden cup in one hand while stacks of thick books lay at his feet.

"You're ready to move forward. Build new experiences."

Suzanne nods and leans in.

Then Franny draws a second card and places it to the far right, leaving space for a pentagram shape to form: this one, Justice.

"If I were empowered to summon the ultimate two cards for you, both would be appropriate. Understand, my friend. It won't be long before your soul seeks justice."

Suzanne frowns and sips her wine slowly. "I'm confused. Isn't my divorce settlement sufficient justice?"

Franny motions for their waitress to bring another round. She grabs hold of the protection medallion hanging close to her heart, one of her many amulets loosely arranged around her neck, and stares directly into Suzanne's eyes. "Please hear me when I say this card does *not* refer to the past, love. Instead, it reveals what's to come. Remember your intention?"

Suzanne places her right index finger on the rim of her glass when their waitress opens another bottle of wine. "No thanks, I've got one last midterm to administer early tomorrow morning."

"The Empress," Franny announces, positioning the third card at the bottom left. "So relieved to see her." She nudges a clean wine glass toward the waitress, happy to accept hers and Suzanne's portion.

How is there another court card?

"Hmmm," Suzanne says. "But the card's reversed. Should I worry?"

"Absolutely not. The Empress, upright, represents femininity and all its strengths. Reversed, she prods you to face what you're neglecting: your true nature, your destiny. This card encourages a re-focus on your empowerment. Own your gifts."

Specifically, which gifts are referenced here? Yes, I'll read tarot and work with crystals. And I've no choice but to speak with spirits. But I'm not Madelaine—under no circumstance will I embrace hoodoo, or any form of spellcasting, in my life again.

Franny draws in her breath quickly, then hesitates to speak.

"Don't hold back now, Franny. Speak," Suzanne says, changing her mind as she reaches for the wine bottle. She estimates half a glass and slowly pours the wine.

"There is another way of interpreting the Empress, reversed. But it's related to unresolved mother issues."

"Well, now that makes more sense than anything else you've mentioned tonight. This is no revelation. I know it; I've lived it. And as you know, Madelaine died before we could resolve one solitary dispute." Suzanne considers gathering her things and leaving the pub. After a day of administering midterms and signing her divorce papers, revisiting lifelong conflicts with her mother is not on her evening's agenda.

Franny waits while Suzanne drinks her wine and calms her spirit. Pressing too soon means the reading ends. And guidance from the cards will filter away, unheard and unheeded.

"Always return to the focus of the reading—the pentagram provides protection and offers knowledge," Franny whispers. "Until you resolve the years of disenchantment with your mother, everything else will remain off-center."

"She's dead, Franny. Not to point out the obvious . . ."

"Then let's address the elephant in the room. If you feel distressed . . . out of sorts . . . unsettled beyond what the divorce is dredging up, it's likely that Madelaine's ghost is tormented, too."

"Let me stop you right there." Surprisingly, Suzanne's wine glass doesn't shatter when she slams it on the polished cedar tabletop. "You believe that Madelaine's spirit has yet to cross over? It's been three years, Franny. Her car crash was in 2008."

Still holding the fourth card, poised to place it within the pentagram outline, Franny stares directly into Suzanne's eyes and says, "Don't look shocked. Neither ghosts nor spirits adhere to a human's timeline. You know better than anyone, love. It's way past time to loosen those protective tentacles that you've wrapped tightly around your heart—regarding Madelaine's death. Because I can guarantee *her* spirit remains loose. Be prepared to meet her energy."

"I'm— I'm really unwilling to accept," Suzanne begins.

"You've little choice in the matter, love," Franny interrupts.

". . . her spirit laying low. Because, dammit . . . I needed her formula for dealing with Carson."

"Where's proof that her spirit *didn't* do just that?"

As Franny flips the fourth card, she hums a Creole praise song that sounds strangely like an old church hymn. Then, revealing the King of Cups, Franny slowly slides the card to the lower right corner. "You'll drift to a dark place if you disregard . . . well, upcoming pleas for help." Then she ceremoniously places the fifth and final card at the pinnacle of the pentagram—the Hanged Man.

Suzanne stares at the card revealing a man hanging upside down from a tree limb, one leg positioned with a foot resting at the other leg's knee, ignoring Franny's take on the King of Cups.

"The Hangman transcends Earth. And the Earth's essences. You'll love again intensely but reach a point of intolerance." As an intuitive, Franny expands her interpretation. "Tough, tough days ahead, Suzanne. You'll need to protect your soul. Promise me you'll stay alert."

Suzanne lightly taps the side of the wineglass. She stares at the pentagram portending her future. Then attempts to pinpoint the specific card that concerns her the most.

Franny leans back and reaches for a final sip of wine. "*All* five cards are Major Arcana. I must be honest. I'm intimidated. I'm supposed to guide you, but these cards reflect energies beyond my pay grade. You've likely ascended to a spiritually higher sphere than me."

"I feel somewhat afloat," Suzanne says, "as though I'm entering unchartered waters." She glances at her phone and realizes hours have passed without hearing from Beau or Kyle. "I need to get home, Franny. Thank you, as always. I don't know what I'd do without you." She rushes to gather her keys and handbag, then stands to slip on her overcoat.

Franny immediately digs into her hobo bag and locates what she's searching for. "Before you go," she says. She stands and presses a medium-sized, super-smooth stone into Suzanne's left palm, then folds her friend's fingers to cover it.

"What's this?"

"Don't pretend you don't know the stone: black obsidian holds protective energies. Carry it, Suzanne. Never be without its security."

On the drive to her home in Lakeview, Suzanne stretches across the car's console to reach into her handbag with her right hand, jerking the steering wheel wildly to the right. When she corrects this move, the car's wheelbase overreacts and swerves, thrusting Suzanne's SUV into the direct pathway of an oncoming pick-up truck. Suzanne glares into its headlights with an intensity never previously summoned. A split second later, her SUV lands on the rocky-pebbled shoulder, off the road, six feet from the right lane.

Yet there's no sense of relief for removing herself from harm's way. On the contrary, as Suzanne's heart beats wildly and sweat gathers at the nape of her neck, she cannot take credit for avoiding a head-on collision. She realizes this has little to do with her and everything to do with Madelaine's stranded spirit, which assumes no time has passed and death has not occurred.

The unmistakable voice of Madelaine's spirit whispers in her left ear: "*Careful, daughter. I won't always protect you.*" Words weighty with advice and threaded with a threat. After three years of silence, an unspoken warning about an impending cataclysm.

Her foot never touches the accelerator. Nor the brake. Her palm never releases the smooth black stone within its grasp. Her right hand still holds a firm grasp on the steering wheel.

Unmistakably, Suzanne's life is spared. *This time.*

5

Max

New Orleans, Spring 2012

Annoyed at his lack of planning, Max slams the door of his convertible BMW and takes the stone steps to his Faubourg Marigny home in New Orleans, two at a time. As he races to unlock the front door to search for his cell phone, Max concedes to missing the moment of surprise at Remé's fiftieth birthday bash.

He doesn't care that Margie, Remé's wife, will be slow to forgive his tardiness. Max has yet another smart-ass retort ready for her: *My next commission, woman, is one phone call away.* But the real reason Max needs his phone begins with an M and ends with an N.

After Max finds the phone tucked in his leather satchel, he takes a minute to respond to a couple of texts. None of them are from Maureen. Finally, he slips back into his car and whips away from the curb. In seconds, Max shifts into third gear, for navigating the potholes of Orleans Parish's streets nearly requires the reactionary skills of a racecar driver. Lost in thought, he plots several ways to negotiate rental space for a client interested in opening a gallery along Magazine Street, where rental space is at a premium and sticker shock is a harsh reality. When he cranks up Steve Tyler belting "Dude Looks Like a Lady," he recalls seeing Aerosmith in concert with Maureen. His original date bailed at the last minute, and Maureen agreed to go with him at less than an hour's notice.

Max checks his phone. Again. No word from his girl Friday. No response from his client, either. Tonight's a first for Max, going solo to his business partner's birthday bash without a gorgeous woman by his side. And a rarity for Maureen to be unavailable as his plus-one.

She's everything to Max, everything but his wife. The arrangement works well for them.

Maureen bloody knows too much. *If I married her, I might have to kill her. And I like her too much to do that.*

Max parks along St. Charles Avenue in the city's Garden District. Once in the house, he snakes his way through a small crowd of friends still gathered in the home's foyer and heads for the tropical backyard to find Remé.

When Max steps onto the lush lawn, he immediately spies a petite woman from behind, sporting a rich bronze tan and long auburn hair that shimmers under the radiance of a nearby gazebo. She wears a sundress the color of Kentucky bluegrass.

He watches as a group of women encircles her, reacting to something she says. They laugh together at a shared secret he'd bet no man could ever understand. Max doesn't notice when Margie walks up with a glass of bourbon, neat. But he's listening when Margie whispers, "She's available, Max. The ink's barely dry on that gorgeous woman's divorce papers."

"Who is she?" Max asks. He turns to greet Margie, kisses her cheek, and thanks her for his drink.

"You're not serious, are you? That's Suzanne Nottingham. We've been friends for years."

"Then why haven't I met her?" Max asks.

"Well, maybe because she's been a married woman. Until

now," Margie says. "Just the sweetest gal ever. Want an introduction?"

At that moment, Suzanne steps back from her friends. When she turns toward the house, she spots Margie first and waves. Then she meets Max's eyes. He returns her smile with an impish grin.

"I got this," he tells Margie. "But thanks."

Walking quickly to intercept Suzanne's path, Max delivers the lamest pick-up line imaginable. "May I refresh your drink?" He cringes at the sound of his hurried offer.

What the hell is wrong with me? Am I effing twenty-two again?

Amused, Suzanne says, "At least your grammar's correct."

Max looks puzzled.

"May I? Instead of *can I*," Suzanne explains. "I know. It's a small detail for most people. But for an English teacher, a man who speaks well, using correct grammar, is damn sexy."

"I'll keep that in mind. So, about your drink?"

"I'll walk with you. You know, it's the funniest thing, but Margie's bartender looks so familiar to me."

"Okay," he says, taken aback, unaccustomed to falling shy of capturing a woman's full-on attention right off the bat. After all, he's Max Martin, by name—real estate broker with million-dollar listings, by trade.

Seriously? Blow me off to check out the bartender?

"A friend?" Max asks. When he feels his face turn beet-red, Max steps back. Rather than risk her lackluster response getting the best of him, he waits.

Suzanne notes his awkward movement but doesn't attach any significance to it, pausing with Max for a second. "It's no big deal. I think he's a former student, so I want to say hello. Then, if you want, you may freshen my drink . . . " Suzanne smiles and winks, wrapping her fingers around Max's right bicep. "By the way, I'm Suzanne," she whispers.

An electric bolt of desire sizzles through Max's body as she continues to flirt. When Suzanne places her palm on his chest, Max smells her intoxicating perfume that mixes patchouli and jasmine with a vanilla scent he can nearly taste. Expensive—and oddly familiar.

"I'm Max. And the pleasure is all mine." He grabs Suzanne's hand to keep it close.

Remé intercepts his friend with a handshake and a slap on the back: He has been rescuing Max from himself for a lifetime.

"Good to see you, man. How'd you sidestep Margie's foyer surprise?" he asks. "Didn't we leave Magazine Street about the same time? What happened?"

"That artist, who wants the loft and storefront frontage, says she won't pay any more than $100 a square foot," Max explains.

"She's dreaming. Put Maureen on it. She'll get the gritty negotiations started." Remé turns to Suzanne, kissing both of her cheeks. "Glad you could make it, babe," he says.

"You know Margie would've dragged me from Lakeview if I failed to come alone," Suzanne laughs. "I'm mingling more these days." Remé nods, ignoring Max standing beside him, waiting to join the conversation.

"Honey, I was sick to hear about your divorce being final," Remé says, sipping his vodka tonic.

Max is in unfamiliar territory, standing awkwardly close to a personal conversation. But he listens closely, attempting to connect bits and pieces of information. Shouldn't they have met in his twenty-odd years of partnering with Remé on real estate projects? While waiting for an opportunity to steal Suzanne away, Max admires an endless parade of luscious women effortlessly floating throughout the garden. He reaches the bottom of his glass before Remé acknowledges him again.

"Enjoy the party, you two. Drink up. I need to find Margie," Remé says, patting Max's shoulder before walking away.

Determined that nothing else interrupts the focus of his

desire, Max asks, "Another drink?"

When they step onto a white wooden gazebo festively decorated with hundreds of twinkling lights, Max imagines running his fingertips along Suzanne's waistline, drawing her closer to kiss the back of her neck, getting lost in her thick hair glistening with copper tones. He refrains. As an overwhelmingly rich vanilla scent snaps him from his fantasy, Max hears Suzanne address the bartender by his name: Jack. And the dude looks nothing like a former student.

"Your drink preference, sir?"

"Sorry, yes. Bourbon, neat."

"Moscato, please." Suzanne adds, "And add one ice cube, Jack—if you don't mind, love." Max's right eyebrow raises. Suzanne explains: "My first glass was warm . . . either insufficiently chilled, or maybe it's just too damn hot out here."

"Right, good to know. Add ice. If things heat up." Max smiles.

They find a bench underneath jasmine vines to sit and watch the stream of guests arriving. Max waves at two friends who are kind enough to say, "Hey," and keep walking.

"Who are those people over there, directly across from us? Max, seriously, are they pointing this way?" She leans into him, so they're sitting shoulder-to-shoulder.

"Oh, that's Remé's brother. And the broad with him, for the record, is not his wife. She's his latest squeeze—and not the brightest of the bunch," he says, clearing his throat.

"Awe, there's always one in every family," Suzanne says, turning her head in the opposite direction. But not before Max catches her eyes rolling.

Laughing, he asks, "What do you mean by that . . . eye thing you just did?"

"It's just . . . well, I know women who've been there. In that position." Suzanne absently swirls her wine glass. "Sometimes, it's best to know the situation before commenting."

Damn, I've stepped in some shit now.

Margie hadn't mentioned the reasons for Suzanne's divorce, had she? Did her husband have an affair? Did Suzanne?

I'm working from ground zero here.

Inching to close the conversational gap, Max says, "I'm sorry. Was that you? Your ex had another woman?"

"Oh, no. No, that wasn't me."

"Then what happened?" Max presses to hear Suzanne's story.

"Nothing happened. And that's the whole of it. Things were great early on—but isn't that always the story? We eroded once the twins hit high school," Suzanne says, still avoiding eye contact. "His career is demanding. So is mine. We found ourselves only hanging out together at the boys' sporting events. After a while, we no longer recognized each other. So, we ended it."

Max doesn't speak for a few minutes. Finally, he reaches for her hand but holds back, deciding to press for more information instead. "Sounds dangerously civilized. So nobody had an affair?"

"No. Other issues break up marriages, Max." Her voice trails off. "Too much drinking, disrespect, hateful behavior . . ." Suzanne stares into the depth of her wine glass as though it holds life advice.

"I'm sorry that happened to you," Max says. But he doesn't buy the story that Suzanne's spinning. In Max's world, someone always cheats.

You're one talented liar, woman. I'll give you that.

"Then the twins head to college in a few weeks . . ."

Hold on. Wait one bloody minute. The twins? Jesus, of course, she's got—kids. Max agonizes over this new information and nervously searches for a server to freshen his drink. Suzanne keeps talking. ". . . staying together is pointless when you're no longer in love with each other." Max nods his head.

When he finally spots a fellow with an empty tray, Max raises his glass and mouths *whiskey*. By now, he neither cares about his drink's quality nor how it's served: He needs the freaking drink because Suzanne is *still* chattering. "About a year ago," she says, "we returned from an overseas trip with three other couples and agreed we'd vacationed as friends, not lovers."

This definitive statement, he hopes, concludes her story.

Max covers an aborted chortle with a pretentious cough. Considering the unrelenting chaos of his former marriage to Farrah, traveling with a wife who morphed into a best friend sounds more like manna from Heaven than emotional torture.

"Don't know what to say, Suzanne. Except that I know next-to-nothing about kid-raising things." When her head tilts slightly downward, Suzanne appears lost in her thoughts. There's no time like the present to reassure this beauty that he thinks she is lovely. Kids or no kids.

"No more talk about the terrors of an ex-spouse," Suzanne adds, looking up to meet Max's gaze. Her deep violet eyes, reflecting a sparkle from the gazebo's lights, invite Max to move closer. He leans in and softly kisses Suzanne's lips, tasting the sweet moscato lingering at the tip of her tongue. "Love your bourbon-whiskey vibe," Suzanne whispers, gently stroking his face with one finger. As her manicured forefinger outlines the contour of his lips, Max takes full advantage of Suzanne's invitation. He presses her lips harder and finds her tongue. When Suzanne uncrosses her legs, shifts her weight, and pulls Max closer, he barely believes the heat that arises within seconds.

Finally pulling back, Max says, "Jesus, woman."

As Suzanne adjusts her posture and straightens her sundress, she notices guests staring at them. "Good Lord, we've drawn a crowd. Max, I really should go."

Holding hands, they walk back through the house to say good night to Remé and Margie. Struggling with unexpected crazy desires, neither one dares to speak. Max feels his phone's vibration in his pocket, yet knows it's the worst time to pick up a call from Maureen.

"Can I walk you to your car?"

"Not necessary. I'm three doors down."

Max lightly kisses Suzanne's forehead and is grateful for no further chatter. "I'll call you soon, Suzy," he says, watching her stroll along a sidewalk lined with live oaks. Despite sharing a pleasant evening, Max feels edgy as he watches the headlights of her black SUV blink twice. When Suzanne turns to wave, Max senses a dark shadow swiftly waft over him, then drift in Suzanne's direction.

If ever queried about a paranormal encounter, Max would surely deny any knowledge or experience with clairsentience, having shown no sensitivity to spirits, either dark or benevolent. Up until this very moment. Yet, Max has no way of gauging the perfect storm that awaits him if he pursues a relationship with this copper-haired beauty, for the ghost energy that continuously swills around Suzanne will eventually impact Max, too.

There's a saying in the spirit world about cavalier people like Max—he'll never see a ghost unless and until the ghost is gunning for him.

Later that night, as he drifts off to sleep, he'll remember the moon slipping behind a darkened cloud when they kissed, as an inexplicable chill brushed against his right cheek.

Yes, a familiar sensation, now in harsh contrast to the freshness of Suzanne's scorching, fiery touch.

6

Addy

Gulf Coast, Summer 1944

By May's end, Addy and her younger sisters began counting down the days until they could trade a New Orleans sultry summer for three frivolous months in Pass Christian, Mississippi, visiting Mimi and Papa. Wealthy New Orleanian families had established the custom of absconding to the Coast more than 100 years ago, so there was no reason to temper tradition.

Anxious for her spring semester at Newcomb College to end, Addy had less than a year before earning a fine arts degree. She dreamt of establishing herself as *the* haute couture designer of the Deep South. She'd have been thrilled with any position that kept her from a desk job at one of Papa's banks, south of the Mason-Dixon line.

Paradise awaited the Lafountain sisters just an hour's drive from New Orleans. Weeks and weeks to sail the Sound and venture beyond the barrier islands, where the emerald-green waters of the Gulf of Mexico beckoned. Time for soirées and teas, hosted in stately homes along the shoreline. And opportunities to meet and flirt with airmen stationed at Keesler's

Army Air Force base in Biloxi. These co-pilots and crew members in training were delighted to oblige the desires of wealthy ingenues before deploying to the other side of the world to fight for their freedom.

Charlotte Lafountain finished loading the family's 1944 Ford Wagon, parked in the driveway of a two-story white house on State Street Drive in Uptown. "Girls, last call for suitcases—time to go," she yelled, shutting the two wooden panels at the wagon's backside, leaving the top window ajar for ventilation. "No telling how far the old wooden Bay Bridge will be backed up. And I've made plans for the evening," Charlotte muttered. "It *is* Friday, after all." The sisters climbed into the back of the station wagon, each avoiding the seat next to their mother. Mama Charlotte fiercely hounded any daughter sitting in the front passenger seat about social propriety when visiting family.

Thank you, Mother, dear, for reminding us. Again. Of our imposition upon your social engagements.

Addy's wavy black locks blew wildly during the drive, distracting Esty's plan to reread several chapters of Carolyn Keene's *The Mystery at Lilac Inn* before reaching the Louisiana/Mississippi state line. And ignored Esty's pleas to bind her hair into a ponytail. Both teens tuned out Macie's bickering with their mother. Addy's imagination drifted to a fictional stroll down the center aisle of St. Paul's Catholic Church in the Pass after exchanging vows with her dreamboat husband. There were days when she struggled to discern the difference between her visions and daydreams: Some days, both merged into one realistic movie reel.

Often, Addy's foresight aligned with reality. Lately, her visions hinted at her connecting with an AAF officer, and portended an encounter with designing ball gowns—a rather prescriptive order for wartime, but one Addy felt entirely plausible.

Since Addy attended a females-only college in New Orleans, her social life was limited to dating the sons of her parents' friends: vetted and stamped with approval. Rebelling against this archaic custom was her first plan on the summer's agenda. Thousands of service guys were conveniently stationed at Keesler, so she'd already set her sights on meeting an officer.

As if reading Addy's mind, Macie, her youngest sister, blurted out, "Addy's falling in love this summer, Mama. Did you know?"

Looking in the rearview mirror, Charlotte glared first at Macie. Then, Addy.

"Explain yourself," she demanded.

"Addy's looking for a beau. She told me!"

Addy grabbed the Nancy Drew books that separated her and Macie, then pitched them over the seat. "Last time I share any grown-up stuff with you, Macie," Addy said.

"I think not," Charlotte said, pulling into Bay St. Louis to buy gas. While the station attendant filled the tank and Macie and Esty went to the ladies' room, Charlotte turned to confront Addy. "I don't know what you have up your sleeve, little missy, but hear me loud and clear. You will NOT spend your summer chasing Keesler boys around the Gulf Coast. If your father or I find out you're doing this, we'll have you back home in a New York second."

Exasperated from the ride and sweating from the heat, Addy said, "Won't be doing the chasing, Mama." She wiped her brow with the backside of her hand. "You still don't understand, do you? He'll easily find me. I've seen him in my visions, so I'll recognize him."

"There you go again, Adelaide, talking foolishness. I fail to understand you. You best be careful, dear. You know, plenty of those Keesler boys are different. They come from backgrounds lower than yours," Charlotte said, taking a hairbrush from her pocketbook to ease her tangles, then offering it to Addy.

"Gracious, Mother." Addy shook her head. *Not this again.* "Why don't you say what you mean?"

"Watch your tone, young lady." Charlotte checked her lipstick in the vanity mirror attached to the sun visor, then adjusted the rearview for driving. After paying for the gas, she tipped the attendant. Then she honked to let Esty and Macie know it was time to leave.

"They're all servicemen, Mama, fighting for our country. But rest assured, I've no intention of running after a guy. I know better." Addy searched under a bag on the middle seat for a ribbon to tame her hair.

"Of course, your daddy wins this one," Charlotte said. "If you girls stayed at my parents' house for the summer, things would be different."

It was a pointless argument for Charlotte to make. When James Jr.'s parents were involved, her mother had no say.

Addy kept quiet for the final stretch of the ride. She no longer bothered with selling a sixth sense to her mother, who knew full well that her daughter had struggled with nightmares cloaked in dreams since childhood. These visions played out often enough for her to trust beyond what *could* happen—Addy saw things that eventually *did* happen.

No one gets to argue with me about what I see. No one.

He was tall, with dark curly hair and piercing blue eyes that held one's attention and never let go. Her serviceman's uniform was olive green, not dark blue, but just the right hue to complement his eye color. His skin reflected a year-round tan, and his touch was strong. Confident. Powerful. Intoxicating.

I haven't met him. Don't know his name. But I'll spot him the second he's nearby.

When they arrived at Mimi Jeanne's house, Charlotte pulled into the oyster-shelled driveway and brushed past the low-hanging magnolia branches before rolling to a stop near the rear of the property. The enormous two-story Greek Revival home blocked the sunlight on the bluff facing the Sound.

Mimi welcomed her brood with her hands on her hips, wearing a wide straw hat adorned in feathers, with a black silk ribbon tied at the back.

"Ms. Jeanne, have you been in the garden all day?" Charlotte asked before demanding the girls gather their suitcases and knapsacks.

"Just the afternoon," Mimi said. "And now it's a perfect time to take a break and drink some of Ida's lemonade. Welcome, everyone." She kissed her daughter-in-law on both cheeks.

"Hi, Mimi!" Addy and her sisters hugged their grandmother before dragging their things into the house. Charlotte rambled on and on about the traffic and the heat.

"Mimi, why do you wear such a crazy hat?" Macie asked, passing back for another load.

"That's what Southern women do, Macie. And, indeed, I am a *proper* Southern woman. Finish moving in, girls, then come down to the porch and get a cold drink. Ida has a gallon jug set aside."

Mimi's definition of a *proper* Southern woman differed dramatically from others in her social league—she was the only one among her contemporaries who practiced hoodoo and led seances once a week in her potter's cottage.

Addy held the screen door open for her sisters' last trek. When she glanced around the trees lining her grandparents' property, a collection of cobalt blue glass bottles dangling from the live oaks caught Addy's attention. Strung together, the bottles created a hypnotic ringtone when a breeze drifted across the low branches.

Odd little bird feeders. No . . . so what are they?

Addy walked toward one of the trees and caught a slight scent of urine as she reached for one of the bottles. Because the dark blue glass disguised its contents, Addy planned to ask Mimi for an explanation before investigating further. But then Ida rang the lemonade bell: time for gossip and sitting a spell.

She smiled at seeing white wicker furniture and crisp linen draperies swaying in the breeze when she stepped onto the porch. The scene, reminiscent of one described in *The Great Gatsby*, was only missing F. Scott Fitzgerald's fictional characters, Daisy Buchanan and Jordan Baker, lounging in boredom amidst the day's heat. Instead, Mimi and Charlotte sat poised on opposite sides of the porch like bald eagles prepared for a fight.

"I surely thought it would be cooler over here, Ms. Jeanne," Charlotte complained, fanning herself despite claiming the most relaxed spot on the porch. No sooner had she said this than a sea breeze blew in from the Sound and drifted across the blue hydrangeas planted along the driveway.

"You're just overheated 'cause of the car ride, Charlotte. You'll cool down directly," Mimi said. Charlotte tried to refrain from rolling her eyes and failed miserably. Addy caught her mother in the act, but chose to sip her lemonade quietly rather than create a scene. Macie and Esty fought over the pillows on the long divan and kept at it until Mimi told them to walk down to the Yacht Club and look for Papa.

"Well, this gives us a second to talk before I head back," Charlotte began, apparently no longer addled by the heat. When she turned to include Addy in the conversation. Mimi smirked, then braced herself. "Adelaide believes the purpose of the summer is to land herself a beau," Charlotte explained with her right eyebrow raised ever so slightly.

"Charlotte, I wouldn't be surprised if that's exactly what she does," Mimi said, nonplussed by this revelation. Mimi knew the girls' hectic social calendar because she'd organized most of their events.

"Don't be harsh, Mama. And please don't talk as though I'm not sitting here. I'm nearly twenty-one, almost a college graduate. I'm capable of making decisions for myself."

"Hard to argue with that, Charlotte," Mimi added.

Charlotte moved to the edge of her cushioned seat and sat up straighter, as if her posture might further emphasize the importance of her comment. "Her father and I don't want her running around with any riff-raff, and I think you *know* what I mean, Ms. Jeanne."

"Oh, I know perfectly well what you mean." Mimi bristled at the idea that she needed instruction on whom her granddaughters would socialize with until Labor Day.

"So, we're clear. You two won't be in cahoots with each other. Correct?"

Addy seized this standoff between her mother and grandmother to inquire about the blue bottles tied with twine hanging from the trees. "What's going on with the blue bottles, Mimi? The ones hanging from the side yard oak trees? I don't remember seeing them before."

"Come with me, love. It might be easier to explain outside," Mimi said. "I've had enough of this interrogation anyway."

Mimi stepped off the side portico and walked toward the yard with Charlotte nearly clipping at her heels. "Jeanne, you can't be serious. Not after James Jr.'s discussions with you."

When Addy reached the tree nearest the house, where most of the bottles were hanging, her mother and grandmother screamed at one another. How could a collection of blue apothecary bottles, suspended from the limbs of century-old live oak trees, be such a big deal?

"Do not yank those bottles off my tree, Charlotte," Mimi said. As Charlotte yanked one bottle, then another, from the branches they were tied to, Mimi's voice escalated. "This is *not* your home, and I won't stand for this brazen behavior. Leave right this instant and go home. I'm sure my son is waiting for his wife to return."

"What's happening? Tell me now, or I'm going to get Papa. He'll settle this," Addy pleaded. She didn't understand her mother's vehement reaction to Mimi's mysterious bottles, nor her grandmother's obsession with protecting them. Didn't these bottles store medicine at one time?

Charlotte whirled around to face her daughter, holding one of the bottles she'd pulled from the lowest tree branch. "Your grandmother's gone mad and made *haint* trees, despite your father telling her to stop." Addy reached for the bottle Charlotte held, only to end up in a tug of war with her.

"If you break that bottle, Charlotte, I won't be able to help you. It'll be out of my hands completely," Mimi warned.

"Shut up, Jeanne. I'm sick of your hoodoo threats, your damn folk magic. None of this is real. It's all malarkey." Nevertheless, Charlotte stopped pulling and relinquished it to Addy, who was surprised to find it heavier than expected. A gentle shake revealed either glass chips or tiny stones within it.

"Leave this instant, Charlotte," Mimi said. Frustrated, Charlotte stormed off to find her keys and purse.

"Mimi, what's a *haint* tree?"

Adjusting her sun hat, Mimi said, "They ward off evil spirits, trap them, keep them from entering our home. I'd been hanging blue bottles for years until *your* father had a fit, so I took them down. But I'm no longer abiding by his wishes. Or anyone else's, for that matter." Mimi paused, allowing her granddaughter a second to absorb her explanation. "When I sense evil is near, love, my bottles will hang."

As Addy watched Mimi re-attach the bottles, she viewed this aging Southern belle differently. In her eyes, any woman who battled Mama Charlotte was a heroine, no question about that—but learning that Mimi practiced folk magic? A forbidden excursion in a small coastal hamlet largely inhabited by conservative, wealthy New Orleanians and descendants of French Catholics.

Mimi Jeanne possessed a rare sensitivity, a unique gift that most would barely notice, much less understand.

Just like me.

"I still don't get why Mama is so mad."

"She's afraid. Of me. Of you. Fearful of what I can teach you that goes against the church's teachings. Your mother doesn't want you to learn hoodoo, conjure, or—as most call the practice—rootwork. It's alchemy . . . born of ancestral trauma endured on plantations, practiced in the swamps, then passed down to generations of women dealing with unmentionable agonies."

It took Addy a couple of seconds to digest Mimi's rushed explanation. The first response that came to mind was that Charlotte was probably more worried about the impact hoodoo might have directly on *her*—and not her eldest daughter.

"What has Papa to say about all this? Hanging bottles from

trees and warding off evil spirits?"

Mimi's response was unexpected. "It doesn't matter if it's okay with your grandfather, young lady, because this is not his world. He holds no dominion here. And when you're ready, if you're ready, Addy, I will share what I know, what my mother, Louisa, and *aunties* taught me eons ago. If you think there's power in your visions, love, you won't believe the power of rootwork."

"Not sure I'm quite ready for all of this, Mimi," Addy said before walking back toward the house.

After twenty years of spending summers with Mimi, how am I only learning today that she's an enchantress?

When she returned to the portico, her eyes drifted to Papa's outdoor bar, nestled in the corner nearest the French door entrance into the dining room. A second after spotting a bottle of Caribbean rum, Addy hurriedly opened it and refreshed her lemonade glass with a sizable pour. Though Addy only intended to settle her racing pulse, it took two more gulps straight from the rum bottle to accomplish that feat.

Charlotte didn't tell anyone goodbye, though she managed a lackluster wave before reversing the Ford wagon. No one noticed if Charlotte had bothered to check for passing traffic before backing onto Beach Boulevard and peeling away.

Except for an opaque figure oddly perched in the live oak tree, who'd witnessed the entire tableau. No one else cared.

Mimi had already stepped into her potter's shed, where dried rosemary and lavender plants hung from a wire strung across two sides of the wooden structure, and fennel seeds lay drying on a windowsill.

No time like the present, she thought, to craft a spell.

7

Suzanne

New Orleans, Summer 2012

Seated on her patio, Suzanne permits herself a break from plotting September's lesson plans to check on her sun tea, now basking for hours in the steam bath of backyard heat. She follows a pebble pathway, ducking through a canopy of magnolia trees, to perform a taste test. Yes, it's nearly brewed. Soon, she'll add pure honey, several sliced lemons, and a touch of Mexican vanilla. While waiting for the sun's final bolster, Suzanne considers potting geraniums and planting monkey grass around the garden's central fountain, then changes her mind when her right wrist snaps back in pain.

The memory of her near head-on collision after leaving Wallaby's eight months ago remains spotty. Yet one thing is clear—an ancestral spirit's quick reaction yanked Suzanne from the throes of a deadly smashup that night. There's no other explanation. Truthfully, Suzanne hasn't summoned the powers that remain at rest within her right hand in the past four years. Not since the night of her mother's fiery death on U.S. Highway 61 at the entrance to Myrtle's Plantation in

St. Francisville, Louisiana, when Suzanne had raised her right hand and commanded the crash's fire to extinguish itself.

Sadly, her command fizzled before the fire and rescue squads arrived, and Madelaine died at the crash scene. Nevertheless, she's now forced to admit that the dramatic touch of her mother's spirit is written all over her recent rescue.

Once determined to navigate her life without relying upon her ancestral spirits, Suzanne changed course on her twenty-first birthday, deeming this resolve an unrealistic expectation. Her clairsentience and gift of communicating with spirits were not easily shared with others. Who could help steer her journey if not the ghosts of those who'd lived before her? Adding Madelaine's demands that Suzanne rightfully should practice the craft alongside her—if for no larger purpose than bragging rights over birthing an expert rootworker—complicated Suzanne's foray into adulthood.

Yes, Madelaine envisioned her daughter morphing into what every other Lafountain sorceress dreamt of: an extraordinary magick practitioner whom others would travel far and wide to consult regarding love, luck, and money. And even protection.

A fruitless rebellion, it turns out, culminating in a broken relationship with the one person who could have aided her the most.

My resistance is of no consequence. I am a legacy in a long line of Lafountain enchantresses, beginning with my second great-great-grandmother, Louisa, born before the Civil War in 1854 at Shelley Plantation near Bay St. Louis, Mississippi, and followed by her daughter, Jeanne, a wealthy hoodoo priestess navigating high society in nearby Pass Christian, who sadly only birthed sons. When Jeanne's granddaughter, Adelaide, was born in New Orleans, the Lafountain women rejoiced because an inherited family gift of communicating with spirits continued, despite her mother, Charlotte's, opposition. Next, in early 1945, Addy gave birth to my mother, Madelaine, in the darkness of a private hospital in Memphis. Cloaked in shame,

Addy was manipulated into giving her baby girl up for adoption.

Finally, there's me, born of an unwed mother while still in college. Like my great-great-grandmother, Jeanne, I have no daughters. Nevertheless, my role is inescapable, for I'm the last Lafountain enchantress, who now must handle a ghost's bidding. Or respond to a roving spirit's nudge.

More than a century has filtered away, a mere brush stroke of time compared to eternity, since the genesis of Lafountain women choosing, at the second of death, to either remain tethered to Earth as a ghostly presence, or drift amidst the In-Between as a loose spirit. To either assist beloveds or haunt ne'er-do-wells in the here and now.

Unless and until an appointed Lafountain enchantress is prepared to cast a final cross-over spell, allowing the lingering Lafountain energies to travel beyond the ether and into the afterlife.

Daydreams about her life's purpose are interrupted when Suzanne hears the house line ring.

Suzanne runs indoors to catch the call, fearing the worst. Perhaps something horrible has happened to the twins. She always fears what she cannot control.

It's Max. "Hey, what are you doing tomorrow afternoon?" he asks.

"Ummm . . . college shopping for Beau and Kyle? Maybe meeting Margie for a late lunch."

She senses some hesitation when he doesn't respond quickly, but to her surprise, he continues. "Boring, Suzy. Super boring. Instead, join me along Florida's Emerald Coast for the weekend. My attorney owns a place in Seaside—three hundred steps from crystal-white sand. It's mine whenever I give him sufficient notice."

His invitation draws a smile. "Tempting, very tempting," Suzanne teases.

"Come on . . . time to disappear. With me."

Calculating her school prep time and considering the possibility of slipping away, Suzanne says, "Give me a second to call my ex and confirm he'll check in with the twins. I'm much more comfortable when their father knows I've left town."

An awkward silence settles between them and cannot be ignored.

"Max, you still there?"

He comes out swinging. "Suzanne, does this man live in a goddamn tent? He does own a house, correct? Don't make this complicated. If you're concerned about leaving your sons alone, tell them to stay at their dad's place for the weekend."

She wonders how Max has turned forty-something years of age and miraculously avoided fatherhood. Who leaves eighteen-year-old kids home alone with no supervision whatsoever? *I did mention the twins when we met at Remé's party, didn't I?*

Max rambles on about several things while she backtracks about the details she has shared about her life since meeting him. When Suzanne returns her attention to their conversation, she hears Max say, "You'll go nuts being solely responsible 24/7 for these kids. You're divorced now. Time to let loose and have some fun."

"Well, I can't argue with that thought. I'll arrange it. When do you want to leave tomorrow?" Suzanne twirls an earring dangling from her right earlobe, then tilts it upward, a habit initiated in childhood that signals uncertainty.

"I'll leave Canal Street around noon and swing by your place. After that, I'm yours."

"Okay, see you soon." Suzanne ignores her second thoughts. At some point, she must trust a sexy weekend away with a handsome man she can't stop fantasizing about several times a day. A drunk-with-desire seventy-two hours—far more appealing than a recent rip-your-clothes-off romp on the sofa before a kid returns home from *his* date.

Simply the idea of a beach escape is intoxicating. And so

very long overdue.

Since Kyle plans to be with his girlfriend until late, and Beau decides to stay at his dad's place, Suzanne allows herself an early turn-in after packing bathing suits, sandals, and an armful of colorful sundresses. A few hours of peaceful sleep pass before nightmares, oddly about jellyfish, jar her awake, and Bimini jumps up from a dog's dead sleep to pace the floor. Suzanne heads to the kitchen and opens the refrigerator to search for sparkling water but instead reaches for a chilled wine bottle and refills her glass left on the countertop. After taking a sip, Suzanne freezes when she hears the faint lyrics of a 1960s folk tune, fragmented and crackling as if struggling to escape from the depths of an old transistor radio. There's no rational explanation for a refrigerator to blast "The Age of Aquarius" from its ice machine.

Gusts of frigid air now billow from the open refrigerator door like a winter storm is brewing. But before Suzanne spies the opaque outline of a spirit lingering at the door's edge, a concentrated earthy scent of a balsamic perfume nearly knocks Suzanne's legs out from under her. Then the shape of the specter quivers before drifting awkwardly to the right—and, a few seconds later, to the left—uncertain of its direction or how to proceed. Suzanne covers a scream and instinctively reaches for the marcasite cross necklace she often wears around her neck.

It's not there.

When she slows her breathing to abate a panicked reaction, Suzanne loosens her grip on the crystal stemware when attempting to calm herself. Unfortunately, it slips from her hand and crashes across the tile, scattering pellets of glass and sweet sticky wine across the kitchen floor.

No stranger to identifying a spirit's urgent request or a ghost's plea for exiting *this* plane of existence, Suzanne recognizes instantly that this one is personal as it encircles her with a forcefield of energy. Eerily aware of the ghost's desire to touch her, Suzanne concentrates on deep, rhythmic breathing to avoid fainting as the spirit tugs against her verve. Suzanne struggles to retain her strength with each inhalation, though she feels it waning the longer the spirit lingers.

As she speaks, Suzanne imagines the words in her mind: *Identify yourself.*

Since visualizing usually prompts a mental conversation, Suzanne grabs a barstool for support. Then, she sits and waits. As the spirit's outline thickens, more details appear. *Denim bell-bottom jeans and a tie-dye shirt? Black platform heels?*

As Suzanne grapples with the spirit's reveal, the refrigerator's light burns even brighter, now deflecting light from an item clinging to the spirit's visage. *No, no, these cannot be aviator sunglasses.*

The woody scent fills the kitchen, threatening to fill Suzanne's lungs with an aroma she can no longer bear to smell. And it's unmistakably Chanel No. 19—Madelaine's signature scent.

Her heartbeat races as Suzanne stands, desperate for a touch . . . and considers a barter: her energy for her mother's. But thinks again. After all this time, Madelaine's spirit appears, rather casually, to drop in from the late 1960s. Suzanne abruptly pulls back her right hand, imagining what's possibly at stake. *Can this be a trap? A way to prompt the transfer of skills, perhaps?*

Suzanne prays Kyle doesn't wake, because if he walks into the kitchen looking for a midnight snack . . . let's say it's not the most suitable time to unveil her family's unique history.

She hears a faint whisper, "*Proud of you, love. You'll start practicing now.*" It's the same voice Suzanne heard several months ago after her near head-on collision.

Only one entity can get away with a jab at Suzanne's refusal to embrace her role as a hoodoo enchantress—her mother. *Stay, please stay, Madelaine.* She wills herself into the lowest level of meditation she can harness: to hold Madelaine's spirit tightly for as long as possible.

Then, Kyle stumbles into the kitchen and flips the light switch, bathing the kitchen in fluorescent light. Instantly, the spirit evaporates and the earthy scent drifts away.

"Mom! Jesus, what are you doing?" Suzanne stares blankly at her son, still shivering from the swirls of cold air blanketing the kitchen only moments ago. "What's that smell?" he asks. "Something from the refrigerator? I don't know, just a suggestion," Kyle says.

"Be careful, love. There's broken glass on the tile behind me. Get me the broom, please?"

Something catches her attention when she stands and pushes the bar stool back under the kitchen island. Her cross necklace is now lodged between a bar stool and the cabinet base, with its velvet ties now entangled—though it had been strung around Suzanne's neck moments before entering the kitchen.

Kyle returns with the broom and rushes to close the refrigerator door, curious that it remains open. He looks at Suzanne with a mixture of concern and annoyance. "Mom, you look like you've just seen a ghost."

How long did you linger near the kitchen, Kyle? What did you hear? Are you next . . . in the Lafountain line of empaths? Could that even be possible?

⁂

By the time Max arrives shortly after noon the next day, Kyle is long gone, cutting grass for one of his preferred lawn care customers.

"I'm disappointed, chér. Thought I'd meet at least one of the twins today." He steps into the foyer, kisses Suzanne's cheek, and reaches for her bag. "This is it?"

She ignores his comment about meeting her sons. Hadn't this been what he'd wanted? For her to easily skirt away at a moment's notice? "We're only away for a few days, Max. If I've forgotten anything, I'll buy it."

"Damn, you're my favorite kind of woman."

Their journey is uneventful, a smooth six-hour car ride along I-10. Finally approaching the quaint town dotted with pastel-colored beach houses, Suzanne imagines disappearing within its watercolor visage, honed with blue, pink, and yellow hues, and floating free of responsibility, if only for a couple of days.

"This is your friend's cottage?" Suzanne asks when Max parks next to a white picket fence. Suzanne admires the three-story coral-colored home with several palm trees dotting the landscaped yard. "This is no cottage, Max. It's a mansion."

"I think John renovated recently," he says absentmindedly. She watches Max stare at the brass address numbers nailed to the white picket gate as though he's seeing it for the first time. Then, while Max checks his phone for the entrance code, Suzanne spots a private entrance to a crystal white-sanded beach. *Perfect.*

Inside, they inspect the luxurious layout.

"Suzanne, come see this."

Max unlatches the sliding glass door, revealing a tropical oasis surrounding a hot tub with a waterfall cascading into a private pool.

She approaches him from behind and encircles her arms around his waist. "Paradise," she says. Then, tilting her head at Max's shoulder, Suzanne notices no neighboring home has an unobstructed view of the pool area. *Hmmm . . .*

Max turns to face her and lightly strokes her neck with both hands before tilting her chin upward. First, he lightly brushes his lips against hers, then sensing her quickened response, Max presses her lips more urgently. Suzanne answers, circling his tongue with hers, then whispers, "The pool's calling my name, Max. I'm jumping in."

She wiggles out of his embrace, kicks off her flip-flops, and unties the back of her sundress, slipping out of its soft colors with ease. Her thong's intact when she hits the water, but it's poolside when Max summersaults his naked entry. He swims the pool's length underwater before surfacing, then tugs at Suzanne's feet, dragging her to the bottom. Max attempts to straddle her, floating atop her, as she struggles back to the surface for air.

"Let me catch my breath," she yells, gasping for air. *What the hell? Rough play is one thing. Nearly drowning me is altogether different.*

She slowly swims on her back to the opposite side of the pool, placing some distance between the two, fully aware that Max monitors her every stroke. She rests on the pool's concrete stairs and gauges which step to sit on, attempting to keep her breasts below the water's surface.

"Such a tease," Max says, swimming into her, his fingers gently arousing her sweet spot. She leans her head back against the top step and watches the movement of clouds, enjoying the interplay of Max's touch. She wants him—deep, deep inside of her.

When passionate kissing passes the point of return, Suzanne guides him inside, consumed with a slow-burning pleasure. She listens to the soft paddles of the pool's intake—mimics its steady rhythm until she climaxes. That's when it feels like the sun, moon, and shooting stars explode in harmony. Afterward, Suzanne slowly drifts to the bottom of the pool, imagining the make-believe life of a sea siren.

Later, they lay across a white wicker lounger. Wrapped together in an oversized towel, Suzanne whispers in his ear: "So good, Max."

"Any time, Suzy."

Suzanne watches the gas flames flicker inside the outdoor fireplace at sunset, threatening to break out yet retracting just enough to remain safely within its perimeters. Suzanne drifts off within seconds, allowing herself to marvel at the steady fire building between them.

Later, through a fog of grogginess, Suzanne fights the sense of someone watching her sleep and bristles at the icy breath upon her neck. It's not Max.

Who's here?

A black opaque mass hovers to her right, then backs away. It quickly morphs into the shape of a human, though it has no eyes to explain the sensation of a death stare. Suzanne squints and resolves the entity to lessen its threat. When she does, its neck stretches oddly to the left, out of sync with the rest of its outline. An immediate rush of sadness envelops Suzanne—to tears. As an empath, she's no stranger to internalizing other people's emotions, including those of trapped ghosts burdened with painful memories. Suddenly, she is awash in a rainstorm of sadness.

As Suzanne moves to sit, the shadow person refuses a confrontation and swiftly flits backward, only to dart past the pool house and into the night, leaving a noxious rose and composted patchouli scent behind.

Two ghostly encounters with two entirely different energies in less than twenty-four hours? One benevolent; the other quite the opposite. Suzanne shivers, despite it being a balmy eighty degrees by the sea. A hostile entity such as this one usually veers away from Suzanne. But not tonight. And she's got a sick, raging headache to prove its malevolence.

Was it searching for someone else? Or does it seek an altercation with me?

That familiar dread, that foreboding anticipation, envelopes her and threatens to disrupt her idyllic weekend. A mandate from the spirit world is imminent. Ignoring ultimatums issued by trapped ghosts has proven fruitless in the past. Suppose this is, indeed, one. Hauntings will continue to escalate until Suzanne complies with whatever imminent demands are placed in her path.

When Suzanne wraps herself in the beach towel and reenters the cottage, she hears two people arguing. Is Max on his speakerphone?

"Who are you talking to?" She follows Max's agitated voice to the kitchen. He's flipping an omelet while staring at his phone screen, now reflecting an aborted call.

"No one. No one at all."

"Don't lie, Max. Why were you screaming?"

"Okay, okay, you caught Remé and me arguing." Max's back is turned while he speaks. "Said he'd handle something so I could get away this weekend. And then he forgot."

"I'm pretty sure I heard a woman's voice," Suzanne says. "Look, I get it if you're still seeing someone else: Be straight with me. This is new for both of us. Seriously, though, I'm not kidding. I'm not dealing with a *bloody* liar."

Though Suzanne hears herself speak, she barely believes her spoken words. Never again will she stand by in silence and endure the torture of a lover's dishonesty, certainly not after struggling with her ex and his host of lies. His years and years of cheating and fabricated excuses to cover his tracks. She'll never tolerate that behavior from a man again. Max will surely learn where she stands, or there will be no relationship.

"You've been sleeping, baby. Probably still dreaming. Nothing to worry about. Remé called." He offers his phone to Suzanne. "Call him back. Check it out."

"God, no, Max. I'm not a teenager. I'm not going through your phone."

"Sit. I made omelets. And the waffle iron's ready for my world-famous chocolate Belgian waffles. You good with breakfast for dinner?"

Suzanne nods her head.

How did I sleep through Max running to the market and cooking dinner? Why didn't he wake me?

She slips into her sundress to join Max at the white-washed table and grabs a shawl from her overnight bag. Her raging headache now seeps into the nape of her neck, further evidence of facing off with a less-than-friendly entity. But this sensation is minor compared to her fury after flipping Max's phone over while he pours chocolate morsels into the waffle batter.

Suzanne reads the person's name at the top of the call list. And it's not Remé.

Who the hell is Maureen?

A gnawing fear tugs at Suzanne. If the spirit world is gearing up . . . to force an unpleasant circumstance in her direction . . . she dreads being wholly under-prepared for the task that awaits.

8

Max

New Orleans, Late Summer 2012

Max impatiently drums his fingers on the oak conference table in his office when a meeting with representatives of a California-based production company turns sluggish. He's on his own to strike a lucrative deal now that Remé is embroiled in a crisis at M & R's coastal office.

No stranger to rolling the die against enormous odds, Max presses on since he cannot risk an impasse. These West Coast movie moguls refuse to let up on their demands for office space in the deepest recesses of the French Quarter, even though Max explains the negative consequences.

He crosses his arms, leans back in his black leather chair, and says, "Guys, I get it. The building is historically enticing, but the logistical hitches outweigh any benefits. First, there's the issue with inadequate storage, and we haven't even discussed the struggle with managing deliveries." Max pounces when he notices one of the head producers, Krauss van Derek, scrolling through his phone, mentally detached from the meeting. "Let's be real: You guys are outsiders. If I were courting old-line

New Orleanians to invest in *my* film project, I wouldn't lease a couple of rundown carriage houses, even for short-term," he begins. The strategy works when Max emphasizes *old-line* New Orleanians and *rundown* carriage houses.

"Exactly what do you mean by that?" Kristoff Dietz, the group's leader, asks.

"It's simple," Max says. "The space is quaint and appealing. I'll grant you that—because you're viewing it from a filmmaker's perspective. But, unfortunately, the rental is unimpressive . . . if you intend to inveigle investors."

"Go on."

"There's no arguing that the Quarter is quixotic, possibly addictive for most people. But that's for tourists who come and go," he explains. "The locals? We know the headaches of sustaining a business back of the Quarter. Problems with parking, limited workspaces, weird-ass people running the streets . . ."

"Max, we're filmmakers," Kristoff interrupts. "Not much intimidates us."

"I get your vision," Max says. "But I'm suggesting that once you're finished with this Storyville documentary and ready to seduce new investors for other projects, it's gonna be one *helluva* challenge."

Max leans forward, clenching his fists underneath the conference table, and allows a few seconds of silence before releasing his final comment. "You won't impress New Orleans old money with meetings in a dilapidated building at the end of Burgundy Street."

Kristoff raises his right eyebrow, glares at Krauss, who's still scrolling on his phone, and says, "Then show us another space. Give us something to compare it with." Krauss slips his phone into a back pocket and nods.

"I've got a spot with Canal Street digits and an impressive view of the Mississippi River available this week." Max jumps to his feet, eases into his suit jacket, then buzzes Maureen. "Grab the file for Suite 25, Maureen," he demands when she rounds the conference room corner.

"Okay," she says, dragging out the *'kay*.

"And I need you to walk through the rental space with us, dear."

"I don't know what condition it's in," Maureen says. "I mean . . . it was only vacated a couple of days ago. Not sure it's survived a cleaning."

"It'll be fine." Max clips Maureen's comment in half. "Just get the paperwork and meet us by the elevator."

"Of course, boss."

"Gentlemen." Max stands to guide the group through the labyrinth of M & R Realty. "Elevators, this way."

When Max picks up the scent of cash, there's little he won't suggest when nailing down a multi-year lease. If he successfully pulls the trigger on this deal, he and Remé sit at the pinnacle of real estate wheelers and dealers in the Crescent City. These West Coast film tycoons have no qualms about paying $20 to $22 per square foot each month for multiple floors of space. It's a minor investment for Kristoff and his partners to establish themselves as premier filmmakers in Louisiana but a career game-changer for Max.

After touring the swanky suite on the twenty-fifth floor of Canal Place, Kristoff responds precisely as Max imagines. But he's unprepared when the group requests an additional 27,000 square feet after walking through the rental space that offers a breathtaking Mississippi River view.

That's an additional freaking floor. How did Kristoff more than double his needs in less than fifteen minutes?

Max panics. This is the only available unit he's contracted to lease in Canal Place. The deal's a bust if he can't make it work. "Any ideas, Maureen?"

She walks toward him, her stilettos clicking against the tile flooring, her hips swaying in rhythm. "Ten minutes ago, they threatened to bail. So why request more than double the square footage? I have a suggestion, but I'm waiting for you," she says.

"I'm not losing this deal, Mo, not after everything I've put into it."

"I hear what you're saying, babe, but I don't see how you'll pull this off. Unless you do something drastic." Maureen glances at her yellow legal pad, then flips back a page or two. She draws a deep breath, then exhales slowly. Taps her pen to the beat of an unfamiliar rhythm.

"For God's sake, Mo. Fess up, what are you thinking?" Max glances back at Kristoff and his group to gauge their restlessness.

"Buy out one of our corporation's leases . . . one of the insurance companies. Relocate them with incentives. It will cost you plenty up front, but may solve your immediate problem."

A devilish smile crawls across Max's lips.

"Woman, you know how to turn a guy on," he says. His hand reaches to touch her, but Maureen is ready for him. She lifts her right heel and steps away.

"I'll start making calls," Maureen says.

Before Max unveils this new strategy with Kristoff, he checks his phone and sees no word from Suzanne. Then, when Max explains it will take an hour or so to pinpoint the actual availability of this additional space, negotiations stall while the movie moguls argue among themselves.

Clinching his jaw, Max dials Suzanne's number. "Excuse me, gentlemen, my partner on the Coast is calling," Max lies.

He's frantic to remind Suzanne about drinks tonight at 21st Amendment, his favorite watering hole on Iberville Street. Max is convinced that an evening filled with boutique cocktails and live jazz is the final touch to convince these Californians to do anything he suggests. But if his new lover could be at his side for a night of New Orleans-style entertaining, that would be pure lagniappe.

Max's call diverts to voicemail three times. Is she still pissed about what happened in Seaside, he wonders? *I didn't ask her to look at my damn phone.* It's still her summer break, right? *Answer my call, woman.*

He texts, "Drinks at 21st Amendment. 5 p.m. Closing the Canal Place deal." Then he adds, "Need your help."

It slips his mind that Suzanne is attending a teachers' conference on reading instruction at the Windsor Court, just around the corner. Sweating, Max walks toward the windows overlooking the river to rejoin the producers and tries to ignore the banging hum that resonates solely in his right ear. He feels dizzy, a sure sign there's a rise in his blood pressure, as his temples pulsate with pain. When Max approaches the group, a swift gust of wind bristles the hair at the back of his neck, then threatens to spin him around.

As Max tries to steady himself, he nearly trips over his feet.

What's producing this? Is it wind from a broken window . . . after pigeons have busted into the building?

Max walks the perimeter of the office space and discovers nothing amiss. But when a deep patchouli, earthy scent escalates, another wave of dizziness nearly brings him to his knees. He grabs onto a column to regain his balance as his throat threatens to close. Max can't suppress gasping for air.

Kristoff watches Max's near stumble and yells, "Everything okay?"

"Of course," Max struggles to answer.

"It appears you're unwell, Max. If this meeting is now inconvenient, we can contact another agent."

"No, absolutely not . . . my apologies. I'm afraid I left . . . my inhaler . . . back in my desk drawer," Max lies again. "Was trying to get in touch with my girlfriend . . . then my asthma . . ." Max explains. "I'd hoped she could meet us for drinks tonight."

Kristoff laughs, walking closer to Max. "What's this? I'm confused. I thought Maureen was your woman. Now there's someone else?"

"Maureen's my executive assistant," Max snaps back. Then regrets his quip. "And a dear friend, of course. We couldn't run our two offices without her."

Before they leave the space, Max reminds the men that the entire floor will be customized to fit their specs. "Whatever you need, we can make it work." The cluster of muscles at the back of his neck throb with such pain that he anticipates a migraine will follow. Quixotically, Max has manifested two previously undiagnosed health conditions in the past ten minutes.

"What about the additional square footage?" Krauss asks, insistent that a resolution be calculated. On the spot. "It was *your* idea, Max, to set our operations upriver, so you need to make this work."

"By the time we meet over at 21st for cocktails, I'll have a proposal," Max says, finally catching his breath. He hopes no one notices his lack of requiring an inhaler.

"Isn't that an old gangster bar?" Kristoff asks.

"Spot on," Max says. "Very impressed that you know local mafia history. You'll enjoy seeing pictures of mob boss Carlos Marcello hanging on the walls. Maybe another Hollywood story for you?"

Max leaves Canal Place and walks to the Riverfront to clear his head. He calls Suzanne again, leaves another message, then sends two more texts. At the bar near the Creole Queen's dock, Max orders a Dos Equis. Then a second one. Finally, a third. Never enough beer to cap his anger when Max fails to get his way—a pointless remedy for a personality trait that had its genesis at a very young age.

He turns the flow of memories from the last day he spent with Farrah on and off like a spigot, though it was the most eruptive clash of his life, four years ago while touring central Kentucky's Mammoth Cave.

A park ranger doubling as the group's excursion guide separated them because of his intensifying argument with Farrah. Nevertheless, something had to be done to keep the group on track. Once 250 feet underground, cave explorers were expected to complete the tour. Max walked to the front of the group as instructed, while Farrah stayed near the back, complaining that her nausea had worsened.

Max plodded along the dark, slippery pathway. Though it seemed to take forever, they finally passed the cave's bottomless pit and headed toward Mammoth Dome, one of the tour's major highlights. After the accident, Max told investigators he didn't realize Farrah was missing until the group reassembled beneath the dome for a scheduled rest stop. The moment Max started an uproar over his wife's disappearance, his spiraling nightmare began.

I can't think of Farrah today.

He watches a series of barges approach the river's bend, each navigating a slight turn to move upriver, with a cruise ship creeping up from behind. He pays his bar tab and makes one final attempt to reach Suzanne. When she finally answers, Max's temper ignites.

Suzanne rushes, saying, "I've ten missed calls from you, Max. Did someone die?"

"Where've you been, Suzy?" he demands. "I've been trying to reach you for hours."

"Why?" she counters, annoyed. "You know that I'm speaking at a reading conference."

"Here in the city?"

"Yes, of course. Where else?" He hears her car key's beeping alarm in the background.

"That's great," Max says. "So, there's no problem meeting me at the jazz bar on Iberville, right?" He waits for her response. When there isn't one, he says, "I'm not going to lie. I need help schmoozing these Hollywood guys."

"Max, I'm meeting my lawyer about Kyle's underage DUI in a few minutes."

"What the hell, Suzy? We talked about this a week ago!"

"Honestly, Max, I forgot. I apologize," she says. "But when one of my sons has an issue, I've no choice but to deal with it."

He hangs up on Suzanne when she starts rambling about

the messed-up twin, who doesn't understand that drinking underage is illegal and driving drunk is entirely insane.

Just when I think I might care for this woman. As much as I can care for anyone. Now, you've made a mistake, Suzy. Never choose your kid over me. This is bullshit.

Max watches the river traffic and attempts to calm his nerves. He soothes himself by re-calculating the commission on a multi-million annual lease, guaranteed over ten years. It's a deal most brokers in his league rarely solidify. The brokerage's commission alone, not to mention the power of referrals, will fund ample opportunities for Remé and him to expand their business along the Gulf Coast.

And make a significant dent in paying off his father's debt that has held a chokehold over Max for years. Of course, that's if he and Remé pocket the total available funds. And postpone recycling everything back into the business.

When his cell rings, he assumes it's Suzanne calling to apologize and is disappointed to hear his lawyer's voice instead.

"Hello, John."

"Got a second, Max?"

"What's up?"

"Need you to fly to Kentucky early Wednesday morning," John says.

"Umm, why?"

"You're not going to like this, just warning you," John begins. "The folks in Edmonson County are re-opening the investigation into Farrah's death. The district attorney is demanding another deposition."

"You've got to be freaking kidding me. I'm brokering a huge leasing deal with Canal Place and have no time for this."

Another cold sweat threatens as he paces from the river's edge to Spanish Plaza's fountain and back. Again, a noxious twist of patchouli envelops Max with a sickening rotten, moldy rose scent. Max gags and struggles against choking. He grabs tightly to the iron railings near the Creole Queen's loading ramp for support—grips his throat for a gulp of air.

There's no reprieve, for his invisible attacker stems from a deep, dark origin. And its message is meant solely for Max.

A gnarly gritty sound, soaked in vengeance, sizzles its inhuman warning that only an angry, trapped ghost may summon to assault its target: "*Gotcha now, lover boy.*"

Max claws at his face when he feels ground clay particles splatter against his cheeks, though nothing is evident when he tries to brush the unseen dirt away.

Tourists boarding the paddle-wheeler's cruise barely glance at Max, for weirder sights have been witnessed in a flamboyant city that champions the unusual. When a New Orleans police officer approaches him, Max shakes his head, then backs away from the tourist crowd.

He forgets that John is still on the phone until he hears him yell, "Max, what's going on?"

"Did you *fucking* hear that? The growling . . . the . . . that *gravel* voice?"

"No idea what you're talking about," John says. "You coughed up a lung. Then some dude asked if you were okay." John waits for Max to speak, then says, "I don't know what's going on with you, Max, but this is no goddamn time to lose your shit."

John explains that the deposition is likely a fact-finding mission. He warns Max that a subpoena will be served at his office later today. Failure to appear and testify puts him in contempt of court. There's no choice in the matter: Max must return to Kentucky to avoid contempt of court charges.

Meanwhile, Kristoff's frown deepens as he observes Max's bizarre behavior from the second-story landing of the nearby Riverwalk shopping plaza. Finally, when his phone call is complete, Kristoff pauses to ensure the Max Show is ending, then opens the door and reenters the hotel.

9

Addy

Gulf Coast, Summer 1944

The acrid scent of magnolia blossoms beckoned Addy as she ascended the steps of Beauvoir, a stately antebellum home set directly across from the calm waters of the Mississippi Sound. Addy's fingertips grazed her ruby-red lips when she scanned two parlor rooms brimming with handsome AAF officers. *Oh, the possibilities.*

Despite the war raging overseas, Addy's sphere on the Gulf Coast remained copasetic, a locale protected by money, legacy, and influence—frequented for years by Louisiana sugarcane planters and Mississippi cotton growers. While the rest of the country coveted ration books, Mimi stored her booklets in a canister on the kitchen counter, not bothering to sign them. If coffee, sugar, and meat routinely appeared at their backdoor, all was well in her world.

Undeniable signs of the war persisted. One clue included Keesler's robust Army Air Force Base, located five miles from Beauvoir, where enlisted men trained in aviation mechanics before heading to cadet school. Because of the increased demand for airmen by the summer of '44, Keesler initiated its B-24 copilot school to sustain America's airborne battles.

Hundreds upon hundreds of these copilots, star-struck with this unprecedented opportunity, were promptly deployed after fast-tracked training. Unfortunately, many never returned with victorious stories.

The reality of war remained the farthest thing from Addy's mind as she and Esty sashayed through Beauvoir's grand entrance atop a sizable flight of stairs. When she spun around to see Esty still at her heels, she realized Mimi was behind them.

"You're not staying, Mimi. Are you?" Addy asked. "Please tell me you'll only introduce us to your auxiliary friends. Then leave. You know . . . the invitation is for debutantes and their friends. *Not* their grandparents."

"Don't be rude, Addy. And by the way, you're not a Gulf Coast deb," Esty snapped at her sister. "Have you forgotten your New Orleans debut?" Esty tartly reminded her elder sister that *she* was the only Lafountain girl forced to forgo her formal introduction to society. Thanks to the war.

"As if it matters, Esty, gee whiz."

"It matters to me, Addy. You know how much I wanted Daddy to present me to society. Don't act like you don't know." Esty stepped behind their grandmother after her sister signaled her to stop talking.

"I'm sorry, Mimi," Addy said. "It's just that I've been looking forward to this party for so long—you know, one with no chaperones." Addy smoothed out her favorite navy dress and checked her lips in the entryway's gold lamé mirror. For touchups, she'd stuck a tube of ruby-red in her left dress pocket.

"Remember, Mimi, we can't forget Addy's plan to meet her one-and-only," Esty said, still pressing to get a rise out of her older sister. "Maybe handsome is here tonight. Who knows?"

Mimi shook her head. "It's going to be a very long summer, girls." She waved at a friend, then turned and said, "One more thing. Addy. Yes, the bar serves alcohol, but that doesn't mean you're required to drink. And Esty, you're not of legal age. So, keep this in mind."

Esty winked. "That warning's for you, sis."

Addy rolled her eyes. When Mimi recognized a group of young ladies from Pass Christian's Yacht Club, she introduced them to her granddaughters, then left to meet Papa for their weekly Friday night dinner date at the Edgewater Gulf Hotel.

It took one Roman punch, offered by a tan and blue-eyed officer, for Addy to claim the piano bench at the Steinway upright in Beauvoir's gentlemen's parlor. She sipped her cocktail and chatted with the officer before warming up the keys. Then, he gladly held her drink when a small crowd gathered to request their favorite songs as Addy's hands darted over the blacks and whites.

"It Had to be You," someone shouted. "No, play 'It's Love-Love-Love.'" Addy ignored both and boldly charged into "Shoo-Shoo Baby." Spirited singing exploded through the antebellum home, still standing after ninety-two years. Esty heard the music from the side porch where she'd run into dear friends from Mobile, Alabama—girls she'd summered with for years. Esty wove through the crowd, stepping around guests lounging on the crowded octagon-shaped sofas in the hallway, because she recognized the sound of Addy's inebriation.

She waited until "Shoo-Shoo Baby" ended before grabbing her sister's drink from the officer's hand.

"Hey, what are you doing?" Second Lieutenant Eddy Whitman sprang from the bench to keep the drink from spilling on his uniform.

"You've had enough, Addy! How will you explain this to Mimi?" Esty asked.

"Mind 'ya own business, Esty, I'm a handlin' myself just fine," Addy slurred. She reached to reclaim her drink.

"Who is Mimi?" the officer asked. "Better yet, who are *you*?"

"Esty, meet Eddy," Addy said. "Eddy, this is my sister, Esty, short for Estelle. Oh, Mimi's our grandmother. She dropped us off before her date with Papa." Addy took two back-to-back sips and drained her Roman punch while tapping the next song's rhythm with her feet against the piano's pedals.

"Your *grandmother* is here?" Eddy asked, searching the parlor for an older female face. "How old are you two?"

"Old enough to be here, or Mimi wouldn't have approved," Esty said. "She's a member of the Junior Auxiliary, the ladies' group hosting the party." She noticed Eddy now had two Roman punches in hand, presumably a fresh one for her sister.

Esty said, "Addy, Mimi had better not find you drunk! Or we won't be going anywhere this summer. Then Mama Charlotte will get involved, and nobody wants that!"

"I'm scared to ask, but who is Mama Charlotte?" For a fellow who was scheduled to leave for Germany, or England, or God knows where to join the war, he was utterly flummoxed by the Lafountain girls. "I honestly have no idea what's happening here." The lieutenant started to back away.

"Our mother!" the sisters answered in unison.

"I'm not drunk, Esty," Addy claimed. "I'm only sipping my favorite drink and playing songs for my new friends."

"How do you *even* have a favorite drink, sis? What's it called?" Esty asked.

The group raised their colorful, fruity drinks in unison. "A Roman punch—isn't it divine? They drank it on the Titanic, 'ya know," Addy said.

"It'll be okay, little lady," Eddy assured Esty. "Now, go find your friends, so we can return to having fun." Addy launched into "It Had to Be You," which reignited the soirée.

As Esty walked back through the home's grand entrance, hoping to rejoin her friends on the porch, Army Air Force Officer Cash Lamar held the door for her before stepping into the foyer. Cash removed his cap and smiled at Esty, sharply dressed in a pressed tawny-tan uniform with the AAF's winged propeller insignia soundly secured upon his left shoulder. Esty's heart fluttered at the sheer vision of one of the most handsome men she'd ever seen.

At first, Cash didn't spot Eddy, though he smiled when he heard the loud singing and decided to follow the music. When a bartender offered him a drink, Cash thanked him.

"This is a gas," Cash said. "And to think, I thought it might be boring." When he glanced over his left shoulder, he spotted Eddy sitting on the piano bench next to a gorgeous black-haired beauty with energetic fingers flying across the keys. There wasn't a single piece of sheet music in sight.

"That lovey's been entertaining everyone since she arrived," the bartender said, nodding toward Addy.

"Who's the pianist?" Cash asked after thanking the guy for his Wild Turkey and Coca-Cola.

"Don't know her name," he answered. "Just know she belongs to some rich family who's important 'round here."

"Lucky me. I know the guy sitting beside her, so I'll introduce myself." Cash thanked him for the drink.

"Bottom's up," the bartender said. "And thank you for your service, sir."

When Addy tired of entertaining the room, she moved the piano bench back and stood, fluffing the netting underneath her skirt. She didn't notice the ruggedly handsome officer standing inches from her. Until he spoke.

"Who taught you to play?" Cash leaned in before his buddy could intervene.

When she heard Cash's voice, Addy's eyes widened. Her pulse quickened. If the mere sound of this man's voice held power over her, what might happen when she turned to face him? Addy slowly spun around, and when her eyes met Cash's, her entire world went still.

Can it be you?

She froze—not trusting herself to move a muscle. Her heart pounded, and she felt dots of sweat gather on her forehead. Despite her visions, despite the number of times she'd anticipated this illusory moment, Addy had never conceived the exact moment of meeting the man destiny chose for her.

An authentic officer. A most handsome man. A lifelong lover.

"Forgive my rudeness, ma'am. The name's Cash. Cash Lamar." He extended his right hand.

"Adelaide Lafountain. My friends call me Addy." She accepted Cash's hand with a delicate brushing of her fingers, withdrawing quickly, conscious of lingering too long.

Their greetings collided.

"What did you ask me?"

"Oh . . . hmmm." Cash regrouped. "No, I asked where you'd learn to play the piano. 'It Had to be You' is one of my all-time favorites."

"Thank you," Addy said. Now that her heart rate had eased to nearly normal, she explained, "I've studied for years with one of my mother's friends who teaches music at Loyola University. Back home."

"Where's home?"

"New Orleans. I'm here for the summer. With my sisters, visiting our grandparents."

Addy felt flushed due to the crowd swell in Beauvoir's parlor rooms. Or because of her second Roman punch. Or was it the third? More likely, Addy felt a fever stirring within because Cash stood entirely too close . . . much too close for Addy to settle her quickened breath.

"Do you mind if we step out? On the back porch for air? I'm so lightheaded." Addy stepped back from the piano and into the main hallway.

"Of course. Excuse me, where are my manners? Let me get you a drink," Cash offered.

"The lady has had a couple, maybe more, Cash. Before your entrance," Eddy said, following them. He'd stood by—annoyed—scrutinizing his best friend's charm while casting a spell over Addy.

Before Eddy could speak his mind again, Cash grabbed Addy's

hand and led her through the hall to the backside of Beauvoir.

It wasn't unusual for Addy to be physically drained following a vision's manifestation. This time, though, she felt weaker than usual, and nearly stumbled into a white wrought-iron chair near the porch's railing, too woozy to stand.

Cash sat next to Addy. "Honey, how many drinks did Eddy hand you? Try putting your head through your knees. It's not lady-like, but it'll keep you from passing out." He held onto Addy's hand tightly.

"No, it's not that. Don't think you understand," Addy said. "I get . . . these feelings that wash over me . . . from time to time. That I can't control." Addy pulled away from Cash's grip, placed her head between her legs, and said, "I'll be better in a minute, I promise." Though she did wish for a cold compress for her head. But when Addy sensed playful fingertips darting across her back, then slithering down her right arm, she abruptly sat up, startled.

Cash was still sitting on her left, his hands resting on his knees. "Maybe something to eat?" he offered.

"No, thank you." *I'm huddled here, wondering how to explain my clairvoyance—then, this touch? From one I can only sense, but not see?*

Far simpler to follow Cash's lead, Addy agreed she was at fault and had consumed more than her share of fruity beverages that were too pretty to pass up. Behaving like a silly party girl who'd lost count of her drinks would buy Addy time to figure out what had just happened to her. Later, that is, when she'd had time to think and mention it to Mimi.

"Maybe if I'd eaten some hors d'oeuvres before those two drinks? But I was having so much fun that I didn't want to stop. I'm overheated, that's all. Everyone kept pushing up closer and closer to the piano bench," Addy said, uncomfortably aware that she was now providing Cash with a good bit of amusement.

Need to get shipshape before Mimi arrives. She'll surely know I'm buzzed!

Cash suggested a walk in Beauvoir's gardens, a stroll to the seawall, and then onto the beach. Since the crowd was thinning, Addy chose to stay on the side porch and trusted the salty air to provide a balance.

When she leaned against the porch railing and pulled her hair together to hold it above her neck, Addy closed her eyes, reassured after spotting a full moon. Cash's right hand barely brushed the small of her back, then lingered to offer support when Addy started to sway and drift with the rhythm of the breeze. Barely a whisper of his touch set Addy on fire. She allowed her head to drift softly onto Cash's shoulder—wished she might rest there for a lifetime. As Cash pulled her into him and leaned in for a kiss, she heard Mimi yell, "Adelaide Marie Lafountain. What do you think you are doing, young lady?"

Jarred, Addy jumped to attention and attempted an introduction. "Oh, Mimi. You're early. Meet Cash, my new friend."

"I certainly will not meet him after what I've witnessed," Mimi said. "Being rather forward, don't you think, young man?"

Cash ignored the woman's slight and introduced himself. "Cash Lamar, ma'am, Second Lieutenant, Army Air Force," he said. "Very pleased to meet you."

"I'm not altogether certain it's a pleasure," Mimi said. When she turned away, distracted with greeting a friend walking past, Cash pulled Addy closer and hurriedly whispered, "Meet me tomorrow night at the Dew Drop around 8 p.m. Take the trolley to Biloxi."

The evening floated to its petulant end after delighting Beauvoir's genteel guests, who basked in the languid language of the South. For hours, the laughter of beautiful, privileged young women rose to the ceiling of this historical setting where former Confederate president Jefferson Davis once lived. What a glorious and carefree evening for the untouchables who embraced an enviable life thousands of miles from utter destruction. They laughed, sang, drank, and danced with abandon while Keesler pilots navigated B-24s and dropped bombs on the other side of the world.

10 Suzanne

New Orleans, Late Summer 2012

Now, why would I agree to entertain Max's real estate clients in the French Quarter instead of meeting with my lawyer to rescue Kyle from his quagmire?

When Max hangs up, Suzanne stares at her phone as if it's embedded with human characteristics. No one person—no child, employee, or lover—deserves a tongue-lashing brushed with hate. Though she tries to deflect Max's harsh words, it's tough. Titillated by a hot, new relationship—overjoyed with embracing the elation of intimacy—Suzanne may have overlooked a red flag in the name of basking in pure pleasure again. Or two.

Four months in, she realizes that overlooking Max's quick temper and pardoning his sporadic jealousy is not working in her favor. No, quite the opposite.

I don't get it. Max has never so much as raised his voice to me. Until now.

Yet she recalls how disappointed he behaved recently after learning he couldn't spend the night because the twins arrived home unexpectedly and were displeased to see him wander out of their parents' bedroom in his skivvies. Then, later, he became visibly agitated after she made plans with friends for dinner or drinks, leaving him out. The more Suzanne mulls over Max's bizarre outburst of anger, the more she lingers over a connection between the sudden uptick in agitated spirit activity and Max's abrupt appearance in her life.

She's a strong advocate for never blaming things on coincidence. To protect herself, she must remain on guard. *The spirit world is stirred up, and it's me in the bloody middle. Did you do something, Max? Or more specifically, what did you do?* That's the next question I need to ask you.

Long acquainted with the power of a phantom that's content to linger or make a return appearance, Suzanne decides it's long past time to exert some control in her life. As a child, she feared falling asleep because a nebulous shape often appeared in the darkness and hovered in the upper corners of her room, watching her sleep. No cowering under the covers magically made the ghost or shadow figure disappear. If anything, her cowardly response only provoked the entity fixated on reaching for a young empath. In time, young Suzanne learned to practice whispering a question as simple as *who are you?* under the security of a comforter before releasing it and sitting in bed. It helped calm her anxiousness.

Her childhood was filled with sleepless nights. Often, she hosted midnight tea parties with the stranded spirits of little girls who'd died suddenly in a car accident or succumbed to a bout with pneumonia. Before she crawled into bed at night, young Suzanne carefully arranged floral bone china teacups on gold saucers atop her bedroom's table and chairs set, anticipating midnight visitors seeking a playmate.

Ancestral spirits often rescued Suzanne from the men Madelaine chose to bring home in the early morning hours, and guided her to recognize the energy of ghosts struggling to cross over, past the ether, into the afterlife. Those deceased Lafountains, lingering in spirit form, encouraged Suzanne to trust her clairsentience. Many spirits attempted to shield her from Madelaine's ugly demands for Suzanne to shift her allegiance from communicating with ghosts to acquiring hoodoo skills instead. Others did not. To note that Suzanne's childhood was dramatically different from her friends' innocent adventures is a gross understatement.

But now, there's a problem. After months of dating Max, she's intoxicated with a heady level of lust she hasn't experienced in decades. *How do I turn away from Max's urgent kisses, resist his fiery touch, and not stare into his endless eyes that sink deep into my soul? Will a spirit demand this of me?* Increasingly, Suzanne questions if her ancestral spirits are behind this, manipulating their encounter, perhaps to resolve an issue yet to be revealed.

When Fleetwood Mac's *Rumours* loads on her playlist, Suzanne sings the refrain of "The Chain" on the drive to her lawyer's office. Clearly, Max cannot be tossed aside. So instead, Suzanne tucks the unpleasant conversation on a shelf to address later.

After parking, Suzanne jumps when she walks around the backside of her SUV and sees the twins casually leaning against Beau's car. Kyle says, "Gee, thanks for coming, Mom."

"Starting to think you weren't going to show," Beau says, needling his mother for a reaction. "You know I'm missing work because of this jackass." He shifts his weight, then points to Kyle. "Why didn't *you* pick him up?"

"You know why, Beau. I'm in the middle of a training session this week. Don't pretend you don't know what I do to help keep this ship afloat," Suzanne says. "Let's go inside."

She's grateful for her family lawyer, who cares enough about her and the twins to help them navigate legal challenges. After being seated in the conference room, Kyle asks, "So, when do you think I'll get my license back?"

"No time soon, son. Mr. Pete will explain. He's trying to broker a deal, so you won't face the heaviest hand of the law."

She shoves her cell phone deep into her purse. Communicating with Max right now is four shades of infeasible.

"Goddamn it!" Kyle slaps his palm on the table.

"Kyle! Honestly, your language." She inches her chair closer to the table and leans in.

"Mom, I drank one beer. One beer before getting into my car!" Kyle's face reddens, and sweat gathers on his upper lip.

"You sure about that, son? You consumed more than you're admitting. Look where you're sitting today."

The severity of the situation sails right over Kyle's head. He *could* serve three months in jail for underage drinking and driving. She prays Pete can get the charge reduced. It would be a godsend if Kyle only faced thirty-six hours of required community services: Even so, a wake-up call is needed to flip his reckless and irresponsible behavior around. Kyle must move in with his father if this life lesson doesn't jolt him into reality.

Is there no bloody escape from a divorce's fallout?

Pete walks in with a thick file under his arm. He kisses Suzanne's cheek and then offers Kyle and Beau his right hand. "Gentlemen, good to see you. Suzanne, always a pleasure."

Sitting, he opens the file and takes a second to review it.

"Okay, Kyle, your hearing is on Tuesday in two weeks. This is how it's going down. You'll arrive on time, nicely dressed. Leave your cell phone in the car. This is non-negotiable. We'll sit at the defendant's table when the clerk calls your case. The judge will ask for your plea, and you'll say . . ."

"Guilty, your Honor," Kyle completes the sentence.

"Right, exactly right. Then the judge will rule and explain the conditions of your sentencing, including the plan to reinstate your license. Since this is your first offense, and your blood alcohol percentage was 0.08 percent, I'm hoping the court will only suspend your license for six months."

Kyle rolls his eyes and lowers his head, shaking it back and forth. Suzanne adjusts her posture, sits up straight, and tries to ignore her phone vibrating in her handbag.

"Kyle, listen to Mr. Pete," she cautions. "I'm losing patience here."

No response.

Pete's not smiling. "Son, this is no joke. Revoking your license for a year and serving jail time is what you face without my intervention. Do you understand the seriousness of underage drinking *and* driving while intoxicated? The court hardly views this offense lightly."

Turning to Suzanne, Pete says, "And there'll be a fine, too. The judge will set the amount, and you'll settle up before leaving the courthouse. But you know this," he adds. With a hard-drinking father and an alcoholic ex-husband, Suzanne has been here before. "Be prepared, friend, to rearrange your life. Set your community service schedule before leaving for school, and pencil in time for the driver's improvement class when you come home during the holidays. See you in two weeks."

Suzanne reaches out for her son's hand. Covers it with her own. There's nothing tentative about her gesture. "Your reckless behavior stops now, Kyle. While you depend on friends for rides around campus, you need to work on your attitude. What if you'd been in a wreck, son? Killed yourself, or, God forbid, others?" She stops there. Losing it with her kid in Pete's office: not the best parenting example to set. "Those plans of yours to attend law school after college? You may have nixed that one." She reaches for her purse and walks to the conference room door.

"Yeah, you might want to tell your boyfriend to stop texting so much," Kyle says. "When you're focused on a life-changing meeting with your kid."

"That's your response?"

Beau shakes his head and says, "Dude. Really?"

"Kyle, I'll see you at home. Beau, text me when you get to work."

Trusting that Pete will handle Kyle's case for the best possible outcome, Suzanne navigates early evening traffic to their home in Lakeview, her thoughts again centered on Max. She's annoyed, thinking of how easily she allowed him entry into her life.

Why didn't Margie warn me of concerns about dating him? Or even Remé, for that matter. Max is his best friend and business partner. Why not suggest caution?

Suzanne will request an investigation later today. To be on the safe side.

Although it goes against every fiber of her being, Suzanne decides it's time to visit Enola's hoodoo boutique in the Marigny, the funky shop on the edge of the French Quarter that Franny keeps begging her to stop by. Slowing down, then turning into her driveway, Suzanne concedes that only *she* can control the puppeteers of her life.

That age-old battle between her spirit guides to fine-tune her clairsentience *or* spellcasting skills *still* conflicts with her now-deceased mother's desire to mold another Lafountain legacy.

Now, from the grave.

Suzanne pulls a bottle of moscato from the wine cooler and a goblet from the cabinet before walking outside to locate a perfect spot to set up a hoodoo altar. No longer can she ignore the need for self-protection.

I'm sorry, Madelaine. I regret not paying attention to your instructions. For the first time in my life, I truly wish I hadn't shoved hoodoo away.

Once she's kicked her heels off, Suzanne meanders through the lush backyard, pausing in front of various stone ledges to consider a spot with sufficient space for candles to burn, then extinguish on their own accord. After she passes the large limestone fountain in the center of her backyard, Suzanne feels an uncomfortable twinge at her temples.

As she circles back around to the brick patio just off the kitchen, the waft of a sickly-sweet vanilla scent takes her by surprise before she notices Jack awkwardly propped atop the back of a wrought-iron lounge chair, watching with amusement. Always thrilled to see the Lafountain family angel, she smiles at his nearly-there glimmer at twilight.

Before Suzanne can properly greet this devilishly handsome being, Kyle appears at the sliding patio door, breaking the spell. Proof that *if* Kyle could see the angel, he's not seeing Jack this time.

"Yeah, your boyfriend's blocking the driveway, Mom. Refusing to move his damn car."

"Are you sure, Kyle? We're not speaking to one another right now," she says, pausing to take a sip from her wine glass.

"Says he's not leaving until he talks to you," Kyle says. "I'm calling Dad if you don't deal with him. This crazy-ass man of yours doesn't get to tell me what to do. He's out front. Are you coming?"

"Don't call your father, Kyle. I'll handle this." Suzanne exhales dramatically. She sets her wine glass on the coffee table across from Jack, who's barely there. Then, before she follows Kyle, she whispers to Jack, "Stay. I have a question I need to ask you. About jellyfish."

"Where else would I be, love?" Jack says. "And I have quite a lot to say about those beguiling creatures."

Out front, Suzanne cannot believe the scene that's unfolding. Kyle's not lying, for Max's vehicle is angled near the entrance to the garage, completely blocking the driveway. He and Kyle are screaming at one another and shoving fingers at each other's faces, only inches apart.

"Max!" she yells to get his attention. "Move your car so that Kyle can park in the garage. Right now."

"Well, isn't this little Miss Suzy Homemaker," Max says, backing away from Kyle, now totally focused on her. "Look at you, so cute, with your high heels off, skipping through the grass, barefoot. I'm surprised you're not wearing an apron."

Managing a firm stance with hands on her hips, Suzanne says, "Have you lost your mind? You can't come to my house and stir things up with my kid," she says. "Move your car, please. Or I'm calling the police."

Not having shifted his eyes away from Suzanne, Max says, "Oh, I like it when you're feisty, Suzy."

She crosses her arms and takes two steps back. "Now, Max."

"I'll move it . . . if you explain."

". . . Not bargaining with you," she interrupts. "Technically, you're trespassing on my property. We may not have a rule book, but I'm certain it's not okay to show up at my house—to confront my kid or yell at me."

"I just complimented you. Didn't you hear me?" A pouty look crawls across his face, a practiced expression that's probably gained him sympathy in the past but is ineffective now. "We'd gotten something started, right? I deserve an explanation."

"Leave, Max." He inches closer. "Now."

Suzanne stomps back into the house and watches Max from the dining room window. He backs up to turn around in the driveway, then topples the rose bushes lining the curb when he peels out into the street. After pulling his car into the garage, Kyle enters the kitchen and slams his body onto one of the bar stools.

"I'm confused," he says. "How's this guy an improvement over Dad?"

"That's uncalled for, son," Suzanne begins. Then reconsiders. "Look, it's been years since I've dated. And it's not easy for me. Some days I feel like I'm still married to your father, so I wonder why I'm bothering to explore a new relationship. Max, well, he sorta landed in my path." Suzanne opens the pantry door and stares at its contents as though sheer eye contact will miraculously produce a quick dinner for them. "It's obvious now I've got a huge learning curve."

"Obviously. I want us to be safe, Mom."

"Of course." Her heart hurts, and her eyes sting with tears when she hears that Kyle believes she is risking their safety by hanging out with Max. *What in the world have I stepped into?*

"Please don't make this a weird mission—like trying to save a jackass from himself."

Suzanne wills her tears away. "Join me in the den for our favorite baked pasta in a few, okay? Then we can tune into that Netflix series we've been watching."

"Sure."

Later that night, after Kyle leaves to see his girlfriend, Suzanne returns to the bricked patio with a refreshed drink and Bimini by her side. Though it's late August and muggy outdoors, a soft, gentle breeze beckons her to stay.

"Jack? Still checking on us? I have questions—I keep dreaming of jellyfish. Any ideas?"

No response.

I'd disappear, too, if I could . . . yet I cannot fathom that kind of freedom.

Every 150 years or so, Jack receives an angel's assignment, allowing him the privilege of weaving in and out of multiple generations of an enchantress's family until the last one's life is extinguished. Or until he crosses over with *the one* he most loves. Then he'll be gone.

Back in 1854, he received his fifth mandate: to shadow the life of Louisa Lafountain, born of a sugarcane planter and a Choctaw fieldworker. And raised by a compliant wife, well-respected as a rootworker.

And Jack is still here.

Suzanne settles into the sofa cushions and immediately spots the ideal location for her hoodoo altar, adjacent to the stone firepit and above the food prep area. Would a casual guest who joins her for an evening drink even notice a few lively-colored candles, a mortar, and a pestle? Suzanne imagines arranging roots to grind and mix, placing crystals around a vial of lavender oil, and positioning at least one blessed item in the mix, with a deck of tarot cards nestled nearby.

Exhausted, Suzanne drifts into a twilight sleep and dreams

so vividly of Madelaine that she senses her mother's cool touch: a fingertip brushing her left cheek, stroking the back of her head. In her dream, Suzanne watches her mom stretch out playfully on the glass coffee table directly across from her, wearing her favorite silk caftan. Suzanne smells a hint of her mother's woody Chanel scent as she dozes in and out of a deep sleep.

Madelaine's spirit whispers: "*He's your destiny. We're stranded, love. Need your help.*"

Suzanne's eyes fly open and widen with both excitement and apprehension. She no longer doubts the validity of this unique voice, engraved long ago in her memory, destined to linger for a lifetime.

Why now, Mother? Why suddenly reach out from the grave?

In 2008, Madelaine died in a fiery car crash along the dark, haunted country road that stretches in front of Myrtle's Plantation in St. Francisville, Louisiana, after she stormed away from a séance that opened an unwelcome portal.

11 Max

New Orleans, Late Summer 2012

Four years separate Max from his chaotic encounter with the Commonwealth of Kentucky. After the horror of Farrah's death, Max swore he'd never set foot in the Bluegrass State again. Yet, despite an initial exoneration in his wife's death, Max will arrive on a Wednesday to testify in yet another deposition.

This state is the worst goddamn place on Earth.

Before leaving New Orleans, Max meets with Kristoff and the Ready, Set, & Roll producers to finalize the Canal Place lease. Somewhere between touring the rental space and drinking Aperol spritzes until 3 a.m., Kristoff and his sidekicks fall madly in love with Max and the entire jazz ensemble of musicians at the 21st on Iberville, including the trumpeter who tap-dances while playing his instrument. Pledging their lifelong dedication to the Big Easy, Kristoff and Krauss sign multi-year leases covering two floors of Canal Place, with an option for a third floor if it becomes available.

"I don't know how they're functioning today," Max tells Maureen as he waits for Kristoff and Krauss to arrive at his office.

"I don't know how *you're* functioning," she says. "I'm guessing you've no memory of calling me. From the bar?" She pours Max another espresso and places three Advil tablets on his desk. Everyone at M & R Realty will celebrate Max's victory today. Once the ink dries on the producers' signatures, generous bonus checks will be distributed.

"I lost count, dahlin'. Sorry," he says, swallowing the painkillers before chasing them with hot coffee. "Suzanne turned off her phone last night, so I didn't talk to her. You know me. I had to call someone." Max glossed over the truth. As per usual. He skipped the encounter at Suzanne's house in Lakeview.

"Always happy to be your stand-in woman."

Maureen steps out and walks to the conference room. "I'll check to see if P.J.'s has delivered our Danishes."

"Confirm my flight, will you? And the car?"

"No need to yell, boss," Maureen says, entering his office again to see if further instructions will follow.

"And Maureen? Not a word of this Kentucky manure to anyone else, especially not Kristoff. Don't need anyone sniffing up my ass right now."

"Of course."

Maureen double-checks that Max has everything for the trip stacked near his attaché. "Your flight's delayed by an hour due to storms circling Nashville," she says.

"Can we change it? Can I land in Louisville?"

"The depo's in Brownsville . . . Kentucky, right? That may work. Since Nashville and Louisville are each about ninety miles away. But you'll need to hightail it after you grab your rental car."

Max slams his fists on his desktop, toppling what's left of his coffee. *I've got no patience for this Farrah bullshit!*

"Seriously, Max?" Maureen asks. She backs up toward the door. "Is John already there?"

"He flew up yesterday to meet with the chief deputy attorney. He hopes to run into one of Farrah's family members . . .

to try and get a read on the haps."

"Okay, Max, let's not go there. Not yet." Maureen turns and steps into the hallway.

But Max keeps talking. Perhaps to himself. Possibly hoping that Maureen will overhear his musings. "You know, I despised them, the whole damn Lamar family, even before we married. Now I hate them even more since I sh—no, no—since she tumbled to her death." He slams his fists again for good measure.

No ringing phones or computer beeps. No printer squeaks or Keurig bleeps. Only silence.

"Wait, what did you say?" Maureen pokes her head through the door's threshold. "Did you start to say that you *shoved* Farrah? Then stop yourself? Which is it, Max? Did she tumble? Or did you shove her?"

Max adjusts his posture, straightens his tie, and buys a second. *How did that slip out?* He clears his throat, takes two more sips from his coffee, and motions for Maureen to get back to work.

"Another shot of espresso, dear?"

"I think I deserve an answer, Max. I'm the one who has defended you against everyone's suspicions or accusations. All because of what happened in that damn cave. Now, this?" Her eyes widen with horror.

Max stares out the large window behind his desk and watches a Carnival cruise ship reach the bend in the Mississippi River. He avoids direct eye contact with his girl Friday.

"So, it's true. It must be true, or you wouldn't say it." Maureen bends over and grabs the arm of a wing chair to catch her balance. "You did it, didn't you? You shoved your beautiful wife into that bottomless pit. *Why*?" Though Maureen doesn't allow time for Max's rebuttal, she expects one. As Max stands eerily still, his back to her as he stares across the expanse of the Mississippi River, a nervous, giddy laugh escapes from Maureen's lips: "Max, do you feel the slightest bit of guilt? How dare you? Now you burden me with a confession when no one else hears it!"

Max whirls around to face her this time, then slams his coffee mug against his desk. Were it not a Rookwood original, it would have shattered into a million pieces. "Goddamn it, Maureen. Why should I confess? I'll have you remember that you are *not* my priest. So measure your importance, chér, and bring my refill to the conference room. Now!"

As Max grabs his suit jacket from the back of the chair and eases into it, there's no slack between him and his rising angst. Today, Max views himself as the pinnacle of local real estate success. News of the deal will be shared across various media, and since Hollywood is involved, videos chronicling the event will be uploaded and shared within minutes. He'll allow nothing to get in the way of finalizing this lease. He grabs his Samsung notebook for last-minute reference and walks across the hall.

Maureen could still spell trouble, but Max is banking on her loyalty. The key to their successful relationship is a commitment to keeping each other's secrets locked and secure—an unspoken job requirement. The idea that Maureen tortures herself because she has long suspected the truth about what happened in Kentucky is inconsequential to Max.

With everything else I've got to manage, he thinks, I need to keep a thumbprint on Mo.

I still need her help.

No evidence has surfaced to gainsay the ruling of his wife's accidental death. She fell to her death in the depths of a deep chasm while walking along the slippery pathways of Mammoth Cave's Domes and Dripstones tour. Max is four years in the clear.

No evidence, no charges. No charges, no trial. No trial, no conviction.

That's my girl. Max watches Maureen, now composed, enter the conference room with another M & R agent, both ready to serve as signature witnesses. Max's notary accepts the security deposit and first and last month's rent: roughly $5 million and some change.

Max holds his breath when he sees the check exchange hands. With the firm's monthly profits, he and Remé plan to develop multiple-family housing for folks who've never recovered from Hurricane Katrina's devastation on the Gulf Coast, particularly in the coastal towns of Pass Christian and Long Beach. He's counting on Remé's willingness to distribute equitable commission checks to them once the deposit clears. Max desperately needs the funds to play catch up with a sticky family debt that predates his birth and has plagued the Martins for generations.

If Remé disagrees, Max will be forced to design an alternative plan.

"Heading out today?" Max asks. "Or will you stay the week?"

"We're auditioning actresses for the lead role in one of our projects back at the Riverfront Hilton this afternoon," Kristoff says. "And you?"

"Going to the great commonwealth of Kentucky, I'm afraid."

"Who goes to Kentucky?"

"From the looks of it, I do."

Against his better judgment, Max reaches out to Suzanne. He's not surprised when the call drifts to voicemail. Was their last communication a text? Max scrolls through his messages.

He locates it. "Still with Kyle's lawyer. I'll call in a few days."

But Suzanne hasn't called. And since Max can't explain Maureen, can't defend blowing up at Suzanne because she missed drinks at 21st Amendment, and can't justify his stupid behavior at her Lakeview house, he sends a text. A gesture Max hopes will keep him in the loop.

"Want to respect your space. I nailed Canal Place. Sorry. If I hurt your feelings."

He waits. Then sends another text: "Out of town for a few days. Up north. Dinner when I return?"

Max stares out the window numbly as the driver exits I-10 at Williams. Curbside check-in is minutes away. He can't shake the sensation that this last-minute journey into his past will backfire.

John calls him as he's boarding his Delta flight.

"Max, we may have a real problem here," John says. "Someone on that cave tour with you and Farrah contacted the DA's office. Claims to be an eyewitness . . . said she'd been sitting on what she knew for a while. The woman's terminally ill or something and doesn't want to die with anything left unsaid."

"What the fuck does that mean?"

"It means she's given a statement to the DA, and now they're looking to follow up on it."

"Jesus."

"Not sure Jesus can help you right now, Max," John says. "But listen to me and listen well. If there's one detail, no matter how small, that you've failed to share with me, now is the time to do so."

"I got nothing else to say."

One damn Kentucky hillbilly, plotting my demise? Don't think that's happening.

Max doesn't see Maureen's text message until he lands in Louisville. "I'm landing thirty minutes after you. Don't leave the airport without me."

12

Addy

Gulf Coast, Summer 1944

In contrast with the rhythm of Addy's racing heart, the drive back to the Pass felt laborious. She settled into the leather seat, smiled, and relived her sweet moments with Cash. But after replaying Mimi's dramatic confrontation, Addy sat up straight, rolled her eyes, and mentally dared her grandmother to turn around and face her.

Try to keep us apart, Mimi. I'll tell you one thing right now—I want nothing more than to disappear inside Cash's kisses. You won't win this battle, not even with your magick.

Addy yearned to embrace a host of sensual experiences now that she'd met the man in her visions: her one and only. She craved the one thing she could least rely upon—time to fall in love. A very tall order since the enlists at Keesler's AAF base left within a few months after training. Could Cash be an exception? Remain stationed here on the Gulf Coast through the summer?

Time to face the music, *sugga'*, as Mama Charlotte would say. Addy braced for Mimi's judgment, for there'd surely be a lecture. Why allow an aborted kiss to slide without making an issue, since it happened in public? The car was quiet. Papa drove in silence. Addy prepared herself for Papa's verbal lashing as he entered the oyster-shell driveway.

"I don't ask much of you two," Mimi began as she turned to face her granddaughters. "Just an ounce of common sense."

Papa turned off the motor and waited. At first, Esty deferred to her older sister for their collective response.

And Addy didn't disappoint her. "Mimi, you'll not get one if you're seeking an apology. Why? Because I haven't done anything wrong. Tonight, I met an extraordinary guy who's patriotic, responsible, and damn good-looking. And I'm really excited for my chance to know him."

"She's over the moon, Mimi," Esty whispered.

"Shush, Esty. I realize this," Mimi said. "But that's not the point."

"That's exactly the point, Mimi!" Addy raised her voice in defiance. "I've told you things I've never shared with Mama Charlotte. You *know* this isn't the first time I've talked about meeting the man of my visions." Her voice rose with her frustration. "And here he is. Finally."

"Calm yourself, young lady. Mimi's only looking to protect you," Papa said, reflecting on the wisdom gained through more than thirty-five years of marriage.

"I know, Papa," Addy snapped. "But I don't think she's playing fair. I figured Mimi was the one Lafountain who'd understand." Addy finished rolling down her window, inviting the evening's coastal breeze to sit a spell. She whispered to Esty to do the same.

Mimi appealed to Papa for support. "James?" Mimi asked.

"How about we go inside, love? It's just too damn hot in the car to argue. You've a long, hot summer together. Find a way to get along."

"She's in love, Mimi, absolutely in love," Esty yelled, racing to be the first one upstairs to run a bath.

"We'll see about that," Mimi said.

"Just admit it, Mimi," Addy said. "You met him. You *know* he's a dreamboat."

Papa headed to the bar, tucked at the far end of the formal dining room next to the screened porch entrance. Liquor bottles imported worldwide were displayed adjacent to the finest Tennessee whiskeys. He poured himself a shot of Jack Daniels over ice and grumbled when he didn't see a jar of boiled-down sugar water or fresh mint for his julep. Finally, he looked at his granddaughter and said, "Addy, get yourself a lemonade to balance what you drank at that sham of a party. This discussion is tabled until tomorrow."

"Good night, girls," Mimi said.

Addy didn't knock before entering the girls' bathroom adjacent to the bedroom she and Esty shared. "I need a plan for tomorrow night, sis. Cash wants me to meet him at the Dew Drop Inn. In Biloxi," she said. "He told me to take the trolley."

"You've clearly lost your damn mind," Esty said. The seventeen-year-old peeked over a cascade of bubbles with eyes wiser than her age. "You're doing exactly what Cash says to do? You can't go to a club with him, Addy. It's not even legal!"

"Of course it's legal. I can drink at a club, even back home. You can if you're eighteen. You *do* know this, don't you?"

"I think it might be different here. We're in Mississippi," Esty said, pointing out the obvious. "Besides, you barely know this guy. You can't go drinking with him."

"I absolutely can. And there's not one thing you can do to stop me. I've waited my whole life for this man. So either you help me plan or keep quiet." Addy lifted a washcloth from a stack of towels in the linen closet, then soaked it in cold water. After wringing it out, she covered her face with it. "I can't remember when I've felt so hot."

"I'll think about it," Esty said, lowering herself deeper into the tub. "I know you have your visions and all, Addy, and you think this Cash guy is super neat, but you need to be careful."

"Why? When I already know he's the one for me?" Addy cranked open the transom windows in their bathroom to let in a breeze, then lowered the toilet cover to sit. She watched her sister slip entirely underwater, then bob up repeatedly. "You're interested in him, am I right? Admit it, Esty."

"Never," Esty yelled. "I've no desire to date an airman. I'm only warning you because I've heard what people say about them. They hunt for the prettiest girls and then take them."

"Take them? Honestly, do you hear yourself?"

"You know what I mean. Have sex and then leave 'em for trash," Esty added awkwardly. The sisters were well-versed in exchanging inaccurate information with one another.

"First, I'm not trash. Second, I'm not having sex with a fellow who'll toss me. And third, we didn't even get a first kiss," Addy said. "Mimi made sure of that."

"But you will. Very soon."

Addy struggled to fall asleep, tossing one way, then another. She sat and looked to see if their bedroom door had been left open. When Addy heard voices, she left her bed and lingered at the top of the stairs.

She heard Mimi ask, "What are we going to do?"

"Nothing," Papa said. "Look, Jeanne, there's not much we can do except keep a watchful eye. Addy's a beautiful young woman, an extraordinary catch for the right young man. Educated, wealthy, and graduating from Newcomb next year."

"You said it. For a *proper*, suitable young man," Mimi said. "There are servicemen everywhere you turn. Walking the streets, crashing social events, lurking behind walls. And they each have an eye for our Addy. Even Esty."

"They're in training to defend our democracy, Jeanne. They're not suspicious characters to be feared. But God help us if they are."

"I love those girls as if they were my own. We don't want a disaster on our watch."

"I'll drink to that." Papa raised his tumbler.

Addy tiptoed back to bed, careful to close the door. Had she lingered a little longer, Addy would have overheard Mimi tell Papa that she'd slipped—explained the blue apothecary bottles hanging on the 'haint tree. Papa grunted and refreshed his drink.

"Why in the world would you bring Addy into your family's hoodoo foolishness? That's all we need 'round here. Do not, Jeanne, I repeat, *do not* have her join your séance circle. And don't even think about inviting her into your potter's cottage."

"You know I wouldn't dream of doing that," Mimi said, averting her eyes. "I know better."

So excited and unsettled about the evening's events, Addy struggled to fall asleep. Then, after she drifted off, Addy had one nightmare after another of Esty and Cash escaping together, hand-in-hand, leaving her behind without a thought as to how their actions would devastate her. Twice, she awoke drenched in sweat, tears running down her cheeks.

It was only a nightmare.

When the girls entered Mimi's kitchen the next morning, they learned Papa had scheduled a day trip out to Cat Island, one of the barrier islands south of the Pass.

"I thought the plan was to go fishing in the Sound. Now it's Cat Island? We'll be out on the island 'til sunset," Addy said, annoyed that her plans to meet Cash were hopelessly dashed.

"So much for the Dew Drop," Esty laughed.

By the time the girls dressed for the day, Mimi had filled an oversized picnic basket with sandwiches, cookies, crackers, and fruit. The girls had less than fifteen minutes to grab a slice of toast and a glass of orange juice.

When they eased into a parking space at Gulfport's Small Craft Harbor, Macie was the first to see the hand-lettered sign: Cat Island excursions canceled for the day due to off-base military training with dogs. An early afternoon charter to another barrier island farther out in the Gulf was available instead to those with military connections. After a brief conversation with the captain of August Moon, Papa announced, "Need a quick decision, mates. Ship Island for the day or back home?"

"Ship Island, of course," Mimi said. "We wait a year for the girls to join us, so we're not missing this opportunity." Seething, Addy turned away from her grandmother.

Please, please, please, Cash, don't be upset with my no-show. I'm not losing my chance with you over this. Don't forget our almost-kiss. And how fast your pulse was racing.

Esty shouted, "Harbor party!" At least one family member was excited about returning late enough to drift in the Sound at dusk. Macie prayed for no seasickness. And Addy silently kissed her evening plans with Cash bye-bye.

Addy watched the harbor while waiting to board, admiring the scale of the piers in Gulfport's adjacent commercial harbor, arranged symmetrically to support the sleek oyster schooners and bulky shrimp trawlers, bopping in their berths. She surveyed the dark blue-gray sparkling water that lapped up against the moorings and inhaled the fresh seafood scents that reeled back from the main wharf where the morning's catch was piled high.

The harbor's harmony lessened the mark of social and economic differences for those living along the Gulf Coast, a fact incomprehensible to outsiders. The wealthy boasted of adventure on their sailboats and chartered crafts, while shrimpers and oystermen trusted their vessels to provide sustenance for their family's futures. In unity, the boats moored in sync with the Sound's lapping water, a testament, a symbol of lives well lived.

How will I leave this paradise come September?

"All aboard," Captain Jack yelled. He offered everyone a hand up, reminding folks that no fishing supplies could be purchased on the island. "Better get your bait, quick, before we shove off."

Within minutes, the engines revved, and the small group headed south through the Mississippi Sound toward the Gulf of Mexico. Esty and Addy huddled beside one another, bracing against the wind and mist kicking up at the yacht's stern, out of earshot from Mimi and Papa. Esty asked, "What about to-night?"

"Not much I can do now, is there?" Staring into the waves the boat created as it sliced through the water, Addy said, "I've got little to go on except a giddy feeling. Don't have Cash's phone number at the base. Can't remember his best friend's name. Have no idea what I'd say if I called."

"If the two of you are destined to see each other again, one of you will find a way," Esty said. She turned slightly away from her sister to keep the wind from whipping at her face. Or perhaps to hide her true thoughts about the situation.

"There's so little time to get acquainted. Airmen, crew-men, they all leave. That's why they're here in the first place. Get trained. Go overseas. Join the war," Addy said. "Honestly, I can't begin to imagine what those guys will face overseas."

"I guess you have to believe . . ."

"Do you?" Addy said. "Officers don't wait. After one eve-ning getting to know a gal? It just doesn't work that way." Esty hugged her sister before they moved to starboard and sat next to a young couple who couldn't take their eyes off each other. As the motor cut, the vessel slowed. Finally, the captain docked near the end of the long pier, leaving sufficient space to tie the line and toss the anchor.

"See the guys over there, near the fort. See the ones who're fishing?" Esty pointed at a large group of young servicemen, some jumping off the dock with wild abandon.

"Shush, young lady," Mimi warned. "Do *not* yell at them." Addy often forgot that Esty was nearly four years younger and infinitely more boy-crazy than she had ever been at the same age.

"Look!"

"Stop, Esty. You're making a fool of yourself," Addy hissed.

"But there're so many of them. And just the two of us," she giggled. "Oh, for gosh sake, if only we weren't here with Mimi and Papa."

Papa led the way off the boat, somehow managing to tote his fishing gear. Addy and Esty carried Mimi's picnic basket, which was heavier than expected, while Mimi and Macie grabbed a couple of beach bags. The Lafountains upheld their family tradition of overestimating a day trip's necessities: They had enough supplies to last a week. When they trudged past Fort Massachusetts, Papa launched into his predictable dissertation of why Confederate prisoners of the Civil War had been detained there.

No one paid him one bit of attention.

When they reached the opposite side of the island, Addy raised her face to the sun, seduced by the island's sugar-white sand sparkling as though tiny diamonds were buried beneath. Papa walked to the water's edge to set his poles while Mimi laid out the tartan-plaid cloth she reserved for day excursions. Addy adjusted her sun hat and leaned back, finally feeling free to relax and watch the pelicans swoop into the waves and grab their fish dinner. She'd lost track of Esty.

Later, she noticed Esty standing atop a small dune with one hand on her right hip and the other adjusting her cat-shaped sunglasses as though she was posing for the cover of *Life* magazine. She watched Esty wink, then smile.

Addy didn't hear Cash sneak up from behind. And didn't expect the passionate kiss he planted on her lips as Mimi watched in disbelief.

13

Suzanne

New Orleans, Late Summer 2012

Suzanne's summer of self-indulgence filters to an end. When she enters Biltmore Christian Academy on a Thursday afternoon in late August, she's refreshed and excited for the new school year. But sadly, these emotions are fleeting. It won't be long before a gifted student demands a higher score on his summer reading test. He'll list excuses to defend his poor performance and request a redo. Naturally, a guidance counselor will be summoned when she refuses to change his grades, and a parental conference with the principal will follow. She'll show up as the sacrificial guest of honor.

Within a week, Suzanne will long for a different career.

She wanders into the school's administration office, hoping to speak to her principal, a balding boss habitually hunched over three laptop computers. But he's not seated in his workspace.

"Justin around?" she asks the school secretary, buried behind a daunting pile of new student folders.

"Hi, Suzanne," the woman answers. "He's in the athletic center. He said something about needing a break from the budget."

"Well, I'm not walking back to the trainer's building," Suzanne says. "When you see him, please mention I stopped by. I'm organizing my classroom today."

"I'll tell him." Ms. Willis adjusts her red-flecked glasses atop her head. "He'll be here late. I'm sure you're aware that the school board meets tonight."

"Thank you, ma'am." Suzanne senses Ms. Willis' hesitation, so she pauses for a moment. She wonders—does the secretary's dawdling concern a specific item on the agenda?

Instead, the older woman asks, "You still seeing the cute guy from the Marigny?" Suzanne regrets posting pictures of her and Max on social media. Too late now.

Suzanne keeps it simple. "Yes, ma'am. We have fun together."

"I'm happy for you, dear. We all deserve love." Ms. Willis, widowed ten years ago, stands up to stretch. "I miss my Satchel every single day."

Suzanne walks through the darkened halls of the high school building, then takes the stairs to the language arts wing, where English, Spanish, and French classrooms encircle an open theater space. As she unlocks Room 10, Suzanne hears her phone's vibration when she tosses her purse on a podium. It's Franny.

"Suzanne, please tell me you're not already at school."

"I am. Summer doesn't last forever." Suzanne surveys the upturned chairs propped on the oversized desks, the stacks of literature textbooks piled next to new bookcases. She wonders if she will have sufficient time to get organized before school starts.

"Honey, you've been on my mind this afternoon. My new Angel tarot deck surely has a message for you." She hears Franny whisper to someone on her end. "Can I pass by your classroom for a minute?"

"Not sure that's a reliable plan." When Suzanne steps back into the middle school complex, home to 200 eighth-grade students, she dreads the progression of hiding her true identity.

Her authentic self.

"It'll be fine, girl," Franny insists. "We won't be in the faculty lounge. I mean, you can do whatever you please in your classroom. Right?"

"Technically, that's true. But privileges can backfire, particularly if board members need ammunition for a teacher's dismissal. For no damn good reason."

"Good Lord, that's frightening."

"Isn't it? Come on, then. If it feels creepy, we'll leave. It's not like we're consulting Ouija."

Suzanne's been an odd fit at Biltmore for a while now. As a literature and writing instructor at a privately funded progressive school, she appreciates the curriculum coordinator ignoring some titles that appear on banned book lists, allowing educators to include novels like Ray Bradbury's *Fahrenheit 451*. Yet school boards set boundaries of what they will and will not accept. Max teases her about tempting fate. *You're asking to be fired.*

Maybe so.

Suzanne has received sufficient warnings, so it's likely Biltmore board members are nearing their level of intolerance. Nevertheless, Suzanne continues to teach Arthur Miller's *The Crucible* to gifted eighth graders, including a mock witchcraft trial. And if that's insufficient evidence to raise more than an eyebrow or two, Suzanne's occasional October pilgrimage to Salem, Massachusetts, confirms she'll never receive a Teacher of the Year nomination.

When Suzanne hears Franny's voice in the hallway, she rushes to catch her friend before any damage is done. "Who are you chatting with?"

"I've no idea," Franny says. "Calm down, Suzanne. We are not criminals." Franny drops her large, fringed hobo bag, packed with good intentions and ominous warnings, by the door. Then sits in a student's chair.

"How's your business in the Quarter?"

Franny sighs. "Tourists converge like moths this time of year, starved to return home with a salacious story. What's better than a tarot reading with someone who looks like me?"

"And that's bad because . . ."

"They're only interested in dabbling with the cards for a few minutes," Franny says. "I spend an excruciating amount of time interpreting. They don't understand a tough call, like Death overlapping a Knight of Swords. When I explain someone's about to die, they don't want to hear that."

"God, that's ominous. That wasn't part of my last reading, was it?"

"No, of course not. But the Knight of Swords *is* destructive. And as for Death, well, it always represents an end. So, connect the dots," Franny says. "For you, I'd interpret a situation coming to its end."

But what if the cards truly mean Death? I need to pay closer attention. Or return to solely reading tarot . . . for me.

Suzanne stands on a step ladder and tapes a white placard over the classroom door's window to prevent any curiosity seekers from peeking in. Then she locks the door.

Franny watches and laughs. "Suzanne, what does this say about you? About your school? If you can't have your spiritualist show up for a friendly tarot reading without subterfuge . . ."

"Taking precautions. Don't judge."

"But that's the point," Franny says. "How do you teach where you're forced to be someone else?"

"I'm not the only faculty member protecting my identity. We've got religious zealots, swingers, divorcées, and a few atheists. And those teachers only top the list. Believe me, there's more."

"Dear God."

"Look, if you're degreed, certified, highly qualified, can pass the sheriff's fingerprint test, and haven't a record of molesting children, you're hired."

"Have to admit, those qualities are essential."

Suzanne moves her desk closer to where Franny's seated and clears the surface. Then, before facing Franny, she says, "If forced to defend you, I'd explain that you're not a soothsayer or a medium. But honestly, if someone walks in on a tarot arc spread across my desk, his first ignorant thought would be . . ."

"That we're summoning spirits," Franny says, completing Suzanne's sentence. She cuts the deck, shuffles the cards, and continues, "Really, though, would anyone here truly understand the role of a conjurer? A hoodoo rootworker?"

"Not a serious question. Is it?" Suzanne glances at the classroom door quickly, imagining the clicking sound of a doorknob jiggle.

"I'd tell the truth and say that you're simply an enchantress. If asked . . ."

Suzanne laughs, then slumps back in her chair. "Well, that would solidify my removal from payroll in a heartbeat."

"Let's see what the cards say." Franny moves forward. "I've brought my Angel deck. It's a bit refreshing, somewhat less daunting."

"Three-card spread?" Suzanne reaches for the deck, holds the beautifully decorated blue cards, gilded in gold, against her chest, and silently offers an intention.

"When you're ready . . ."

Suzanne chooses the first card and places it face-down on her desk in the left corner. This card represents the past. Franny flips it face-up.

"Four of Air, my friend."

"These illustrations are different from what I recognize—I'm lost."

Franny explains: "In the past, you've needed more time to make decisions. That's changing."

"Won't argue with that," Suzanne says, drawing the second card, representing the present. She places it slightly to the right and admires its intricacy of fairies and unicorns surrounding a mermaid against a cerulean blue background. "The card's exquisite," Suzanne says.

"Ahh, the Page of Water," Franny says, cocking her head slightly. "Someone's in the wings. Waiting to play a more prominent role in your life. Not sure . . . of its identity. A spirit? No . . . no, perhaps an angel." Franny's ambiguous interpretation of the second card is irritating, partly because Suzanne already knows it's true.

Jack is back, and that's not necessarily a reassuring sign.

Resting her elbows on the desk, Suzanne lowers her head and massages her temples. As she raises her chin, she feels stymied from turning her head to the right or left. She cannot resist staring directly at a light orange aura drifting in her direction. As its color shifts from orange to yellow, Suzanne hears the unmistakable sound of Madelaine's spirit voice: "*Stay . . . with Max . . . he's the skeleton key.*"

Suzanne shivers as the chilly room temperature drops dramatically, her teeth chattering uncontrollably. Franny senses the room's energy shift and reaches for her friend's hand. She's no stranger to a trapped spirit's dramatic entrance.

"It's Madelaine, dear, isn't it?" Franny whispers. "We'll stop. If this is too much."

Suzanne shakes her head, then reaches for another card with her trembling right hand. Often, specters are fleeting, so there's no reason to believe Madelaine's spirit will linger for more than a few seconds—if it is, undeniably, Madelaine, and not a trickster ghost. Franny flips it, revealing a Seven of Earth with a majestic dragon in its center. The card represents the future.

Rushing to complete the reading, Franny explains, "Seeds are planted, Suzanne. Time to claim your legacy, your future. If you fail to do so, there'll be repercussions."

An avalanche of emotions slams through Suzanne's entire being, flooding her mid-section, her heart, with an overwhelming sensation of love. In her mind's eye, Suzanne watches her mother lighting candles on a birthday cake and hears her sing.

Then, she sees Madelaine holding the twin boys shortly after their birth. Suzanne struggles to breathe. A wave of dizziness threatens a fainting spell.

Franny's hand covers hers. "What's happening, honey?"

Suzanne whispers that she's okay. A hand appears on her left as she holds on tightly to the desk's edge. A hand with nails decorated in bright coral polish. She knows this hand. A familiar marcasite ring encircling the left ring finger dispels any doubt. When the sleeve of a silk teal caftan slowly emerges, seeping with the scent of Chanel No. 19, Suzanne is awestruck when Madelaine's spirit fully reveals itself. Struggling to maintain her composure, Suzanne feels the brush of a whisper in her left ear: "*You are never alone, my love.*"

Then, it evaporates. The bottom half of Madelaine dissipates first, leaving her silk sleeve dangling near her daughter's hand. Within seconds, only the trail of her scent is left behind. An intense movement of energy slams through Suzanne's core, pressing into her ribs. She wonders if her heart will burst after feeling fully embraced by her mother's love: an engulfing sensation, unlike anything Suzanne experienced when her mom was alive.

"Did you see her?" Suzanne asks, breathless, as the mother-daughter reunion passes.

"No, honey. But you did. Savor it, my dear. Few are as blessed as you."

Suzanne tells Franny that Madelaine's spirit has been hovering for a while, since even before meeting Max. "I smelled her perfume, sensed her presence before I left for Seaside, then again after an awful row with Max at the house. And now, today."

"I suspected as much," Franny says. Then, gathering the tarot cards into one stack, she says, "As you acknowledge your mother's spirit today, understand that she's been with you all along. From the exact second Madelaine's soul lifted from her body at the crash scene, if I had to guess."

"Perhaps. But I didn't think of her choosing to linger . . . and not reach out. Franny, today is the first time I've been convinced this hovering essence is truly my mom's spirit. So why now, do you think?"

"I'd say you're about to receive an assignment," Franny begins. "Her spirit will likely be the forerunner of communication with others. Be patient. You'll learn your role soon enough."

Befuddled by the spirit reveal, Suzanne checks the caller ID when her phone rings. Finally, her private investigator is getting back in touch.

"Got a second to talk?"

"One second. What's happening?"

"I've some info," the PI says. "Rather . . . disturbing news."

"Good God, man." Suzanne sighs. "Just get to it."

"Max didn't divorce his wife, Farrah. She died. Tragically."

"Explain." She tries to swallow her fear.

"On a family vacation exploring Mammoth Cave. Do you know it? It's a monstrous cave system in central Kentucky."

"Oh, my God." Suzanne hears her heartbeat resonating through her ear canals.

"It happened four years ago, back in 2008," Oscar says. "Wait, honey. It gets worse. The DA's office in the county where the accident happened reopened an investigation into her death. New evidence has surfaced."

"What the hell?" White-faced and weak-kneed, Suzanne slumps over her desk and faints. Franny, always prepared for similar reactions when she reads for a querent, reaches for her bag of smelling salts.

"Suzanne? You there? I'm sorry, sweetheart."

"She'll call you back," Franny says, ending the call.

Suzanne moans as she regains consciousness.

"I'm going to run and get you some water, Suzanne. You'll be okay for a minute?"

Suzanne nods. When Franny returns, she explains. "Guess I forgot to mention I hired a PI to investigate Max's past. After he went nuts because I didn't show up to meet his West Coast clients for drinks at 21st."

"Yeah, you didn't mention *that* information." Franny twists the plastic cap off the bottle. "Anything else happening that's got you on edge?"

Suzanne takes slow sips, brushing her damp hair away from her face. She doesn't notice that Franny leaves the classroom door cracked open. "Not just one thing, a series of things. No, not even things. A string of reactions. Negative ones. Max becomes irate when situations don't pan out as he imagines. And he imagines a lot of impossibly perfect scenarios. Then blames me when things don't add up."

Franny listens, then whispers, "Has he hit you? Violent in any way? Suzanne, you've got to pull away from him if he's hurting you, threatening you. Don't take this one step further."

"He hasn't." Suzanne pauses.

"Why do I hear an unspoken word?"

"I may very well have no choice in the matter, Franny. You *do* understand . . . when a spirit *commands* . . ."

"Surely not, my friend. Surely no stranded spirit, no trapped ghost, will expect you to risk everything, perhaps even your life. To ensure their safe passage to the afterlife."

According to her investigator's report, that's precisely what may be at stake. Couple that horrifying information with Madelaine's command for her to stay with Max because he holds the key to unlock many things, possibly freeing her mother's spirit.

Are there other spirits that remain trapped and stranded, perhaps not by choice? If so, who are they?

A noise in the hallway jostles Suzanne back to reality. She hurries to shut her classroom door. Her heart drops when she sees her principal, Justin, hustling down the dark hallway.

What did he see? More importantly, what did he hear?

14

Max

Edmondson County, Kentucky, Late Summer 2012

The late-afternoon sunlight filters through the maple trees, blanketing the Edmonson County Courthouse in Brownsville, Kentucky. Max paces in front of the nineteenth-century brick building while Maureen walks up and down the courthouse steps. They are getting in a workout while they wait for John DeRouen, Max's attorney, to arrive. While the structure lacks the intimidating aura most urban courthouses covet, the judgments leveraged within these walls carry sufficient weight to destroy Max's charmed life.

While he sits and mopes, Maureen reads the local names engraved on the war memorials erected in front of the courthouse, a tribute to the county's lost lives in both world wars, Korea, and Vietnam.

"Max, come see this," Maureen says. "Look at all these names. Brownsville has certainly paid her dues."

"I've seen it, Maureen. Remember? I've been here before. I've paid my dues, too."

He'd returned to collect Farrah's remains once the coroner's office released them. But by the time he'd arrived, Farrah's father, James Lamar, had handled everything. So Max flew home to Louisiana—empty-handed. Then, after responding to his first subpoena to testify in an official investigation into his wife's death, Max swore he'd never step foot in this one-horse town. Ever again.

"Either John's late, or we're early," Maureen says. "Should we wait inside?"

"We're not early," Max says. "And I'm not going in that hellhole without my lawyer." He's edgy, looking to lash out at her. "Remind me, why are *you* here?"

"Max, this is what I do. You create a fiasco that screams for help, and I show up as reinforcements." She brushes the lint from her black pencil skirt, then turns and checks her backside.

Max ignores her comment. "When we were on the phone in Florida, Suzanne heard you in the background. It's now a problem for me, Mo."

She glances at her watch and laughs. "Honey, you've got bigger worries than me. See where we're standing right now?" Maureen waves her arm dramatically at the scope of the courthouse and its supporting buildings. "Try being straight with your woman. Honesty might work for you," she suggests.

"I don't have much success with the truth, love. I tried honesty with Farrah, and she ended up at the bottom of a cavern." He stands and begins pacing again.

"Maybe it wasn't the best time or place to tell her you wanted out. If that's what happened," Maureen says, slipping out of her left high heel to shake out a small rock. "No one would argue against your genius in striking real estate deals, but you've got lots to learn about handling your women. It needn't come down to life-or-death situations."

John pulls up in a leased Lexus. He grabs two leather trial cases from the trunk, one fairly beaten up, the other brand new.

Max tightens his tie and walks toward the stairs, anxious to get inside and start the proceedings. He opens the door for their entry. "What's the game plan?"

"Whit Buster, an assistant district attorney, will question you about the day of the accident. This will require simple answers, Max. The DA's office wants to nail something down, but you aren't the primary target. Just the bait."

"You're not anticipating new charges to stick?" Maureen asks.

John points in the direction of the conference room at the end of a long hallway that honors local war heroes. "Not yet. Farrah's family cites negligence in their wrongful death suit against the management group that operates Mammoth Cave. They're seeking a decent pain and suffering settlement plus reimbursement of expenses for recovering Farrah's body, then transporting it back to Louisiana. But that's the civil suit."

"No rejuvenation of criminal interest?" Max wonders aloud.

"I don't think so," John says. "Someone has offered sufficient information for the DA to reopen Farrah's death inquiry. But from what I can tell, the new information should strengthen the Lamar family's case. I believe your position remains stable."

"I hope you're right," Max says. *Because, no matter what, I'm not effing going to jail.*

The court reporter sits by her steno machine in the middle of the conference room and glances at the clock on the wall. After Max swears an oath to tell the truth, he sits beside John. Maureen is seated close by.

The deposition starts.

"It's 10 a.m. on August 31, 2012, and we are on the record," the court reporter notes. Max states his name.

"Mr. Martin, what recreational tour were you and your now-deceased wife, Farrah, taking when you visited Mammoth Cave National Park roughly four years ago in 2008?"

It takes one question to catapult Max into the past. Naturally, he'll never forget the name of that damn tour because he and Farrah argued for hours over which one to schedule—way back when they originally planned the trip.

"Domes and Dripstones," he answers. Max lowers his head, sighs, and rubs his temples to ward off a massive headache. Stay with the basics, he tells himself. "Farrah wanted to take a lantern tour later, but I disagreed." Before the words leave his lips, Max winces at an unbearable buzzing in his right ear. It's so loud that he hears nothing else. Then as suddenly as the racket begins, it stops.

John nudges Max's knee beneath the table. He writes "answer THE question" on an index card. Shoves it within Max's line of vision. Then writes another message on the next index card in a stack. "Stop bobbing your head."

"Why is it such a vivid memory for you?"

John weighs in. "Objection. Leading."

"I'll rephrase. Mr. Martin, why did you and your wife take a rigorous walking tour in an ill-lighted cave that she'd expressed disinterest in taking?"

Do I say that Farrah felt too ill to take any tour? No. If she was too exhausted for one excursion, she was too exhausted, period. Farrah had no business even being in the cave that day.

Sweat forms on Max's upper lip as he feels flushed and dizzy. He reaches into his jacket pocket for a handkerchief.

Get a freaking grip!

"Sir? Answer the question, please." Buster rests an arm on a stack of leatherbound state statutes, leftover from a paralegal's recent afternoon of research, as he waits for Max's response.

"Look, it was my turn to choose a tour. I felt we'd already spent too much time with her family . . . for *our* vacation."

The assistant DA smiles.

"Did you and Farrah argue?"

"Objection. Leading," John counters. Holds his breath. Word jousts like this are Max's nemesis.

"I'll rephrase. Did you argue with your wife because you thought . . .?"

"Again. Objection. Relevance," John interrupts. "Mr. Buster, how is this relevant? Please explain how my client is expected to remember the scope of an argument with his dead wife four years previous?"

"I'll move on," Buster says.

"Do you recall a park ranger issuing a warning before the tour started? Do you remember any heads-up on areas anticipated to be slick or slippery?"

"Yes, I do recall that," Max answers. "Some girls were left behind since they didn't have proper shoes." He remembers Farrah's annoyance with the blonde twins standing near them, wearing short shorts and cheap flip-flops. The intense buzzing sound returns, even louder this time. In pain, Max grabs hold of his right ear as if he might rub away the noise.

John nudges his client. Max shrugs his shoulder, still gripping his ear. "Get ahold of yourself, Max," John hisses into Max's other ear, the one not throbbing in pain.

"Are you okay, Mr. Martin? Are you unwell, sir?" Buster demands.

"I'm fine."

Max is far from feeling fine. In his mind, he hears, "*Did you plan to see your wife at the bottom of the cave's deepest cavern?*" Instead, Buster asks, "So you and Farrah believed the tour to be safe, despite warnings offered by the park rangers?"

"Yes."

"At any point did that sense of safety change?"

"Yes, it did," he says. Fearing the worst, Max's heart rate skyrockets as his blood pressure shoots up right alongside it.

"When did it change?"

Max's dark eyes plead with John, who briefly touches his client's forearm and tells him to answer the question.

"One of the rangers demanded I walk to the front of the tour. He told me I couldn't stay with Farrah." Max is uncertain how to produce a catch in his voice, but he does.

There's no end to Buster's rapid-fire questions, for he's throwing one zinger right after another: "Did you understand why the ranger separated the two of you?"

"Not really."

"Do you believe separating the two of you placed Farrah in imminent danger?"

"Yes, absolutely."

"I request a five-minute recess to speak to my client." John hustles to break up the inquiry before Max meets a question that spirals him further.

"We'll regroup in five," Buster says.

"We're taking a walk. Outside," John says. Max pushes back from the oversized conference table and glances at Maureen, seated in the corner.

"You're okay. Stop worrying so much," Maureen whispers.

"Front steps," John says, pointing down the hallway toward the glass doors.

Max's mind isn't in the here and now. Instead, he's reliving the Saturday when he and Farrah entered the cave. Fourth tour in three days. Their relationship's rocky ground had tilted from slightly tricky to simply impossible. They argued over the tiniest details, like where to eat, what to order, and even how to chew properly. The bottom line: Farrah suspected Max of cheating, and Max feared Farrah was pregnant. A colossal mess that offered no solution in sight. Until a particular slippery condition in a million-year-old cave system presented itself.

"Are you listening, Max?" John asks.

"Of course."

"Then what did I just say?"

"Sorry. Repeat?"

"What the bloody hell is going on with you? The head jerking needs to stop, man. You look demented. Is this a medical issue? Does a physician need to examine you?"

"No, no, I'm okay. With this damn screeching noise in my ear, I can't hear the questions." Max taps his right ear, which feels hot to the touch.

"I'm running out of patience. Max, it's unnecessary for you to provide anything but the basic facts. These boys are now on a mission, and you running down rabbit holes with the ADA is not helping." John takes a long draw from his unfiltered Marlboro. "Whit Buster is a master at weaving a complicated web, so I'm betting he'll use your testimony to focus on the rangers' incompetence. Both are named in Lamar's lawsuit."

"Okay, okay." Max grimaces, for the increased pressure in his ear delivers a shrill, repetitive beat along with the warning, "*Payday, Max.*"

Max wonders if he's beginning to lose his mind.

John's grimace deepens. "Are you listening, Max? Deposing you today is simply a means to an end. Now get your shit together before you come back inside." John stomps his cigarette butt into a cracked red brick on the sidewalk before turning to walk away. "Got to hit the loo."

Maureen catches up with Max, edging closer to him after John walks away. "Anything you want to get off your chest?"

He jumps back from Maureen. "Jesus, Mo, do you *ever* stop?" Max yells, holding both hands over his ears. He turns from her, looks toward the town's main intersection, and focuses on the systematic flow of First Street's traffic, hoping to calm the pounding noise inside his head.

"I'm always going to be here for you, Max," she says as he walks away.

Back in the conference room, Buster picks up where he left off. "Before the break, we addressed the ranger who separated you from your wife during the tour."

"Yes, correct."

"Did he explain the reasons for his actions?"

"My wife and I were arguing. I'll admit it. Our voices echoed. I mean, we were in a damn cave . . ."

"What did the argument concern?"

"Objection. Leading," John says.

The ADA continues. "What happened next?"

"The head ranger kept the tour going. I was in the front of the group with him."

"Could you see Farrah from where you were?"

"No," Max says, "but I heard her. Or 'least, thought I did."

John presses Max's knee sharply, then taps his pen on the table.

"Continue, Mr. Martin."

"I thought I heard her throwing up, vomiting."

"Had your wife complained of a sick stomach earlier that morning?"

Max lies. "Not that I recall. Farrah said she felt tired. That's what I remember."

"Did you attempt to move to the back of the group? To help her?"

"I did. I kept to one side as best I could and let others walk in front of me. It was tough because of the dark, narrow passages. But the ranger caught me."

"Caught you? Explain."

"Yes . . . hmmm. The ranger said the female in the back would handle things. And to keep walking. I'd meet up with Farrah later in the main dome."

Though it feels like hours pass before the deposition winds down, it only takes a few minutes. Max barely remembers what he says. Then, finally, the court reporter relinquishes the recording. It's finished.

Max spots his former father-in-law lingering at the conference room's entrance when he stands to shake Buster's hand. He recognizes Sophie, Farrah's mother, standing next to him. Max rounds the conference table and steps into the hallway.

"Hello, Max. Good to see you," Sophie says, the first to approach him.

Max's handshake with Jay is friendlier than expected. "I regret dragging you back here, son," Jay says. "And apologize for my silence over the years." Max doubts the authenticity of Jay's words, but nods his head anyway.

"What's up?"

"Farrah's autopsy, the third one we ordered, revealed Farrah was two months pregnant."

Max's jaw drops.

"Son, we lost more than our daughter. We lost our first grandchild. And *someone's* going to pay." Jay's furrowed brow, long deepened with sorrow, is immovable as he stares coldly at Max and struggles to control a left-eye twitch.

Addy

Gulf Coast, Summer 1944

Addy succumbed to Cash's passionate kiss before pushing back his shoulders. When she opened her eyes and looked past the officer's shoulder, she saw Mimi standing over them, hands on her hips. Mimi wore her Southern belle propriety like a war medal. Before Addy could attempt another introduction, her grandmother demanded, "Just what do you think you're doing, young man? Of all the audacious things I've ever witnessed."

"Cash Lamar, ma'am. United States Army Air Force." Cash flashed his intoxicating smile before extending his right hand. "I missed the pleasure of meeting you at Beauvoir."

"I wonder, officer," Mimi said. "Is this behavior befitting your rank?"

"Probably not, ma'am, but when a guy is sweet on a gal . . ." Cash slipped his hand back into his shorts' pocket when Mimi ignored his gesture.

Addy stood and brushed the sand off the gathered front of her bathing suit. "Mimi, please do not embarrass me with one of your *in-my-day* stories. I tried introducing you at the soirée." She faced her dark-haired, blue-eyed officer and exaggerated the belated introduction. "Cash, meet my grandmother, Mrs. James Lafountain. We call her Mimi Jeanne. Or Mimi, for short."

Mimi adjusted her floppy sunhat. Then, squinting against the blinding sunlight, she said, "I'd have preferred it if Addy had asked you to dinner first for a proper introduction. But here you are."

"Yes, ma'am. Here I am. Some of us had a day's leave, so we came to the island. You might have noticed our boat?"

"Yes, you boys made quite the impression on more than one of my granddaughters."

"Addy has sisters?" Cash asked, looking around.

Addy jumped in too quickly to explain, sounding childish. "Yes, Esty, my middle sister, was super jazzed. She's seventeen and boy crazy." Addy felt her skin flush with embarrassment while Mimi ignored them both, busying herself with arranging a tartan beach blanket. "Join me in the surf?" Addy asked."How 'bout spreading some Coppertone across my shoulders while you're thinking it over." She handed Cash the brown glass bottle of tanning lotion, pleased at her grandmother's reaction.

He's my guy, Mimi. My handsome officer, the one I've envisioned for so long. You best get used to him, because he'll be around for a while.

Cash broke the spell. "Let's go swimming," he said after grabbing one of Mimi's beach towels to dry the lotion from his hands. Addy stood on her toes to kiss Cash's cheek, then laced her hand with his.

Mimi had watched Cash and Addy's performance and observed more than she let on. "Cash, you do seem familiar to me. You two met last summer, didn't you?" she asked.

"No, ma'am," Cash fired back. "I was pre-training at Kelly, the Army Air Force Base in San Antonio, last summer."

Addy looked puzzled. "Why do you ask, Mimi?"

"The two of you don't behave like strangers. Interesting."

Cocking her head slightly to the right, Mimi stared at Addy, then Cash. Addy locked eyes with Mimi and willed the matriarch to stop talking.

Cash saved them. “It’s my first day off in weeks, Mrs. Lafountain. Don’t know when I’ll get another one. Come in the water with us.” He positioned himself between Addy and her grandmother before taking a step.

“Call me Mrs. Jeanne,” Mimi said. “I’ll go as far as where Papa and Esty are fishing . . . check on their haul.”

“Sure thing.” Cash stooped down to greet Macie as she was sunbathing. “I’m Cash, by the way.”

“Oh, I know,” Macie said. “We all know about *you*.” She turned over on her stomach to sun her backside.

“How’s that? I only just met your sister.”

“She’ll explain.” Macie grabbed a handful of sand and flung it in Addy’s direction. “Here comes Addy’s new beau, Papa,” Macie yelled to her grandfather.

Focused on helping Esty angle an ornery redfish, Papa didn’t respond.

“Shut up, Macie,” Esty yelled against the wind.

“Don’t lose ‘em!” As Cash ran through the shallow water to help, he watched Esty slip, exhausted from her efforts.

Laughing through her tumble onto the sandbar, Esty gladly accepted Cash’s hand. “I couldn’t hold on for another second,” she said. “Papa will be thrilled you showed up. He’s fed up with this family of girls. I didn’t expect a redfish to weigh that much.”

Papa swore. “Damn schnook. If we keep wading these waters, lots more will be close behind him.” When he turned around and squinted against the sun’s glare, he saw Cash. “Do I know you, son?”

“Name’s Cash Lamar. Army Air Force, stationed at Keesler.” Cash’s personal information rolled off his tongue, by rote, as if he were addressing a superior officer.

Papa stared. “Good God, man. Anything else you want to add?”

Cash's nervous laugh did not go unnoticed. "Just started co-pilot training. B-24s, sir. And I'm a friend of Addy's."

Addy caught up with Cash, who'd run into the surf like a bolt of lightning. "Oh, good, you've met each other."

Cash nodded, then continued chatting with Papa. "I don't know how long you've fished these waters, sir, but if you want to hit pay dirt, I'd suggest the grass beds on the island's north side. Better for this time of day," Cash offered.

"I've heard that. Not quite ready to give up my spot here."

Is it possible? That Papa and Cash might become, well, friends? This might be my ace.

As she lingered at the edge of Cash's and Papa's fish tales, with Esty adding her two cents, Addy fought against a ping of jealousy. Duh, maybe Cash loved fishing more than anything else in the world, she thought. Though Esty had spent a lifetime fishing with Papa, Addy considered playing catch-up. *Guess I'll learn to fish.*

But when Addy reached for one of Papa's fishing poles, Cash pulled her away and said, "If you don't want to swim, let's walk."

Having gained some distance from her watchful family, Cash eased his arm around Addy's shoulder, then slowly slid his hand down her right side, resting at her hip. They waded through the surf and searched for shells as the high tide rolled in. Addy practiced considerable restraint and decided against asking a host of questions.

While Cash knew little of Addy, she knew even less about him.

With the salty Gulf breeze at his back, Cash lifted Addy's hair away from her face, stared into her violet eyes, and kissed her forehead. When his lips first captured hers, Cash held back from pressing further. Until Addy's tongue softly brushed his. This magnetic couple could have been mistaken for two Hollywood actors prepping for a romantic movie scene with the sun perfectly positioned. The Gulf provided the enchantment of a blue-green backdrop. Their energy, a slow yet steady burn. Altogether, an orchestra of sensations.

"Oh, my God, Cash," Addy whimpered. Their intense embrace—separated only by the thin material of their bathing suits—ushered in a fresh era of sensuality for her.

Cash waited. "You okay?"

"I've never . . . been kissed . . . like that." She nearly tripped over a pile of oyster shells set upright in the sand when she stepped back to regain footing. "I thought I'd lost my breath for a second."

Cash shifted his stance, his expression puzzled. "Hey, your sister said a weird thing to me when I introduced myself—something like . . . she'd known about me for a long time. What's that mean?"

Addy smiled. "You're so much more than I'd envisioned."

"Wait. You conjured up some dream of a fellow who looks like me? To spend your summer with?" Cash turned and walked into the surf, running his fingers through his wavy black hair. "Is that what your sister meant?"

"No, no. She's only tired of hearing me talk about my visions."

Cash stared toward the horizon and laughed. "So that's what schoolgirls do. Imagine their next boyfriends. And, snap, there he is? He could be anybody. Just any guy who comes around."

"No, it's not like that." Addy immediately regretted sharing the tiniest little detail about her clairvoyance. It was the sole reason she rarely discussed her gift. Most people got huffy and brushed off talk about seeing into the future. No one ever validated her experiences. Except for Mimi. Despite her disappointment, Addy bolstered herself against his rudeness.

"You're in school, aren't you?" Cash kept teasing.

"I'm in *college*, Cash. My sisters are still in school. There's a huge difference. Have you ever dated a college girl before, or do you only hang out with local working girls?" Addy's sarcasm met Cash's jabs.

"Working girls? Whatcha mean by that?"

"Girls, you know, who work in town, at the market, the soda shop, or one of the seafood canneries."

"I don't think that's what you meant, Addy. But I get your point." Cash changed the subject quickly. He reached into the surf wash and grabbed a shiny flattened oyster shell, pretty enough to be polished into a piece of jewelry. He handed her the shell. "I bet you've left a string of broken hearts from here to New Orleans." His quick smile offered to smooth things over.

"Maybe, maybe not." Their quixotic moment had drifted to sea, detaching a chunk of Addy's vision that floated away on a receding wave. She walked alone on the beach for a few minutes before joining Cash, sitting amidst the sea oats.

"Was that supposed to be my next line?" Cash asked. "I've been waiting my whole life for the right girl?"

Addy eased down to sit next to him, crossing her legs. "I've no idea. Have you?"

Cash was older than the young men she'd dated back in New Orleans . . . aged with roughened life experiences. Addy had never met anyone like him.

"It's perfect here, 'ya know?" he said, avoiding an answer, scooting slightly to the right to give Addy plenty of space. "I don't think I've ever been on this side of the island. My buddies and I either swim where we've lowered the anchor or walk through Fort Massachusetts."

Addy followed Cash's conversational lead, grateful to have the focus off her for a few minutes.

"It's tough on you guys, isn't it? Not having much time off during training?" She didn't want to pry, but it occurred to her that airmen had little time to spare for girlfriends.

Cash answered her indirect question. "To be honest, I've never had a serious girlfriend. Always had to concentrate on fending for myself, which left no time to dawdle. I've been on my own since high school."

Addy didn't know if she should believe Cash, so she offered no response to his confession. She hadn't intended for their conversation to take such a serious turn. But then, she'd seriously underestimated Cash's maturity.

"Is it always so hot here?" Cash asked, changing gears. Again. "Don't think I'll ever get used to this Mississippi humidity," he said, revealing more personal information than he'd probably intended. *Wasn't it terribly hot and humid in Texas, too?*

"I can assure you it's going to get a lot hotter. It's only early June, Cash."

"Sitting here with you, baby, watching over the blue-green water, it's impossible for me to imagine there's a war raging across the Atlantic," he said, raising his face to greet the sun's beams.

"It's hard for *me* to imagine. But I don't understand how you'd say that. It seems you guys live for war. Right? You train, learn to be experts, then go overseas to do an enormous thing and come back as heroes."

Cash reached for Addy's hand. "You don't know how lucky you are, Addy, to have a safe place to live your life." *Again, such seriousness.* "Have your grandparents lived here for a while?"

She curled her fingers around his. "For as long as I can remember. Mimi inherited their home from my great-grandmother, Louisa. At first they only spent summers in the Pass, but now this is home. My sisters and I always summer here, so my parents can travel."

"Naturally," he said.

Addy shook her head. She didn't appreciate the tone of his voice, but kept the conversation flowing.

"Have you met many summer girls since you've been stationed here? I might know them. Most of us come from New Orleans or Mobile, even Jackson, Atlanta, or Memphis."

"No, none worth mentioning. But I'm damn certain, Addy, you're the only girl I'll never forget."

Cash looked down at their clasped hands for a good while. Her soft palms and shiny, lacquered red nails starkly contrasted against his weathered, worn fingers. They stopped talking and quietly watched the pelicans swoop into the Gulf's water to catch their prey, take to the skies, and repeat the cycle.

She felt a letdown, staring at the sinking sun in the western sky. Maybe Esty and Macie were right. Maybe her visions were complete rubbish. Sensing that Cash was restless and more interested in leaving than staying, Addy charged forward, despite her better judgment. "Have you ever considered there's one perfect person for each of us?" she asked.

"One specific person? For an entire lifetime?" Cash continued, "Are you talking about a soulmate?"

"More than a soulmate." She kept going. What did she have to lose? "That one person you're supposed to be with who's part of a larger picture, a bigger plan."

"I think you're talking about destiny," Cash said. "I've never really understood that concept. How would you recognize that one person, intended only for you?"

Addy brushed Cash's cheek with her fingertip and ran it along his jawline. "You just do," her hypnotic voice whispered. "I know you've little reason to believe me, Cash. But I've always known you'd be waiting for me here. On the Coast." Cash, an airman training to co-pilot B-24 liberators, struggled to keep his cool against the tease of Addy's magnetic touch. Her family nearby, within shouting distance.

He jumped to his feet and wiped the sweat dripping from his face. "I have to go, Addy. Right now. Goddammit, if the fellas already left for Biloxi without me . . . I'm screwed."

"Okay," she said, "It's all right if you don't understand."

Addy reached for Cash, expecting him to give her a hand up. But when he didn't, she stood and brushed away the sand clinging to her shorts and the backside of her legs. She quickened her step to walk him back to the pier, but finally gave up when Cash began sprinting after he passed the fort.

Realizing he'd probably not hear her, Addy yelled into the wind anyway, "Looks like I won't be able to meet up with you at the Dew Drop tonight." She watched him board a Coast Guard vessel filled with sunburned servicemen and waved goodbye.

When she turned to walk back to her family, she saw Mimi sitting on a brick ledge that surrounded Fort Massachusetts, talking to a handsome man, oddly wearing a tan fedora hat adorned with a feather.

"Come meet Jack, a dear friend of the family," Mimi called out to her.

Addy smiled and waved. "Another time, Mimi."

She'd experienced quite enough for one day.

16

Suzanne

New Orleans, Fall 2012

Suzanne navigates St. Philip Street alongside local cyclists, weaving between cars in New Orleans' Tremé neighborhood. The last thing she wants to do is hit a biker. Didn't Franny say that Enola's Boutique is near the corner of N. Miro Street and St. Philip?

Within minutes she spots Franny's car and squeezes in behind it. As she walks toward Enola's, Suzanne notices how its shopfront blends in with other Caribbean-colored houses on the block. There's no front signage. Nothing that beckons curiosity-seekers to step inside. Enola's might be the best-kept secret in the Tremé. Only those who covet the Creole shop owner's wisdom and guidance are invited beyond the Bahama-shuttered doors.

Once Suzanne crosses the shop's threshold, there's no turning back. She'll no longer lie about her knowledge of elemental spells—Suzanne's self-proclaimed stance since Madelaine's death regarding all things relative to hoodoo. Her mother instilled sufficient spellcasting basics when Suzanne was young enough to comply, but as time passed, Suzanne chose a different path—one that did not center on the practice. The last spell she agreed to participate in took place on the night of Madelaine's death. Afterward, she swore against casting another spell.

Unless and until Madelaine's trapped spirit reached out for assistance.

Now, with the spirit world demanding an action she has yet to fully comprehend, Suzanne seeks stronger incantations and guidance with rootwork as she adjusts to a life filled with sage cleansings and casting charms. Most urgently, the slithering malevolence that's complicating her life must be handled head-on. She's savvy enough to recognize there's no choice in the matter, for this situation may be life or death.

There's no escaping my destiny.

Franny meets Suzanne just inside the entryway. "Enola's ready for you," she says, her voice solemn. She leads Suzanne into the first large room of this converted shotgun house and leaves her with an older Creole woman wearing a bright yellow and brown head-wrap, standing behind an enormous mahogany counter. Her arms stretch out, hovering over an expansive glass case. She's decorated in layers of tiny black onyx beads wrapped around both wrists. Various amulets dangle at different lengths from her neck.

"Welcome, Suzanne," Enola says, smiling widely. "Come closer, love."

When Enola's hands reach for Suzanne, she wonders if steam might rise from the woman's palms. Beyond warm, bordering on hot. "You no newcomer, are you? I know you . . . I know your people."

Suzanne cannot escape Enola's black piercing eyes. She is spellbound.

"It's my first visit here," she says.

"You sure?" Enola rubs Suzanne's palms, then extends one arm to indicate a waist-level height. "You're a Lafountain, and you've been here. When much younger."

"Perhaps," she says, having no memory of the occasion. "Even so, I'm sorely out of practice. Madelaine . . ."

". . . Madelaine?" Enola interrupts. "Of course, you're Madelaine's. This explains so much." Tears form in the corner of her eyes. "You next in line."

Suzanne abruptly pulls back her hands from Enola's grasp. She stretches her fingers to relieve the tingling sensation, the pulsating energy that's racing through her right hand, to her forearm, all the way to her shoulder. A source of energy, filled with intention, that Suzanne will learn to welcome. When the time comes to cast spells.

"Time to begin. Tarot will guide us," Enola says before disappearing behind the thick burgundy brocade drape that divides the front of the store from the reading room in the back. Suzanne hears Enola call out for her husband, Adetope, inquiring if he's prepared to start. While waiting, Suzanne inhales the heavy lavender scent that permeates the shop and admires the colorful assortment of candles, including novena candles—the very ones that line prayer vestibules of churches—sitting on shelves next to those used for spell casting. A perfectly natural display, since hoodoo *crosses* with established religions when prayers need a boost and spells need extra power.

Enola creeps up behind her and whispers, "Adetope can see you, love. Come this way."

Suzanne follows Enola into a darkened room furnished with early nineteenth-century antiquities. Tall black candles lit within cast-iron candelabras provide the only light source. A dark-skinned man sits alone on one side of an antique mahogany table, his fingers outstretched.

"Meet my husband, Adetope," Enola says.

"A pleasure," he says in a thick Jamaican accent. He motions for Suzanne to settle into an oversized tufted chair directly across from him. "Franny will join if you're agreeable."

"Of course." Suzanne extends her hand to greet Adetope as Franny steps into the room and pulls a chair closer. "An honor to meet you," she says. He responds with a firm handshake.

"How about the sword?" Adetope asks. Suzanne nods. He shuffles the deck one more time and hands it to Suzanne. "Proceed, my friend."

Suzanne closes her eyes and holds the deck close to her heart, between her hands. She draws in several deep breaths, then exhales slowly. Suzanne doesn't notice when Enola swoops in to light more candles on a mantle across from the table.

Adetope begins: The first card flipped is the Nine of Pentacles. "You fail to embrace power that's offered you. Why?"

I should have known. This is going to be an extremely contentious reading. Probably one controversial card after another. Because I've left my calling unheeded for far too long.

He places the second drawn card to the left. "Four of Wands . . . awe. My lady, why so much contradiction between you and others? How *do* you manage?"

Suzanne laughs, though she feels the threat of tears. "That's just it. I'm not managing very well at all." Her laughter: a trained response designed to cushion layers of turmoil.

"Max," Franny weighs in. "Her man is problematic. One contradictory son-of-a-bitch."

"Won't disagree with that. Go on."

"Two of Wands." He sits back for a moment. "Hmmm . . . does this card surface often for you?" Adetope asks.

"More times than I'd like to admit."

"Then, you've failed. Two of Wands offers encouragement. What must you now acknowledge?" he demands.

"My identity—my purpose."

Adetope puts down the fourth card, positioning it above the first to form the shape of a sword's handle. *Third of Pentacles.*

"Are you sensing a theme, Suzanne?" Franny whispers.

Suzanne hesitates. "Yes . . ."

"Why, love, are you so afraid?" Adetope presses.

"Answer him, Suzanne."

“Loudly,” Enola yells from the back corner of the parlor.

“Speak, woman!” Adetope yells. When the candles burst into a blaze, threatening to inflame the cloistered parlor room, Suzanne rushes her words that have remained dormant for far too long: “The truth is . . . that I *am* an enchantress. From a long line of resilient Lafountain women who’ve been root-workers, conjurers, hoodoo practitioners. Now it comes down to me, for I’m the *one* who remains—and am empowered to right many wrongs.”

“Don’t stop now, Suzanne,” Franny says. “Own your legacy. Share your truth.”

“Just as my mother and her mother before her. And my grandmother, Jeanne, and God knows how many women before my great-grandmother, Louisa. I see and I know—both as a conjurer and a clairsentient,” Suzanne announces, her eyes raised toward the ceiling of the century-old structure. Her inner core shudders—infused with the vibrant energy of ancestral spirits, unleashing all that’s been submerged for many lifetimes.

Suzanne turns to Franny, “You’ve known all along, haven’t you?” she asks. “This explains some of your responses during our readings.” Covering Franny’s hands with hers, squeezing them gently, Suzanne’s gesture speaks to gratitude and sisterhood.

“Since the night of your near collision. Remember? I handed you the black obsidian for protection and felt your spiritual energy exploding.” Suzanne nods, remembering her close call.

“I could’ve died that night months ago. There’s no reasonable explanation for my car moving six feet away from a head-on collision within seconds.”

“Oh, there’s a *reasonable* explanation. You still have work to do,” Adetope says, reassuring Suzanne. “Though it’s impossible to determine if your gifts saved your life or if a spirit intervened. Energies work together to provide protection. Guidance.”

Three additional cards complete the sword’s length. The

Page of Pentacles is followed by the King of Cups. Then, Two of Pentacles clarifies the balancing act Suzanne must finesse.

Until the demands from the Spirit World are met.

"Thank you, Adetope," Suzanne sighs. "I feel Madelaine's spirit is with me, but recently it's overwhelming. I'm struggling . . ." Her fingertips massage the throbbing in her temples, a sure sign that she's emotionally spent. "It's a huge undertaking to jump from rebellion to full immersion."

"How will you proceed?" he asks.

"Cautiously. I'm managing a difficult, dangerous man," Suzanne says. "I've got to keep my emotions in check as I determine his role in all these spirit reveals I'm experiencing."

"Rely upon your spiritual ancestors. They can assist you. Remember, the family cord that connects us is the strongest bond of the universe," Adetope says.

Suzanne nods in agreement.

"Yet, you still hesitate."

"Another spirit hovers in the background. Perhaps not born of malice, but now filled with it. I'm uncertain . . . about this dark one. It's been a very long time since I've faced such malevolence." She doesn't mention Jack, because that's an entirely different issue.

"Sometimes we never understand a dark spirit's intention," he says. "Often, it filters away—content to pass by. Enola can share a protection spell with you before you go. Chant it often. Before complications escalate."

Before Suzanne leaves, Enola opens a bottle of 1947 vintage Bordeaux. Together, they share a toast within the comfort and security of a house that settled souls built 200 years ago.

"I challenge you, Suzanne, to answer this: As an enchantress, what is *your* desire? Take time with answering the question—it will provide a template for the rest of your days."

Suzanne smiles. She hugs Adetope before following Enola along the narrow hallway back to the shop's front room, leaving Franny and Adetope to visit.

As she watches Enola prepare a spell bag, Suzanne asks,

"Are many of your customers churchgoers? I noticed the vast collection of novena candles on your shelves."

"Lordy, some of my best customers are sneaking in here after church services." Enola laughs and adds, "Plenty crossover in hoodoo with different faiths. Call upon your saints, your beloved who have passed, as you start your spells. We are one in spiritual existence, love."

Precious pearls of assurance to an eccentric who has *never* fit within the boundaries of organized religion.

There are no Bible study groups for those who talk to the dead. And respond to the pleas of the trapped ghosts who are stuck here after death. Or the lingering spirits who've chosen to stay close to their beloveds.

"What's your worry today?" Enola asks, adjusting her head scarf.

Suzanne positions her forearms on the glass counter for support. "Beyond what we've already covered during my tarot reading? Well, I've just learned my lover may have killed his last wife."

Enola throws her head back and laughs uproariously. "Then leave him! No folk magic to solve this, woman!"

"He's not the kind of man a gal gets away with leaving, if you know what I mean. For now, I've no choice but to deal with him." Suzanne's face scrunches, then relaxes. "My spirits are unrelenting about this."

Enola stops chuckling. "Is that all?"

Suzanne shakes her head, clears her throat. There is another concern that she must share. "A dark spirit hovers—more disquieting than managing Max. First, it appeared as a shadow person, which isn't new to me since I've dealt with them since childhood. But this one is *different*. Its energy is unkind. And I'm certain that it's personal."

Enola places her hand over Suzanne's as they linger across the counter.

"Too dark to recognize?"

Suzanne nods.

Enola reaches for sage and thyme leaves nestled in a small compartment. She tucks them inside a white cotton pouch, then adds rose petals. Last, she grabs a basket, adds lavender and sage oils, then tosses in lavender buds for spiritual healing. "More spell work you do, the more you adjust. That is why you're here, yes?" Enola stops. "Otherwise, what's the point?"

"You're correct."

"Hmm, what am I missing?" Enola mutters. She gazes among the crystals and stones displayed in the glass case and says, "Yes, black obsidian, of course."

"I'm very familiar with the stone."

"Your shield," Enola says. "Blocks the negative." Enola loops a thin copper wire over its slick surface, then weaves a necklace-length black cord around the wiring. She walks from behind the counter and approaches Suzanne.

"May I?" she asks before hanging the amulet around Suzanne's neck.

"Of course." Suzanne touches its silky-smooth surface. Enola gathers everything in a black velvet bag, adds a handwritten sheet of instructions for casting the protection petition, and ties it with a thin satin ribbon. She places a thick six-inch black candle and an ornately carved candle holder in a brown bag.

"Come see me soon." Enola is now pure business.

"Thank you for today."

"Don't wait for Franny to return. You *will* need more potent spells. Remember the saints: Saint Christopher, Saint Joseph, and St. Agrippina. Put them to work. I guided Madelaine during difficult times. I can help you, too."

Suzanne feels unsettled, searching for a memory of that time period. "I'm sorry. I really don't remember."

"How could you, love? You stayed with your father most of the time."

Her safety, her future, her mission. If not now, to set the spirit world right, then when? Suzanne hears the tinkle of the front doorbell as she turns to leave. Franny rushes in, out of breath.

"There's a man out front demanding to speak to you, Suzanne," Franny says. "But he refuses to step inside the shop."

"So, it's not Max?" Suzanne asks.

"Oh, no, honey. Certainly not Max. He's blond, blue-eyed, and about six feet tall. Super pale. Smells like freshly baked vanilla cookies."

"Never mind, I know who it is," Suzanne says, following Franny outside. "Jack! What on earth are you doing here?"

"Hey, doll," he answers. "Looks like I've just hit your car's back bumper. Why did you park across the street from my house and not stop to say hello?"

So, now Jack owns a house in New Orleans?

17

Max

New Orleans, Thanksgiving 2005

When Max met Farrah, he had already divorced his first wife, Lily—the mother of his twelve-year-old son, Jacob, the boy hardly anyone knew existed. The family court demanded a six-month mediation because a minor child was stuck in the couple's custody battle. But after several sessions, including Max's refusal to apologize for many adulterous affairs, he relinquished custody of his only child. Financially and emotionally drained, he did what many people do when there's no longer a place to call home.

Max went home.

There, chopping onions alongside his mother in the kitchen and sharing a nightly brandy with his father, listening to jazz favorites and Ol' Blue Eyes, Max tried to make sense of his life. He'd accepted there was no path to redemption after losing his job, wife, child, and half of his retirement account.

As Max and his mom prepared dinner one evening in late August, he'd switched from brandy to whiskey and was on his third Jack and Coke while they watched WWL-TV's forecast for

Hurricane Katrina. Meteorologist Carl Arredondo announced the predicted Category 5 storm would make landfall along the Mississippi-Louisiana Gulf Coast by August 29, only three days away. Max knew the drill: pick up plywood from the hardware store, hoist it, and nail it across the windows of their two-story family home in Lakeview. His folks would be challenged to shore up the family business in the French Quarter. Max had no alternative but to appease his parents now that he was broke and back to living at home.

Annoying. How many hurricanes effing follow the weather guys' predictions?

Paxton and Martha Martin had survived preeminent Gulf Coast hurricanes like Camille and Betsy, 100-year storms no one in his generation could fathom. That is, until Hurricane Katrina's threat. Max didn't argue with his parents' evacuation decisions. Paxton still rambled about the days he spent stranded on a rooftop after Hurricane Betsy, helplessly watching the water rise, as if it had happened five years ago instead of forty.

"You know, Max, we can always use you full time at Tuttle's," Martha said, spinning the spice rack on the counter. "Weddings haven't gone out of style, and people keep dying. Some days we're so busy we turn away customers. It's all we can do to keep up with our regulars." Regulars were the third or fourth generation of Paxton's grandfather's customer base established in the 1940s.

Tuttle's, named after Max's great-grandmother, who'd immigrated from Mexico in the 20s, had two identities: visible to all and veiled for a select few.

On the surface, the floral shop was a legitimate source of pride and income for three generations of Martins. But secretly, Tuttle's served as a mecca of money laundering for Papa Martinez's financial enterprises back in Mexico.

"Who's calling to make reservations, Mom?" Max had appeared to be hypnotized by the ticker-tape notifications running across the kitchen's television screen. Evacuation orders were imminent for New Orleans residents. "You or me?"

"Our conversation isn't finished, Max. Book a couple of hotel rooms in Houston while I finish the roux."

Maybe for a short stint. But I'll be goddamned if Tuttle's is my end game.

For weeks following Hurricane Katrina's unfathomable rage against coastal Mississippi and southeast Louisiana, the Martins were denied access to their flooded Lakeview neighborhood, thanks, in part, to a failed levee system that was woefully outdated for a storm the size of Katrina. Once allowed back on their street, neither Max nor his parents recognized the foul-smelling pile of rubble previously known as their home. Only two surviving items looked familiar: an antique desk and armoire, both thickened with black-greenish mold, propped at the curbside by a well-meaning neighbor.

That was in early September. Nearly three months had passed, marking the time from Max's nadir to his renaissance. His journey paralleled that of his beloved New Orleans. The city and the man refused to be crippled by circumstances or natural disasters.

On a Wednesday afternoon near Thanksgiving, when Max was helping his mom organize delivery orders in Tuttle's workroom, a petite brunette, bubbling with energy, rushed into their showroom and announced her immediate desire for a harvest arrangement.

"I know it's short notice, but can I order a holiday table arrangement? With cornucopias, cute little pumpkins, maybe burlap bows?" the young woman asked. She stopped talking when she saw the amused facial expressions on both Max's and his mom's faces. "I'm sorry, is that asking too much?" Farrah's infectious smile confirmed that her wish would be granted.

Martha Martin deferred the request to her son. With a wink.

"Probably depends on when you need it delivered," Max said, stepping to the counter. "If you can wait until Thanksgiving morning, I'll add you to my final route." He waited for the young woman's response before turning to his mom to confirm.

"Perfect. I'll need it delivered to my grandmother's house. Thank you so much," the woman said, searching Max's lapel for a nametag or form of identification.

"I'm Max," he said.

"Farrah. Pleased to meet you."

Max nodded and grabbed a pad off the workbench.

"I'll take the order, son," Martha said. "Go ahead and start on today's deliveries."

Max missed his family's dramatic Thanksgiving meal that year. And never heard the end of it. Although the Martins had lost their beloved home near Lake Pontchartrain's shore, they'd learned lessons in both humility and gratitude. Unlike countless others, they still had a source of income. Located on Royal Street in the French Quarter, Tuttle's hadn't taken on water after the levees broke. Built on slightly higher ground, the Quarter was spared. Martha planned an enormous celebration to honor their blessings.

Max had other things on his mind the moment he met Farrah.

The delivery to Farrah's grandmother's house on State Street Drive in Uptown was the last one on Max's schedule. Max heard chaos on the other side of the front door as he rang the bell, centerpiece in hand. No one had shown up early to help cook and set up tables, and Mama Esty, Farrah's spunky grandmother, was flustered.

Max, naturally, volunteered his assistance.

Years later, as the story of Max missing the Martins' post-Katrina Thanksgiving dinner circulated, no one remembered if Max had ever called home to apologize for eating turkey elsewhere. Yet, that Thanksgiving Day in 2005 changed Max's life immeasurably.

Once Max helped Mama Esty arrange the settings and chairs around an enormous dining table, he joined Farrah in the kitchen, where she feverishly chopped celery and pecans.

"Can I help?" Max asked, glancing around the countertops laden with grocery bags and unopened containers.

"Thank you, but you've done so much with delivering the arrangement and helping Mama Esty. I'm sure your mom is expecting you." Farrah looked up long enough to scratch her nose with the top of her wrist, only to irritate her eye with an onion shaving.

"My mom and grandma have been cooking since sunrise. They'd be happier if I weren't in the way," Max said. He'd spotted a bag of green beans that needed to be washed and sliced. "Where does your grandmother keep a paring knife?"

"A man after my heart. You know what one is?"

"Of course. Point to where one's kept, and I'm at your service." Max explained that he was an only child, the son of two hardworking parents, so he'd learned early to fend for himself in the kitchen.

The two worked side-by-side for hours, sharing life experiences and post-college plans. It didn't take long for Hurricane Katrina to prickle their conversation—so many opportunities swept away, like receding water lines, leaving a mark.

"Do you think we'll ever stop talking about Katrina?" Farrah asked. He enjoyed watching her stir stuffing ingredients in her grandmother's country French bowl.

She's gorgeous, educated, and cooks like a chef. Maybe something here . . . ?

"Never. Twenty-plus years from now, people will still bitch about Katrina. I'm freaking exhausted from the whole mess. Sick of living with my parents—tired of working for them, too." Max shoved a bowl of prepped green beans in Farrah's direction. "Too damn much, you know?"

"If you say so," Farrah said. "Thank you, Max, for all of your help today."

He dried his hands on his jeans, ignoring the tea towel Farrah had placed on the counter for him. Then, he noticed Mama Esty dragging another chair from the side garage into the driveway. "Probably none of my business, but why are *you* making

Thanksgiving dinner for a crowd that's growing by the minute?"

Farrah laughed, at first, but then became very quiet. "Everyone in my family, except Mama Esty and I, lived in Pass Christian when Katrina struck . . ." Farrah struggled to complete her sentence. But there was no need to finish it. Max's horrified expression filled the gap of her missing words. A nearly thirty-foot storm surge had slammed along the coastline by the time Katrina made its third landfall along the Mississippi/Louisiana border, decimating Mississippi's beach towns beginning at Bay St. Louis and including other coastal communities all along the coastline to Biloxi.

In Katrina's wake, little remained in its thirty-plus-mile swath of destruction but concrete slabs. Homes were ripped apart, while the evidence of lives hurled miles away like matchsticks. Slaughtered power lines. Unrecognizable debris. Yachts tossed onshore like Matchbox toys. Smashed vehicles stacked on one another. Trucks teetering in tree branches. Boats upended at the bottom of swimming pools. One-hundred-year-old live oaks uprooted.

A completely unrecognizable landscape.

"Damn, Farrah, I wish you'd said something . . . before I put my foot in my mouth. Your family lost *everything*."

Farrah nodded her head. "Mimi Jeanne and Papa Lafountain, my great-grandparents, lived on our family estate across from the beach in the Pass. My dad, Jay, inherited the property when Mama Esty said she'd never return after her sister, Addy, died. Our entire family's legacy. Gone. My parents still haven't decided if they want to rebuild."

Max didn't hold back. He opened his arms and embraced this tiny waif of a woman, hellbent on creating a Thanksgiving meal worthy of their family's long-held traditions. As he thought of kissing her, Max looked through the kitchen's bay window behind them and reconsidered: Esty sat on a dining chair in the middle of the driveway, tussling to open a hand-carved wooden box.

"Looks like your grandmother still needs help, Farrah," he said.

Farrah gasped when she saw Mama Esty fighting to unlock Mimi's spell box and followed Max outdoors.

"No, no, Mama Esty. Let's not do this right now. Remember? Guests are arriving soon, and we're not ready." Farrah rescued the spell box before Max could question it, returning the family treasure to a shelf in her grandmother's potter's cottage.

"Madelaine's amethyst bracelet is in that box, Farrah. It's yours," Mama Esty whispered, tears gathering in her eyes. "I should have given it to you a long time ago. And Mimi's spell book is tucked on the bottom too. It belongs to you."

"I don't understand, Mama Esty. But you can explain later, after everyone leaves," Farrah said. She assumed her grandmother was exhausted with holiday preparations and confused with the family line. There'd be no reason for any of Madelaine's treasures to be passed on to her. Her mother was Sophie, Mama Esty's daughter-in-law—not Madelaine. Didn't Aunt Madelaine have a long-lost daughter, anyway?

By late afternoon, Max and Farrah pulled a luscious brown-glazed 20-pound turkey from Mama Esty's oven, balanced it on a platter, and ceremoniously delivered it to the dining table. When the doorbell rang, a string of Farrah's relatives crowded through the front door, including her parents: Jay and Sophie Lamar. One introduction followed another, and Max lost track. Later, he was the subject of the evening's last toast and heralded the savior of the holiday.

He was impressed by Farrah's family's capacity to laugh and share stories in the wake of such a monumental loss: a generational coastal treasure, swept to shreds by a storm boasting at least 120-mile-per-hour winds. It forced Max to reevaluate his family's experience. His dad had finally settled with the insurance company. The house gutting was nearly complete. Meanwhile, his aunt, who lived on the Northshore, insisted the family move in until their home was rebuilt. His aunt had even quit her job, and now rode into New Orleans with them each day to help design floral arrangements.

No one in the Martin family had died. No one had lost an estate—a place multiple generations had cherished for decades.

Once the last platter was washed and hand-dried and the crystalware was lined up against the blue-green backsplash of the kitchen counter, Max and Farrah looked at each other and laughed.

"Wanna grab a beer?" Farrah asked, brushing errant strands of hair from her eyes. "It's the least I can do to repay you for today."

"You have a favorite spot?"

"Carrollton Station, over on Willow Street. You know it?"

"Think they're open? I mean, it being Thanksgiving and all?"

"Let's go see."

Farrah hugged her parents and told Mama Esty not to worry. She'd check in with her tomorrow. Everyone thanked Max and encouraged him not to become a stranger. "You're welcome here anytime, love. You saved our Thanksgiving," Mama Esty said, hugging Max tightly.

Max and Farrah didn't arrive at the bar. Instead, when they stopped at Farrah's apartment for a change of clothes, they stumbled through the hallway in a frenzied version of foreplay that began with hurried disrobing and ended with Max entering Farrah, balanced against a wall. Afterward, they crawled into her canopied, four-poster bed and sipped tequila for hours. When Farrah eventually slipped into the bathroom, she heard Max's phone vibrating atop the chest of drawers.

"Max! Oh my God, wake up," she shouted.

When he didn't respond, she nudged him repeatedly. "Something's terribly wrong. You've got thirty missed calls. Wake up. Answer this," she said, shoving the phone into his face.

"What the hell, Farrah?"

"Answer your bloody phone. Something has happened."

Max sat up. “Hello,” he managed. “Wait . . . what? Mother, slow down. I can’t understand a word.” A second later, Max threw his phone across the room, screamed, then punched a hole in the bedroom wall.

Farrah rushed to pick up the phone. “Are you there? I’m sorry. Can I do anything . . . to help?”

“Bring my son to me. Immediately. I’m at Tharpe’s on Canal Street.”

“Okay, but he has his car. It’s here.”

“Who are you, exactly?” Martha asked.

“Farrah Adelaide Lamar,” she answered, uncertain as to why she felt compelled to roll out her proper name in its entirety.

“All right, little miss Farrah. Max’s father keeled over in his plate of turkey and mirliton dressing last night with a heart attack. The man’s dead. I’m sure Max won’t be in the best shape to drive himself. Get over here with *my goddamn son*.”

Farrah quietly answered her. “Yes, ma’am. And I’m very sorry for your loss.”

Max listened to his mother’s screams and Farrah’s response as he huddled behind the bathroom door, sweat dripping from his brow.

The Cartel debt’s now mine to settle? Fuck me.

18

Addy

Gulf Coast, Summer 1944

When Addy awoke on Friday morning, she checked the calendar propped against the vanity mirror in the bedroom she shared with Esty. Then she sprayed Mademoiselle Chanel No. 1 on her inner wrists and behind her earlobes, just as Mimi had modeled a few weeks ago when she presented Addy with her first bottle of exquisite perfume. Such a remarkable flourish of extravagance, even for Mimi.

Two months had passed since their first lazy afternoon spent in the Pass. Addy counted thirty days until her parents returned from their annual summer stint in New York City. That's when Addy and her sisters were expected back at State Street Drive in New Orleans, ready to start school shortly after Labor Day.

Summer days frittered away like the drops of rainwater from a leaky spigot. Here. There. Split. Splat. *Gone.*

"Esty, wake up!" Addy yelled. She threw a pillow at her sister's head to rouse her. "I'm finally meeting Cash at the Dew Drop. You're coming with me." Addy sat at the end of Esty's twin bed and nudged her feet. "Say yes, sis."

"Did you tell Mimi yet? That's twenty miles away."

"No," Addy said. "But she won't object if you say we're going together." She stood and admired her reflection in front of the full-length mirror, pulled her locks to one side, then ran her fingers through the tangles earned during a restless night of sleep.

Esty smirked. "It depends on why you want me there, Addy. Not interested in being a third wheel."

"Summer's nearly spent," Addy said, unclasping their bedroom's only shuttered dormer window. "And I don't have much more time to spend with Cash."

Seconds after rolling out of bed, Esty smoothed her pink chenille bedspread at all four corners until it looked just right. "What's wrong with you?" she asked. "You act as if Cash is off on a business trip, like the ones Daddy takes." Someday, Esty will make an extraordinary wife for a lucky man, Addy thought, noticing the contrast between her unmade bed with pillows scattered on the floor and Esty's.

Addy frowned. "How am I supposed to act?"

"Scared to death, for starters. That's how most girlfriends feel, right?" Esty quickly ran a brush through her straight blonde hair. When Addy didn't answer, Esty turned and asked, "What will you do if Cash dies?"

"Don't be ridiculous. Cash won't die." Addy's clipped words sounded like the click-click rhythm of high heels hitting the concrete.

Both hands on her hips, Esty rolled her eyes. "I wonder about you, Addy. Army Air Force guys always leave—the WAAC leaves, too. Why do you think he's training hard after getting admitted to that special co-piloting program? That's why you barely see him. He's preparing for air combat."

"Who are you? Cash's agent?" It didn't make sense that Esty knew considerably more about Cash's training opportunities than she did.

Esty searched for a red halter top in the bureau and avoided meeting her sister's eyes.

"You see things the rest of us don't see, Addy, but sometimes you don't recognize what's right before you," Esty said, gathering her hair into a ponytail.

"Enough, Esty. You've said enough."

Addy sat on the window seat in the room's alcove and gazed across the Sound. She loved getting lost in the sparkling diamond-like reflections after low tide. She had faithfully followed her vision and found her handsome officer here on the Gulf Coast. Wearing his olive-green uniform. Flashing his million-dollar smile.

Now, the future loomed with enormous uncertainty. She'd paid close attention to her visions' details and followed them. Then watched as fate played its hand. Maybe more foresight than Addy'd allowed herself was crucial. Following a vision was one thing—ensuring its successful development was another matter entirely.

Am I meant to be with Cash? Forever?

Addy pulled away from watching the water. "Are you coming tonight or not?"

"I'll go, Addy. But only because I don't want you stuck alone in a bar. Especially if Cash doesn't show. Plus, there'll be plenty of cute airmen around. You know you're not the only Lafountain beauty who can snag an officer," Esty said.

Mimi yelled from downstairs. "Hurry up, girls. We're off to Henderson Park."

Oh, no, we're not.

"Mimi, we are *not* spending another hot day in the sun," Addy argued, racing down the steps. "Esty and I both need new dresses. We're meeting up with Cash and his buddies at the Dew Drop tonight."

Mimi frowned and squarely faced Addy. "Are you asking or telling me?"

"Both?"

"That place is a dive. You know exactly what I'm saying, given the kind of music they play. So, has it come to this? For you to see Cash?" Mimi shook her head. "Hanging out in a juke joint to have a Friday night date. In my day, we set expectations high. We didn't settle for less, Adelaide."

"Good Lord, Mimi, no more lectures from your day. The Dew Drop's not a dive. Please tell me you don't hear things like that in your ladies' circle. It's one of the bars in Biloxi where Negro jazz musicians are allowed to play." Addy looked back up the stairs, wishing Esty would hurry along. *Is she talking on the phone with someone?*

"Those jazzers are . . ." Mimi interjected.

"Talented musicians," Addy completed her interpretation of Mimi's thought. "The only people of color allowed in the place *are* the musicians, Mimi," Addy said. She realized her grandmother had carved herself a reasonable distance from the Coast's day-to-day doings. *Why?* Either Mimi was spending more time in her potter's shed, mixing potions, or her social contacts were limited to yacht club luncheons and church socials. Addy hoped her first assumption was correct.

Esty caught up. "It'll be fine, Mimi," she said. "I'm happy to be the tag-along. Besides, Cash is already expecting her."

"He'll be getting his orders," Addy said. "To leave for Europe soon. I don't know. Cash keeps avoiding the conversation." She noticed Papa's unusual silence emanating from the living room. Felt him avoiding her eyes. Maybe *he* knew something.

"That young man doesn't strike me as one to hold back words," Mimi said. "Or anything else, for that matter."

By early '44, the Army Air Forces' impressive tactics with its allies had boomeranged a blast across Germany. Their efforts had made headlines in the papers and movie newsreels. So it didn't add up that Cash remained at Keesler. Unless Esty was correct, given the war's increased demand for pilots. Maybe Cash was in line for more training.

Addy's frame of reference was askew—she was tired of waiting for Cash to make a move. *You do feel the same way, don't you?* She craved one crazy romantic night of lovemaking before returning to New Orleans by summer's end. One final chance to wake up in Cash's arms and watch the sunrise. Anything short of that felt like a failed vision. Anything beyond felt like an impossible dream.

After they spent the morning shopping for new dresses in the Pass, Mimi drove Addy and Esty to the trolley stop on Second Street. They shared a seat and a breeze from the trolley's open window, a welcome relief from the day's steamy heat. Pulling into Biloxi, the sisters spotted the Dew Drop and its long entrance line just north of the beach. They hopped off, crossed the street, and stood in line, waiting for Cash and Eddy to find them.

Esty spotted the men first. "Here they come," she yelled, waving dramatically.

"Calm yourself, Esty." *Geez.*

Cash kissed Addy's lips, then Esty's cheek. Addy watched Eddy introduce a couple of other guys through a haze of anxiety after witnessing Cash's lips linger too long against Esty's ear. Then wished she could pretend Esty's hand had not pressed against Cash's chest, a gesture far too intimate for her sister to display.

"Let's get a bite to eat here, then head to the Tivoli. They've got plenty of slot machines in the lobby and a swing band headlining their ballroom tonight."

Eddy chimed in, "Man, wouldn't you love cleaning up on 'dem slot machines before flying over?"

Addy doubted her presence mattered to Cash, who was distracted by cutting up with Eddy and their pals. Yet the two had talked about meeting in Biloxi since the night they'd met at Beauvoir a few weeks ago.

Esty whispered, "What've you got us into, Addy? Are they even happy to see us?"

"Do *not* say a word!" Addy hissed. Determined to hide her

disappointment, she said, "It'll be fine. He's showing off with his friends. I don't want to ride back just yet, so let's try . . . and enjoy ourselves."

Listen to your advice, she thought. And put a lid on the jealousy jar. Still, she wanted to scream at Esty.

Leave my guy alone! He's mine.

Esty agreed. "Let's find a table of gals at Tivoli's. That's if the guys stay in the lobby to gamble instead of joining us in the ballroom. This might be our last party night before we leave for New Orleans."

Their extravagant steak and shrimp dinners were more than Addy had expected. She met some of Cash's friends, and Esty hit it off with Eddy. Still, Addy felt disappointed. She hadn't received star billing tonight. Cash and his friends needed to release a week's worth of stress following rigorous training. He deserved to live it up before leaving, she finally decided.

Then Cash grabbed her shoulders and pulled her up to her feet, catching her off guard. "Let's dance, baby," he said. The brass ensemble blasted "G.I. Jive" from their huddle in the club's corner as everyone at their table crowded onto the dance floor. "Why so quiet?" he yelled in her ear, competing against a loud trumpeter.

"It's nothing," Addy paused, gauging whether she should say more. "It's just that . . ."

"We're out of smokes, pal. Walk over to the gas station with me?" Eddy interrupted. He had a tight grip on her sister's hand.

"Let's get 'em on the way. You girls ready for more action?" Cash yelled.

Addy met his enthusiasm with a half-smile. Fighting back the tears, she fell in line with the group as they left the Dew Drop and strutted into the night, bound for Tivoli's hot spot. When they walked past Biloxi's Main Street, she saw guys laughing, smoking, drinking, and joking. Shopfronts were brightly lit, and music filled the street. Even the streetlamps blazed brighter than ever. Big news must have come down at the base earlier in the day.

Keeping pace with Eddy, Esty turned back to spot her sister. When she realized Addy was trailing far behind, she ran back and grabbed her by the elbow.

"Are you sick or something?" Esty slurred through her s's. "I thought you wanted to come out tonight."

"I'm fine. I just imagined tonight would be . . . *you know* . . . personal. That's all."

"You don't mean romantic, do you?"

"Maybe."

"If Cash had wanted romance, you'd have known. And he wouldn't have invited his friends to watch. Try having some fun with your dreamboat, why don't you?" Esty ran to catch up with Eddy.

Maybe Esty said something to Eddy, for within seconds, Cash circled back, grabbed Addy by her waist, and spun her around. "Time to party, my beautiful Southern belle. Got any change in that pricey purse of yours?"

"Maybe." She smiled. "You're sure excited tonight. What happened this week?"

"A lot," Cash answered, beaming with pride. "Finished B-24 training. Now they're talking about B-32s, too. But I'm ready to let loose tonight!" Cash jumped on the trolley's foothold, then offered her a hand up.

Addy perked up when she heard a saxophonist glide through a twelve-bar blues set as they entered Tivoli's. She felt homesick, hearing the blues. Maybe it really was time to head home to New Orleans after all.

A steward wearing a brass tag on his lapel, simply engraved with his first name—Jack—escorted the sisters to a table close to the band, and motioned other women to join them. Cash, Eddy, and several friends stayed in the hotel lobby, as predicted.

The sisters completely lost track of time. And eventually

lost track of one another. After hours of dancing, a hotel manager approached Addy and insisted that she accompany him. *Did I hear him correctly? A guest of mine behaving rudely, even belligerently?*

She heard Cash's drunk and agitated voice before they entered the lobby. "It's rigged. Everything's rig...geed, Addy," he yelled as a couple of hotel bouncers struggled to restrain him.

"You're not leaving here until this matter is settled," the manager said.

"I'm not going anywhere until you explain what's happened." She looked around for another hotel employee to provide an explanation, since the manager seemed solely concerned about compensation.

"What did you *do*?" Addy demanded, after coming face-to-face with Cash, her glare piercing his eyes.

Before Cash could respond, the manager yelled, "This crew of yours destroyed one of the slot machines because it didn't pay out as they expected."

"I don't have a crew . . . I have a date," Addy offered. "And if you're blaming *this* officer, I doubt he is solely at fault, because it looks like any one of these fellas could be responsible."

"You're not expecting one of us," Esty chimed in, appearing at Addy's side, "to reimburse the hotel, are you? I've already phoned our grandfather."

When the manager learned that James Lafountain was en route to the Tivoli, he changed his attitude. "This rogue," he said, pointing to Cash, "and his unruly friends, are no longer welcome here."

"We're leaving," Addy announced.

As they approached the hotel's front entry, Addy turned to Cash, "You're on your own here. Never, ever put me in a position like this again." He snickered at Addy's reaction, which fueled her anger. Addy slapped Cash squarely across his face, then stepped back. "My family . . . has lived here for generations . . . I've summered in the Pass for my entire life. Do you not see how humiliating this is? We've reputations to uphold."

Cash's expression didn't change until she asked, "So, who *are* you, anyway? Looks to me like another Keesler boy simply passing through." Then changed dramatically when the steward punched Cash in the nose as the sisters breezed through the doors and out into the summer evening air.

The Lafountain sisters were ill-equipped to salvage the night, much less save themselves from an outsider who had insidiously entered their realm. Though unbeknownst to them, the Lafountain family angel had his protective eyes on the sisters and their best interests at heart.

19

Suzanne

New Orleans, Fall 2012

No one notices the small hoodoo altar Suzanne sets upon the ledge of her white-bricked patio in the backyard of her Lakeview home. It's nestled between caladium pots and powder-blue chrysanthemums. A cast-iron fence with cornstalk posts provides its backdrop. When Franny weighs in on authenticating the altar, she questions Suzanne about its location since it's hiding in plain sight. It's okay for the altar to be a bit more front-and-center, Franny says.

How 'bout a little credit for a start? I'll get there.

White candles are harmoniously aligned, with one exception. A thick, waxy black one is positioned dead center atop an ornate hand-carved candleholder that Suzanne bought at Enola's. Once the shop owner shared the story about purchasing it in Tervuren, Belgium, at the Royal Museum for Central Africa, there was no question that Suzanne wanted it for herself. To an uneducated observer, the black candle is out of sync. But for a spellcaster, it's the most significant one.

To complete the altar, Suzanne places an ivory cross to the

right of the candle. She adds a marbled set of praying hands to the left and sets a diffuser in the center. Circling the diffuser, she places several black obsidian stones and, at right, a large block of selenite to cleanse her aura before beginning a spell. Ceremoniously displayed are the tarot cards from her reading at Enola's. Finally, Suzanne adds novena candles to honor Archangel Michael, Archangel Gabriel, and various saints. Sprigs of freshly cut rosemary, for empowerment, and lavender, for cleansing the atmosphere, are bound together with a black satin ribbon, providing a final touch. Stepping back to examine the altar, she smiles, satisfied.

If Sister Rosa Mae, her first-grade teacher at the small Catholic primary school Suzanne attended a few blocks away, peered in on this scene from the other side, she would die—if she wasn't already deceased. Any clergy supporting tarot and hoodoo working in tandem with the saints—offering suppliance—is the rarest of gems.

The altar provides comfort. It pays homage to a simpler time when folks paid closer attention to the care and well-being of their souls. Suzanne inhales and exhales serenity. She prays that her renewed zest for incantations will safeguard her against a throng of unknown adversaries.

Suzanne reassesses where things stand. *Farrah is dead.* Not an estranged ex-wife, as Max would have her believe. When her PI reports that Max is still Edmonson County's number one person of interest in his wife's untimely death, Suzanne is disheartened.

You are an unforgivable liar, Max.

Suzanne is far too entangled within her spirit web to dismiss Max—then, of course, there's the burning complication known as lust. When asked, she denies falling in love with Max. Friends question Suzanne's motivation, possibly her sanity, for the risks of teaming up with Max are increasing tenfold. No one could possibly understand the contradiction of seducing a man for the sheer purpose of delaying his harm.

In the bleak darkness of nights filtered with arguments, followed by make-up sex, Suzanne lies awake as Max drifts off, watching the four upper corners of either of their bedrooms. Any night can result in a ghostly encounter, so she'll remain awake as long as possible, just like she did as a child, until exhaustion finally takes over. Her routine is not unlike the lookout millions of other women craft for themselves to protect their children and themselves from men like Max, who thrive on control, no matter the cost.

Then there's the big question to mull over as sleep evades her: If Max *is* guilty, will he kill again? Has he killed more than once? *Would Max kill me?*

In these stark moments, Suzanne nearly convinces herself that this situation is normal—for her—and entirely within the bounds of management. But, then again, she must reflect upon her worth. *Exactly how valuable am I?* Destiny cannot be altered, she concludes.

After all, I am the daughter of a woman who nearly abandoned me to a father who refused to make her his wife. Because she refused to give up magick.

After two glasses of moscato, Suzanne prepares the incantation. First, she anoints the black candle with sage oil, then coats its center with ground-up thyme and sage. Adds drops of lavender oil to the diffuser. Lights the tea candle beneath. Soon, her entire backyard wafts with the scents of lavender and sage.

She lights the black candle first, then the white. Then, softly, Suzanne pronounces gratitude for her protection, repeating her mantra until she feels confident that this is true.

Holding Enola's velvet pouch open in her left hand, Suzanne removes the obsidian stone necklace she's been religiously wearing and tucks it inside, along with other spell items, including the sage and thyme leaves, rose petals, and lavender bud.

She passes the bag through the smoke of the black candle ceremoniously. Then, chants:

Cleanse my soul, I ask of thee/cleanse my soul of all negativity/Energy, and wishes, thoughts, and deeds/ Cleanse them all/So mote it be/And as you cleanse, protect my soul/Through day and night, and the morning dew/Protect from harm and negativity/ Cleanse it now, and leave only purity/It is done.

She repeats the chant three times. Finally, when the white candles' flames extinguish themselves, Suzanne remembers the relevance of leaving the black one lit. She recalls Enola's instructions to carry the velvet pouch until the black candle is completely extinguished.

Suzanne must trust in the spell and be content with not wearing her talisman until the charm is cast, a feat destined to last several days.

Bimini, bored with watching her movements, wanders out to the back side of the property. Suzanne notices his halting gait and, even at a distance, sees her faithful companion standing stock-still, at attention.

Looking back at the black candle's flames, Suzanne stares hypnotically. She prays the charm works its magic. Then, as she begins her Thursday evening grading papers, seated on the patio sofa, Suzanne catches the aroma of jasmine, Turkish rose, and citrus, and her senses shift to high alert.

Who's this? Indeed, it's not Madelaine.

Suzanne feels her chest tighten each time she inhales. She stacks the ungraded essays on a table, anchoring the pile with a stapler, and walks into her yard, searching for the scent's origin. Each time Suzanne clears her throat to swallow, she tastes an infusion of mandarin orange and white musk. While she perceives a swift movement by the fountain, she sees nothing upon approaching it.

Struggling against the pressure building in her throat, Suzanne returns to the patio, searching for a glass of water left by the altar. She takes slow sips, hoping to settle the spasms gripping her larynx. Standing by the altar, in the shadow of the candlelight's protection, Suzanne whispers her mantra and fights to settle the rhythm of her racing heartbeat. There's confusion, for this citrus, musky smell is *not* Madeline's scent. It's thicker, with a heavy rose aroma, and smells like a much older woman's perfume. Perhaps from decades ago.

Suzanne fears an evil spirit is attempting a connection and hesitates to wander the garden's perimeter. But when Bimini senses more shadow movement, again near the fountain, Suzanne follows her golden retriever's path, nudging past the stone encasement surrounding the backyard pond and pushing against overgrown foliage. She's startled when a large, leafy white blossom jumps out at her from a magnolia tree's long-hanging branch.

But there's nothing here.

Suzanne walks the fence line as the afternoon wanes into dusk, her eyes darting between the fountain and the property's cast-iron border. *Naturally, when I gather the courage to cast my first spell in years, a phantom steps forward.*

Within moments, an opaque apparition appears and hovers in the middle of the yard. The air is magnified with electric energy as the white wisp of a woman's figure unfolds. As a chilling breeze swirls through the yard, Suzanne feels bound by its force field, unable to move. She's inexplicably drawn to the figure.

Concentrating, willing the apparition to linger, she forms a question in her mind: *Who are you?* Suzanne closes her eyes, tilts her face to the heavens, and listens for a non-verbal response.

Instead, faint notes from a saxophone lament a blues tune from long ago.

Suzanne speaks aloud this time. "Please identify yourself." Experience has taught her to confine an initial communication to three-or-four-word statements.

The uneven white form glides effortlessly past Suzanne toward the fountain, seemingly unaware of her presence. Then the deafening clatter of water crashing against rocks or wood—a sound Suzanne does not usually hear in her garden—beckons the phantom steadily and with purpose.

Though unnecessary, Suzanne dramatically steps aside to accommodate the ghost's movement. "Live by the sea? In a past life?" she asks. In response, the white opaque form shakes violently. Then raspy, throaty sounds spring forth as though water is gurgling.

Is this specter choking on water? Gasping for air?

"I mean no harm," Suzanne says, softly stepping closer. She stretches out her hands, palms up, to underscore her promise. But her gesture is premature and much too intimate. When Suzanne feels the phantom tug against her energy, she reaches for the marcasite cross necklace around her neck.

With this gesture, more detail emerges. Though the phantom faces Suzanne, its façade remains blurred. Long, luscious black hair gathers at its neckline and whips around the spirit's outline as sudden gusts of wind blow across the backyard. Suzanne glimpses a bright red fabric reflected from a cocktail dress worn long ago, maybe during wartime. Perhaps the 1940s? She memorizes every detail.

"Let me help you," Suzanne whispers. The ghost's power is exhausting, draining Suzanne of her ability to remain standing. She wonders how much more she can handle, short of passing out. When Suzanne drops to her knees, a garbled response resonates against the sound of crashing waves, though there's only one fountain in the yard built near the trunk of a magnolia tree. And *no* angry sea in sight. The clamor in her backyard is so deafening Suzanne fears it could wake the dead.

Suzanne doesn't consider the fact that only *she* can hear the clamor of discontent.

"*Pay.*" The ghost's voice is throaty and hoarse, as though years have passed since last it spoke.

Her connection to this specter shocks Suzanne—it emotionally outdistances any other communication with those who no longer breathe the Earth's air.

"*Make him. Pay.*"

"Who?"

When Suzanne stands and steps forward too quickly, its departure is swift, swirling upward in a bizarre wind twist, dissipating within seconds.

Physically drained and emotionally spent, Suzanne sits cross-legged in the grass as she grapples with the most heart-rending emotions. It's as if she has just learned of the horrible death of a beloved. Tears run down her cheeks as she assimilates the events of the past five minutes. She's dead certain of one thing: This is an angry, trapped ghost seeking payback.

Before Suzanne can fully collect herself, Max's insistent voice splits through the stillness. "Suzanne! Who the hell are you talking to out here?" He slams his way through the side gate. "You don't answer my calls, don't answer your door."

Oh, dear God. What is he doing here? How much did Max see? Or, worse, hear?

"Get off my property right now before I call the police," Suzanne shouts.

Max scrutinizes the backyard, trying to locate her voice. When he finds her, she's stretched out on the lawn. "Not very hospitable of you, Suzanne. Considering how worried I am." He stoops down to examine her situation. "Jesus, what the hell are you doing, Suzy?"

"I felt like I was going to faint," she says.

"I've been watching you stagger around your lawn for ten minutes, trying to figure out this mess. Where's that massive dog of yours? Bimi? Bimini, whatever its name is . . ." Max looks around, puzzled that her golden retriever is nowhere to be seen.

"It's best that you leave, Max. I'm not myself tonight."

"No. We need to talk," Max says. "Too many weird things are happening, and after what I've witnessed, weirdness isn't confined to me."

Max reaches to help Suzanne sit, then joins her. "I came over to explain some things. But after this?" The man has no reference point for describing the past few minutes. "You've some explaining of your own, Suzy Q."

After tonight's events, there's no more time to waste. Suzanne gets right to it. "Did you kill your wife, Max?"

"No, absolutely not." He edges closer. "I'm the victim here, Suzy. Farrah's family always hated me, so when she died in Mammoth Cave, her dad went hellfire crazy. Decided someone had to pay for his only daughter's death. And guess who? *Me*."

Suzanne wants to believe him. Sorting ghost visits would be less ambiguous if truth played its hand.

"I'll give you the time it takes to knock back one Jack and Coke," she says. "That's all I've got left for crazy. But then, you go home and stay there."

"Fair enough." He offers his hand and guides her to the patio. Suzanne appears disoriented, somewhat disheveled, and perhaps even ill.

"Do you mind making your drink?" she asks before easing into her favorite overstuffed chair. She notes the black candle, still burning, on the brick ledge directly across from her. What might have happened if the protection spell had *not* been cast? If she had yet to light the tall black candle?

"May I pour you a glass of wine?"

"No, thanks. Just water."

Max sits on the sofa, with the altar situated behind him, slightly elevated over his head. Suzanne can't help but relish the poetic justice of the moment, for Max looks demonic.

"You don't have to say it, Suzy, so I'll say it for you. I fucked up." Max hands her a glass of ice water. He sits, crosses his right leg, and continues. "I didn't tell you that Mo joined me for the deposition because she surprised me . . . had no idea she'd be on a later flight." He lies with the slick ease of a carpetbagger. Then he gulps his three-finger bourbon, neat.

"Wait just one minute. You think I'm upset that Maureen

joined you? I didn't even know she'd gone with you." With her head pulsating, Suzanne can barely sit up, much less hold a serious conversation with Max. Still, she tries. "Let's discuss the rumor, you know, that you murdered your wife. You didn't think to mention it?"

"Don't say it doesn't matter to you, Suzy. Me and Maureen, together in Kentucky. Believe me, nothing happened. In case you're worried."

Suzanne leans her head back and nestles into the sofa's cushions. "And four years ago, you were charged with killing Farrah," she says, nearly whispering, as though she's speaking to herself.

"No, you're wrong about that. I've never been officially charged." Max pours himself another bourbon, ignoring Suzanne's one-drink rule. She's too wiped out to notice.

"Max, I hired the same detective I used when I needed dirt on my ex. And so far, my PI has not let me down."

He doesn't take the bait. "You're imagining the worst," Max yells. "Woman, I didn't kill my wife!"

Suzanne slumps down deeper in the cushions, fighting sleep, and resists curling into a fetal position. Yes, it's been that kind of night. "I don't know how to gauge your worst lie because there're so many of them, so don't know where the bar's set," she says. "The night we met at Remé's party, you said you were divorced. Remember?"

Max deflects her question with ease. "Maybe I need a PI to poke around in your skeletal closet. Huh? I need someone to explain the creepy things that happen in your backyard. In the middle of the night," he says, wiping the sweat from his face. "And explain all the stupid shit I don't get. You know, love, you're not an easy woman."

"Don't bring my issues into the mix. Tonight's not the night."

"I love you, Suzy." Blurted in quiet desperation, Max's confession of love falls flat. Nevertheless, she believes it's likely that he loves her as much as he can love *anyone*. But, sadly, love alone won't establish solvency between them.

Max drinks another bourbon. Suzanne watches her lover's bravado fade as an odd glow crosses his face, not stemming from the candlelight. A darkened vignette now frames his countenance. She shudders at the sight, his perfect posture, his legs crossed, calmly drinking his bourbon. A thought crosses Suzanne's mind before sleep threatens to overtake her, despite her best efforts to keep it at bay.

The shadow figure . . . that confronted me in Seaside . . . whom did it seek?

"Go home, Max."

20

Max

New Orleans, Fall 2012

Max calls Maureen a few minutes after Suzanne throws him out. He's annoyed when his girl Friday doesn't answer. He sits on the curbside adjacent to Suzanne's driveway, too drunk to drive. All he needs is for one of her smart-ass sons to come home and whip into the driveway.

Max knows something's off with his Suzy. But as far as pegging the specific issue, he's clueless.

She's a freak, dammit. Not sure how that's going to jell with my strategy.

He redials Maureen's number.

"I'm rather tied up right now," Maureen says, answering Max's tenth attempt.

"With whom?"

"None of your business." Max may be soused, but he's lucid enough to recognize the sounds of interrupted sex. "Get to it, Max. Your timing sucks."

"We've got a problem." He's pacing in front of Suzanne's place, hoping he can wrap up this call before she realizes he hasn't left and calls the cops.

"We? You mean *you* have a problem. This can't wait . . . because?"

"I need help. Then you can get back to your whomever." He stops walking and stares at the heavens, pretending he believes enough to barter a plea deal.

Maureen sighs. "Talk. Quickly."

"Suzanne's gone bat-shit crazy and kicked me out after I went over to her place to explain everything." Max paces for 500 yards, dragging his fingers through his sweaty hair, then turns on a heel and walks back to his car.

"How much of *everything* can you explain?" Maureen asks in between whispers to someone on her end.

"Right. So . . ."

"Let me guess. She wants to break things off."

"Worst timing for it, when I'm so close to getting my hands on . . ." Max says. "Not sure about following through—Suzy's killing me with her craziness."

"She freaks *you* out? Shouldn't it be the other way around?" Maureen asks. "The Max I know would already be on top of things."

When Max leans against his BMW, he fails to notice the spiffily dressed man lounging atop the car's hood, his elbow poised against the windshield. Jack smiles, amused at Max's acquiescence. For once, Max agrees with Maureen's take on the situation. She's right. There's no reason for Max to relinquish his presumed upper hand with Suzanne. No reason to get off track now. Had Max managed to control his emotional responses to Suzanne, he wouldn't be questioning his motives.

"I let myself in her backyard—first mistake. But then, I hear her talking in that shrill, high-pitched voice. The one she uses when she's wound tight. Then, I nearly trip over her stretched out on the lawn, staring at the sky. Then her damn dog finally shows up, running circles around the garden, acting just as cuckoo."

"You *do* realize she's a spiritualist. She reads tarot, consults a spirit guide. Your Suzy's likely a sorceress, Max. And I highly suspect that she talks to the dead."

Max rambles on. "Yeah, maybe that explains a few things. Okay . . . and she's burning candles and shit around her patio . . . God—do you think she's holding séances in her backyard?"

"And that would be the worst possible thing? Ahh, I get it. You're afraid she'll summon Farrah, aren't you? Max, time to get over yourself. You're nowhere near getting your hands on Suzanne's entire fortune. My advice? Get on your knees and beg for forgiveness if that's what it takes to stay in this woman's life. Too much is at stake."

"I didn't count on her learning about the deposition. Now I'm thrown."

"If you can sell property along the Gulf Coast to fools clueless about hurricanes, you can handle Suzanne," Maureen says. "Use some damn common sense. Good night."

He gives Suzanne space to simmer down and lets two weeks pass before stopping by her school. Max lingers in his car until he hears the final dismissal bell. Then he whips into the parking lot when the last school bus leaves. Her vehicle is easy to spot at the back of the campus.

Their conversation begins with Max pleading for another chance and ends with Suzanne's declaration: "Absolutely the last chance I'll give you, Max. Ever." No opportunity for a sexy ending tonight if he doesn't shift the odds right now.

Damn it, woman, why must you be so goddamn complicated?

Suzanne agrees to meet him at Crazy Johnnie's in Metairie for the restaurant's celebrated filet mignon dinner. And drinks.

Max arrives first and rehearses what he's willing to explain. His favorite waitress, Laureen, leads him to his usual back corner booth and promises to watch for Suzanne. He downs back-to-back bourbons while waiting to marvel at Suzanne's sashay into the restaurant. He dismisses one call after another from Remé.

"Am I safe? Here. With you?" she asks, sliding into the booth.

"I could ask you the same goddamn question, Suzy, given your bizarre behavior I witnessed the other night in your backyard." He watches the amber swirl of his drink skate around ice cubes. "You're misinformed, sugga'. I don't know what kind of crackerjack PI you hired, but he stinks."

"You're such a liar, Max," Suzanne fires back. "I've no recourse but to hire others to get the information I need. And deserve. Because you're shamelessly dishonest." She waves at Laureen. "Have you ever thought of playing it straight, Max?"

"You misunderstand. I speak the truth about many things . . ."

Suzanne interrupts his foray into honesty. "Then lie about things that matter most to others. In the name of getting what you want. There's a label for that, but I'm not giving it voice."

Laureen delivers a decanter of Suzanne's favorite wine to the table and places it at the table's edge. There's a reason she has seated the couple in the back dining room.

"Okay if I start with a few questions, or do you plan to unfold your defense first?"

"How 'bout I begin." Max raises his glass for another bourbon. "Farrah and I married with little thought and less planning. We flew to Vegas one weekend six months after we met. It was right after Hurricane Katrina had annihilated our lives. Farrah came into the florist shop my family owns that first Thanksgiving after the storm, and we got married the next May because she told me she was pregnant."

Max pauses after unpacking that nugget.

Their steaks arrive on par with Crazy Johnnie's premier standards. Max watches Suzanne cut into her flamed filet and is grateful for the respite. Anyone else would be unnerved by a silent dinner date. Suzanne empties her wine glass and reaches to refill it.

After digging through his twice-baked potato teeming with butter and sour cream, he continues with his Farrah fable.

"So, a few weeks after we got married, she calls me at work

in the middle of the afternoon—mind you, I'm still slaving for peanuts at my family's florist because my dad died on Thanksgiving. She's screaming. Says she's at the hospital, and the baby's gone."

"Gone?"

"Yeah, gone. A miscarriage, she tells me." Max shakes his head. "I'm saying, hey, put the doctor on the phone. I got some questions of my own."

"Did you? Talk to the doctor?"

"*Fuck*, no," he says—too loudly. "She's hysterical, hangs up on me. So that was that. We never spoke of it again. First, there was a baby. Then there wasn't one."

"I'm sorry, Max. I had no idea." As the evening spins on Max's version of the truth, he watches tears pool in the corner of Suzanne's eyes. Bolstered by her reaction, Max embellishes facts for his protection. "Everything changed for us after that. Farrah was sickly and depressed. Had no interest in leaving the apartment or going back to work. All she talked about was getting pregnant again."

"What did you want?"

"Not to repeat the nightmare. That much I can tell you."

Pisses me off, the way women get dreamy-eyed about babies. But if that's what it takes . . . I'll keep at it. That Martinez debt won't disappear on its own.

Laureen escorts the dessert cart to their table. Max smiles, knowing that Suzanne loves this fawning attention when dining out. She chooses a slice of coconut meringue pie and orders a cappuccino. Then the floodgate of questioning opens. Building a relationship with Suzanne is as excruciating as constructing an Egyptian pyramid.

"You were married," she starts.

"You knew that."

"I didn't know you'd lost a baby, Max. That's information worth sharing." Is it his imagination, or is Suzanne hissing her words as she leans forward?

"I don't think guys share shit like that, Suzanne. That's not first or second date material."

"Okay, I'll give you that, but concealing your wife's death and pretending you divorced her just because you learned I was divorced, too . . . that's a stretch. Why lie?"

Max lowers his eyes and rearranges the remaining pieces of steak on his plate. "Because in my mind, I was divorced. Our marriage was over. I'd already hired an attorney by the time we took that trip with her family. My plan was to end the nightmare."

"Go on."

"If you'd been through what I have for the past four years—dealing with Farrah's family, the DA in Edmonson County, everyone on my ass—you'd understand why I'd avoid sharing the gritty details of my life on the first night we met."

"Or the second or the third, *yes*. But not after several months." Suzanne thanks Laureen for placing a slice of pie, topped with a three-inch meringue, in front of her, and her cappuccino, at her right.

As for Max, well, he has lost his appetite.

This mock interview is slower than ass molasses. Here's to a delicious dinner, now flushed down the drain. He raises his tumbler for Laureen, bracing for Suzanne's further interrogation. No doubt years married to an attorney helped her hone this skill.

"Whose idea was it to vacation in Kentucky? Mammoth Cave is a bizarre choice for a getaway. Why not the Bahamas? Cozumel? One of the Sandals resorts?"

"It wasn't mine. I enjoy a good cave excursion like the next guy, but I wasn't stoked about spending a week bent over like a hunchback, wandering through musky caves. Or stomping through horse dung from one equestrian farm to the next. Her family wanted to meet in a central location as far away from hurricanes as possible."

"Why worry about hurricanes?"

"The Lafountains, her family, had owned a beachfront home on the Gulf Coast for generations. Back in the '40s, her grandmother and great-aunts summered in the Pass. Their adventures were legendary," Max explains.

Does he imagine her gasp? Suzanne nearly chokes on a mouthful of filet coated in sour cream-soaked potato before grabbing the glass of water at her left. She doesn't stop drinking until the glass is drained. Max doesn't look up from his plate or detour from his monologue until Suzanne pours and guzzles another glass of moscato.

Max, confused by her deer-in-headlights expression, asks, "Did I say something . . . disturbing? What's wrong with you, Suzy?"

She clears her throat and stutters, "So that explains your love for the Coast. You two spent considerable time there."

"A good bit." Now anxious to end this inquiry, he sums up a mountain of valuable information in a couple of sentences. "The family lost everything to Katrina, and they're still searching for their footing. Her grandmother, Ms. Esty, lives here in New Orleans, over on State Street Drive, in the home she grew up in."

"This is the definition of a major mess."

"Effing nightmare. Still, to this day." Max pushes his plate to the center of the table and tucks his napkin slightly underneath it. He stands to stretch his legs and adjusts his trousers before sitting again, crossing one leg over the other.

"You get one more question, Suzy. Then, goddammit, that's it."

"Fair enough," Suzanne says, taking the edge of her napkin to dab at sweat gathering along her hairline and across the bridge of her nose. Max cannot fathom what has caused Suzanne to become so disheveled within minutes. She manages to say, "It's a big deal that you were a suspect . . ."

Max interrupts, tiring of her questions: "Husbands are always the number one suspects. It's simple. I was the last person to see Farrah alive. We had an obnoxious argument on the cave tour, so tourists in our group fingered me during their interviews. No evidence. No charges to support the DA's suspicion."

Before covering her mouth with her napkin, Suzanne stutters, "Wait . . . wait . . . wait. What argument?"

"*The* argument. Farrah didn't want to take the tour that morning because she claimed her stomach was upset. She was being a little bitch, whining about everything." Suzanne frowns, revealing a wrinkle between her eyebrows, which Max notices for the first time.

It annoys him. "What's up with you tonight?"

"I'm tired of feeling like I need to stay one step ahead of you." She finally shoves her plate toward the center of the table and tosses her napkin over it. "Seems like we're playing a cat-and-mouse game, though I can't figure out why."

After the table is cleared and they've declined an after-dinner brandy, Max reaches for Suzanne's hand. "I want to get back to where we started, Suzy. Not waste any more time—fighting."

"I'm ridiculously attracted to you, Max. That's never been the issue."

"Then, what *is* the issue?" Max leans in.

"It's simple: You're not good for me. There's the constant lying and manipulation of facts, and a general feeling of being unsafe with you," Suzanne says. "Hate to break it to you, Max, but these aren't the characteristics of a positive and healthy relationship."

Often falling short of empathy, Max does recognize that Suzanne is sufficiently upset to end their relationship tonight. "I fucked up, Suzy. I don't know what else I can say to smooth things over." He motions to Laureen. "Honey, can we leave Suzanne's car parked here overnight?"

"Absolutely," the waitress answers.

"Aren't you assuming a lot?" Suzanne asks.

"No, I don't think so. You and me, Suzy, we're broken. Suffered because of things beyond our control. We've been wounded, but we're not blameless. We've hurt others, too." Max knows he's speaking to Suzanne's heart as he watches her darkened violet eyes struggle against tears. "If you could step down from your pedestal for one minute, you might admit we have more in common than not."

For the first time since they started seeing one another, Suzanne has no reply. Her poignant stare voices the imbalance of what she feels and what she knows. As Max reaches to help her stand, he realizes her right hand is nearly scorching hot to the touch.

"Make no mistake, Suzy. I know you're hiding secrets of your own. But I trust you'll tell me when you're ready. Come home with me and stay the night."

Max embraces Suzanne with desperation. It's not until he pulls away from their deep kiss that he realizes Suzanne is shaking. He interprets her small whimper as one of pleasure and a signal to proceed. Max has all he needs for the night: a win for this round.

He speeds off into the darkened Louisiana night after Suzanne buckles in. Max not only hangs his hopes on reconciliation, but he's also banking on it. As he leaves Jefferson Parish and merges onto I-10 east, Max realizes his BMW is accelerating on its own. He yells, "I've no control of the car. Goddamn it, Suzanne, if this is you playing around, stop now."

In the piercing darkness of the night, Max cannot distinguish Suzanne's wicked smile that widens. Nor does he notice her raising her right arm over her head and its ever-so-slight movement toward the car's floorboard. "Relax, Max. It won't last long. So that you know, I'm not doing a thing."

It's not until he veers toward the Vieux Carré exit that the brake pedal responds to the slamming pressure of his right foot. And his heartbeat doesn't slow until he careens to an abrupt stop in front of his house.

21

Addy

Gulf Coast, Summer 1944

Mimi's right eyebrow arched as she sliced a peach: "Yes?"

"Cash asked me to dinner at the Edgewater for Saturday night," Addy said as she scraped the last peanut butter from the Peter Pan jar and smoothed it across a slice of white Bunny Bread.

"Surely you're not thinking of going, Addy," Mimi said. She slowly arranged the peach slices on a serving platter before meeting her granddaughter's eyes. Although it was Ida's day off, Papa still expected lunch to be served in the dining room at noon. Mimi's curt response could have commanded a gathering of coastal conjurers: "You'll need a protection spell, Addy. Have you forgotten what happened the *last* night you went with Cash? That Papa was summoned to Biloxi? Most likely, we're no longer welcome at the Trivoli."

Addy smirked and jutted her shoulders back. "Esty and I handled that the best we could, Mimi. You're right. I hadn't planned on seeing Cash. But Keesler co-pilots just graduated from B-24 training. And have their orders. Tonight, they're celebrating, then leaving in a few days."

"Why must this involve you?" Mimi said. She slammed the paring knife against the counter. "Cash's behavior is intolerable. Beneath you, Addy. Visions or no visions, you deserve more."

Addy sat on the bay window seat and ate her sandwich. She admired the blue apothecary bottles dangling from the oak tree, swaying against the morning ocean breeze as if an invisible maestro were conducting nature's response.

Do I dare ask Mimi to teach me a spell or two? To make things shiny and new again? Probably won't work since you must believe that it will. If only I'd accepted her offer weeks ago, Addy thought.

When Addy turned from the window to face Mimi, she said, "I want to say goodbye. Good luck. Try not to get killed over there."

"I don't feel good about this, Addy," Mimi said. "Not one little bit."

Addy held back tears. "Mimi, I thought Cash was the *one.* My forever fellow. But I can't make him stay. He must go."

"I'm sorry, love. But you've known from the first second you laid eyes on him that *this* moment would arrive." Mimi scurried around the kitchen, tidying up the counters. "I'll cast a protection spell for you tonight, if for no other reason than to help me feel secure about you being with Cash again. It doesn't matter that you're not ready to learn one for yourself."

"Whatever you think is best, Mimi."

Addy carefully slipped into her taffeta red and white polka-dot dress six hours later. Then, after adding a touch of blush and bright red lipstick, she spun around in front of the full-length mirror and winked at her reflection before sliding her tiny feet inside red patent leather pumps. Esty, who'd been stretched out on one of the twin beds reading, looked up and said, "You've never looked more gorgeous, Addy. I surely hope tonight is everything you want it to be."

The doorbell rang, and Macie rushed to answer it before

Papa could get there. Addy's eyes only focused on Cash as she slowly descended the stairs to greet her officer, perhaps for the last time.

"Addy, my girl, you are a dream," Cash said.

"They look like movie stars, don't they, Papa? Like on the cover of *Life* magazine?" Macie asked.

"You two make a stunning couple." Papa kissed his granddaughter's cheek, then reached for Cash's hand.

Awkwardly, Cash responded, "Sir, I want to apologize for my behavior at the Trivoli. I was out of line. I swear it won't happen again." He then turned to Mimi. "My apologies, ma'am," he said. Mimi's smile waned as she tipped her head in Addy's direction.

"Addy, I'm sorry. I never meant to embarrass you or your family." The three Lafountains stood quietly in the foyer and watched Cash escort Addy to Eddy's car.

As soon as Mimi closed the front door, Macie responded to her grandmother's troubled expression. "What's wrong, Mimi?" she asked.

"I so wish she'd decided not to go with him."

"What are we to do, Jeanne?" Papa asked. "Addy wants a proper farewell. Cash will be overseas within hours, and there's no guarantee she'll see him again." He returned to his wingback chair in the formal living room and reached for his brandy snifter.

Mimi pursed her lips and began pacing the floor in the foyer.

"I know that look," Macie said. She sat on the stairs in her favorite spot, one step below the first landing, which offered an excellent vantage point. "If you're going to the potter's shed, I'm coming with you."

Even if Addy rejected the chance to learn hoodoo, if for no other reason than for her personal protection, Mimi had two other aspirants possibly agreeable to learning the family's mysterious ways.

Even before they entered Edgewater's large banquet room,

the belting strands of Benny Goodman's "Bugle Call Rag" beckoned Keesler's airmen and their sweethearts inside. Once Addy wove herself onto the dance floor, she barely stopped to sip the Coca-Cola that Cash insisted she drink and only nibbled at the seafood platter filled with raw oysters, boiled shrimp, and cocktail sauce. That is, until Cash yelled, "Addy, stop."

As a guitarist plucked the beginning strands of "Bésame Mucho," Cash seized his opportunity to coax Addy into the fresh night's air. She twirled through the side door, her red pumps barely touching the ground. "I have something important to say, Addy. Stop moving for a minute."

Please, no, don't tell me you're leaving. Let this night be perfect.

Cash led her along the wooden pier stretching from the hotel to the beachfront. Addy's heart pounded, for she hoped to hear him speak three simple words.

Cash leaned closer and held her hands in his. "I'm in love with you, baby girl," he said. "I've loved you from the first night we met at Beauvoir."

Tears streamed down Addy's face. "You just don't understand how long I've waited to hear you say the words, Cash." Addy bounced up on her toes, hugged Cash's neck tightly, then kissed his cheek, neck, and lips. "I love you too, baby."

Cash grabbed Addy's wrists and pushed her back. "But there's something else I need to tell you."

"I don't want to talk right now. I only want to be alone with you," she pleaded.

"No, I need you to listen . . ."

Addy interrupted. "I loved you before I even met . . ."

As a sea breeze skipped across the lapping waters, whipping around the two of them, Cash rushed his words. He spilled his announcement with one gigantic effort. "I got my orders."

"*What?*"

"I'm off to Germany in a few days."

"No . . . no. . . . No! Did you and Eddy cook this up? Just to see how I'd react? Don't joke about this, Cash."

"I'm sorry, baby. It's no joke. I've been at this for months . . . to earn my co-pilot's assignment, and it's a doozy. Right in the thick of the action."

Cash's voice filtered away like a disintegrating echo, with the splashing waters beneath the pier providing a steady beat. Addy stood stone-cold still as her vision tumbled into the dust pile of a broken dream. Despite the warmth of the night, she started shaking. She made no effort to control her avalanche of tears.

"Addy, baby," he tried again. "It's the Army Air Forces, honey. I've got no choice." He tightly folded her into his arms, as though a hug would soothe her distress.

Inconsolable, she struggled to catch her breath before the next bout of sobs began. Cash spotted Eddy leaving the hotel lobby and motioned for his buddy to help.

"Do you still have the key?" Cash demanded.

"Really?" Eddy countered.

"Yes. The key?"

Eddy stood still with his hands in his pockets. "You're *not* taking a Lafountain girl into our hotel room. Do you know who you're dealing with?"

"We can't stay out here on the pier, Eddy. Addy's hysterical. Give me the goddamn key!"

"Okay, okay. Don't take forever. Other guys want the room, too."

"Goddamn you. I can't take her home like this. She's in shock or something."

"You have an hour, Cash. Then I'm coming in."

Later, Addy said she had no memory of entering Room 111. She was dizzy and confused when she forced herself to stir nearly forty-five minutes after Cash carried her into the room. As she struggled to lift her head off the pillow, Addy realized she was only wearing her slip, her silk panties looped around one knee. One red pump dangled from her right foot, ever-so-slightly. Her polka-dot dress lay damp and wrinkled near the foot of the oversized bed.

Horror struck hard.

The hotel room had been tossed. Addy saw the contents of her clutch scattered across a dresser and onto the floor. As bile gathered at the back of her throat, she ran for the bathroom and hovered over the toilet's rim until her nausea passed. Addy's head throbbed horribly with an inexplicable pain immeasurably worse than her migraines. She managed to prop herself against the cooling relief of the bathtub. Elbows on her knees, head in her hands, she resisted the vile sensation building from the back of her head, threatening to make her pass out. This must be what Mimi had always described as wooziness.

Addy felt the urgent need to pee. Bracing against the sink's vanity and the wall, Addy pulled herself onto the toilet seat. That's when she saw lines of caked blood trailing her inner thighs. A scream paralyzed Addy's throat, desperately seeking an escape.

Cash raped me.

Struggling to pee, Addy wrestled through her foggy mind to understand how she ended up inside an Edgewater hotel suite. *Did Cash mention a room? Because if he had . . .* She retraced the evening's footprint, including Cash dropping the bomb of his overseas assignment. The rest drew a blank. Addy had no memory of making love.

Because she didn't, at least not willingly. Consciously. Her body was there, plenty of evidence of that. But her heart, her mind, missed the event completely. Addy's consent—to losing her virginity to an airman bound for war—had been summarily denied.

"Where is that sonofabitch?" she whispered through her tears.

As if on cue, Cash knocked on the bathroom door.

"Addy, you okay? Time to go. Eddy needs the room." Cash's voice rang hollow, as if he'd spoken from the end of a misty, imaginary tunnel. "If you don't step out, I'm coming in," Cash said when he realized the door was unlocked. He found Addy sitting naked on the side of the tub, scrubbing away the caked blood with a bar of Ivory soap and a stack of pure white face-cloths.

When Cash reached out to touch her, she slapped his hand away.

"Why?" she asked tearfully. "You didn't have to take me by force, Cash. Can't you see I'm hurt? Bleeding?"

"Didn't plan for things to turn out this way. I'm so, so—sorry, Addy."

"You're sorry about everything, aren't you?" She reached for another washcloth, turned on the tub's faucet to soak it, and resumed her scrubbing. "Is a woman supposed to bleed this much? I don't know, Cash, because I've never had sex. Tell me what happened because I don't remember anything." When she twisted the washcloth over the tub, squeezing more blood from it, she whimpered, "You didn't put something in my drink, did you?"

He lowered the toilet seat and flushed the blood away as if the mere touch of a lever could cleanse this nightmare. Again, Cash reached for Addy, but she'd tucked her hands between her knees.

He started to explain. "When we were dancing, you were having the best time. I've never seen you so happy. Then I started to panic, thinking how ugly the night would end, how upset you'd be when you found out—you know . . . that I was leaving."

"You're not answering my question. You did, didn't you? Put a drug in my drink. Because you thought I'd be upset you were shipping out?"

"Well, yeah, kind of."

"You're insane, Cash," she yelled. "You're in the AAF, so of course I understand that you're leaving. That's the point of it, isn't it?"

"Lower your voice, Addy, please."

"No, I will not. I was ready, didn't you see? I've dreamt of making love with you all summer," she cried. "It didn't have to be like this."

"Dammit, that's not why I did it!" he yelled back.

"Then why?"

"I figured you'd be upset when I told you the news, so I bought a little pill from one of the guys back at the base, a nerve pill or something. They told me it would be fine. So I put it in your Coke when you were dancing with Eddy, so you'd be settled when I gave you the news." The situation worsened as Cash attempted to justify his actions.

"I need you to explain why we had sex without me being conscious. Did you propose, too? Or did I miss that?"

"I didn't expect the pill to be so powerful. I didn't think it could knock you out. When you wouldn't wake up, I went to find Eddy."

"Before or after I lost consciousness?" Addled from the drug, Addy tried to stand but was confused. She grabbed a folded towel from the back of the toilet, then sank back onto the cold tile floor.

Cash watched and offered no assistance. "You sounded like you were okay."

"But did I *look* like it was okay . . .?" Addy couldn't fix a clear thought on anything.

"I dunno. It was dark when we stumbled into the room. You were kissing me like crazy. You grabbed my uniform. Addy, the things you said . . . made me think you wanted this as much as I did. Besides, it's not so unusual for a girl to want her man before he ships out."

"You took my choice away. When you drugged me, Cash. I don't recall what I said. I don't remember a single thing."

Addy felt a new resolve begin to grow, the kind that starts at the tips of a woman's toes and then surges through her veins, her muscles, boils her blood, shakes her bones until it reaches her mind, explodes in the center of her essence, and reminds her of what's right and just in the world.

Tonight, Addy placed her right hand over her heart and pledged that no man would ever possess complete dominion over her. *Ever again.*

"God, what if you'd killed me? Did—did you even think about that?"

"You're missing the big picture, Addy. I love you."

"Fuck you. *This* isn't what love looks like."

"I don't know what love looks like," he said, barely audible. "I haven't had it in my life, 'least not 'til I met you."

"Won't argue with that."

Addy heard someone pounding on the hotel room's door and loud voices in the hallway. Cash left to investigate while Addy stayed glued to the side of the tub. When she looked up again at the partially-open bathroom door, she noticed her dress hanging on a hook, still somewhat rumpled.

Who in the world hung up my dress?

Cash poked his head in the bathroom and said, "We have to leave."

She stared blankly at this handsome young officer she'd once envisioned as her prince, her hero, her protector.

Now, a liar and a thief.

"Not before I scrub the lipstick smears from my face. And put on my dress. Brush my hair. You owe me time to do that, Cash."

22

Suzanne

New Orleans, Fall 2012

Sleep eludes Suzanne. She pulls the thick black duvet to her neck and replays their heated race to reach Max's four-poster king bed before climaxing. If only sex could *be* sex. Untethered. Uncomplicated. Feral. Orgastic.

Any confusion over Max's sudden presence in her life, just when spirit reveals are at an all-time high, is quelled after their inquisition dinner at Crazy Johnnie's. Turns out that Max married a Lafountain, connected in some way to Suzanne's family of enchantresses. Now, sorting the branches of an unfamiliar family tree seems pointless. Madelaine spent a lifetime estranged from her people. And Suzanne spent years separated from her mother.

You're playing with fire, my friend. Suzanne recalls Franny's warning, flashing like a neon sign. *You know I can't escape from myself, Franny.*

Max *is* a lot to manage. Though he has yet to demand an explanation for the bizarre events that surround her, he's clearly aware that something is askew. Suzanne knows a day of reckoning is coming—the day when she'll be forced to explain why she talks to entities others can neither see nor hear. *Unless*—unless a particular ghost has a specific person in mind . . .

Here's my story, Max. You see, I'm clairsentient. Trapped ghosts, bound to a beloved person or horrific event here on Earth—even loose spirits who choose to linger, at the precise second of their death—smother me with unreasonable demands. Warnings often follow. And right now? It's taking everything within me to handle an uptick in ghost reveals. Not to mention my twins, my job.

And you.

Suzanne created a public façade as a child to balance her psychic abilities with everyday activities. Madeline aided and abetted for a time when Suzanne was a little girl, playing off her beloved ghost friend, Gigi, as a long-lost cousin who rarely visited. This narrative was more manageable than explaining her daughter's predilection for running circles around child spirits on the playground, trapped and desperate for interaction with the living. But that was years before the battle between mother and daughter ignited—when Madelaine insisted that Suzanne favor rootwork and learn hoodoo instead of fine-tuning her clairsentient gifts.

It's very difficult to explain to others—the ones who will listen—that a purpose lurks behind each specter's reach. Suzanne faces retaliation if she fails to honor its demand for action: repetitive hauntings until the issue at hand is resolved, at the very least. Usually, Suzanne only experiences a brief threat if she bears no attachment to a trapped ghost, for it will flit away in search of another clairsentient willing to assist in its bidding.

But when she and a phantom share a personal connection, trouble surely awaits. After hearing Max describe Farrah's death, Suzanne fears the worst.

It's him. Max is the one. The one Madelaine's spirit and the garden ghost both say —must pay.

Suzanne lays in the arms of a man she barely knows and understands even less, powerless to resist his caress, the pressure of his fingertips, the slip of his tongue, the rhythm of his hips when he's inside her. She can only pray that Farrah died accidentally, as Max claims. She has little choice but to heed the warnings from the spirit world and remain in Max's good graces until she can sort it out. Because *her* life may hang in the balance.

She reaches for her earbuds left on the bedside chest. After pulling up a Dave Koz playlist on her phone, Suzanne closes her eyes and drifts off to the sounds of saxophone-infused jazz. At the twilight edge of drifting off, at the precipice of a dream inviting her in, Suzanne senses a ghost's energy.

A fierce plea forms quickly in her mind. *Please move along. I've nothing left for you. Not tonight.* She concentrates and wills it to turn away. When she spots a slight brush of white light hovering in the upper left corner of Max's bedroom, she holds her breath.

Be gone. There's nothing for you here.

It's not uncommon for a ghost to watch her sleep. Sometimes it sits at her feet or on the opposite side of the bed. Even dares to relocate precious belongings, like her beloved marcasite cross necklace.

Suzanne readjusts the duvet, sinks into the saxophonist's notes, and falls asleep. After an hour or so, a wisp of air playfully crosses her cheek. Perhaps an invitation to play? She props up a couple of pillows and glances at Max, sleeping deeply, snoring softly.

"Still here?" she whispers to the ceiling.

No response.

Then a strong scent of patchouli and musk swarms the room with a vigorous stir. Not the same aroma, though, as the distinctive one that had recently slammed through her backyard in Lakeview. She wonders why this patchouli smell is so familiar. Within seconds the room turns bone-chilling cold. Suzanne watches her breath in the vibrating glow of a ghost that hovers near the ceiling.

Something's wrong.

You're not the same one that just tickled my cheek.

A shield of malevolence coats the bed and thickens as it surrounds her. Panicking, Suzanne peeks over the duvet toward Max and prays he'll keep sleeping. Then the ghost swoops down and hovers at Suzanne's bedside.

Please don't wake up until I can get this . . . this furious energy to leave.

Suzanne whispers a protection spell and instinctively grabs for the obsidian amulet that Enola gave her. Then remembers it's still in her spell bag! She tries maneuvering from beneath the covers to sit but struggles against a force field.

Her racing heart pounds its echo in her head.

"What is . . ." she stutters. "Who are you?" she demands, this time aloud.

The ghost growls an unintelligible response.

When Suzanne reaches to open the bedside table's drawer, praying there's a cross or a Bible tucked within, the ghost's energy smacks her arm away. Slams her back against the bed's headboard.

"You terrify me," Suzanne whispers.

Its malevolent energy shifts again. Though the bedroom's atmosphere is blue-black dark, Suzanne watches its misty form drifting above the floor to the foot of the bed, then to Max's side.

Oh, God. Could it harm both of us?

"I need something," Suzanne says, concentrating on a quilted backpack perched on a bench nearby. This time, when Suzanne tries to sit, she's successful. Measuring her pace, she moves quickly to grab her bag. With hands shaking uncontrollably, Suzanne struggles to unzip it.

A wicked intention seeks her from behind. First, a burning

sensation starts at her waistline and then moves upward to the back of her neck. Suzanne grabs her black velvet pouch from the backpack and slams it against her chest.

It's all I've got to work with.

Suzanne raises the spell bag above her head when she stands and turns abruptly. She chants the words of the hoodoo spell recently cast in her garden with the confidence that she would if she'd been doing so for all the years Madelaine had commissioned her. Then, using every ounce of mystical energy she can muster, Suzanne pushes back the entity dripping with vengeance.

Within seconds, a framed picture of her and Max from their weekend in Seaside topples from the chest of drawers and crashes, shattering shards of glass across the hardwood floor. Despite her efforts, the ghost lingers.

Max jumps up, jarred from his deep sleep. "What the hell?"

"I bumped into the dresser coming out of the bathroom, Max." She struggles to keep her voice steady. "Go back to sleep. I'll pick up the mess."

"Well, I'm awake now."

"Be careful if you're getting up. You'll cut your feet."

"Too late for that, Suzy." Max yells one expletive after another as he tiptoes through the glass chips. He hobbles into the ensuite, leaving a trail of blood behind, then slams the door. Suzanne grabs a wooden cross hanging on the wall. She summons every degree of conviction, holds it high, and yells, "LEAVE NOW, IN THE NAME OF ALL THAT'S HOLY."

Refusing to back down, the ghost's response is garbled and very difficult to decipher.

"*Makkkkeee,*" the inhuman voice snarls, "*hmmm paaayy.*"

Blown-glass figurines rattle atop a bookshelf with the vibration of the ghost's proclamation—an echo so utterly guttural, so terrifying, that Suzanne fears an upended life filled with hauntings if this ghost is not banished. Threatened and angry as never before, Suzanne extends her right arm and points her forefinger, seared with heat, directly at the vindictive visage.

Then, unleashing her maximum dominion held dormant since the night of Madelaine's death, she screams, "Begone!"

Within seconds, the dark specter scatters, and in its wake, a horrible, rotting, earthy stench is left behind.

"I need a hand, Suzy. I'm bleeding!" Max yells from the bathroom. "Stop screaming into the air and come help me."

The spirit world has spoken: The horrific wrong once foisted upon this vengeful ghost must be righted. An avenging message now delivered by two separate entities—one benevolent, the other unmistakably malevolent.

"Max, you imagine things. See what happens when you drink too much?" Suzanne says, adjusting the tone of her voice as she steps into the bathroom. She's shaking so violently that it's challenging for her to open the first aid kit.

"I heard you screaming. Who had to leave now?"

If that's what he heard . . .

"I was talking to Beau. He needs to take Kyle home. Make him leave a party."

"I get it. Before *he* drives drunk. You and those damn twins of yours," Max mumbles.

"They won't call again."

"Unless they're in jail," he says.

"No. Their dad will handle that call. He's the lawyer."

Suzanne cleans and bandages Max's feet. They sit quietly on the ice-cold ceramic tile. She's in no rush to leave the safety net of a marble bathroom bathed in soft, reassuring light.

"You've finally stopped shaking," Max says, holding her tightly. "You need to block your kids' bloody numbers. If your ex can't handle things, then I will."

"I can't block my children's phone numbers, Max."

"I'm going downstairs for coffee." When Max tries to wipe smeared blood from the white tile, he makes a bigger mess.

"Make us a pot," she says. "I'll clean up here."

Max kisses her cheek, then whispers before closing the bathroom door, "You enjoyed last night, didn't you, love?"

Suzanne stares vacantly into the ornate silver mirrors hanging above the vanity. She searches for the apparition to reappear—no sign of it now. *Thank God for mirrors.* Locating a sponge and bottle of Clorox in the lower cabinet, she stoops to scrub the pooled blood. Then she returns to the bedroom to sweep up the glass.

The stench of latent decay is gone. Only the patchouli scent lingers next to a large dresser near the door. That's where she spies a Miss Dior Cherie fragrance bottle. It's not hers. As with every Lafountain woman before her, she exclusively wears a Chanel scent—a long-respected family tradition since numerous French ancestors worked for Coco Chanel as nosers, or so she has been told through the years.

But Suzanne's attention is quickly shifted to a gorgeous African amethyst bracelet placed on a jewelry stand next to the perfume spritzer. It's the most beautiful blue-purple collection of stones she has ever seen, aside from a museum piece. Oddly, when she reaches to touch the bracelet, it's warm to the touch. She misses an opportunity to place it on her wrist, curious about how it might look, when she hears Max yelling from downstairs, "Come get your cappuccino, woman. Stop cleaning!"

After Max hands her a coffee cup, he leads her to the courtyard.

"I see you've repaired the fountain. It's exquisite, Max."

Suzanne settles into the wicker sofa and recalls Max telling her that his mom owns a florist shop. Maybe that's where he buys his tropicals like the banana plants overtopping the back corners and yellow canna lilies circling the fountain.

Perhaps the bracelet belongs to his mom, though it's so oddly displayed—almost like a trophy. She's still visualizing the exquisite piece of estate jewelry on display in Max's bedroom.

"If I didn't know better, Max, I'd guess you're about to list your house on the market."

"Don't be ridiculous, Suzy. I'll never sell. It's likely on the historical registry. Drink up. Think about what you're doing today."

How quickly Max changes the topic of conversation when a sensitive subject is raised.

"You look sickly," Max says, balancing his coffee cup on his knee. "Drained. Pale. You have a similar appearance . . . very much like you had the other night . . . after that fiasco at your place when I found you outstretched on your lawn."

"I didn't sleep well." Suzanne pats the cushion and says, "I'd like to discuss something with you. Could you sit next to me, please?"

"Don't do this."

"It's not an inquest, Max. I want to share something about myself. Before we go further." She avoids saying the word *relationship* since she's uncertain how to label this *thing* between them. The description of what they share needs an altogether new category crafted, for it defies explanation.

Max shoves a throw pillow aside and joins her. "Okay, I'll bite. What's up?"

"By now, Max, I'm sure you've noticed. That I have traits other people don't have. Sometimes, I feel blessed. Lately, I feel cursed." Suzanne moves her hand along his thigh and scoots a little closer to lock in his dark eyes, forcing Max to stay focused. "I see energies others cannot see. I see trapped ghosts—phantoms who've died violent deaths and often don't realize they're dead. And lingering spirits who choose to stay . . . and remain attached to loved ones. They need resolutions before they can cross over. I communicate with them."

Max says nothing, at first. Suzanne waits, holds back on compounding information until he responds.

"I can't say I believe ghosts are real, but this sure as hell explains a lot." Max takes her hand and squeezes it. "Last night was terrifying. I don't know what all went down . . ."

Suzanne pauses to sip her coffee, taken back by Max's vulnerability. *Pretty sure that won't last for long.*

"Last night was unusual. I don't willingly subject anyone

to this madness, which is why I'm flummoxed this morning. If a ghost manifests itself when I'm not alone, then the connection often involves whomever I'm with. I'm no newcomer, Max. I've dealt with spirits since I was a child."

She allows this fact to sink in for a few seconds.

"Didn't think to mention this early on, did you?" Max stares across the courtyard. The reference to a ghost's desire to communicate with him seemingly soars over his head. Or he chooses to avoid dealing with it.

Suzanne's not finished, though she'd love to wander back into the kitchen for another cup of cappuccino. Instead, she plunges forward. "I'm not sure it's much different from withholding information about your wife's death. Is it? Both of us have complicated issues hanging over . . ."

"Let me get this straight. You see, but I can't?" Max interrupts, a beat behind the conversation's flow. A smile builds when she realizes he's still holding onto her hand firmly.

She nods. "Yes, that's correct." Max wants specifics, like how Suzanne talks to the dead when others have no clue it's remotely possible.

"A ghost *speaks*? With words?"

"The sounds are unfamiliar. Not recognizable like your voice or mine. When I was a little girl, I learned to understand non-human voices with help from my mother, Madelaine, also a clairsentient." But, of course, she leaves out a pivotal piece of information—the woman was a world-class conjurer. *And somehow or other, Max, you're related to her by marriage.*

Max's eyes widen. "Like a growling sound?"

"Well . . . yes. Sometimes. Odd that you would mention it, though. Because that's not the sound of a benevolent spirit." Max appears more intrigued with this morsel than anything else mentioned earlier. Suzanne watches his face before saying more. "Most of the time, the spirit and I share a version of telepathy. I listen, then answer in my mind."

"So how do you know it gets through? That you didn't imagine the whole damn thing?"

"I repeat things aloud. To confirm. Unless . . ."

"Unless what?" Max asks.

"Unless the spirit is hateful and seeks vengeance. Then . . ."

Max stands abruptly. "Okay, Suzy, I've had enough." He storms back into his house. "I can't—I just can't."

Suzanne follows Max indoors and finds him leaning against the gray granite counter, watching her like a Cheshire cat. It's hard to tell whether there's fear or concern in his eyes, but before she can decide, Max grabs her around the waist and hoists her onto the low kitchen island. He responds to Suzanne's confessional the only way he knows how: seduction.

Max deadlocks Suzanne's eyes as his forefingers slowly slide up her inner thighs, first along the right side, then the left. He senses her go-ahead when her head tilts back and her eyelashes flutter. Then he shoves back the length of the Oxford shirt she's wearing and disappears between her legs. Suzanne wraps her legs around his neck and ignores the crash of the ceramic coffee creamer hitting the kitchen tile.

Her sighs sing a symphony of pleasure, allowing Max the honor of lifting her far beyond the natural and unreal worlds that haunt her. In these intimate moments, she releases the stress of a stark night and the pressure of living simultaneously in two worlds: one in the here-and-now, and the other at the fringe of the spirit world, where those cloaked in residual energy grapple with unfinished business.

For now, the dark spirit's command is a distant memory. She sees nothing, notices nothing—not even her phone vibrating nearby.

She doesn't notice that Jack is calling.

23

Madelaine & Farrah

The In-Between

Farrah's ghost and Madelaine's spirit drift through Max's bathroom wall and linger in the hallway. Madelaine's smoky mist slithers down the staircase, then back up to check on Farrah, whose opaqueness darkens. Then down again. As the eldest of the two—stranded by choice between here and passing through the ether to an afterlife—it's her responsibility to guide Farrah, as it should have been when both were alive.

That is, if Madelaine had embraced the task of motherhood instead of considering it an onus and sluffing off parenthood, relying on Suzanne's father to be the responsible party for her, and Mama Esty to handpick a surrogate mother for Farrah.

With her quick and lively movements, the light of Madelaine's white maxi skirt flashes. Her platform shoes, though of no function now, grant her renewed confidence.

"*Does she know?*" Farrah's ghostliness swirls to a corner in the twelve-foot ceiling, then alternates between curling up and hovering at large. "*That we're both attached to her?*"

"If Suzanne has figured it out, she likely doesn't understand the reason."

Farrah's ghost is more secure if she's tucked in the corners where the crown molding meets, where she finds comfort. "*She's terrified.*"

"*Your fault. You took it too far.*" Madelaine's spirit still drips with maternal condescension. Schooling Farrah's energy is an exercise in futility, a temporary inconvenience.

"*Look in the mirror, Mother. You took everything too far, Madelaine.*" Farrah's ghost lingers at the highest point of the foyer's ceiling. "*It's always been about you.*"

Madelaine whirled upward to comfort Farrah but was quickly rebuffed. "*She wouldn't be frightened if she knew me. You made a big mistake separating us.*" Farrah's ghost whimpered like a child. "*So angry to see Max asleep. Like a baby. No troubles.*"

"*Oh, he has troubles,*" Madelaine's spirit corrects. "*I'm warning you, Farrah, you must behave,*" she says. "*Time to go. Enough harm for one night.*" Madelaine waits. "*Come down.*"

"*No. Not falling.*" Farrah's ghost circles the stairwell. Picks up speed—shifts to reenter Max's bedroom.

"*Oh, no, you don't.*"

At the end of Max's bed, Farrah's ghost hovers, intent to leave an imprint upon the duvet. But, before she spots the amethyst bracelet dangling like a dare, Madelaine's spirit whips her energy around the younger ghost, precisely as she encircled Farrah's departing energy when the young mother-to-be took her final breath in 2008.

Madelaine, whose life tragically ended just two months before Farrah's, waited to greet Esty's granddaughter in the In-Between. It was the least she could do for the woman who'd rescued, adopted, and raised her.

"*Suzanne's handling Max.*"

These tired, trapped forces of energy—ripped from their human existence due to no faults or plans of their own—whirl together and spin out into the predawn atmosphere. But they are not alone: this infinite space also holds Louisa, Jeanne, and Grace. They wait for Suzanne, the only remaining Lafountain enchantress, to complete their bidding.

Madelaine speaks sharply. "*You nearly frightened Suzanne to death, Farrah. We're all bound for Hell, all our souls. If she dies before the job is done.*"

"*Spoken like an enchantress, Madelaine. Let's have some faith in our Suzanne.*"

Addy

Gulf Coast, Summer 1944

After Addy gathered her things from the Edgewater hotel room, she sat in Eddy's car and waited for Cash to finish talking to his best friend. Trying to eavesdrop on their conversation, she only heard Eddy say, "Get rid of them. We'll be in a shit load of trouble if anyone finds those pills."

Neither Cash nor Addy spoke during the ride. Addy felt increasingly nervous the closer they got to her grandparents' home. It didn't help that cobwebs still cluttered her mind, muddling her thoughts and making it impossible to rehearse what she would say. She anticipated Mimi demanding an explanation and feared Papa summoning the sheriff.

I'll tiptoe up the stairs without waking anyone. No one will know.

An unlikely scenario, considering her disheveled condition. Addy resembled a woman who had clawed her way out of the losing end of a catfight. *If only*. If only she had been conscious.

If only I could remember.

Tell or don't tell. Who'd believe her if she skipped confiding in her grandparents and later learned she was pregnant after Cash left for Germany? There was the distinct possibility that her grandfather might murder Cash, Addy considered. But he'd reassess the likelihood of serving time as too high a price to protect her honor. *Cash couldn't die a war hero if he'd been murdered.* Her mind filled with jumbled thoughts, and sadly, Addy lost the thread of what-ifs.

Cash turned slowly onto the shell driveway. When Addy saw the warm, welcoming porch lights of her grandparents' house, humiliation slithered through her veins. He tried putting his arm around Addy's shoulder, but she scooted further away, her arm edged against the car door. "Addy, please stop your crying."

"Can't. And you're damn lucky, Cash, because I'd rather scream."

"Pull yourself together. I can't afford this kind of trouble."

"And *I* can?"

"I love you. And you love me. Think. Don't stir up a scene, make this a bigger deal than it needs to be." Cash grabbed her arm and squeezed it too tightly. "We had a misunderstanding. It's between us."

"Are you threatening me?"

"Keep in mind, baby," pointing his forefinger at Addy's face. "I didn't force you into that hotel room," he hissed.

"Okay, maybe not to go in. But what about the rest of it?"

Inching closer to her on the front seat, he said, "You can't deny that you were making sounds, moaning and all. Sounded to me like you enjoyed it. Addy, you never told me to stop."

With a hand already poised on the door's handle, she said, "You drugged me, Cash. Good Lord, how could I tell you to stop if I didn't realize what was happening? I don't remember a damn thing after I collapsed on that bed." She didn't hide her tears, rejecting Cash's offer of a handkerchief. "My head hurts horribly, and my stomach's upset, so I'm going inside."

"Do you want me to walk you to the door?"

"If you don't, I'll have to explain," she said. "There's a chance Mimi's still awake, waiting for me. Maybe watching us right now through one of those living room windows."

"I won't kiss you."

"No. Cash, you're right about that. You'll never kiss me again."

Cash grabbed Addy's hand before she stepped from the car. "Before you go, I need to know."

"What?" For one second, Addy feared a stumbling, hurried marriage proposal. Much different from the one she had naively imagined before tonight's nightmare.

"Are you going to tell your grandfather? I need to be prepared."

"I don't have to answer that."

"Don't be a bitch, Addy."

"Never mind walking me to the door." She slammed the car door and scurried up the front pathway, sensing more blood dribbling down her legs. At the screen door, Mimi greeted her with arms open wide.

"Papa just got a call, Addy," Mimi said, hugging Addy tightly. "A commotion at the Edgewater? With hotel guests calling the police. Officers running girls in and out of the first-floor rooms. What in the world?"

Addy dissolved into Mimi's embrace. "Oh, no, why did they call Papa?"

"Honey, he's got friends who're always watching out for us, particularly after what just happened at the Tivoli. And you left your clutch behind, which had your ID tucked inside. Please tell me something dreadful didn't happen to you."

This sick-to-the-stomach moment was unavoidable. Forced to face her beloved grandmother, who held her in the highest esteem, was nearly as excruciating as the event itself.

"I wish I could, Mimi."

"Sit here on the stairs right now. Talk to me."

When Addy turned around, Mimi gasped. Her hands covered her mouth and muffled a scream. "Adelaide, there's blood all over your dress. And it's running down the back of your legs. Dear God, child."

"I'm sorry, Mimi, I didn't know," Addy said.

"You didn't realize you were bleeding?"

"I did. When I woke up. I tried cleaning up in the bathroom before we left."

Addy raised her skirt and saw fresh blood now mingled with the darkened caked residue she missed. "I thought it had stopped. Mimi, I'm really not feeling well. I need to sit." She grabbed the banister to keep her balance and landed on her behind with her legs sprawled, the sticky blood dribbling onto the steps and into her red patent pumps.

"Why didn't someone at the Edgewater help you?" Mimi asked. Flustered beyond measure, Mimi now realized the man who'd foisted such implausible pain on her granddaughter was no longer there.

"He's not coming inside, Mimi. He left."

"What are we to do . . .?" Mimi yelled, "James, we need your help!"

"I don't want to tell Papa. You'll tell him, won't you?"

"No, I certainly will not! How can I, Adelaide? I don't know what happened, myself." Mimi had yanked the soft rollers from the ends of her hair out of sheer desperation. She sat with Addy, hugged her tightly, and sobbed. It wasn't until much later that Mimi realized her housecoat was smeared with Addy's blood.

When Papa hovered at the upstairs landing, his view of the most beloved people in his life was horrifying. Esty and Macie crept up behind him on tiptoes. He summarily dismissed Addy's sisters back to bed.

"James, Addy's been involved with that mess at the Edgewater."

"I can see that. What happened, Addy?" Papa asked, slowly descending the stairs.

The fine lines on Mimi's forehead looked more pronounced since Addy arrived home. She frowned, crossed her arms, and glared at Addy. "Talk."

"I didn't want to go to the hotel room, Mimi," Addy lied. Her grandmother nodded. "Go on."

"When Cash said he was scheduled to leave early Tuesday morning, I couldn't stop crying. I couldn't catch my breath." Addy avoided Mimi's eyes and didn't dare turn to face Papa.

"Go get her a soapy towel, James," Mimi said. She finally sat near Addy on the lower step.

"Let's wait, Jeanne. From what I'm hearing, she needs to be examined."

"I don't want the police involved, James."

"Let the girl talk, woman!"

Addy couldn't comprehend her grandparents arguing with each other. Their voices sounded far away, like a resounding echo from a long metal tunnel. She stared straight ahead and spoke in a monotone. "I got dizzy. And confused. Everything started to spin. Honestly, I may have passed out on the pier. The one in front of the hotel?"

"If that's so, I still don't understand. Someone must have seen this and come to your rescue." Mimi gathered her granddaughter's thick black locks behind her neck and encouraged her to keep talking.

"When I woke up, I was on the bed. All I had on . . . was . . . my slip . . . and I couldn't find my . . . panties . . ." Racked with sobs, Addy folded into her grandmother's lap. "I thought I'd lost my dress . . ."

"So that son-of-a-bitch *raped* you?" Papa yelled. "Where is he?"

"Hold on a minute, James," Mimi said. "I think there's more. Things aren't adding up here. Addy, were you drunk?"

"No, Mimi, not at all."

"Then, do you think it's possible . . . that he spiked your drink?" Papa asked.

Addy nodded her head, then grappled with sitting up. "Cash told me he did—he put a little pill in my Coke at dinner. So that

I wouldn't be upset when he told me he was leaving."

"For the love of God," Mimi cried.

They sat motionless at the foot of the elegant staircase in a home that had championed the legacy of privilege and propriety for generations. Though the low-hanging chandelier in the foyer provided some illumination, it left three Lafountains in the dark about what to do next. The family myth propelled by mistruths—that money and influence resolved everything—was decimated on the night of Addy's rape. And exacerbated by the fact that an AAF officer had assaulted her.

What was the probability that Addy's interpretation of events would ever be taken seriously, ever believed? Particularly since drugs, and possibly alcohol, were involved.

"What do you want me to do?" Papa asked. He took several puffs off his wooden tobacco pipe. "Because I'm going to do something. This is assault, which is a crime. I'll not allow it to go unreported."

The truth. Declared.

"She needs to see a doctor, that much I know," Mimi said. She looked at the porcelain pendulum clock resting on the living room's mantel to confirm the time. It was 2 a.m. "I can't call Dr. Lemoine for another three or four hours."

"At the very least, I need to contact the chief of police," Papa said. He paced in the foyer and kept looking out the front windows as though answers rested beyond the beachfront cloaked in darkness, past the Gulf waters, beyond the horizon. He placed his hand on Addy's shoulder and asked, "You okay, dear?"

Addy shook her head in the negative.

"Did you scream? Call for help?"

"No, Papa. I was knocked out."

A swift glance toward Mimi acknowledged their doubt that this nightmare would end well.

"Go upstairs and bathe, Addy. Put your clothes in the hallway outside the door. I'll gather them for you," Mimi said.

"My favorite red and white polka-dot dress . . ."

"Yes, even the bloody dress. We may need it."

When Addy reached the top of the stairs, she nearly tripped over Esty leaning against the wall, crying. Her sister had heard everything.

"I'm so, so sorry this happened to you, sis. I'm never forgiving myself for not going with you tonight. Do you want to be alone?"

Addy didn't answer as she quietly shut the bathroom door.

The next few hours merged into a whirlwind nightmare that lasted two days. Addy's efforts to stand against the powerhouse of James and Jeanne Lafountain failed. By dawn, both Mimi and Papa had started making phone calls. As Southern aristocrats, their behavior was predictable, for they'd stop at nothing to protect a legacy, a reputation, and a dark secret that would remain hidden for generations.

By noon, Addy had been examined by Mimi's gynecologist, who confirmed Addy's virginity loss. Only a few stitches were necessary, and the minor bruising at the source of entry would heal quickly. Mimi called her son, James, Addy's father, and left word at his hotel in New York City. An urgent situation with Addy required him to call immediately.

Cash, accompanied by his superior officer Capt. Duce Whitman, arrived at the Lafountain's first, and was quickly ushered to the screen porch. The Harrison County police chief entered next, prepared to handle matters officially, with handcuffs if necessary. Papa's brother Ben, a noted criminal defense attorney, arrived minutes later, along with Walt Matterson, a circuit court judge.

Addy sat cross-legged on the carpeted floor of the dining room, right outside the porch's entrance. She listened to the threats against Cash from the judge, Papa, and her Uncle Ben. She'd never heard this gathering of men she'd admired for a lifetime speak in such angry and threatening tones.

When Papa announced the matter settled, Ida entered with

a crowded tray of favorite cocktails. Judge Matterson raised his bourbon-on-the-rocks and proposed a toast to behind-the-scenes Southern justice. The type of justice that never saw the interior of a harsh yellow-blazed-lit courtroom for any juror named Tom, Dick, or Harry to pass judgment on.

Judge Walters quickly grew weary of Cash's cockiness, so he shifted his weightiness in the chair, allowing his thick spectacles to glide along the bridge of his nose. He asked, "Son, are you remotely aware of your predicament? You'd be in jail if Adelaide's grandfather didn't intervene."

Cash deflected the question. Instead, he said, "I'm grateful, sir. I realize I could be court-martialed for this misunderstanding."

"*Misunderstanding*? I can't say this decision we've come to doesn't sit in my craw." Papa echoed the judge's take on the situation.

"A price must be paid . . ." the judge said.

"An immoral crime, no less," Papa added. Turning to his brother, he asked, "Are we certain the two of them getting married is the best solution, Ben?"

"Before final decisions are made, remember this mess will reflect on you and Jeanne," Ben said. "Rape and assault charges will be made public. Folks will find out. And no one will ever look at Addy the same way."

Addy collided with Ida, serving her famous pimento cheese sandwiches and chocolate chip cookies as she charged onto the porch. She didn't stoop to help pick up the mess when the maid's trays toppled.

"When's it my turn to speak?" she yelled.

Ida crawled around Addy's feet to rescue the cheese sandwiches before the mess stained the rattan floor covering.

"I hope you're feeling better, young lady," Judge Walters said, looking up from his third drink. "We're taking proper care of you, though you may not realize it right now."

"By plotting my entire life?"

"Imagine what's probably going to happen . . . you'll turn up pregnant in a few weeks. Have you considered that?" Judge Walters asked.

Papa hadn't counted on his granddaughter joining the conversation. Since she did, he asked her to take a seat.

Instead, she whirled around to face Papa, releasing a rage she'd never felt.

"What if I don't want to get married?" she demanded. "From the looks of it, he doesn't want to marry me, either." Addy glared at Cash and found him shaking his head.

"I'm okay with marrying you, Addy," he said, repeatedly folding his AAF cap. "Does it matter? I'm leaving for Germany soon."

"With no guarantee of coming back alive or returning in one piece. He'll be co-piloting the most dangerous missions yet," Duce added.

"It matters to me," Addy whispered.

I'm heartbroken, and nobody seems to care. One minute, she hated Cash. The next, she was terrified for his safety.

"Where are your parents in this, Addy?" her Uncle Ben asked. "What does James Jr. say? The girl's father needs to be here."

"He's not returning our phone calls," Mimi said, appearing at the door frame connected to the kitchen.

"I'm not waiting on James," Papa said. "Cash is scheduled to leave within days. I'll not have my granddaughter saddled with raising a bastard child. Can you get the minister on the phone, Jeanne? Arrange everything?"

"Of course, love."

Papa stood, his movement signaling the end of their meeting. The men exited quickly, except for Cash, who hung back to speak with Addy.

"You don't know how terrible I feel, how sorry I am." He tried to kiss Addy's cheek, but she turned away, wishing she could slap his face instead. But because she knew Papa was watching them, she refrained.

"You will never know, Cash, how deeply I *once* loved you," Addy whispered.

The sound of the blue bottles knocking against each other in the *haint* tree across from the porch played Cash's symphony of departure.

Mimi, I need to learn me a spell.

Suzanne

New Orleans, Fall 2012

Exhausted by a dark spirit's negative energy that hovers nearly every time she's with Max, Suzanne heads back to Enola's shop to bolster her spell knowledge. She parks on St. Ann since she plans to stop at Jack Reynolds' place before leaving the neighborhood. And ask him why a Lafountain angel requires a permanent residence.

Hurrying to arrive before the shop closes, Suzanne walks the sidewalk opposite Jack's shotgun house, still standing since the early 1800s. When she hears his thready voice—"Hey, pretty lady"—she spins around to see the barely-visible man completing his late afternoon jog. When Jack's hands seem to flow straight through his legs as he bends to stretch his calf muscles, Suzanne laughs, nonplussed, for she has dealt with his kind for a lifetime.

"Well, there you are, Jack. How are you?"

"Much better now that I've run into you," he says. "Up for a drink?"

Suzanne watches him glide effortlessly across the street,

then along the wrought iron handrail of his front steps to sit on the porch stoop. "Maybe after I consult with Enola. Got an issue I can't resolve on my own."

"Not my area of expertise, so I'll leave it to her. I've no interest in conjuring. But you already know this, love." She's puzzled, watching him reach under the doormat to grab a key. Perhaps for the benefit of a neighbor's prying eyes? "Offer stands when you're finished. Don't worry about knocking. Come on in." She doubts anyone else notices Jack morph through his locked front door.

When the little bell on the front door signals Suzanne's arrival, Enola peeks up from behind the counter between a stack of dried lavender that needs to be cut and cloves of garlic that require packaging.

"I thought I might see you today," Enola says. "How can I help you, dearie?"

"I need considerable assistance."

Enola frowns. "Did the protection spell work? Against that crazy man of yours?"

"It's either working beautifully, or Max is behaving admirably. Honestly, I'm still figuring things out. Max is . . . well, he's a complicated man." Suzanne pauses. Her gaze searches the shelving behind Enola. "But something tells me you understand my challenges without me explaining."

"What else?" Enola takes a sharp blade and dramatically smashes the lavender blossoms from their stems.

"I'm dealing with more and more unsettled entities," Suzanne explains. "I'm an educator, Enola. I need a way to control all of this. I can't have ghosts popping into my classroom."

"How recently did that happen?" she asks.

"It hasn't yet. But I'm bracing for it." Suzanne adjusts her neck scarf that's off-center. "One, I've identified. Another, I'm somewhat certain of its identity, but then there's an ever-present dark one hovering in the background that I fear is a loose cannon . . . very unpredictable and somehow associated with Max."

Enola stops chopping. "Didn't we discuss your *abilities*?"

"Did we? No, I don't think so."

"Dark one is worse? Since you cast a spell?"

"Yes, exactly." Suzanne walks to the counter and admires a gorgeous piece of amethyst stretching nearly two feet in height, untouched, uncarved. *I absolutely could use this beauty.* "The dark one, Enola, threatens in a way I'm unprepared to handle, and solely appears when I'm around Max."

"When he's alone, is he threatened?"

"Well, I've no idea," Suzanne says. "Never thought to ask him. It's highly unlikely he'd recognize one. This spirit's anger and desire for vengeance is terrifying."

"But, what *if* the threat's for him? Whether he recognizes it or not, whether he has told you or not, it's likely there's been an encounter," Enola says while examining the contents of an oversized button armoire. She faces Suzanne and says, "Something's working because the dark one isn't with you now. If attached, I'd know." Enola reaches below the counter and pushes a button to summon Adetope.

"During the most recent encounter, I ended up clutching the black pouch—the one you made for me—the same one I used in the protection spell, to dismiss it."

"What aren't you telling me? 'Cause that spell wasn't near strong enough to keep an entity like this at bay."

"A large cross. Hanging on Max's bedroom wall. When everything else failed, I yanked the crucifix off the wall and screamed for it to leave us alone in the name of all things holy." Suzanne shudders as she remembers the night of broken glass, when an overwhelming rotting stench mixed with patchouli filled the bedroom. "I didn't know what else to do."

With hands on her hips, Enola nearly shrieks, "Keep going, what else?"

Suzanne slowly raises her right hand and extends her index finger. "By pure instinct. I extended my arm in the ghost's direction and commanded it to leave. I've not trusted an attempt to banish anything. Not since Madelaine died."

"Since childhood, you've had this gift." Enola laughs uproariously at Suzanne's reluctant acceptance of what others can only dream of possessing. "At last, your journey truly begins. You did well, love." Enola asks a couple more questions before concluding, "Your man has a vengeful ghost haunting him, even if he doesn't know it yet."

"It's an untenable situation. I've refused to trust magic, but I get it now. I need it—if nothing else, to protect myself from this slew of ghostly attacks I can't seem to crawl out from. I do feel better when I speak with you, Enola."

"Finally, you see, my dear. Speaking to the non-living. Practicing hoodoo. Reading tarot. Raising your hand, summoning your power. Full circle. Madelaine is proud, now."

Suzanne brushes back a loose strand of hair and reaches for Enola's hand, patting it lightly. It's hard to determine who's more reassured by the gesture. "I hate to admit it, but I've outgrown Franny's guidance in many ways."

"Her sister, Calpurnia, will take it from here. She'll appear when you need her." Suzanne nods, having anticipated a shift with Franny backing away from her. While she doesn't recall a lot of details of her early years with Madelaine, she does remember the sisterhood of conjurers, rootworkers, tarot readers, and seers who seemed to take shifts hanging out in their living room for extended weeks that turned into months.

Enola smiles, and for the first time it occurs to Suzanne that the woman is also a mind reader. "Before you go, there's a stronger spell I can offer. But you must be all in, or it may do more harm than good."

"I hear you."

Enola pulls a black card from a wooden cubby behind the counter. The following words are printed in white scripted lettering: *Ashes to ashes/Spirit to spirit/Take this soul/Banish this evil.*

After Enola wrenches a large bag of sea salt from another cubby, she begins her instruction. "Draw a pentagram on the ground, the floor, using the sea salt. Center it in all the places you've encountered this dark one." Suzanne listens as though her life depends on this information. Enola continues, "Space tall black candles at the five endpoints of your pentagram. Light the candles, sit in the center."

Suzanne writes the instructions in a small leatherbound notebook she now carries. "Okay, then what?"

"Meditate. Imagine a wall of protection building from under the ground, the dirt below the house, into the heavens. The energy for protection originates within you. Chant the words on this card I've given you exactly thirteen times."

"I can do this," Suzanne says.

"Of course you can," Adetope says, entering the front room. "One thing to add: If you cast this spell on sacred ground, the protection more than doubles. Maybe tenfold." When Suzanne's half-smile reflects confusion, Adetope asks, "You do know? Your people's sacred ground?" A slight shake of her head answers his question.

Adetope helps Enola search for Suzanne's black candles. They're tall, thick, and sturdy. As he packages the salt and includes the chant card, Enola reminds Suzanne about the absolute importance of closing the spell.

"After you've meditated, embrace the change in energy. To extinguish the candles, begin with the upper right pentacle corner flame. That one represents water. You'll follow the pentagram around and end with the fifth one: spirit."

Adetope writes a number on the back of the chant card. "Call if you get into trouble," he says. "And talk to Jack, even Franny, about the Lafountain's sacred ground."

Suzanne reaches for the spell bag. "How much more trouble can there be?"

He pauses with the bag in midair. "Don't ever ask that question. You're the one who opened the portal. Now you, and only you, must face what comes through."

Exactly when did I open the portal? Take this soul/banish this evil.

As Suzanne heads to her car, she hears Jack call out to her. He never forgets.

"You promised to step in." Jack's oddly suspended inches above the stoop in front of his red front door. "Come have a drink. My courtyard's divine, darlin'."

Suzanne crosses the street. "You're relentless. You know that, right? I'm only agreeing because I have questions to ask you."

"What could you possibly need to ask me? We've known each other for a lifetime," he says. Suzanne remembers Jack dropping in unannounced to see Madelaine. God only knows how long this angel had been attached to her mother. Perhaps to other Lafountain women, too.

"Yes, but do we really *know* one another?" Suzanne asks as Jack leads her along a narrow alleyway that hugs the side of his shotgun house. When he opens the gate, Suzanne is amazed at Jack's tropical Garden of Eden. Pebble walkways, palm trees, banana plants, lilies, and caladiums fill the bricked courtyard as two fountains funnel aqua-colored water over limestone rocks. Butterflies dart in and out of the milkweed.

"Truly, an angelic paradise, Jack. It's breathtaking."

Set amidst cobbled stones, two ornately fashioned chairs flank a bistro table. He pulls one out for her and invites her to sit. "Some wine, love? How 'bout a bottle of white zinfandel?"

"Thank you, that's lovely."

After pouring her drink from a cozy glass bar bound with Swedish ivy, Jack tops a highball with Captain Morgan rum—simply to be sociable. "I must ask. What's the deal with you and that hoodoo shop?" He brings the rum to his lips yet refrains from sipping. "Do you practice now?"

Suzanne tucks the velvet spell bag under her chair and adjusts her posture. "It appears I've no choice but to refresh my knowledge. And embrace Enola's guidance."

"Interesting," he says.

Suzanne laughs. "I know what you're thinking . . ."

"No, I'm pretty sure you don't."

"Yeah, I do. Why solicit Enola's wisdom when I had the best resource anyone could ever desire: Madelaine, my mother."

"Your words, not mine." Jack moves his drink to the middle of the table, then leans back in the chair. His golden retriever squeezes through the back screen's doggie door to investigate a new voice.

"You have a golden!" Suzanne says. "I do, as well."

"Meet Bentley."

"That's perfect. We call mine Bimini, or Bimi, for short. He's English cream, too."

"Odd name, don't you think?"

"You know Bimini, Jack. It's an island in the Bahamas—the one closest to the States. I'd love to live there one day."

Bentley snuggles on top of Suzanne's feet.

"Back to what I was saying. I'm simply confused." Jack lifts his drink to catch the late afternoon reflection of the sun. His beverage appears to be more of a plaything than anything else.

"About?"

"Hoodoo," Jack begins. "I can't say I ever understood Madelaine's obsession with it." He tops off Suzanne's wineglass. "Since it's spiritually entrenched in the African culture, I'm curious if you believe that conjures are nearly pointless if you don't share that heritage."

Suzanne sighs. "I'm not sure practitioners since plantation days would agree with you, Jack. Hoodoo has been trusted and relied upon here for centuries. Even Enola will tell you that her best customers visit the shop after church services to learn how to augment their prayers."

"Why not call upon the power of the Saints, if you will? Why not harness traditional tools?" Jack inches his chair closer to her.

"I'm learning it will require a combination of elements to deal with what's in front of me," she says, scooting her chair back. Jack's movement feels strange, perhaps intrusive. Bentley adjusts to her movement, then lays on his back, still sprawled across her feet and blocking her exit. She feels trapped.

"I've said too much, Suzanne. I apologize." The scent of deep, pure Mexican vanilla radiates from Jack's entire being, and today it's overwhelming. It's as though Jack flipped an internal switch and released a vanilla concoction.

He shifts topics. "How did you explain recognizing me at Remé's party?"

"I told Max you were a former student, which he didn't believe," she says, looking down at Bentley again, now certain it's time to go.

"Because it's a ridiculous explanation," Jack teases. "Couldn't think of anything else?"

Suzanne sidesteps the subject, hoping to reduce the electricity in the air. "How do you know Remé?"

"I hung out at his high school and pretended to be a student. Didn't he become an architect? You may not know this, but I studied to be an architect nearly a century ago. Now, I migrate between here and Pass Christian, where I stay on my yacht. And check in on mortals like you."

"I should have remembered your ties to the Coast," Suzanne says. "Didn't Madelaine's mother's family have a place in the Pass for generations? Until wicked Hurricane Katrina wiped the town down to its slabs." Suzanne empties her wine glass, and Jack instinctively refills it.

"You don't favor Madelaine as much as I'd imagined that you would, as an adult woman," Jack says. "Though I'd recognize those violet eyes of yours anywhere."

"My mother's eyes," she adds.

"And the color of *her* mother's eyes, too," Jacks says wistfully. As dusk approaches, she remembers the question she wants to ask Jack.

"Can you tell me where my family's sacred ground is? I'm embarrassed to ask . . . for it seems like I should be knowledgeable about that."

Jack's visage takes on a golden hue as the sun inches closer to setting. He laughs and says, "Surely, you're not serious. You just mentioned the place a moment ago, silly woman."

"It's in the Pass? Yes, of course, it is." Suzanne feels the turn of a valuable key in its lock. Click. Click. "And I'm guessing you've spent decades there over time."

He ignores Suzanne, stating the obvious. "I'd love to share an evening," Jack begins. "Better yet, show you the sacred area, even take you out on the Sound the next time you're on the Coast."

She leaves his awkward invitation unanswered. She is cautious, considering Jack's predilection for jealously attaching himself to Lafountain enchantresses. "I need to head home. At least one of the twins will be there tonight." When she stands, Bentley lumbers back indoors. "Thank you, Jack. This has been lovely."

He walks Suzanne to the side gate, his fingertips resting at the small of her back, his touch so light she barely feels it. How does he know *her* spot, the most erogenous part of her being? Suzanne fights against grabbing Jack, pulling him to her, and melting into him.

As she opens the gate latch to leave, Jack slams his hand against the wooden panel, effectively preventing her exit. He lightly kisses Suzanne's neck and encircles his arms around her. Jack's warmth embraces her like the coziest quilt on a bitter-cold winter night, wrapping her in love and security. Suzanne could easily hold onto him tightly if nothing else needed her attention. And stay forever. She'd easily banish all the chaos in her life to drink in the essence of the family's angel.

Kissing Jack tastes like melting molasses—the most delicious kiss that ever brushed her lips or welcomed her tongue. Softly, at first. A fire sizzles, bursting with a passion that threatens to consume her, transporting her to a place she has never known.

Try as she might, Suzanne cannot imagine why Madelaine fell out with her angel.

26

Max

Gulf Coast, Fall 2012

Max moves to Pass Christian on the weekend in September when Suzanne plans a girls' trip to Hilton Head, South Carolina, with Margie. Time is a thief, shifting far too rapidly through Max's hourglass.

The threat of being arrested and charged with Farrah's death hovers like a live, frantic chicken some fool on a Louisiana swamp tour dangles over an alligator's mouth. A feeding frenzy awaits him if charged, tried, and convicted of Farrah's untimely demise. In the unlikely event that forensic evidence is discovered within Mammoth Cave's most cavernous pit, Max expects John to defend him against a second-degree murder charge.

Max leaves his legal concerns in his attorney's hands and concentrates on fast-forwarding his relationship with Suzanne. Thanks to Maureen's sleuthing skills, he learns that Suzanne's considerably wealthier than estimated. Max knew about Suzanne's lawsuit that followed her mother's fiery death in a crash on U.S. Highway 61 four years ago—in front of Myrtles

Plantation in St. Francisville, Louisiana, one of the most notably haunted plantations in the South.

But he didn't know that her attorney's wrongful death suit against the drunk driver who eviscerated Madelaine and her then-husband won a record-breaking settlement. Suzanne made her lawyer an exceedingly wealthy man.

And here I thought I was only chasing a fat divorce settlement. Instead, I'm hitting pay dirt with this broad.

Even before Max learns the extent of Suzanne's wealth, he morphs his original plan of seducing her, then cleaning out her investment accounts. He wants Suzanne all to himself despite her sage-burning ways. Despite her midnight ghost conversations. Despite her bratty, spoiled kids. Max plans to propose. He decides to tolerate weirdness if it means he can enjoy a great life with a sexy, dripping-rich woman. But first, Max must settle Dad's debt—then he'll be free to enjoy the fruits of his labor.

Maureen warns him not to push too hard. "She's fragile, Max. Don't you see this?"

"No, I disagree," he says. "That fragile shit of hers? It's an act. She knows what she's doing every second of the day. This gal loves the brass ring." Tired of waiting for the moving van's arrival from New Orleans, Max squints against the sunlight before checking his phone for messages. "We're both survivors, Suzy and me. It's the number one thing we have in common."

"Move too fast, and you risk everything."

"That's why I have you, Mo. To keep me in check," he says. He pulls two Coronas from the small retro refrigerator on the back patio of M & R's rental house on Davis Avenue in the Pass. The leasing agent who signed off on Max's six-month commitment said it's the original one from the first kitchen, built in the 1940s.

Maureen sips her beer and watches the goldfinches linger on the white picket fence posts. "I remember when I stumbled upon this cottage for M & R . . . what was it . . . three years ago? I fell in love with the salmon-colored stucco. And the magnificent Lady Banks Rose bushes planted along the fence line. This place could be featured in *Southern Living*."

Max leans back in one of the Adirondack chairs placed in the side yard, encircling a stone fireplace. "This is exactly what I need to entice Suzanne to leave that nightmare job of hers and go coastal with me. Seriously, though, why does she work? Time to live *the* good life. Share her money. With me, here on the Coast."

"That's rough, Max. Even for you."

"Life's rough, Mo." When Max stands and stretches, he notices an older woman wandering along the sidewalk in front of the cottage, carrying a white bowl billowing with smoke. He charges to the front gate to confront her.

"Ma'am, what the hell are you doing?"

"Calm down, Max. Meet Calpurnia, Franny's sister. No need to overreact," Maureen explains. "She's here to cleanse the house with white sage."

"I swear, Mo. If I didn't know better, I'd think you and Suzanne are now best friends."

"It's protocol when a previous owner dies a horrible, violent death. It's been nearly impossible to lease the cottage for decades because locals know the story," she says. "That's one of the reasons M & R had no trouble snatching it up. But since there's a new lease agreement . . ."

"Yeah, yeah, yeah. I know about disclosures. Do you have any idea how many times I've slept here?" Max interrupts. "And had no clue it's haunted?"

"Calpurnia has an excellent reputation for coaxing restless spirits from these older homes. So, please. Don't make a scene," Maureen says. "It's starting to look like fate—you and Suzanne. For reasons no one fully understands. Least of all, me."

They lean against the fence and watch Calpurnia's methodical work. She walks the entire width and length of the front and side yards, guiding the white sage smoke. Neither understands the indiscernible words the old Creole woman speaks. Then, when Max starts for the porch to get another beer, he hears his son Jacob's voice shout from the curbside.

"Where have you been, Dad? I thought we were meeting at the office."

"Damn, son. I totally forgot. Why didn't you call?"

"What difference would it make? You don't answer your phone," Jacob says. He gets out of his truck and walks over to greet Maureen, kissing her on the cheek. "Good to see you, Mo."

"Likewise, hon."

"Has Dad explained why he's moving over here?" Jacob asks, adjusting his Atlanta Braves ball cap.

"He's worried about Remé's latest housing development, as he calls it. It's a larger headache than either of us imagined."

"I won't argue with that," Jacob agrees. Though a junior in college, he works part-time at M & R's coastal office and keeps tabs on several projects for his dad. When he sees Calpurnia approach the front entrance, he turns to Max and asks, "Who's this?"

"Calpurnia. Franny's sister," Max answers matter-of-factly. "She's cleansing the house."

"Of what?" Jacob shakes his head in disbelief. "And who's Franny?"

As Jacob follows his dad to the cottage's front door, Calpurnia's already in place to block his passage. She's a large, immovable fortress when she leans her back against the threshold. "You don't go in there, boy. It's not properly cleansed."

"Ms. Calpurnia," Max says, turning to allow his son inside. "It's okay."

"You don't understand. I say *I'm* not stepping in this place, Mr. Max," Calpurnia says. "Spirit's too strong for me."

"Good God, woman. Just come inside. Maureen will walk through the house with you."

"You don't get it, do you?" Calpurnia's face, creased with wrinkles, crunches up even more as she stares at Max in disbelief.

Max frowns. "Now, ma'am. No need to be rude."

Calpurnia reaches into her pouch and removes a small jar filled with dried red clay. She carefully unscrews its top and retraces her steps, sprinkling a line at the first small step by the gate's entrance and again at the home's entry. When Calpurnia tentatively steps inside, she sees Maureen standing across the room.

"I know you're not her, are you?"

"Not who?"

"The one. The one who will help."

Maureen laughs. "Calpurnia, what are you talking about?"

"You're not her. I'd know her. I sense her, smell her."

"Woman, you already know Maureen's not Suzanne. Just finish the job, so I can get my girlfriend moved in."

"She must be the one, then. Your girlfriend," Calpurnia says, walking into the house, searching for more sage in her handwoven pouch, frayed at the edges. "Franny's little friend."

Max leaves Maureen to deal with the cleansing. When he closes the front door, he steps over Calpurnia's protective squiggles of red dirt—but not before he overhears the older woman warn Maureen that a priest must be called to the house for a blessing with holy water.

When Max climbs into his son's truck, he faces Jacob's disdain. "You're unbelievable, Dad. So you're moving to the Coast with Suzanne but still hanging out with Mo? I don't get you. By the way, when do I meet Suzanne? Does she even know I exist?"

Go ahead, Jacob. Deliver your laundry list of complaints. What else is new? How 'bout getting more creative with your questions. Ask why the cottage needs a cleansing and a priest's blessing before anyone can move in?

"Don't get fired up, Jacob. There's a lot you don't understand." Max lowers his window to catch the sea breeze. "Suzanne hasn't a clue that I moved here this weekend, so I get to deal with that, too."

Jacob turns his car around in the driveway. "Why not marry Maureen? She's the one you love."

"Mo's my best friend, son," Max says. "I can't marry my best friend. Besides, I don't love her. These are things you've yet to learn. But you will."

"I can guarantee Mo loves you. No words, Dad. No words."

As they turn off Second Street onto Market, Max asks, "What's so all-fire important at the office?" He should be uncomfortable about nosing around at M & R on the weekend without Remé on site, but he's not.

"You need to look at some discrepancies I've found. Now that you're going to be here full time, you can be the one to keep tabs."

"Why wait on something that important?"

Jacob looks at Max's profile, gauging his father's reaction. "Because it's a touchy subject, Dad. It concerns Mr. Remé's son. I've suspected him of stealing for a while, but I wanted to be sure I had proof before saying anything."

"That's a serious charge, Jacob. You've been onboard since we opened the coastal office, and you're just now coming to me about this?"

"Come on, you can't claim this is the first time I've mentioned it. Everybody knows you won't challenge 'ya boy Remé."

"Some respect, son. He's your boss, too, and a family friend," Max says. He considers Jacob's news. "Goddamn it. I've known in my gut we shouldn't have put Sawyer in charge of leasing the Long Beach project."

"Yeah, but there's something else you need to look at," Jacob says.

"Jesus. This is turning into one seriously messed up day." Max opens his door before Jacob comes to a complete stop in

M & R's parking lot.

They take the stairs two at a time and enter Sawyer's office after clearing the office alarm.

"Check out the book Sawyer keeps, not the one the accountant runs or the one you and Remé monitor in the computer program." Max jams his hands in his jeans pockets and works to control his frustration. He's not good at taking direction from anyone, much less his son, despite the young man's math-whiz capabilities. "Look in the bottom right drawer of his desk. Under that thin layer of wood."

Max opens the drawer's false bottom and retrieves the leatherbound ledger. Why would Remé's son record entries by hand when a computer program generates figures more efficiently?

He flips the ledger pages back and forth. First, he logs into the software that keeps the office books current using his access code. Then, he rechecks the ledger's pages.

"Skimming from the profits," Max concludes at first glance. He's enraged. While he spends months courting Hollywood moguls into signing a multi-million-dollar lease at One Canal Place in New Orleans, his partner's kid is stealing from them. Max wants to punch a hole through a wall.

Max demands, "Tell me now, Jacob, are you in on this? Are both you and Sawyer stealing from your old men? Are you squealing 'cause you thought I'd catch you first?"

"Goddamn it, Dad!" Jacob yells. "No, sir. I'm not stealing from my father. I'm not stupid enough to piss you off. Or lose my job. Or break the law. I'm showing you what I found, so I've done my part. Now, you guys resolve this."

Manipulation is an insidious and demanding business. It's hard to determine whether Max is more flummoxed about the underhanded thievery or being outfoxed by one craftier than him. It had been his intention all along to have Sawyer take the fall for *his* embezzlement of company funds. "Look, son, I'm sorry. I'm exhausted with keeping up with finances, 24/7, for both offices," Max says.

"You and Remé figure this out. Either way, he needs to know what his kid is doing." Jacob replaces the ledgers just as he finds them. When he looks at Max, he says, "You and Mo are welcome to crash at my condo tonight if your furniture doesn't arrive."

"Thanks." Max hugs Jacob. "But we're staying at our usual B & B for the next couple of days."

"I don't get it, Dad. Is any woman ever enough for you?" Jacob asks. "Suzanne is gorgeous, at least from the pictures on Facebook I've seen. I'm sure she's perfect in person."

Max overlooks the dig. "You know, I've messed up many things in my life, kid, but thank God you're not one of them. Thank you, son, for this."

"See you soon, Dad. Bright and early on Monday morning." Three beautiful words. Words that Max will yearn to hear as time moves forward.

Never underestimate the power of three little words: see you soon.

When he hears the office door open and close fifteen minutes later, Max thinks nothing of it and assumes Jacob forgot something. But before he reaches down to shut the bottom drawer, he hears Sawyer ask, "Why the fuck are you going through my desk drawer, Max?"

Sawyer races into his office to grab Max from the swivel chair, then slams him against the wall behind the desk. "Stupid bastard," Max yells, kneeing Sawyer in the balls, throwing the younger man off-balance. "What am I doing? You're asking *me*?" Max yells. "I'll ask you the same goddamn question, you idiot." Max leans over Sawyer, lying on the floor, curled up on one side. "You think you're getting away with stealing from me and your dad, you stupid m'ffer!"

Max aims a punch at Sawyer's jawline but misses it, hitting Sawyer's nose instead. With blood squirting from his nostrils, Sawyer bolts back up. His punch grazes the side of Max's face, hits his temple, and sends him reeling to the floor. He's not finished. Hands on his knees, Sawyer waits for Max to right himself before punching him again.

"What the fuck?" Remé yells, racing down the hallway. He grabs his son by the scruff of his shirt collar to separate him from Max.

"Where'd *you* come from, Remé?" Max yells. He points at Sawyer. "Your boy right here, he's a thief! Your kid's a fuckin' thief. And I've got the digits to prove it."

His partner offers Max a hand up. "We'll discuss it later, Max. But for now, I'm taking Sawyer to the hospital. I think you've broken his nose."

"Goddamn, you." Max walks to the breakroom, leaving a trail of blood dripping from his face.

Max sits on the cold tile floor in the office's kitchen, facing the open refrigerator door, with bloody rags scattered around him. He pushes the ice button on the exterior panel to keep the cubes coming. With his head tilted backward and a makeshift cold pack balanced across the bridge of his nose, Max wonders how he let Sawyer punch him. That fist came out of nowhere. Strangely in slow motion, it held a power that puzzled Sawyer, too.

Max hears the office door chime. Again.

"Now what?" he mutters, spitting droplets of blood into a wadded-up paper towel.

He looks up through a swollen eye to see a shadowed presence hovering in the small kitchen. It sucks the air from the room.

Am I hallucinating? No way that kid hit me hard enough to start seeing things.

He tries to back away. But there's nowhere to go. It's impossible to escape the shadow, whose figure fills the depth and width of the doorway. When he dares to look up, he sees that it's Suzanne. And she's glaring at him.

"You moved to the Coast and forgot to tell me, Max? Let me guess. You're not here alone. Is your trusty assistant with you?"

"Jesus, woman. I thought you were the devil."

"That's amusing, Max," she says. "Since you're pale enough to have seen a ghost. You need to see a doctor. Let's go."

How does Suzanne show up when least expected? Yet rarely when anticipated.

27

Addy

Gulf Coast, August 1944

After privately meeting with Papa in his study, Addy walked out with a plan: She'd stop fighting with her grandparents and adopt a new point of view. Simply put, her marriage to Cash served as a short-term solution to a lifetime of disinheritance. So, with this arrangement in mind, Addy exchanged wedding vows with her officer at Trinity Episcopal Church in the Pass on Monday evening, just two days after the Edgewater incident and several hours before Cash, Eddy, and their entire squadron departed for Germany.

When she entered the small sanctuary, she couldn't resist smiling. Addy recognized Mimi's style of arranging violet hydrangeas and white roses around the altar. On second glance, she discovered spell bags placed in each of the potted hydrangeas. Macie had mentioned the hours she spent observing Mimi in her potter's shed, casting one protection spell after another. What failed to protect Addy two days ago must be urgently summoned to shield her now.

Apparently, the best way to deal with deception was to combat it with magick.

After tripping over a half-length white runner centered up the church's middle aisle, Addy ripped it up and stuffed it underneath one of the back-row pews. She had no intention of walking up the aisle in an empty church. Alone, no less. Her father hadn't returned her phone calls, clearly now refusing to attend. Addy no longer had the patience for the civility of a Southern belle's rite of passage. She'd spent a lifetime dreaming of this moment—now, it'd quickly disassembled into a nightmare.

The pristine white candles topping the church's antique candelabras, symbolizing purity and holiness, were also unacceptable. She found an altar boy who promised to remove them before anyone else arrived and gave him the change in her pocket to seal the deal.

This feels more like a funeral than my wedding.

Esty stood as Addy's maid of honor. Cash's commanding officer, Major Duce Whitman, served as the best man. Addy wore a drop-sleeved princess gown layered with cream lace. She agreed to wear a simple dotted-Swiss veil because it hid her eyes. A mere phone call to Mimi's seamstress had resulted in an overnight wedding dress creation. Cash wore his white dress uniform.

Addy grasped a cascading bouquet of orchids and lilies—Esty held only lilies. Mimi and Papa stood slightly off to Addy's left while Macie huddled between her grandparents. Two of Cash's squadron buddies, including his best pal, Eddy, stood with Cash. Though Addy's parents had refused to cut their New York City trip short, James Jr. had managed to contact his attorney. Papa had warned her to expect retaliation from her father, but recommended that she remain true to their agreement. James Jr. planned to move for an annulment.

None of Cash's family members attended. No one. Not even a favorite uncle. Papa wondered if the young man had been orphaned, for he never once spoke about his people.

Reverend Evan Faucheux, the Episcopalian priest, shortened the wedding script, yet still interjected his thoughts about the circumstances of war and the realities of marriage.

"In First Corinthians, the Holy Bible teaches us that love is patient, love is kind; it protects, trusts, hopes, perseveres, and never fails," he said. His attention seemed directed to Mimi and Papa more than the bride and groom. "These words the Lord delivers through St. Paul, the Apostle, explain what love is, what love will do." When the priest addressed her and Cash, he said, "God expects you both to commit a lifetime to each other, to think, grow, and serve in His name."

With a distorted, twitch-like movement, Cash looked blankly at the priest, then quickly back at Addy as if to disagree or request further explanation. At that moment, Addy feared Cash might race to the rear of the church, slam through the massive double doors, and disappear into the night.

Addy nervously shifted her high heels that fit too tightly and tried to lock her deep violet eyes with his. She doubted he'd heard anything the priest recited.

Why's Cash staring at Esty? Instead of me?

She caught Mimi's attention, shook her head, and mouthed, "I can't do this." Father Evan sensed something amiss, so he sped up the ceremony. He was no stranger to uniting couples a few hours before the war split them apart.

Mimi stepped away from Papa and walked behind Addy. She placed her hand on her granddaughter's shoulder and whispered, "Take Cash's hand."

After Father Evan asked Addy and Cash to face each other, he said, "Our prayers for you two, who will wed and become one, are the prayers for all Americans who serve. Cash, we pray fervently that you will safely return to American soil unharmed. Addy, we pray that you find strength. And we pray the war nears its end."

Addy glanced at her great-grandmother Louisa's silver marcasite wedding band, now nestled on her left ring finger. She looked for lost love in Cash's eyes. And pretended she'd miraculously found it when he winked and whispered, "It's going to be okay. I promise."

"By the authority committed to me as a priest, I declare Addy and Cash are husband and wife, according to the ordinance of God, in the name of the Father, and of the Son, and of the Holy Spirit. Those whom God has joined together, let no man put asunder. Cash, you may kiss your bride."

Are we going to kiss? After what has happened?

Cash's lips lightly brushed against Addy's. He caught a tear sliding along her left cheek so quickly that no one saw it. "My Addy, please believe that I love you."

As her eyes locked solidly into his baby blues, she whispered, "Never hurt me again, Cash."

And with Father Evan's pronouncement, Addy and Cash became man and wife. The tiny group of celebrants encircled the newlyweds with hugs and handshakes as the organist began playing a recessional designed for a church filled with jubilant family and friends. Addy saw the priest motion to the organist to wrap it up.

Naturally, Mimi had contacted a photographer at the last minute. When she busied herself with setting Addy's veil, just so, for a final bridal shot of her granddaughter, Papa pulled Cash aside and handed him an envelope. Perhaps the older man's furrowed brow spoke more fervently than his words. "Mimi asked me to book the White House Hotel's finest honeymoon suite for the next two nights. With you leaving early tomorrow, she wanted Addy to stay for some extra pampering."

"I can't thank you enough, sir," Cash said. He fervently shook Papa's hand. "Mr. Lafountain, I want you to know, sir, I won't let you down. Understand that I love your granddaughter, no matter what you think of me. I'd never lie about that." Cash tucked the envelope into his uniform's inner pocket. "And when I return, sir, I'll spend my life making this up to her."

"If I didn't believe this Cash, I can assure you none of this wedding business would've been arranged." The two men shook hands. "In the meanwhile, Godspeed."

Mimi waited patiently for her turn to speak to Cash, giving his uniformed attire the once-over. When she clasped his hands between hers, she said, "Today, tonight, tomorrow, and all the days to follow, there will be no more hurt for Adelaide. Do you understand me?"

"Yes, ma'am."

"We've entrusted our most prized possession to you. And we will be watching."

"Of that, I'm certain, ma'am."

Addy hugged Esty closely. "Thank you, sis, for standing in my wedding. I know it wasn't easy for you." Somewhat puzzled by Esty's tears, Addy thought her sister's emotional reaction had more to do with losing a sister than anything else.

"We'll spend some time together before I leave for New Orleans, Addy."

When the newlyweds spun from the parking lot in a glossy red '44 Mercury Coupe convertible, on loan from Cash's Keesler buddies, an evening sea breeze lifted Addy's veil. Her long, luxuriant dark locks whipped around her face, creating a cocoon-like image of a woman wrapped within her post-nuptial bliss. Cash rested his arm around her shoulders.

"You okay?" He tried to separate the strands of Addy's long black locks from her face while driving the car.

"I'm working on it."

I did what everybody expected. I married you. But I can promise you, from this day forward, that any future decisions will benefit me. Without interference from Mimi. Even Papa. And especially not from you, Cash.

Addy thought about her chat with Mimi when her grandmother helped her dress in the church's parlor.

"If you keep crying, Adelaide, it'll seem as if we've forced you to marry."

"Because that's exactly what you and Papa are doing!" Addy

cried out. "I haven't been able to talk to Mama or Daddy or tell them my side. This is *not* how I imagined my wedding."

"Life has a way of stomping on our dreams, Addy. We leave those dreams behind when we become adults." Mimi reached into her beaded clutch and gingerly removed a white gold bracelet dotted with deep blue-purple amethyst stones, ornately encircled in marcasite. "I want you to have this as a token of my deep gratitude that you're willing to protect this family's legacy. As the only granddaughter who possesses special gifts, it's yours. And it will suffice as something old: a protection bracelet worn by generations of Lafountain women."

The bracelet appeared to have life-affirming qualities within its magical sparkles.

Addy extended her arm and allowed Mimi to fasten it around her left wrist. "It's breathtaking, Mimi. I don't know what to say . . . don't feel like I deserve to wear such a treasure." She ran her fingers over the delicate marcasite designs encompassing the brilliant stones, hardly believing her grandmother would trust her with such a gift. "Thank you."

"Of course, love. It's your turn," Mimi said.

Addy jiggled her wrist, amazed by the bracelet's perfect fit. "I'm terrified of losing it, Mimi. I don't know about this."

"You may misplace it once or twice, but the bracelet will never lose track of you. Or the person it needs to adorn." Mimi hugged her eldest granddaughter tightly. She closed her eyes and said a silent prayer for Addy's future. "One more thing. After Cash leaves and you've had time to adjust your plans, please reconsider learning more rootwork, some candle magic—just a few simple spells to start, like love, protection, even wealth."

Will it ever end? This demand to uphold a legacy started more than 100 years ago.

"How, Mimi, will I work that in alongside everything else? Right now, I'm worried sick over marrying a man I no longer trust. How many women do that?"

"Many more than you know, love. Sometimes it's the only choice. But you're a fortunate woman, for you have resources." Mimi double-checked her reflection in the church parlor's mirror, patting the backside of her updo with hands covered in white lace gloves.

Fortunate. Not an adjective Addy would have chosen to describe the past forty-eight hours. No matter how Mimi dressed up Addy's circumstances by ignoring the obvious challenges, not one bit of it fell under the guise of reining in a fortune.

Can I rewrite history? Right the wrong of two nights ago?

She tossed her bouquet from the convertible and watched the sea breeze whisk the blossoms into the night sky toward a full moon that cast a gorgeous pearl-like glow.

"Can we pretend, Cash?"

"That's for kids, Addy."

"Just for one night?" she said, undaunted. "Pretend that this nightmare . . . was a bad dream." How desperately Addy wanted to recapture her losses.

Cash thought about his wife's request for a minute, then said, "Okay, it'll be our first night." Perhaps he recognized her fear that it might easily be their last.

A bellman hurried to greet the couple when Cash stopped at the white-columned front entrance of the hotel. When they entered, the hotel concierge explained that a seven-course wedding dinner would be served in their suite within an hour.

Addy waited patiently in the lobby as Cash signed the hotel register. It wasn't until several hotel guests continued to stare that she realized her wedding veil was miraculously still pinned in her hair. She thought of the hundreds of war brides who'd stood in this very same spot, restless for their hurried wedding night. Not uncommon in the summer of 1944.

Finally, Cash had the key in hand. She shoved back the flash of a memory from the Edgewater when Cash had screamed at Eddy to hand over the room key. Before everything went dark and her life had changed forever.

"Ready?" Cash asked.

She laced her fingers between Cash's, and they walked along a first-floor hallway to find their suite. After Cash opened the door, he stopped his bride from stepping inside.

"No, wait. Let me get this right," he said. Cash swooped Addy in his arms, his hat falling back to the hallway carpet, and dramatically swung her into their room. Her high-heeled foot kicked the door shut. Once righted, he twirled Addy around a large open living area. "I want to do everything right tonight, baby."

He led her to the bedroom and slowly unzipped her wedding gown. When she turned to face her husband, Addy searched for the spark in Cash's eyes that had captured her heart two months ago. Then they surrendered to an unbridled passion that summer had ignited. Together, they rewrote history.

Not long after, a cart filled with steak, oysters, champagne, and chocolate-covered strawberries arrived. When the waiter left, he placed a "do not disturb" sign on the doorknob and propped Cash's cap against the door jamb. Cash set a loving pace for the night, and Addy followed his lead. Neither one planned to drift off to sleep.

"I have to leave before the sun comes up, Addy," Cash said, hugging Addy tighter.

"Keep talking. I want to feel your breath against my neck until the last minute."

"I'll wait 'til you fall asleep, then I'll slip away."

Addy's eyes threatened to close after the day's exhaustion. Yet, she said, "I won't. Fall asleep."

"Yes, you will."

Already, she felt his weight shift—pulling away and taking his heart along. "I *do* love you, Cash. I've loved you since our first night at Beauvoir."

"I love you, baby," he said. He watched her expression as he edged the palm of his hand effortlessly from her thigh, to the curve of her hip, to cup her breast.

"Come back to me, Cash," Addy whispered. "After all this, I don't want to lose you."

Cash circled his hands around Addy's waist and glided her to straddle him. He entered Addy once more before kissing her goodbye.

Once the hotel door closed, she threw back the thick hotel bedspread. Unable to sleep, Addy decided to run a bubble bath. She grabbed what was left of the oyster platter, set it atop a cloth napkin on the side of the tub, and placed the champagne bottle on top of the toilet seat. Slipping into the hot bubbles, she threw the bottle back, sucked the butter drippings from the platter, and contemplated life without the man who'd waltzed into her life at the beginning of the summer and abruptly walked out a few minutes ago.

Bombs away.

28

Suzanne

New Orleans, Early Winter 2013

Suzanne locks her classroom door at noon on Friday for Mardi Gras break, grateful for a reprieve. While other faculty members head to the mountains for their winter resort experiences, Suzanne anxiously anticipates a stay-cation with a man she resists loving one minute—and attempts not to despise the next.

She's spent. After weeks of handling ghost encounters and Max's mood swings, Suzanne's barely functioning.

The hauntings in Suzanne's world have more than doubled. Stress and a lack of sleep have created a professional crisis for her. Approaching her car, she's puzzled to see Ms. Willis waiting with an envelope in her hand.

"Justin had to leave early for his trip, so he apologizes for missing you. But he asked that I get this to you before you leave." Nervously, the older woman places a legal-size envelope in Suzanne's hand before scurrying away.

"What's this? He didn't have the guts to talk to me himself?"

She turns the envelope over and notes the school board president's signature across the envelope's sealed flap. Suzanne's heart sinks when she makes the connection. It's a summons to appear before the school's governing body at its next meeting. Her battle with the board is past the festering stage and now a boiling point of combustion.

Threats to cancel her annual teaching contract now appear to be accurate.

Suzanne has continued to teach *The Crucible*, Arthur Miller's dramatic interpretation of the Salem Witch Trials of 1692, to a class of gifted and talented eighth graders, despite the risks of losing her position if she didn't rein in her controversial curriculum. Suzanne doesn't have to open the envelope to know its contents. While she must attend the meeting and mount a defense, it won't make a difference. She'll stand before the board, with administrators seated nearby. Then, after she's allotted ten minutes to speak, she'll be instructed to clear her classroom—not at the end of the school year, just three months away, but right smack in the middle of the third grading period.

I cannot back down. I'll leave the school before censorship slams me into submission.

The theme of Miller's play is far too important to ignore. People lied, manipulated, and falsely accused others, resulting in senseless hangings for crimes they didn't commit. A seventeenth-century life lesson still carries a bold message for young people. Too strong of a statement for students at a small private school in Southeast Louisiana? She's willing to concede this ideology. Or has gossip about Suzanne's *extracurricular* activities cycled through the school community, and now folks fear a conjurer among them?

Suzanne craves New Orleans' positive energy to flush her anger and frustration. She needs a break.

To kick off the Mardi Gras holiday, Max invites Suzanne to a glitzy weekend at the Roosevelt New Orleans Hotel, one block off Canal Street, where Carnival krewes will parade over the next four days before Ash Wednesday. Not an uncommon practice for native New Orleanians who hate traffic and parking challenges when a million guests land in their city to celebrate the frenzy of Carnival. Predictably stuck in a line of immovable vehicles, Suzanne considers how to introduce her news about possibly being unemployed.

I'll be jobless, but please do not worry. You see, I'm financially secure. Oh, and I forgot to mention one other thing. The lone dark spirit that hovers when I sleep with you keeps demanding that I make you pay. So, I must ask: Did you do it, Max? Did you kill your wife, Farrah? I do need to know.

What a colossal mess. And to think, most people only face decisions about what to wear to work on any morning and when to knock off for a four-day holiday late in the afternoon. But not Suzanne. No, Suzanne must balance the demands of the spirit world against a dangerous lover *and* retain her competency as a parent, without losing her mind.

Suzanne misses Bimini the minute she boards him at the veterinarian's office. High-stress times demand her golden's sweet, reassuring touch and funny arched eyebrows. Right now, though, Bimini is frazzled from warning Suzanne of impending ghost manifestations. Poor pup needs a break, too.

When Suzanne turns off Common Street in New Orleans' congested central business district, she immediately spots Max pacing back and forth in front of the signature red-carpeted entrance of the Roosevelt. Naturally, his cell phone appears attached to his ear, and he's shouting.

A porter approaches curbside as soon as she swoops into the first available parking spot. Max finishes his conversation and runs to greet her, giving the man their room number. He grabs Suzanne's hand and heads for the hotel's entrance.

When they walk past the magnificent conical nineteenth-century pendulum clock that marks the hotel's main entrance, magically keeping accurate time with its circling bob, Suzanne notices the door to its famous Blue Room gaping wide open to her right. She pauses before taking a step toward the door.

"No, no, Suzanne," Max says, guiding her to stay on course. "We're in a rush. I've got us a suite. And a surprise is waiting upstairs."

"Max, the Blue Room's open. Are dinner reservations possible? I need a peek." Then, when he urges her to keep apace, they brush past the Sazerac, the city's most iconic bar, without hesitation. "Oh, surely we can stop for a drink here, Max," she says.

"Time for that later. Here's the elevator." Suzanne doesn't recognize Max detouring from his bourbon and branch, served in a classic upscale bar, where the skilled bartenders ceremoniously pour the world's finest bourbon into ridiculously expensive crystal highball glasses.

"An explanation would be appreciated. Jump in at any time," she says, double-checking her appearance at the polished elevator door.

Max smiles and looks down at his feet, which are crossed. Leans against the wall.

The elevator climbs. When they enter the suite's double doors at the end of a long hallway, Suzanne is greeted by a sequined, bejeweled full-length rose-gold ball gown hanging on a vintage dress form in the foyer.

"It's not my birthday, nowhere near it. This is rather superfluous, even for you."

No response. Max watches Suzanne wander through the hotel suite, checking out an enormous bedroom on one end with living and dining space on the other—a suite healthy enough to host an intimate party.

"Are we entertaining clients this weekend?" she asks.

Given the intoxicating draw that Mardi Gras offers, it makes sense to invite a bevy of people he needs to impress.

"Nah, this weekend's all yours, babe. Check out the bathroom."

A massive chandelier dangles over a marble spa tub with gold-plated fixtures. Towel warmers are placed between the stone-floored shower, large enough to fit a family of five, and the toilet and bidet. There are two flat-screen televisions: one mounted above the vanity, the other over the tub.

"It's not the anniversary of when we met," Suzanne says, returning to Max, who's still standing in the foyer. "Is it? Wait a minute . . . is this a honeymoon suite?"

"Let's call it the surprise suite," he says. "In the most eclectic city in the world. And ours for the weekend."

Still bewildered by Max's flagrant extravagance, Suzanne asks, "And the evening gown?" She flips the tag at the back zipper to see if he has purchased the correct size. Sure enough. "It's a gorgeous dress I'd easily choose for myself. And the perfect size, no less. Excellent job."

"I had help." The bellman rings. He delivers Suzanne's bags. Max tips him while she wanders back into the bedroom.

"What are tonight's plans? May I wear the gown?" she murmurs, kissing his cheek. She runs her hands around his waistline, dips her palm inside his trousers, then pulls him toward the bed, tugging at his belt buckle.

"I thought you'd never ask," Max says. Then he checks his phone for the time. His hand stalls her from further exploration. "I can't believe I'm saying this . . ." Max refastens his belt. "But our reservations in the Blue Room are in less than twenty minutes. Can you be ready? I can't reschedule."

"No way! So that's why you wouldn't let me peek inside. Didn't want me to see the blue lighting, did you? Or the table decorations."

"Only one table, babe. For you and me." His smile is entirely too broad. Nearly a caricature of itself. "And the gown is for you to wear tonight."

When the bellman knocks twice to escort them downstairs, Suzanne's standing in the suite's foyer, helping Max with his tux tie and cufflinks. She's worried that she doesn't have heels, hoping the dress can cover her black ballet flats. Then, when she opens the door, the bellman solemnly hands her a pair of gold, sparkling stilettos, precisely her size.

What's the occasion? Nothing seems natural. Everything's orchestrated.

Suzanne feels like she's riding a fantasy wave, admiring the gilded mirrors and golden columns on their walk through the hotel's central corridor. She catches their reflection in one of the elongated mirrors behind a grand piano and recognizes what others see when they're together: Suzanne and Max are an extraordinarily striking couple.

The protection spell is working. There's no other explanation for Max's complete turn-around.

The maître d' at the Blue Room's entrance bows and welcomes them inside. With Suzanne's first step onto the exquisite azure-blue carpet, she enters a cloud of make-believe—prisms of light twinkle from low-hanging fixtures, mimicking a flood of fireflies amiss. The pastel décor, reminiscent of the '30s, returns them to the years when jazz vocalist Ella Fitzgerald ran the room. A five-string quartet positioned in the far-left corner floats the notes of Frank Sinatra's "The Best is Yet to Come."

Max reaches for Suzanne's right hand and leads her into the East Coast Swing around one solitary table in the center of this elegant space. On the third tour of the dance floor, Suzanne whispers in Max's ear, "I know better, but no matter how much I try, I cannot resist you."

Max smiles and pulls her closer.

If this is what a fairy-tale ending feels like, keep me here forever.

After her final pirouette, a waiter standing nearby pulls out her chair. As plates of caviar and crab cakes arrive in a flourish, another waiter pours two glasses of Armand de Brignac Rosé champagne. When the strings begin to play "The Girl from Ipanema," Suzanne envisions Sinatra teleporting to the famous dining room, microphone in hand, stopping by their table to invite them to dance before taking the stage meshed into a corner-curved wall. Only in a dream.

With such a delightful evening unfolding, Suzanne relaxes and ignores the probability that once she's content, a stranded ghost will pounce from nowhere—to gouge a hole in a captivating experience.

As though on cue, Suzanne recognizes a familiar cloaking presence as she reaches for her champagne flute. *Not here, please. Not here in the Blue Room, where I've dreamt of dining for a lifetime.*

But perhaps she's experiencing a bizarre reaction to the head steward dimming the lights along the blue walls . . . and has purely imagined a threat.

Ask nothing of me tonight.

"I thought you wouldn't mind skipping your wine tonight." Max raises his glass.

"For this gorgeous champagne? You're absolutely correct." She meets his glass. "What are we toasting?"

"Us."

"Then, to us." The faintest clink of fine crystal starts small, then echoes. And re-echoes. As if Suzanne is listening from the bottom of a tall, resounding drum.

A smile. A sip. A perfect moment she knows will be ruined within seconds.

Then, the smothering sensation stops.

Two formally attired waiters serve lobster, filet mignon, Creole green beans, and truffle mashed potatoes. With flair. On gold lamé platters. Suzanne eats like a glutton, as if days have passed without a meal. She prays that the quicker she chews and swallows, the faster these weird sensations will disappear.

Suzanne extends her left hand to protest when the maître d' announces that a baked Alaska flambé is coming.

"I'm gasping, Max. Please, I need a minute. To catch my breath." She takes several swigs of champagne and lifts her flute for a refill. "This is . . ." She falters. "So very overwhelming. It might help if you'd explain what's happening."

"No, no. No more explaining myself, Suzy. We've no more time to waste. We haven't a second to spare."

"What are you saying?" Suzanne feels lightheaded, as if the music, the champagne, and the circular room with blue swirling everywhere now threaten to envelop her in a sinkhole from whence she'll never return. Though a medium February chill blows outdoors, the threat of frostbite seems tenable here in this famous supper club, past its prime.

Suzanne shivers, her teeth chatter. She rubs her hands over her bare arms to warm herself. The walls seem to squeeze inward as she watches Max charge forward as if nothing is amiss—he's drinking champagne. And whiskey. And shoveling mounds of food into his mouth. In the most gluttonous way imaginable. Her stomach turns.

She won't bother asking Max if he sees or hears a thing out of the ordinary, because she already knows the answer. He'll never perceive what Suzanne accepts as commonplace.

The moment the head waiter majestically rolls in an exotic dessert cart and prepares to light a fire to several delicacies, Max pulls a ring box from his tuxedo pocket, snaps it open, and slides it across the table to Suzanne. The result of his vigor upends her champagne flute, toppling its contents.

"Marry me, Suzy. You know that I'm in love with you. And just tonight, you've said the same to me."

"*What?*"

His voice echoes as if Max is miles away, drifting out to sea. *This man, did he ask me to marry him?* Suzanne squints through her darkened tunnel vision and attempts to focus on his facial features. She's dizzy, and likens her weakness to a sudden onslaught of the flu as she battles a feeling that she's plummeting downward. *Out of control.* Suzanne senses her body twisting grotesquely as rocks fly from the sides of an unknown cavern, a place she's never seen nor been remotely interested in visiting.

How does Max not see that something is terribly wrong here?

Following the bass's four-bar entry, the violins and viola join "The Way You Look Tonight." As multiple string instruments layer their notes and the cello steps forward, Suzanne hears the anticipated ghost's voice she fears the most.

A gravel sound from the same dark phantom she encountered in Max's bedroom now exhales in her right ear with an icy cold breath.

"*Yes, yes, YES!*" it screeches as the Blue Room's walls waffle and appear to squeeze inward. But, then, there's a whimper—an ever-so-gentle infant's whimper, with a plea of desperation that engulfs Suzanne.

The harsher spirit hovers. The tiny soul softens its hatefulness. Suzanne closes her eyes—her mind pushes back against the phantom's impenetrable energy. As it vibrates and threatens, Suzanne feels a foreboding penumbra overtake her while she watches the three-carat diamond ring, exposed in its black velvet box, turn in circles.

Overwhelmed, Suzanne loses consciousness when her head tumbles into the baked Alaskan pie. Max screams for the waiters to call 911, horrified to see the engagement ring wrapped in a meringue topping.

29

Max

New Orleans, Spring 2013

Max lounges in his Marigny home on this lazy Thursday morning, propped up on pillows, reading the morning's e-edition of *The Wall Street Journal.* He smiles as Maureen walks to her closet in the spare bedroom, wearing only lace tap pants.

"Have you scheduled the transfers?" he asks.

"Yes, everything's set."

He sets his laptop aside. "Come back to bed."

Maureen whisks a wrap-around dress off its stand and faces him. She effortlessly winds the dress ties around her waist, then creates a knot. "I'm needed in the office, at least for a few hours. Your damn Hollywood guys have a list of complaints about the carriage house they ended up leasing on Burgundy after the Canal Place deal."

"I knew those jackasses would be trouble from the beginning." Max sighs. "They're a goldmine, but they're complete pains in the ass." Then, realizing he can't change Maureen's mind, he pulls his shorts on. "Mo, what would I do without you?"

"Good thing you'll never have to find out." She leans in for a kiss. "Do you think Suzanne suspects anything?"

"Not a thing. She's redecorating the Davis Avenue house, even though it's only a rental. And planning the wedding."

"How will she react? When she discovers, well, a declining balance?" Maureen glances across the room to ensure she hasn't left anything behind. "Wait, redecorating? Shouldn't she be teaching in her classroom?"

"Says she's on some kind of personal leave right now. But by the time she realizes the amount missing, she'll be sunk." Max tucks his wallet in his back pants pocket and grabs the phone charger from the outlet.

"How long did she stay in the hospital?"

Maureen must have a daily quota for questions. *Please. Shut. Up.*

Max moans. "I'm tired of talking about her damn freak show in the Blue Room." Yes, Max described Suzanne's eyes rolling back and her body shaking as he popped the question, but he omitted how terrifying it was to watch Suzanne turn the blue-white color of death. "They kept her overnight at East Jefferson. For observation or some other bullshit reason, because they couldn't figure out what was wrong."

"Thank God she didn't die." Maureen brushes back her burnt umber hair, pulls it over one shoulder, and applies one stroke of lipstick. "You'd have a huge problem if that had happened." Then, switching topics quickly, she asks, "When will I see you again?"

"You *do* understand what's at stake. Right? We won't meet up for a *very* long time," he says. "I'm serious, Mo—no texts, calls, no emails. Nothing whatsoever. As far as you're concerned, I'm dead."

"Okay, okay." She turns out the bedroom light. He walks her downstairs to the front door and kisses her cheek. "Take care, love."

"See 'ya soon, boss."

No reassurance is offered. As far as Max is concerned, this

is a forever goodbye. He has no plans to see Maureen again.

Stay in your lane, Mo. Finish the goddamn job.

She heads to Canal Place to mitigate Dietz's mess while Max returns to the Coast. When he reaches the halfway point on Bay Bridge, he's less than one mile from the construction site of his and Suzanne's permanent home in the Pass. Less than 1,000 feet from the water, the design crafted by a coastal architect boasts every house amenity a woman may desire—a dream home designed to make up for a dream.

Max's wedding gift—secretly financed using Suzanne's money.

He had started stealing funds from her investment account, using his limited access as one of her financial advisers, to cover construction costs long before he proposed. At about the same time he'd started narrowing the gap on the remaining balance of the Martinez family debt.

Thank God Suzy said yes.

The builder's sluggish performance in meeting their agreed-upon completion date is wreaking havoc on Max's plan to surprise Suzanne before their wedding. He interrogates the man about a finish date. "When can I move my bride in?" he asks.

"We're a few weeks out. The paint crew only finished this morning, and your appliances are running behind schedule," he said.

"I need Suzanne set up in that house, like, yesterday."

"Talk to Remé. My best subs were yanked over to M & R's project in Long Beach early this morning. It's damn clear 'ya partner is pissed about keeping your new place a secret."

"I'll take care of him," Max says. "Just finish the house."

On days like this, when the tentacles of his deceptive life become entangled with reality, Max dreams of being free of it all. The type of freedom that stems from a disappearing act.

After entering M & R's coastal office, Max knocks on Remé's office door. Before confronting his partner about pulling a construction crew away from his new build, Max must discuss Sawyer's charges against him.

"Time to talk?"

"I've got a second," Remé answers. "Maybe two." He glances up from a balance sheet.

"Whose idea was it to file charges? Yours or Sawyer's?" Max stands near the open door with his arms crossed in defiance. He'll delay a full-blown confrontation until he hears what his partner says.

"Sawyer's decision. And I didn't argue with him, Max, because you behaved like a jackass." Remé pushes back his swivel chair yet makes no effort to stand. On the contrary, he leans back with an air of confidence that doesn't sit well with Max.

"Sawyer swung first. What was I supposed to . . ."

"Not swing back," Remé interrupts. "Goddammit, you know better. Help me understand. You beat up my son because you *imagined* money was missing from the corporate account? Without first talking to me? If the situation had been reversed, I'd have called you immediately. And never, ever would I have hit Jacob."

"He's your kid, so I get it. But being blood-related doesn't give him the right to steal from the company."

Remé shakes his head, removes his reading glasses. "I've asked our accountant to check for discrepancies. We'll have answers in a day or so." His calm demeanor is enough to set Max off. "And for the record, I've no reason to believe that Sawyer is a thief. Think about it. Why would he steal from what he stands to inherit?"

After months of manipulating Sawyer to take the fall for Max's blatant pilfering of the company's general account, an auditor's examination is unwelcome. Considering the length of time Max has been siphoning profits from M & R, it should've been glaringly apparent weeks ago that money was missing. *Why didn't anyone notice?*

"Meanwhile, I've got a court date to answer these damn assault and battery charges."

"Take a plea deal. That's probably John's advice, too." Remé stands, a signal that their conversation is ending. "Looks like more legal problems for you, my friend."

Turning away from Remé's office door, Max says, "Well, the other ones I brought on myself. I'll admit to that. But this one shouldn't have happened. If Sawyer hadn't . . ."

"Enough!"

"So, you won't demand he drops the charges?" Max pushes on.

"Hell, no." Remé stuffs a file folder into his briefcase. He's running low on patience after spending decades making excuses for Max—the guy he met standing in the lunch line on the first day of high school thirty-five years ago. "I'm done covering for you, Max. Finished." Then, matter-of-factly, Remé switches gears. "There's an issue with a live oak standing in the way of progress on the Long Beach site, so I'm heading there before the contractor levels it and leaves us with a stiff fine. I could use your help with that."

"I'll see 'ya in a few," Max says, though he has no intention of wasting one more minute in Long Beach.

Instead, he heads home. Suzanne is bent over in the side yard, pulling weeds. He parks in the driveway and sneaks up on her.

"Hey, I didn't hear you drive up." She stands, removes her gardening gloves, and kisses his cheek. "You remember Calpurnia? Franny's sister."

"Right. Would have thought you'd finished the job last time you were here."

The two women face each other and laugh. Max has no idea what's so amusing.

Suzanne hands Calpurnia a tray of rosemary and lavender plants, then points to where she wants them placed. "I need to discuss a couple of things with you, Max, though I'm uncertain of your afternoon schedule," Suzanne says.

"I'll be around for the afternoon," he says, walking the property's fence line, looking for a new hoodoo altar that he's convinced has been tucked between the rose bushes. With Calpurnia nearly moving in with them, he believes something's surely amiss. He'd love the reassurance that no folk magick is being practiced, but considering Suzanne's demeanor and abundance of free time, he suspects that's an impossible dream.

He stretches out on his favorite outdoor lounger, feet up, his hands clasped behind his head. When his cell phone rings, Max sees that John is calling.

"You seated, Max?"

"In my lounge chair, watching two crazy women pretend *not* to practice hoodoo."

"Really?" John asks. "My favorite great aunt was a conjurer, back in the day. Didn't know it was still a thing."

"You have it on good authority that it's still very much a *thing*. What's up?"

"Look, I tried. But Remé's son is being a butt, not budging. Sawyer's hellbent on sticking with the assault and battery charges. Fingers crossed that nobody here in Harrison County gets wind of your troubles back in Kentucky." When John hears no response, he allows his comment a couple of seconds to sink in. "Lay low and stay out of trouble. I'll be in touch."

Suzanne walks to the back porch and grabs two cold drinks for Calpurnia and herself. Max expects a confrontation is imminent, but hopes she'll grab two Dr. Peppers and return to the herb garden.

"You all right, babe?" she asks before walking away.

"Not a good time, Suzy," he mumbles.

She doesn't hear him. Places her hands on his shoulders, offering a brief midday massage.

He explodes. "What the fuck do you want, Suzanne?"

"Jesus, Max. I'm just checking on you. Never mind, though."

"No, you started this. *What* do you want?"

Since Suzanne has Max's attention, she presses forward. "Because you asked, I'm apprehensive about my investment account, Max. Money is—evaporating."

"How is this *my* problem?" he counters.

"It's your problem because I asked for advice, gave you access, and now thousands are missing. And I don't understand why. Look over the account and help me understand?"

"If I have time." Max rubs his temples, sensing the blood pulsating through his veins.

"So, this a burden for you? I've invested over the years to make withdrawals, when necessary, for the twins' education and other expenses. I'm terrified there won't be sufficient funds left when I need money."

"I'll pull up the account and check it. But I'm not taking any responsibility for your bad judgment with investing. It is what it is," he says.

"I really regret giving you access. That would certainly explain why I might be heading to the poor house," she says.

Max jumps from his chair and attempts to grab her, barely missing Suzanne's forearm. Calpurnia notices their interaction from a few steps away. She immediately reaches for something in her pocket, voicing a protection chant using indiscernible language.

Max checks himself, offers a half-smile, and walks into the house.

"Goddamn it straight to hell," he says. Max cannot explain the genesis of his anger, the way it suddenly rises, taking him unaware as it boils beneath his skin. Having addressed his uncontrollable outbursts when an outsider mandated that he gets things under control, it seems reasonable to assume Max should have adopted a skill or two to tamp down his temper.

The final image of Farrah's horrified expression surfaces with no warning.

Her shocked, stricken, terrified visage—as she tumbled to her death—haunts him. Sadly, Max has yet to realize that it's Farrah's spirit, accompanied by the spirit of their unborn child, who remains attached to him.

Farrah's Ghost

The In-Between, at the Cusp of the Ether

There would be no abortion. Our baby would have her chance at life. None of Max's demands would change my mind. The Lamars had suffered enough at the hands of Lafountain manipulation. I'd raise Grace on my own, coveted in abundant love for the two of us.

Max. So furious that day.

"You're pregnant, aren't you?" Max demanded a confession.

"I don't know for certain, Max. I haven't taken a pregnancy test or seen a doctor yet."

He charged me with plotting against him.

"I knew it! And after we talked about waiting. You bitch. You did this on purpose. Answer me! When did you stop taking your pills?"

Terrified, I needed to escape from the cave and into the fresh air.

"You can't just decide to leave the damn cave, woman. There's no special exit door for Farrah. Get your shit together and stop complaining."

His face contorted—his eyes flashed with hatred—the instant he decided to kill me. Callously, my husband flung me over the railing and into the blackened crevice. My body broken, my voice paralyzed—I couldn't find my scream.

No one heard the thud of her body slamming against the limestone and gypsum walls of the cavern as she and her unborn daughter tumble to their deaths. Beyond their broken bodies, their spirits clear the cave's summit. Farrah grasps her infant's spirit, protectively swaddled in a sweet, soft vapor, bound tightly within her arm, to remain joined in death until a peaceful crossing may be arranged.

If and only if their murders are avenged.

Addy prepared for Grace and me. When our spirits soared, Addy soothed our broken hearts and wrapped us in love's warm embrace. When we lifted through the harsh world, we swirled above the atmosphere— toward the ether—and met Madelaine, who'd just been freed of her physical body. In an instant, I knew Madelaine's heart—her love, maternal.

When I screamed, "You'll pay," an angel magically joined us. To guide our journey.

I think his name was Jack.

31

Addy

Gulf Coast, August 1944

Addy closed her eyes and drifted into a jumbled slumber. Then, forcing herself awake hours later, a cruel reality awaited: Her pilot was gone. Addy grabbed the bedsheet that Cash had wrapped around his waist earlier and inhaled his scent. Only a marriage certificate and a few awkward photographs proved that she'd married Cash one minute, only to lose him the next. She wondered how long friends would wait before voicing the question lingering on everyone's mind: How *do* you love . . . and hate . . . the man you just married? She had no answer.

I can't explain something I don't understand myself.

Addy stared at the white-enameled telephone on the nightstand beside the bed. She considered calling Mama Charlotte, despite the sting of her mother regarding Addy's predicament as a mark of shame. Still, she longed to hear her mama's voice. Hear someone else say *it was for the best*. Addy picked up the receiver and asked the hotel operator to dial The Plaza in New York.

"It's a beautiful day at the Plaza. How may I direct your call?"

"The room of James and Charlotte Lafountain, please."

"I'll try that extension," the operator said. "Hold, please."

"Thank you." Addy's heart raced, nervously anticipating the most intimate conversation she would ever share with her parents.

The operator returned. "I'm instructed to request who's calling, ma'am. Whom may I say is on the line?"

"Their daughter."

The operator's next question was too quick: "Which one?"

Mimi had been honest. It appeared neither her mom nor dad wanted anything to do with her.

"Tell them Mrs. Adelaide Lamar is on the line."

"Thank you. Hold for a moment."

After a minute passed, Addy considered disconnecting the call. Then she heard a click.

Her father said, "Are you all right, Addy?"

"I'm okay, Daddy." Determined not to cry, Addy held to her words. *Why didn't you come? Why didn't you call?* She waited for the quiver in her throat to stop and prayed for the strength to demand answers.

"Your mother," James Jr. explained, "cannot speak with you just yet."

Addy pulled the sheet to her face as tears threatened, prepared to dab her eyes. "I figured that out when she didn't show up at the church for our ceremony."

"We didn't have sufficient notice, Addy. You are aware, I assume, of my usual schedule of meetings and social commitments that cannot be canceled or postponed." Her father's explanation rang with a business tone usually reserved for his financial clients. "Perhaps if we better understood . . . what had actually happened."

"Mimi and Papa took hold of everything, Daddy. I've barely known what's been going on myself," she said. "Cash and I followed their plan and did what needed to be done. We were left with no other option."

Blank silence filled the other end of the phone line. Then, James Jr. said, "I'm proud of you for not fighting your grandparents and going along with reason. I must say, I'm rather surprised you didn't rebel and run straight home to New Orleans. We'd started to prepare ourselves for that . . ."

"Daddy, there were considerable threats," Addy explained. "And since I've no desire to live like a pauper, and Cash didn't relish a court-martial, we did what was required of us."

Again, a blank expanse of silence.

Addy continued, undeterred. "I have plans, Daddy. This isn't going to sink me." She took a deep breath, gathering courage. "I'm coming home to finish at Newcomb, of course, since Cash will be overseas, he says, for at least a year."

"Well, now, here's trouble. Returning to New Orleans is no longer an option for you, Adelaide."

She sprung from the bed and stood erect, with one hand on a hip. "What are you saying, Daddy? I can't come home at all?"

"That's precisely what I'm saying," James Jr. said. "There've been dramatic changes since we last saw you. You're married now, likely pregnant. What makes you think you can waltz back into Newcomb, an elite college filled with the daughters of our dearest friends, after what's occurred? No longer an option, dear."

Her voice collapsed. With a tremor, she asked, "What exactly . . . do you expect me to do? About finishing college?"

"Since you're an adult, it's time to make tough decisions and figure out your life. Take care of yourself. Goodbye, Addy."

The call disconnected. No affirmation of love. Not one ounce of support.

The White House Hotel's honeymoon suite, heavily scented with hurried and desperate lovemaking, now pulsated with a fear of failure and a sense of shame. The dawn of a bride's new life—predictably cheerful, exciting, and filled with hope for the future.

Not a woeful morning of sadness.

After stuffing cosmetics and her white wedding peignoir into a small suitcase, Addy picked up the receiver she'd just slammed on the bedside table. She needed Papa to collect her earlier than they'd planned. He answered on the third ring.

"Can you pick me up, Papa?" Addy asked.

"Right now?"

"Yes. Cash is gone. I don't want to stay here without him."

"The suite's paid for, Addy, and so are your meals for the next couple of days. Why not stay and get some rest?"

"I can't stand to be here. Besides, I need to make new plans."

"Mimi and I think it's important for you to stop and catch your breath, Addy. A lot has happened."

"There's no time for that, Papa. I've got to figure out what I'm going to do about school. Daddy just told me I cannot return to Newcomb. And here I am, so close to graduating."

"Everything doesn't have to be decided today."

"I'm going to the dining room for breakfast, and then I'll be ready to go."

"If you insist. I'll be there soon."

Perhaps Papa knew the importance of choosing his battles with Addy. He'd won the big one: getting Addy married before her name and reputation could be besmirched. Picking her up from the resort hotel a day earlier than planned was probably the least he could do in return for what she had given him. For now, the Lafountain's dignity remained intact.

When Addy paused at the entrance to the hotel's large dining area dotted with white tableclothed tables, she noticed the room was filled with young women, all seated individually.

She followed the hostess to a small table and walked past a woman she recognized from the Dew Drop juke joint. Addy asked, "Did your husband, boyfriend, leave this morning?"

"Husband, honey. And he surely just left."

"Can I join you for coffee?" Addy asked.

"Sure thing."

"I'm Addy."

"I know who you are. I'm Laura." The woman's eyes were red-rimmed. She met Addy's outstretched hand.

"How long were you married?"

"One week."

"I was married less than a day."

"Lord, honey. It looks like you take the cake," Laura said. "Can't think of anything more tragic than that," she added, pulling another cigarette from a red leather pouch that matched the color of her painted lips.

When Laura offered a cigarette to Addy, she declined. "Oh, I hope there aren't more tragic stories than ours," Addy said, looking for a waiter with a carafe of coffee.

The two barely spoke while they stared blankly at the menu selections.

"So, can I ask?" Laura ventured curiously.

"Ask what?"

"You know."

Addy lowered the menu to meet Laura's eyes. "No, I don't know. I have no idea what you're talking about."

Her new acquaintance refused to let up. "Are you?"

"Am I what?" Addy countered, placing the menu on the table.

"Then you mustn't be. Otherwise, you wouldn't act so sore about a little bitty question. It's just that some of the guys told my husband that you're pregnant, and that's why Cash had to hurry and marry you."

"What?" Addy exclaimed, horrified to learn she had become the object of discussion at the base. Even among girlfriends and wives. "No, I am not pregnant! And I'm insulted you would assume it's the only reason Cash married me."

Addy volleyed the obnoxious assumption back to Laura and demanded, "Are you?"

"We'll see. Won't know for a few weeks," Laura winked.

Addy stood up quickly and shoved her chair back from the table. "I'll see you around, Laura."

"Whatever suits you, honey." The woman winked and took an extended draw from her cigarette before stubbing it out in the crystal ashtray.

Addy found Papa in the lobby, patiently sitting in a wing-back chair, chatting with another fellow near his age.

"Here she is! Our beautiful new bride," Papa announced to his friend, Walt—the circuit court judge who'd been consulted about how to deal with Cash's assault a few days ago.

"Mornin' Papa," Addy said, leaning in to kiss her grandfather. "Thank you for coming so quickly."

Judge Matterson stood to extend his congratulations, then checked himself and chuckled. "Forgive my manners, Addy, but I'm uncertain if the customary kiss on the bride's cheek is okay."

"It's fine, Judge."

"I'm so sorry, my dear," he said, facing Addy. "For all that's happened to you." Her lips quivered while her weakened smile reflected her fragile demeanor. She'd already begun to feel herself disappearing.

"I left my wedding dress back in the room, Papa," Addy said. "It'll just take a minute to run back to get it."

When Addy walked down the front steps of the luxury hotel with her wedding dress and veil draped over her left arm, Papa was by her side, his strength providing much-needed support. He nodded to the attendant to retrieve his car, then signaled another young man to fetch his granddaughter's suitcase, which she'd left inside the hotel's front doors.

"You okay, dear?"

"No, not okay. I'm sad, Papa. Cash and I—we didn't even have a chance."

"We'll pray, every day, for his safe return." Addy was becoming accustomed to the platitudes, the expected responses to Cash's quick exit.

"I'm pretty certain at least one member of my family is working against that being the case," Addy suggested. "And since

Cash may not return, I need a plan."

They stood side by side near the hotel's signature fountain, watching the rise and fall of the water's spray. Last night, the fountain lights sparkled like magic when she and Cash approached the hotel's magnificent front entrance.

But in the morning light, Addy no longer believed in the magic of love.

She broke their silence. "Mama and Daddy aren't going to let me come back home."

"I know, Addy. Your father called me this morning. I'd give him a few days. If I know my son, he'll settle down and call you with a different decision."

"He's not going to change his mind, Papa," Addy quipped. "I just talked to him. It will take years for him and Mama to get over their disappointment in me. And I won't have a chance at forgiveness if I'm carrying Cash's baby. Daddy told me I couldn't come back home. What's next, Papa? Can they disown me?"

Waiting for the valet to bring his car to a complete stop, Papa abruptly turned to face his granddaughter and said, "Let me make one thing clear, Adelaide. You will never be disowned. I'm the patriarch. And I'm empowered to make sure that never happens. It's likely your father is truly an idiot if he's threatening that type of action."

"He didn't say anything about that today. I'm going by what I overheard Mimi say."

Addy watched Papa during the ride back to the Pass. The older man, who'd been more of a father to her than her own, appeared weary and worn. While Addy hoped her behavior during the summer months had not singularly aged him, Addy believed that she was responsible for the sadness in his eyes.

Six weeks later, Addy successfully transferred to Gulf Park College for Women in Long Beach. During a mixed-medium class in mid-September, she felt lightheaded and grabbed her easel to steady herself. A few minutes later, she managed to get to the ladies' room in time to lose her breakfast in the sink nearest the entrance. Addy raised her head to face a pasty-white reflection when her nausea quelled. Mimi's and Mama Charlotte's greatest fears had come to pass.

Addy reached for two towels stacked in a basket on a nearby shelf and ran cold water over them: one for the back of her neck, the other to cover her face. With her back nestled against the wall nearest the door, she slowly slid down to sit on the cold tiled floor, no longer attempting to hold back her tears. Her new friend, Dotty, came rushing in to check on her.

"Are you okay, Addy?"

"No," Addy began. "I think I'm . . ."

"Pregnant," Dotty finished the sentence.

"With a husband 5,000 miles away. And not certain to return," Addy said.

"I'm here for you, honey. You won't go through this alone."

32

Suzanne

Gulf Coast, August 2013

Suzanne and Max exchange wedding vows beneath a white tulle canopy on Biloxi's expansive sugar-white beach. Fifty or so friends gather on this hot mid-August Saturday evening to witness the curtain falling on a humid day and a heated courtship. As a sherbet-orange sun dips behind the clouds, the unity candle atop a makeshift altar loses its flame as the short ceremony ends.

Looking gorgeous in a white crepe sundress with daisies woven through her hair, Suzanne glows in the early evening sunlight. Max wears a beige handwoven Guayabera and a Panama straw fedora. At the ceremony's end, the couple stands at the water's edge, hands entwined, their toes sinking into the wet sand as they watch the sun lower on the western horizon. Their gaze across the Sound's gently lapping water reflects an uncertain future.

She gets it—her position is untenable. How does one even consider proclaiming love for a suspected murderer? To others, her stance is impossible to defend. As she watches Max shift his gaze toward the east, he is lost in thoughts that exclude her, already separated from the vows they exchanged only moments ago. Suzanne cannot concern herself with inconsequential details, for she must focus on the embedded plan that has been percolating for generations.

Her mother's spirit, and the ghost of her mother's *mother*, will remain trapped until Farrah's violent death is avenged. And perhaps the spirits of other Lafountain enchantresses, who chose to remain on Earth at the time of their deaths, will be freed to cross through the ether and discover peace on the other side. Suzanne doesn't understand all the overlaps that connect her to each of them. But she surely recognizes a mandate from the spirit world when it's issued.

The Lafountain women: Louisa, Mimi Jeanne, Addy, Madelaine, Farrah, and Suzanne, represent five generations bound by blood and destiny. Six, if Grace's tiny existence is considered, though she never received the privilege of life. Whether these Lafountains accepted their hoodoo legacy—or embraced their clairsentience—they were each offered a choice to decide independently which path to follow.

Tonight, Suzanne's journey of unbinding the webs of a trapped spirit world begins, for only she, an authentic Southern enchantress, can rescue those who choose to seek liberation.

Wedding revelers gather on Beauvoir's grounds, directly across the street. Suzanne watches her twins smile as they approach, hand in hand. She meets Jacob, Max's son, for the first time, and though their introduction is awkward, the young man seems amiable to his father's change in circumstances.

Waiters balance platters filled with crab cakes, fried catfish, and lobster mac 'n cheese, displaying the finest in Southern culinary tradition. An energetic bass saxophonist leads a jazz ensemble to jumpstart the reception as Tennessee whiskey and Jamaican rum flow through the summer night like creek water racing past an abandoned mill. No expense is spared.

"You put on a good wedding, Suzanne," Jacob says. "I'll give 'ya that."

"Thank you, dear." Suzanne almost says *son* but reconsiders. She's not Jacob's mother, nor his stepmom. She's simply the woman who just married his dad.

"Where'd you drift off?" Max asks, hugging her closer.

"Nowhere. I'm still here."

"Happy?" Max asks, unfastening the top two buttons of his Guayabera.

"Absolutely."

"Better than your first wedding?" She finds that Max's need for affirmation is unsettling. Too many years have passed to make a valid comparison.

"Easier, I'd say."

The wedding photographer interrupts. "Smile, y'all. Look this way, please. At the count of three . . . one, two, three."

Neither one of them listens. The photographer captures Suzanne staring dreamily toward the beachfront while her groom admires her from behind. But her smile widens as she spies Jack's airy gait moving toward her. There's a photograph of that too, though no one could ever identify the recipient of her grin. She rushes to consider how best to deal with his unexpected appearance.

"Perfect," the photographer says. Neither the bride nor groom asks to see the photo in the camera's viewfinder.

"I'd love a glass of champagne, Max. Please?" she asks.

"It's not time for the toast yet. I thought someone was to alert us," Max says.

"Never mind, I'll get one from the bar. I need to speak to someone quickly, babe. Be right back." She leans in to give Max's cheek a peck, but he intercepts with a full-on French kiss.

I'll need an entire bottle to manage this night, not just a glass.

Suzanne waltzes away from Max, knowing Jack will follow her lead. After swinging by the bar for her drink, she walks past the back side of the antebellum home and hurries down to Oyster Bayou. She'll leave it to Jack to navigate his way without detection: an effortless task, she's certain.

She sits on a rock buttress near the lagoon, surrounded by live oaks. When a rustle in the azalea bushes makes a good deal of racket, Suzanne looks up from watching tiny ripples in the water. Jack gradually appears on an adjacent pebbled pathway.

"They're looking for you," Jack says, laughing. "No less than a half-dozen people are circling the grounds, all searching for the bride." Jack hoists himself atop a chunk of chert rock filled with ossicles. "You find this utterly amusing, don't you? Cloak and dagger at the wedding of a clueless groom and an aloof bride. He has no clue, does he?"

"That he's responsible for creating a debacle? No, he has no concept of repercussions. And rarely accepts responsibility for his actions." Her eyes widen when Jack hands over an entire bottle of champagne. She tops her flute with a fresh pour.

Jack adds his take on the situation. "Well, let's be fair. Others are complicit. In fact, a slew of deceased Lafountains can claim credit for several issues impacting you. Quite a gifted family, I might add. And I can speak with authority, since I've been attached to your people for more than a century."

Suzanne laughs. "I *do* love watching you suddenly appear wherever you wish to be."

"Tricks of the trade," he says. "Though, I admit. I still work hard to master my movements."

"Have you brought an extra glass?" she asks. More laughter. "Sorry. Since I'm the only one here drinking, I guess it doesn't matter."

"You're right." Jack's hand glides smoothly through Suzanne's hair, loosening a couple of the daisy blossoms that have become tangled. His skin reveals a sparkling iridescence in the dusk's approaching moonlight, with the same diamond-like shine that's celebrated for reflecting off the Mississippi Sound.

"Were you here for the ceremony? I didn't dare turn around." Suzanne feels dizzy, this time completely related to the delayed effect of three back-to-back champagne flutes.

"This step is necessary—to fulfill your destiny."

"Still . . ."

"It's nothing. You won't be stranded here much longer, Suzanne. We can be together soon enough. If that's what you desire."

What are you talking about, angel? I've not agreed to anything.

Jack's words are utterly confusing. How does an aborted kiss in his garden warrant this assumption? *I am not stranded. How could I be? I'd have to be dead to be a stranded ghost.*

Suzanne doesn't plan to experience her first panic attack, on her second wedding day, but she fears it's at bay: a racing heartbeat, excessive sweat, blurred vision. *Could this be what's behind the spirits' demands? Is there a preordained order that I pay with my own life?*

Though she yearns for the reassurance of an angel's touch, Suzanne considers the impossibility of this situation. When Jack leans in to kiss her underneath the glow of a summer's moon, Suzanne pulls away quickly, nearly slipping from the rock she's teetering on. "This crosses the line, and you know it. I don't have a lot of memories from my childhood, Jack, but I clearly recall, even from a young age, that you belonged to Madelaine."

The energy of the moment shifts immediately as Jack's visage filters away. She's nearly finished with the champagne bottle when Max finds her.

"What are you doing way out here, Suzanne? Our guests have walked this entire plantation searching for you. Who's out here with you?"

"Nobody," she answers. "I needed to breathe."

"Don't lie. You've been missing for at least an hour. And I just heard you babbling something about your childhood." He asks, "Again, who were you talking to?"

"An old friend," she answers. "I only wanted a word with him."

"It must've been one hell of a conversation, Suzy." Max takes the handkerchief he stuffed in his shirt's front pocket and wipes the sweat from his face and neck. "Classic Suzanne behavior, that's what this is."

"Calm down, Max. No harm's been done," Suzanne says. "Let's go have our toast. Cut the cake."

"Much too late for that," Max fumes. "People started leaving some time ago." Suzanne assumes Max is exaggerating because she hears music and laughter tumbling from the direction of the antebellum home. The sounds of a jazzy saxophone drift from the gazebo as they head to the big house.

"I want a word with your friend. His behavior is highly unacceptable."

"Might be a challenge," Suzanne says. "He's gone."

"Gone? Nobody's completely gone, Suzanne. Where does he live? I want to talk to the man."

Suzanne keeps walking.

Max stops. "Of course, I get it. He's that kind of friend, so not officially in *this* world. It's our wedding night, Suzy, and here I am, out searching for you in the dark instead of enjoying myself. And when I *do* find you, you're sitting at a creek's edge, celebrating with a ghost. Why did I ever believe marriage to you might work?"

Suzanne takes Max's hand. "Stop overreacting. I wasn't gone that long. Let's go back to the party. And for the record, he's an angel, not a ghost."

The steps of Beauvoir beckon Suzanne and Max, the steps thousands have climbed for over 150 years. Their wedding guests, lining the front porch railings, cheer and applaud them as they step onto the gallery. Suzanne feels joy lift from within as they cross the threshold into the historical home's main parlor—she senses that generations of her family have fallen in love in this very place. She hears tunes from the late nineteenth-century lift from the piano in the corner as a banker's son proposes to his sweet girlfriend, Jeanne, sitting on a circular tufted chair. She sees a World War II co-pilot stealing the prettiest pianist in the room from his best buddy after listening to her play a beloved '40s song.

Get ahold of yourself, honey.

Margie signals that it's time for the toast and cutting the cake. Suzanne follows Max's lead. For now, she's incapable of handling more. Embraced by an overwhelming ache of love inside this magnificent home, Suzanne feels as if she has truly come home. Tears pool in her eyes as she presses a hand over her chest to ease the pressure there.

"Don't cry yet, Suzanne," Margie says. "We haven't toasted you two."

Suzanne and Max reach for their filled flutes and await Margie's tribute. Poised, ready to celebrate, Suzanne hears the piano in the parlor trickle out the melodic notes of "I'll Be Seeing You" loudly and clearly—she might as well have time-traveled back nearly seventy years.

Max looks at Suzanne as if she has lost her mind when she starts to hum the same tune. He follows with a smart-ass quip about Suzanne surpassing her alcohol tolerance for the day.

"Let her alone, Max," a friend shouts. "She's already tired of you." The comment draws a laugh and buys Margie the second she needs to regroup her toast.

"I'd like to remind everyone these two met at Remé's fiftieth birthday bash. And I take full credit for introducing them to each other. There's never been a couple more deserving of a second chance at love. Congratulations, you two. To Suzanne and Max."

They raise their glasses to meet the group's toast. Over the top of Suzanne's champagne flute, she spots the shimmering specter of a woman wearing a red and white polka-dot party dress, poised at the piano near the home's entrance. When she senses a less benevolent phantom hovering in the background, appearing to embrace something on its side, Suzanne panics, for simultaneously facing both is overwhelming.

The apparition seated at the piano bench rapidly flits toward Suzanne, then soars through her midsection, rendering her nearly breathless. If Suzanne hadn't grabbed onto Max's arm, the force of the ghost slamming through her, consuming her energy for its purpose, might very well have knocked her to the floor.

Though Suzanne barely taps her crystal flute against Max's, it shatters and bursts. Either the ghosts garnished sufficient energy from the wedding guests to stir up a dramatic exit, or Suzanne has yet to harness the latent energy of her right hand that merges the past with the present.

It's far past the time to *right* a wrong and set the spirit world straight.

33

Addy

Memphis, Tennessee, Winter 1945

The small, hardening bump beneath Addy's waistline defied camouflage. Addy shoved her skinny, belted A-line dresses to the back of her closet. They no longer fit. Though relieved about a decrease in weight gain during the past two weeks, Addy feared it was a sure sign of trouble.

Only recently, Addy had tried to build an emotional bond with the tiny life she carried. When resentment surfaced, she fought to set those feelings aside. Her child, Cash's child, deserved to enter a world filled with love and endless possibilities.

Is there any hope for me to love this baby?

At the end of her next appointment, the obstetrician asked her to join him in his office.

"Come in, dear. Shut the door." Dr. Lemoine paced back and forth in front of the bay window of his home office.

"What's wrong, doctor?" Addy asked nervously. "It's bad news, isn't it?"

"My dear, there's no easy way to say this," he said. "Your

baby's measurements have not increased since your last visit." Dr. Lemoine's glance topped his spectacles, confirming that she was listening.

Addy felt the entire room grow dark and sad. She fought back the tears. "Go on."

"You must go to Memphis and consult with my colleague, Dr. Winn. He has an excellent reputation for handling . . . well . . . this type of complication."

"And if I don't go? See Dr. Winn?"

"Your baby has little chance of surviving a full-term pregnancy." Dr. Lemoine's voice lingered like a doomsday proclamation. "Everything's been arranged for you," he continued. "I understand you have an aunt who lives in Memphis, right? Plan to stay with her until we transfer you to a girls' home near the hospital."

"I don't understand," Addy said. "What do you mean everything's arranged?"

"I've spoken to Jeanne and James. They're prepared to help you. Your grandfather has already contacted Dr. Winn and discussed what may be ahead for you."

"Dr. Lemoine. Look at me, please!" she yelled. "This is me. Addy. My body, my baby. Not my grandmother's baby. Certainly not Papa's. I deserve to have a say in what's happening."

"Of course, dear. You see, I needed Jeanne to help prepare you—from a woman's perspective," he explained. "Nothing about what awaits you will be easy."

And here I thought I'd solved my predicament—I married Cash.

He rubbed his eyes after removing his glasses. "The simple truth is that your child may not survive. Supposing the baby can be saved, you'll likely deliver by Cesarean section. And that's if, and only if, *your* health can be sustained."

Addy choked on a sob. *Did he say we both could die?*

Dr. Lemoine sat, then moved his chair closer to Addy. He

placed his hand paternally on her knee. "You need to be prepared for another difficult possibility. Your pregnancy may require termination if a miscarriage doesn't occur naturally. Of course, you'll be sedated. Probably won't remember a thing." He rolled his chair back and said, "Perhaps this is for the best."

"This *does not* make any sense, Dr. Lemoine."

The obstetrician scratched his head and avoided direct eye contact with Addy when he said, "I don't perform any form of abortion, but Dr. Winn does. Nonetheless, we're not focused on that today. If you can carry to term, Dr. Winn is the finest specialist in the South to deliver your baby. You'll stay near the hospital and his office, at the Mockingbird, where he can examine you often."

Numbly, Addy rose and walked to the door. Before she placed her hand on the doorknob, she turned and said, "I don't want an abortion, doctor. I want to have other children."

"Only if your life is at risk. Your records, dear?" Dr. Lemoine rose from his chair and handed Addy a thick brown envelope with large numbers taped to the flap on the backside.

"Thank you."

"Safe travels, Addy. I look forward to seeing you again, here in the Pass, in a few months."

After listening to Dr. Lemoine's dire warnings, Addy feared the worst. Not only did she carry a baby conceived during a non-consensual sexual encounter, but the baby's life, and now her life, were no longer guaranteed. And even if she and the baby both survived her pregnancy, a risky childbirth and difficult recovery period followed.

I only wanted to follow my visions. Wanted to fall in love. Who could have predicted this nightmare?

Cash kept writing letters, and Addy read each one yet refused to answer the *only* question for which he demanded a response. Would there be a child with thick, silky black hair and cerulean blue eyes, a little person who'd admire him and call him Daddy once he returned home?

Even if the baby survived. Even if Cash returned from the war unscathed. Even if Addy ignored Papa's proposal to turn the infant over for adoption, the family secret had been uncloaked by a mere appointment with an obstetrician. With more than 100 years of history in the Pass, this aristocratic clan would never embrace a child conceived in violence and without consent as their own. Papa had made that abundantly clear.

The officer. The rape. The marriage. The baby. The monumental mess.

Addy accepted Mimi's offer to take the L&N Coast Train to Memphis, stopping briefly in New Orleans. They decided to leave by January 6, before Twelfth Night celebrations would be privately held. Despite the war, Mimi predicted Mardi Gras krewe members from New Orleans to Mobile would secretly reignite their revelries.

A wave of dizziness washed over Addy while stuffing a pajama set and housecoat inside her jam-packed suitcase. She grasped the knob of the footboard for support. "Honey, are you okay?" Mimi placed her hand against Addy's forehead as if she were a child suddenly spiking a fever.

"Please don't do that, Mimi. I'm only lightheaded. The spells come and go." Addy shook her head back and forth quickly to will away the fuzziness in her head. "I need to sit for a moment." She had felt a tightness in her chest earlier, but failed to mention it. "I'm afraid to ask you something, Mimi, but I just don't think I have a choice," Addy began, folding and refolding a bulky sweater on her lap. "Did you cast a hoodoo spell on my baby?"

"How dare you ask such a thing, Adelaide," Mimi yelled. "You know very well that rootwork's not for harm." Mimi rose from sitting next to the suitcase and began pacing, attempting to rein in her anger. "I conjure for health, protection, love, and money, but you already know this."

Addy fired back, "That's not an answer, Mimi." She lifted

the folded sweater for Mimi to include in the suitcase. "Maybe you started with a protection spell, then decided Cash needed punishment instead. But now I'm hurting," she cried. A pointless effort because Addy knew no honest response would follow.

"The fact that you're suggesting such a thing, granddaughter, is ludicrous." Mimi slammed the door on her way out of the girls' bedroom.

Slam all the doors you want, woman, but I've been to the potter's shed. I've seen what you've hidden there. Sage, fennel seeds, lodestone, lemongrass, graveyard dirt—and that's just for starters.

Annoyed on the ride to the train depot the next day, Addy glared at Mimi's head from the backseat. How did she *always* have a solution? Serving as the eldest Lafountain enchantress entitled Mimi to boundless matriarchal power as she orchestrated their world. Papa thought he was in control, but he was sadly mistaken.

Early the next day, Addy handed her ticket to the conductor and stepped into the first-class passenger car with Mimi right behind her. Once they found their seats, Addy settled against a window to watch the billowing engine steam blow past. She silently prayed that no one onboard would organize a war sing-along between here and the Crescent City.

Addy's heart pounded as the Coast Train rolled into the L&N Station at the foot of Canal in New Orleans. Even for an hour or two, being back in her hometown thrilled her. Addy swore she spotted Esty standing on the platform as the train rolled to a stop. She grabbed her coat and hurried to see if her eyes had deceived her.

As soon as the conductor released the car's door. Esty raced to greet Addy and Mimi.

"What are you doing here, Esty?" Addy yelled, throwing her arms around her sister's neck. They had not seen each other since Addy's wedding.

"Not so hard, you'll choke me!" Esty said, stepping back.

"Surprise! Spin around, sis. Let me look at you, Addy. Honestly, you're not showing. How do you feel?"

"Sometimes I'm dizzy, sometimes queasy."

"Let me buy you a Coca-Cola. There's got to be a vending machine inside the terminal. Then we can sit and talk until it's time for your next train," Esty said, grabbing Addy's hand and swinging it back and forth. "Oh, hi, Mimi!" Esty turned to greet her grandmother with a wink. Addy gazed across the three-tracked platform to see if her parents were nearby, wondering if they'd come to greet her, too. The gesture wasn't lost on Esty.

"I asked Mama to at least ride the streetcar with me to Canal, but she refused," Esty explained. "Said she couldn't stop me, but she didn't want to see you until you'd taken care of . . . everything."

"Honestly, I don't have a disease, Esty. You know, I *am* a married woman," Addy said. She waited until Mimi went to search for a restroom before saying, "I've no choice but to follow the doctor's instructions. And then there's Papa's mandate. What good am I, God forbid, if Cash doesn't return? And I'm left penniless, raising a baby alone."

Esty frowned. "Nobody's giving you much choice," she said.

Addy learned Macie had turned boy crazy, and Esty's high school graduation was scheduled in the spring. Mama Charlotte still worried she'd be ousted from the Junior League, and their father spent more time in New York City on bank business. Oddly, Esty slipped and confessed that she and Cash had been exchanging letters since he left the States.

"I don't appreciate that, Esty," Addy said. She'd taken too many gulps of her Coke, so now her stomach felt upset.

Esty glared at her sister. "Why ever not? Cash wrote to me first," she said. "I thought it was important to answer him. I mean, he *is* overseas fighting for all of us. It'd be cruel to ignore him. *You* need to answer his letters, sis."

"Just because I don't answer quickly doesn't give you license to write my husband, instead." The fogginess in Addy's head worsened. She struggled to grab hold of the correct words in her head before speaking.

"I might agree with you, Addy, 'cept you're not writing him at all."

Addy rolled her eyes and stared straight ahead. She now wished her sister had gone shopping with Mama Charlotte instead of meeting her train.

"What if I were writing notes to your boyfriend?"

"Don't have one, so it doesn't matter," Esty snapped. Something's up, Addy thought. Esty *always* had a boyfriend.

"It's not right, Esty. Please stop."

"Your problems are much bigger than me writing to Cash," Esty said. "Think about it. If you answered his letters, he might not be so lonely and less interested in corresponding with me."

My husband is writing letters—to my sister!

"You do understand what happens when girls check in at the Mockingbird, don't you? What will Cash do if he ever finds out?" Esty looked at her wristwatch, checking the time.

"Kill me," Addy said, as Esty's words sliced straight through her heart. "Or leave me."

"If this were happening to me, Addy, I'd keep my baby."

"Well, it's not." Her sister's criticism smacked of ignorance. Esty had no concept of Addy's muddled situation. "Promise me, Esty, never a hint of this to anyone."

"Or?"

"Or I'll reveal your dirty little secrets. Like how you lost your virginity to Duncan Wilkes four years ago and are still sleeping with him. I'm surprised you're not the pregnant one."

"That's a bitchy thing to say."

"To one who's being one."

They sat in silence. A barely cordial farewell sent Addy and Mimi on their way, northbound to a city Addy had only visited once. They were exhausted when they reached Memphis. Aunt Lou met their train as promised. She served a hot meal of seared roast and vegetables after they'd settled in and unpacked.

Sitting on the examining table in the doctor's office the following day, Addy hoped to hear good news. Dr. Winn was very thorough as he consulted several large medical books—he jotted notes in-between examining and measuring her abdomen. She handed the nurse her urine sample and turned her head when blood was drawn.

"Please get dressed, miss. I'll join you and your grandmother in my office in a moment," Dr. Winn said.

Addy glanced at her grandmother, who looked puzzled. "He doesn't know I'm married?" Addy asked.

"Of course he does."

"Then why did you look as confused as me just now?"

"I never made a connection until Dr. Winn asked about my pregnancies," Mimi said. "I had extremely high blood pressure when I was expecting your father and spent the last three months of my pregnancy laid up in bed."

Dr. Winn did not report that everything was fine.

"Your blood pressure is dangerously high, my dear. I'm diagnosing you with toxemia of pregnancy. Your life, I fear, is very much at risk."

"Oh my God." Here was the confirmation she'd dreaded.

Mimi moved her chair closer to Addy's to provide comfort and moral support.

"What does she do now?" Mimi asked.

Facing Addy, Dr. Winn said, "Miss Lafountain, you absolutely must rest. No housework, no chores, no pressures whatsoever. Bedrest is probably in your future." He offered a bit of reassurance to Mimi. "Since your granddaughter's staying at the Mockingbird, I'll check on her at least once a week until she delivers. You can count on that."

"Thank you, doctor. My sister lives around the corner, so she'll be looking in on Addy, too."

Dr. Winn nodded his head. "If there's a dramatic change, I'll take the baby. I won't risk your granddaughter's life."

The OB's words bleated like squawking seagulls, a sound

that generally comforted Addy but now prompted abject fear. She summoned her maternal instinct, vowing to take every precaution possible to ensure her baby had a fighting chance at life. Which meant she had a better chance of surviving, too.

As Mimi helped Addy get settled at the Mockingbird, she said, "No one uses her real name here, Addy. That way, if you ever meet up again with anyone you've met here, it'll appear that you've been mistaken for someone else. It would be best if you chose a name," Mimi said.

"Bess. I like that name."

Mimi shook her head. "But that sounds quite close to your sister's name . . ."

Addy spent her days watching the other girls complete their chores. The cold winter months disappeared as the spring of 1945 promised a fresh start. In idle moments, Addy sketched evening gowns in a notebook, shading in the folds of satin cascading to the floor while clasping the amethyst bracelet Mimi had given her on her wedding day.

One evening, Aunt Lou stopped by with a large envelope. Enclosed were several letters from Cash, one with a postmark dating from September '44, written a month after he'd deployed to Germany. Within, she read the truth of Cash's ordeal.

War is horrible. Death is everywhere. Nothing like what I'd imagined. It's not any safer from the air. If I don't make it back home, please know how much I love you, Addy. I've never been prouder than on the day we married. You agreed to be my wife, even after I hurt you so badly. Please write to me. Let me know. Am I going to be a father?

Four months after Addy's initial examination with Dr. Winn, she reached for the nurse's hand to steady her when he announced, "You're nearly there, Addy. I've scheduled you for a C-section at Worthington General on Friday. There's simply no other choice. I'll send a car to pick you up at 5 a.m.," he said.

"Okay."

"A couple of things you need to know. You won't see the child."

"Why not?" Even though the girls at Mockingbird had warned her, Addy didn't believe she might not meet her baby. After diligently caring for herself so both she and her child had the best chances for survival, how could she be denied seeing her infant?

"We believe it's best. This way, you won't form an attachment," Dr. Winn continued. "It's easier when you return home. Easier to pick up your life right where you left it."

Tears slid along Addy's cheeks. She no longer envisioned Adelaide's Designs, the haute couture dress shop she'd yearned to establish, now assured of Papa's assistance. Instead, she leaned her head back and sobbed, gripped by the pain of never laying eyes upon the child she had fought so hard to carry.

On April 29, 1945, she gave birth to a five-pound, four-ounce girl she insisted upon calling Madelaine. Dr. Winn disappeared immediately following her surgery. Hours later, after the twilight anesthesia had worn off, Addy woke up and begged his stand-in obstetrician to let her hold her daughter. The older physician obliged. Two nurses kept close watch when he stepped away.

Nearly half an hour later, a woman in a white jacket walked in to collect the infant. Addy kissed her daughter goodbye. "I love you, sweet Madelaine," she whispered. "I'll love you forever." As she held her newborn, Addy delicately wrapped the amethyst bracelet around Madelaine's tiny wrist and told the nurse that the heirloom must accompany her child. Addy believed she was protecting herself and her future by gifting Madelaine with a perfect life filled with adoration and love—intangible jewels she couldn't provide when the patriarch of the Lafountain family held the purse strings and called the shots.

No granddaughter of Papa's would raise a child born of rape and filth. Not on his watch.

So wrapped up in her farewell was she, Addy neither saw nor sensed the benevolent presence hovering in the corner of the delivery room. Jack cast a glowing ray of warmth to comfort Addy when she felt her heart ripped in half. Nothing had prepared her to part from her infant child. No words could describe her pain, her gulf of regret.

She had no way of knowing that her decision to relinquish Madelaine would dramatically change her life and affect future generations in ways no one could fathom.

As Addy slipped into a feverish sleep in her private hospital room later that night, it occurred to her that rebuffing Mimi's offer to learn conjuring, the folk magick Lafountain women had passed down through the ages, may have been the worst decision of her life.

34

Suzanne

Isla Mujeres, Mexico, August 2013

On Saturday afternoon, Suzanne and Max plow through the grueling immigration process at Cancún International Airport. After they clear customs with no incident, a sea of salespeople peddling zipline adventures and Mayan day trips press toward them. Max issues a two-word predictable response that starts with an "F" and ends with one, too.

The heat is oppressive here—so oppressive that it's challenging to breathe deeply. It's August, with a heat index inching over 110 degrees. Suzanne doesn't remember one single conversation about traveling to Mexico for a wedding trip. Max informed her of their honeymoon location. And that was that.

After spending fifteen minutes trying to locate their driver, Suzanne spots a man waving a whiteboard with awkwardly printed letters: "Hola, Señor Martin!"

"Max, look." Suzanne motions for him to follow. "To the left. See the driver's sign?"

"I got it, Suzy." Max dramatically signals for the man to

grab their bags.

The driver pours two shots of silver tequila and hands them back as they buckle up—his official welcome to Mexico.

"Hola," Suzanne says. "What a lovely way for you to welcome visitors."

"Salud."

"It's added to the fare, don't kid yourself, woman," Max says.

"You've reservations, yes?" The driver collects their shot glasses and tucks them away in an old leather bag poised on the passenger seat. "You know where you go?"

"Of course, of course," Max says. "Gran Puerto. We need the ferry to Isla Mujeres."

"First time in Cancún?"

"Goodness, no. We've been here before," Suzanne says.

"But not with each other. It's our first trip together," Max adds quickly, touching Suzanne's hand. She smiles, then settles in for the ride. Max continues to text someone as if his life hangs in the balance with each message.

She thinks of Jack—wishes their last encounter had not been so . . . unsettling.

They barely arrive in time to catch the island ferry, so the only remaining seats are atop the deck, where tourists sing loudly and compete for a local guitarist's attention. After disembarking, they weave a pathway through the island's port entrance, each pulling one suitcase filled with beachwear, t-shirts, and shorts. When Suzanne passes a shop that smells of coconut oil, she pops in to pick up more sunscreen.

A beach breeze blows through her hair as she exits and meets Max curbside. He flashes an intimate smile that only lovers share. Suzanne knows how much he loves watching her walk, her curves teasingly visible through her white cotton sundress. She can't help but return one.

If only you weren't so wicked, Max. Surely wish Madelaine had left behind a spell book to handle falling out of lust with a man who must be admonished. But lust knows no logic. And love knows even less.

Here in paradise, Suzanne can only hope for a respite from trapped ghosts. Thank God the phantom who slammed through her midsection on her wedding day has not resurfaced. She gets that there's an intense connection between her and this ghost, but fails to understand its desperation. She is certain that the entity is *not* Madelaine. Though the scents have something in common, the aroma traveling with her mother's spirit is fresher and rounded with nature scents, compared to an older, heavier, more intoxicating bouquet associated with the strong ghost's presence.

She arrives on the island prepared to begin Max's ending. Brides don't usually pack a small spell pouch and several ounces of diluted belladonna oil in a cosmetic bag. Far from home, and on her own for this leg of her journey, there's reassurance with drops of nightshade at her fingertips in the event of an emergency.

They're already in a cab when Suzanne regrets not requesting a different route to the other side of the island. She looks up in time to see them whip past the entrance of Seaside Cemetery on the way to the eastern side of the island. Suzanne clamps her eyes shut and pushes against the sudden rush of discordant voices—those stranded and searching for an agent who'll speak for them and set them free.

Leave. Me. Alone.

The driver screeches to a stop at the foot of a villa topping a hill. Overlooking the cerulean blue waters of the Caribbean Sea, where it meets the Gulf of Mexico, the vacation home offers a spectacular view of blended blue and green hues.

"This is breathtaking, Max," she says.

"Only the best for my bride." He tips the cabbie and quickly thanks him. In Spanish.

"You speak the language, Max? How do I not know this?"

"Probably a few things you don't know, Suzy." He grabs

both suitcases. "It goes both ways. Bet they're a few things I don't know about you." Max squints his eyes against the blinding sunlight here at the edge of the island. "No elevator here, babe. We're taking the steps."

A harsh, blunt chill in Max's stare slices through her. Suzanne senses a shift in their relationship balance. Are her calculations off? Lately, Suzanne has banked on having the upper hand with Max as she works with spells and trusts her spirit guides to project a timeline. Now, she must consider that Max may harbor harmful plans of his own. And it doesn't help that communication with others is hampered since his command of the local language is impressive while hers relies upon a translation app. Suzanne must proceed with her plan to slowly add toxins to Max's drinks while not letting down her guard for one single moment.

And that includes keeping Max satisfied, so no suspicions arise.

He pauses at the foot of the uneven, cobbled steps, one foot poised on the first one. "Are you coming?"

"Yes, of course." She begins the climb to the entrance of the villa. And only glances down once to gauge the depth of one's potential fall.

When they reach the bedroom, Suzanne opens the French doors facing the sea to air out the room. She hears the pop of a champagne cork, the sparkly bubbles as the liquid hits the cut glass. Max saunters onto the balcony with his predictable panache.

"To my Suzy," he says, handing her a glass.

They lightly tip the flutes' edges. "And to my Max. You leave no stone unturned. An excellent touch after our 700-mile journey."

Max wraps his arms around Suzanne's waist. They watch the soft movement of the deep blue water, small waves lapping against the blackened coral at the second low tide. She doesn't pull away.

"How long have you been fluent?"

Max laughs. Gulps his champagne. Suzanne knows he'll become bored with this feminine drink and soon uncap the bourbon he bought in Miami. She'll be ready when he makes the switch.

"Odd question, love. You *should* know the answer."

"Well, I don't. Or I wouldn't be asking."

His grip around Suzanne's waist tightens. Max kisses the top of her head when her hair whispers in the wind, its golden highlights reflecting in the sun.

"I've spoken Spanish all my life."

"During the entire time I've known you, Max, I've never heard you speak one word of Spanish."

"There's no reason for me to disguise being bilingual. Suppose that's what you're implying. That's crazy."

Suzanne reaches for the champagne bottle Max has set atop the mosaic bistro table and pours herself another glass. As she leans against the balcony's railing, Suzanne imagines how much more she'll learn about Max during their wedding trip, in addition to watching his confidence and ease increase by the minute.

Thank goodness for the stand-in minister willing to perform a ceremony but delay the marriage license's final signature. And willing to procrastinate with filing the paperwork. For a handsome fee, of course. She has no choice but to stay focused while straddling life in two worlds: one of the living, the other of the dead.

"Where are you, Suzy? You've quit listening to me."

She doesn't answer his question. Instead, Suzanne takes Max's hand and walks to the bedroom.

"Join me in bed. Leave the doors open so we can watch the sunset."

Suzanne slips from her dress and crawls into bed seconds before Max pins her against the white leather headboard. She grabs onto the top groove of the board and hopes it holds.

Max enters her hungrily and climaxes within seconds. She's not far behind him. Never desirous of much foreplay, Suzanne falls asleep, satisfied. Sex with this man is aggressive, hot, and selfish. And unabashedly addictive. Sustaining their erotic relationship is Suzanne's insurance policy for lingering long enough to complete her directive.

An hour later, she wakes, startled—a breeze of Caribbean air drenched in salt-water vapor fills the bedroom suite. When she calls for Max, there's no answer. Has he gone to pick up groceries? While he's out, it's the perfect time to prepare for the final stretch. Reaching to the bottom of her cosmetic bag, she locates the bottle of liquid nightshade and double-checks the strength of its plastic wrap. After pulling on a pair of latex gloves, she unfolds the nightshade plant wrapped in a red flannel pouch, including its root and berries, then unpacks the mortar and pestle tucked in her suitcase. She remembers Enola's strict instruction that three or four grains ground from the root, or five smashed berries, is an excellent place to start.

As Suzanne grinds the root down to tiny grains, she hears Enola's voice—slipping into the dialect of her Creole people—repeat in her mind: "Jast a liddle, or 'da man will go cray-cray. That stalk make hallucinations."

No part of Suzanne's heart, mind, or spirit wants to kill Max. Fulfilling the demands of her ancestral ghosts is all that's necessary. Making someone pay for a past transgression is surely open to interpretation. She'll begin the process at her end and trust the appropriate retribution will follow at another's behest. Several days of doctoring Max's bourbon will make him very ill, and with any luck, prompt the spirit world to seize upon her efforts and collectively determine what's next for him.

Suzanne locates the bottle of bourbon Max purchased at the airport, opens it, and taps a few grains of the ground-up root through a tiny funnel. After sloshing the bottle for a few minutes, there's no evidence of the nightshade.

When Suzanne is reminded that there's only champagne in the refrigerator, she grabs her purse and locks the front door. She remembers a small market across the street from Iglesia de Concepcion Immaculada, an alabaster white Catholic church within walking distance of the villa. When she hears the voices of men arguing loudly in Spanish, she quickens her step.

"Tienes que pagar! Miles, debes miles!"

"Estoy trabajando en ello, no es fácil ahora."

"Estás fuera de tiempo, amigo."

Suzanne immediately recognizes Max's voice, discernable above the others, as she approaches the corner at Plaza Principal. Even with her limited knowledge of Spanish, she understands that he's being threatened about paying thousands of dollars. Unnerved by the tone of their voices, she ducks along an alleyway one street over and slips into the back of the church. She sits in the last church pew nearest the door propped ajar, where she can watch the men arguing with Max when she turns slightly to the right.

In deference to her surroundings, Suzanne crosses herself and kneels. Within moments, a strong vanilla scent emerges. At the opposite end of the pew, the kneeling bench squeaks when it's lowered. She opens one eye to see who's intruding on her meditation.

"Jack?" She whispers loudly. "What are you doing here?"

He flips the kneeling bench and slowly glides to her side of the church pew. "Look, I don't have much time to explain . . ."

"I'm in the middle of something here, Jack," she hisses.

"Bullshit. Come outside and talk to me."

She doesn't budge.

"Now!"

Sensing his urgency, she has no choice but to leave the church and follow him. They quickly pass the basketball goals set up for neighborhood children and enter another alleyway, farther from Max's loud and heated argument.

"Explain why you are hiding from your husband. In a church," Jack demands. "You do know about the generational debt Max is buried under, yes? The Martins have been involved with some very unsavory people for decades," Jack says hurriedly.

"Who does his family owe money to?"

"Men you don't want to mess with. I'm guessing Max never mentioned his grandfather's connection to the Mexican mafia?"

"The Martins are mafia members?" Suzanne can't help but laugh at Jack's allegations. "This is outrageous, even for you."

"No, the *Martinezes* are involved with the mafia." Jack provides a missing puzzle piece and allows the information to settle. "Don't know the details, but I'm fairly certain Paxton Martinez changed his last name to Martin when he became a U.S. citizen."

"Ahhh, of course he did."

It has taken a trip to Mexico for Suzanne to connect the loose ends of Max's life story. Clearly, Max targeted her some time ago. He must have learned about Madelaine's accident, and the multiple cash settlements disbursed. Not to mention her divorce settlement, still paying out.

In a word or two: her fortune.

"Don't you see, love, that you're in serious danger?" Jack asks. He embraces her affectionately, with a warm-all-over, covered-in-quilts feeling only an angel can invoke. "Let's get you back to the States before something horrible happens. There's an available flight from Cancún into Houston tonight."

"I can't leave, Jack. I'm on my *wedding* trip, for Christ's sake. Remember?" Her reasoning falters when she listens to his voice. Suzanne shudders. "I've got roots to work with, spells to complete. Unsettled trapped ghosts demanding action. I cannot leave yet."

"Explain this to me again?"

Suzanne runs through a year's worth of inexplicable events. She describes the malevolent spirit who hovers and threatens when she's with Max. She recounts several encounters with Madelaine's spirit, which vacillates between warning and praising her. She tries to explain the power of the phantom whose presence nearly engulfs her, the one from decades ago that steals her energy and her breath.

Yet, none of this is news to an angel.

"But you don't love Max," Jack says. "Yes, I've heard your reasons for feigning a marriage to him, but in the end, it makes no sense to me. I'm a spirit, too, so I should know!"

"No, you're *not* a spirit, Jack. You're an angel. And a family one at that," she whispers. "You know our Lafountain history better than I do." She calmly explains that her motivation involves more than blindly following instructions mandated by her ancestral ghosts. "It's about honoring my mother and assisting her journey—to exit the In-Between and arrive beyond the ether—to cast the cross-over spell that will offer her a peaceful afterlife."

"Have you ever considered . . ." Jack hesitates. "That you may be misinterpreting? Do you believe these ghosts, your mother's spirit, have your safety in mind? Is there an evil intention?"

"My mother?" Suzanne hisses. "My mother is not an evil spirit, Jack." Suzanne turns away. "Go home. You're not needed here. I can handle this." She returns to the church and slides into the back pew.

Jack follows her and flips up the bench again to make his point. "I love you, and I'm very concerned. Surely you realize this."

"You love every woman in my family, Jack. It's what you do."

"I'm not leaving this island until you do, Suzanne. I don't trust that son of a bitch. Think of what I'm saying."

When the priest walks from the confessional, he heads directly to Suzanne. Neither one notices Max waiting in the shadows of the church's vestibule or rinsing his bloody hands in the holy water when no one is watching.

Only Jack watches the priest place an exquisite hard-carved cross choker in the palm of Suzanne's right hand before kneeling to pray with her. It's the same one Jack handed to the cleric earlier—the very same one he presented to Louisa, on the night her daughter, Jeanne, was born.

A family heirloom worn by Lafountain enchantresses for more than 150 years, designed to protect and comfort.

35

Max

Isla Mujeres, Mexico, August 2013

Max narrowly evades running into Suzanne after beating up one of the goons who followed them to Isla Mujeres. He slips into the tiled vestibule at Iglesia de Concepcion Immaculada to seek sanctuary. That's when he spies Suzanne kneeling on a prayer bench. With a priest praying at her side.

Freaky weird. What is Suzy—a woman who reads tarot, talks to the dead, and suddenly owns her family's hoodoo heritage—doing in a Catholic church in Mexico? Kneeling? *Something's not right.* Max hasn't practiced his faith since his father's death, yet he readily admits his shortcomings in refusing to attend Mass. He doesn't cloak his lack of faith in a masquerade.

Max doesn't lie about hating God.

This church scene is the wackiest Suzy thing he has witnessed. It might even be sacrilegious. Is she confessing? Why not meet the priest in the confessional? Here's a thought: Maybe she's trying to leave her conjuring ways behind.

Max ducks out before Suzanne spots him and jogs back to their villa. He's showering when he hears a splash in the pool outside the main bedroom, signaling his bride is back from the church. When he walks onto the veranda surrounded by pink Mandevilla creeping through panels of white lattice, he trips over Suzanne's clothing strewn across the planked flooring. She's swimming laps in the nude. Again. *What is the deal with Suzanne getting naked in a pool? Probably does some freaky hoodoo when no one's looking.*

"You couldn't wait for me?" he asks. Max throws his towel to the side and jumps in.

Suzanne plunges underwater and swims to the opposite side. Not to be outdone, Max follows her. She retaliates by swimming laps. The chase is on until Suzanne pauses to catch her breath. Max sighs as though the world's burdens lay upon his shoulders when he stops swimming, mid-pool, and announces, "I know you're in love with the island of women and are having a freaky relationship with swimming naked, but I've got some bad news: We need to relocate for a week or so."

"We just arrived. Why do we . . .?" She whines just enough to irritate him.

Max snaps back. "Look, if we need to leave sooner than planned, Suzy, that's God's truth. We're not safe here." His phone rings, and he eases quickly into speaking Spanish. As the conversation ends, he returns to English. "Your tan is as gorgeous as it's going to get, and I'm damned tired of dodging iguanas by the rocks."

"Okay, Max. No need to get yourself worked up."

"Is it ever enough?" Max yells. Suzanne hoists herself from the deep end to sit at the pool's edge. Max climbs out, reaches for his towel, and instead of wrapping himself, he pitches it toward Suzanne.

"Cover yourself, please," he says. "I've no idea who's watching the villa." Suzanne snuggles into its oversized softness as dusk falls. Still, she doesn't budge from the poolside.

Max's mood sours after returning from the bedroom, clad in one of the villa's guest robes. He plops on a lounge chair facing the sea. His twilight meeting with two Latino men failed miserably. Despite spending most of his adult life working against the endless pit of debt he inherited when his father died, Max learned tonight that much more money is owed. It's never going to end. And he's running thin on resources, even after accessing some of Suzanne's fortune.

"So, who were you talking to a few minutes ago?" she asks.

"No one that you know." Max turns to watch her swim as she reenters the pool. "We'll stay . . . in Mexico . . . for another couple of weeks, but it's urgent, Suzy, that we leave the island as soon as possible. One of my associates has found a secluded house near the Mayan ruins in Tulum, where we can disappear and have privacy."

"It's a lot for me to digest. Since I don't think you're being fully honest with me," she says.

"I'm asking you to trust me. Some things are impossible to explain because, let's face it, you're a latecomer. We'll take the first ferry back to Cancún tomorrow morning. A driver will be waiting to escort us safely to Tulum."

Suzanne swims to Max. When she comes up for air, she says, "You might be happier if you didn't expect too much from people."

"And you might be happier if you didn't settle for too little," he counters. "Ever think of that? You expect everyone to have your back; instead, people take advantage of you. Even the dead."

"You and I disagree on what's important in life. We may have a problem with that. In the future."

Max stands, then gives Suzanne a hand to ease out of the pool. "We have a problem with that now." After he drapes his robe around her shoulders and wraps himself in an extra towel, they walk the perimeter of the villa's property. He's looking for anyone who may be lurking along the narrow road. Or sitting on the stone wall by the sea. Or weaving on scooters, slowing down when they pass the villa.

"Want a glass of bourbon before bed?" Suzanne asks.

"Only if you pour it for me. I've got nothing left today."

Suzanne watches him secure the villa's doors and double-check the lower-level windows before they retire for the night. Despite the warm and balmy August night, she pulls the covers to her neck and asks, "Wake me early enough to pack?"

Max watches her fall asleep, her damp hair circling her cheek. She smells of aloe vera and coconut oil. He wishes the night had no end, for he knows what lies ahead. Max knows what he must do to survive.

I didn't plan to fall in love with you, Suzy. Now, I must let you go. And it will be the hardest thing I'll ever do.

The following two weeks in Tulum are the best days of Max's life, even though it costs him a fortune to lease and guard the house nestled in the mountainous area near the Mayan ruins. They swim in the Caribbean, walk along the beaches made famous in Corona beer advertisements, and charter a ferry to Cozumel for a day. And make love for hours. That's how Max views their physical relationship: founded in love.

The Monday morning after they fly back to Mississippi, Max calls his builder to inquire about the house in the Pass. He learns it's finished. After completing a punch list of minor things that need to be addressed, he texts Suzanne the address on West Beach Boulevard.

He flushes the toilets, runs the faucets, flips the light switches on and off, and locks and unlocks each door. There's nothing awry with the place. He's happy the stained-glass transoms are authentic, for he knows Suzanne will love this feature. She'll be set for life, owning the beach house she always desired. And hopefully, she'll never discover that her wealth entirely funded the project.

As Max waits for Suzanne to arrive, he tries to convince himself that this gesture will balance any future distress Suzanne faces as his wife. Suzanne doesn't spot Max until she's halfway up the front staircase, designed to resemble a Louisiana plantation entrance.

"Whose house is this, Max?" she yells.

"Yours." Then he adds, "And mine." With a mischievous smile.

She pauses at the oversized leaded-glass French doors, standing ajar with a puzzled expression.

"Step inside. I'll be up in a second."

She shakes her head. "Explain why I need to see this client's house."

"You're the client," Max says, rounding the landing on the stairway. "Go on. Explore your wedding gift."

"If it's a joke, Max, I don't think it's amusing. We have a house. Why do we need another one?" She opens one of the French doors and takes a step. The scent of fresh paint is intoxicating.

"The cottage on Davis is a rental for M & R clients. You know that. It was never meant to be home. This is your home. Deed's in *your* name."

Max enters the great room and watches her reaction to the winding staircase in one corner balanced against a kitchen designed for a master chef in the other. A massive stone fireplace that stretches to the ceiling centers the room, along with white leather sectionals that complete a seating formation.

He reaches for Suzanne's hand and leads the way to their main bedroom and en suite. The views across the sparkling white beach and blue-gray water are breathtaking. When Max's phone rings, their honeymoon officially ends—within the walls of a house Max boldly built using stolen funds.

It's John. "Here we go again, dude," John leads with a sigh of disbelief.

"It's never gonna freakin' end, is it?"

"The Harrison County DA refuses to budge on the assault and battery charge, my friend," John says. "I'd hoped that since it's your first official offense, he'd be open to probation, community service."

"Would M & R's construction of low-cost condos in Long Beach count in my favor? You know, as a sign of community service? We're taking a hit with that project."

"Not helpful," John says. "DA's got full knowledge of your charges up in Kentucky. I'm assuming they weren't planning to show their hand before your appearance in court." And then, naturally, Max fails to appear. On the advice of counsel, of course.

"Okay, and?"

After so many years of jumping through hoops, pushing John to create delays, and flat-out lying to everyone, including himself, Max struggles to believe all options are coming to a dead end.

"You're looking at a jail cell, Max. Between these assault charges and what's pending in the Bluegrass state, there's no way you'll avoid serving time."

"I'm paying you to resolve this." Max sees that Suzanne's on the balcony facing the water, lounging on a chair, and missing the crux of his conversation.

"It's what you've been running from for years. I can't fix it anymore," John says. "My hands are tied."

"So, the bullshit over the depositions taking place for Farrah's father's civil suit is just that: *bullshit*?"

"My advice? Do *not* return to your office in New Orleans. Make it impossible to be found."

"What are you saying, John?"

"You know exactly what I'm saying. I don't want to hear from you again until you resurface somewhere else. Safely. Understand, I can't be involved with your disappearance."

"Right."

"Goodbye, my friend."

Max struggles for composure. John hangs up. By now, his attorney has deleted their texts spanning several years. By nightfall, John will have a new cell number and be on his way to putting serious space between himself and his most nefarious client.

There is no fucking way I'm going to jail. For any reason.

For any crime that didn't deserve to be committed.

Farrah knew I didn't want kids. Knew it from the start. One son is enough. Kids take up your life. Ruin your plans. How dare she go behind my back? Refuse to take her birth control pills? Got pregnant on purpose. Not a secret she could hide forever.

Mammoth Cave provided the perfect opportunity for Max to handle his angst with Farrah. During the cave tour, the enormous pit he stumbled upon begged for something—or someone—to fall deep into its abyss. Who stumbles on that type of luck?

Yeah, I did the deed. Left no evidence. No regrets.

36

Addy

Gulf Coast, Summer 1946

They were worlds apart for nearly two years—Addy and Cash.

Safely anchored on American soil, Addy attended classes at Gulf Park College to complete her studies and earn an art degree. Cash ascended to piloting B-24s shortly after landing in Germany because he was so highly skilled, and the demand for pilots was unprecedented. Separated by more than 5,000 miles, they lived dramatically different lives. While Addy battled familial and societal odds to achieve her dream, Cash's bombing missions fought hard to ensure American democracy.

Both were seemingly impossible tasks.

Tragic updates arrived daily in the coastal communities from Bay St. Louis to Ocean Springs. The news of young men's deaths or their life-altering injuries came often. Time marched forward, and with it, the inspiration Addy needed to create a good life for herself, since she had no assurance of Cash's return.

She wrestled with thoughts about Madelaine. Whenever she envisioned her baby's face floating in the periphery of her mind's eye, she brushed the image away along with the tears.

Buried her guilt and forged forward.

After earning her art degree, Addy continued working at Madison's Boutique in Gulfport. Then when she returned from Memphis, Addy started again from the bottom: in alterations. A promotion to head salesgirl followed quickly when Addy displayed talent in courting high-end customers.

Once she'd convinced the shop owner to grant her a little freedom in designing sharp suits and stunning cocktail attire, Addy created one original design after another. She and Dotty made a perfect team: Dotty sewed and helped fit the custom designs for each woman. Soon, Addy's original designs became window dressing at Madison's and outsold everything else in the shop. Theirs was a captive market. When the war's end jumpstarted recovery, Southern women who lived along the Gulf Coast demanded gorgeous fashion for their re-emerging society events.

Cash returned home in the summer of '46, a mere version of the man Addy's chiseled adolescent visions had strummed up. Though his limbs remained intact, he was not the same carefree officer she'd frolicked with at Beauvoir and on Ship Island.

Folks in town talked about the miracle of Cash's survival. During conversations with strangers on the street, Addy responded with a smile while Cash stared straight ahead. Even his best friend, Eddy, acknowledged how dramatically Cash had changed. Addy only learned bits of information about Cash's experience during intimate moments after they'd made love.

Stretched out on the bed in their house on Davis Avenue, which Papa had purchased for them a few months ago, Addy curved the backside of her body next to Cash. Though it was an oh-so-hot-and-humid night, Cash covered her with a sheet and remained eerily still. She glanced over to check if he'd fallen asleep only to find him staring at the ceiling with blank eyes.

She whispered, "What do you see, Cash, when you're quiet?"

Replaying the horrors of war? Night after night?

Cash released a deep breath, born in the depths of his soul. "Bombs. And chaos. Bombs from our plane, bombs from all the planes flying the mission. And houses. Houses with children. Screams. Screams that never stopped. Smoke," he answered, barely audible. "Death. Destruction. Death everywhere."

"Do you think the pictures in your head," she whispered, "will ever disappear?"

"Not likely. They're in my . . . nightmares. No matter how hard I try, I can't push it away. What I did." Addy turned, curled into Cash, and hugged his chest tightly. "Every sight, every smell will stay with me 'til I take my last breath. That's my biggest fear." He turned to face Addy, their bodies skin-to-skin. "But I thought of you and the baby I believed we'd made. It was the one thought that kept me from losing my mind. That and coming home to the Coast."

His palm caressed her abdomen. Addy held her breath. Cash's hand stopped, then his fingers skipped across her belly. This was *not* an intimate gesture. His fingertips didn't tease her skin with desire. Cash repeated the movements as though he was searching, not discovering what he'd expected to find.

Addy reminded herself to breathe and willed her husband's hand to stop exploring. The tears pooling in one eye threatened to slide along her cheek. But she steadied herself.

You won't find what you're searching for, lover. Not where your fingertips wander.

Dr. Winn made a low transverse incision in her abdomen when it was time to wrench her baby out. Much discussion surrounded this effort before Addy's Caesarean. The surgeon took enormous pride in ensuring that any incision scar would be well hidden in the regrowth of her thick black hair.

Then Cash pulled Addy so close it left little room for more than heartbeats between them. He kissed her deeply with a desperate, unsatisfied yearning, and whispered, "We have all the time in the world now to make a baby." The assumption of impending parenthood, which led to their vow exchange nearly two years ago, remained unvoiced.

Cash refrained from asking: *What have you done with my child?*

Instead, he moved expectantly atop her, pressed her legs apart, and kissed her breasts. "I don't want to wait, Addy," he whispered. "It's time, time to be a family." And with this pronouncement, Cash entered her, matching her response with his as her body joined his melodic rhythm.

He must never learn the truth. It would hurt him irreparably. Destroy what remained of him. But if Cash had suspected his wife had been pregnant and given birth, there was no evidence to prove that assumption. Acting as if he were engaged in wartime subterfuge, Papa had covered their trail of deceit. And Addy had cooperated, even adopting a different name while staying at the Mockingbird Home for Girls. The name *Bess* was purely a figment of Addy's imagination. At least, that's what she told herself.

The following day, after a breakfast of eggs, bacon, smoked ham cutlets, fried-green tomatoes, and golden-baked biscuits, Addy suggested plans for the day.

"Papa's friend wants to meet with us, Cash. If you're ready." She began stacking dishes to set in the deep farm sink to soak.

"What about our picnic at Henderson Point? It's Saturday, Addy." His coffee had cooled, so he motioned Addy to top it off. "I've missed being at the beach."

"Papa has a proposition for us."

"So? What of it?"

"He wants to ensure we're set up with a good future." She placed the first of several dishes on the sideboard to dry. She despised discussing finances with Cash. Predicted he'd be defensive, even suspicious of her family's offer of assistance.

Uncertain how to proceed, Addy watched Cash hide behind his newspaper. "Am I so bad off that you think I need help? It's only a little while since I've been back." He folded the sports section in half. "Yeah, it's taking more time to get easy with life, but after what I've experienced . . . Believe me, there're guys much worse off than me."

Addy dried her hands on the tea towel, then draped it over its hook by the window. She looked across their side yard to the white picket fence that served as a backdrop for red rose bushes planted along the property line.

"Do you know who I am?" Cash stepped to the stove to grab the coffee percolator. "I've lost count of combat missions. I . . . *me* . . . I killed people. Helped to destroy at least one city. *Why?* Because I'm an airman, and that's what airmen do." He spun around to face Addy, still standing at the sink. His face was strangely contorted. "But I can't do that anymore," he yelled. "Is it too much to ask for time to figure things out?"

It was too hard to watch Cash, so Addy stared out the window. Cash had returned later than some of his buddies, who'd reported elsewhere for more training after the Germans surrendered. But Cash eventually came home to the Pass.

She finally turned to face Cash. "What did they offer you before your discharge?"

"Like what?"

Addy couldn't help herself. She kept pressing. "You're a pilot, Cash. And a damn good one. Why wouldn't they want you to return to base . . . and maybe teach others?"

"Haven't you heard? The goddamn war is over, Addy. I'm out. I'm discharged. It's finished." He walked outside and slammed the screen door shut.

"Then listen to what Papa and Judge Matterson have to offer. Papa can be here in less than ten minutes, and we can ride to the bank with him," Addy called after him.

Cash stood at the end of the driveway, then turned toward Addy's voice. "Whatever you say, Addy." He exhaled the smoke from his cigarette and threw the butt into the street.

When Papa pulled his '42 black Lincoln Continental parallel to the house, Cash was waiting at the curbside, dressed in a black suit and gray tie, with Addy by his side. For their financial meeting, she'd chosen to wear a blue-and-white striped dress with a cinched waist. When Cash opened the car door, she climbed into the back, leaving the passenger seat open for her husband.

"Good morning, sir. Good to see you. And thank you."

"Don't thank me yet. Not until you hear Walt's proposition," Papa said. He greeted his granddaughter in the back. "And Addy, I have a surprise for you, love."

"You've done so much for us, Papa. You don't need to do anything else."

"Oh, this little nugget isn't coming from me," he said. "Wait and see."

Davis Street was around the corner from The Merchant Bank and Trust on Market Street, so walking to the meeting was possible. But if they had done so, it would have eliminated the shock of watching James Lafountain Jr. approach Papa's car to greet them when they parked.

"Daddy's here?" Addy's excitement bubbled over into nervousness. "Papa, Cash hasn't met Daddy. Is this the best way to introduce them?"

"No time like the present to meet one another. Since you're considering a business deal together," Papa said.

While still somewhat stilted, communication between Addy and her father had improved over the past two years. She had to accept that things would never be wholly right between them, because she recognized disappointment in her father's eyes when it boldly stared back at her.

Since the judge's family had started the bank, he kept an office there. After Papa introduced Cash, they were seated around a cedar conference table. He explained the proposal in detail, because neither Addy nor Cash knew its scope and reach. When Papa reiterated their strategy to take over an established oyster cannery in the Pass, their confused expressions disappeared. Cash provided value to the deal as a returning military member, for he was eligible for low-interest loans. All the other three had to do was name the amount they wanted to borrow, and the deal was essentially locked in place.

Judge Matterson drafted an agreement for Cash to purchase the cannery located along the most extensively developed wharf in Pass Harbor. As local fishermen unloaded their oyster and shrimp haul daily, Cash would oversee the canning process and arrange for the seafood to be shipped worldwide. Papa, the judge, and Addy's father planned to remain silent partners.

As the three men continued to talk around the conference table, Cash released an audible gasp, and Addy's handbag dropped to the floor. She'd had no idea about the extravagance of their proposal. Her eyes immediately darted to her husband, sitting upright in the wingback chair next to her. When she reached for his hand, he withdrew it. She dreaded the aftermath, for Cash had pegged her as a co-conspirator.

The meeting turned into a shouting match.

"You've got to be kidding," Cash yelled. "How long did it take for y'all to hatch this brilliant plan? I want nothing to do with it." He stood. Then looked down at Abby, who stared toward the Gulf's water, searching for endurance. "You knew, didn't you?" he demanded.

"No, I did not," she whispered. *How was this déjà vu?* It surely felt like that impromptu meeting on Papa's and Mimi's side porch—on a sweltering summer night in August 1944 two years ago, when decisions were being made on their behalf with little to no consultation.

"Sit down, Cash. You're embarrassing me."

"Don't be a fool, son. This is a great opportunity. We have the richest oyster reefs in the world located right here in the Pass." The judge rattled off more statistics, but Cash had stopped listening.

"Believe us when we say the demand for oysters and shrimp goes straight up through the Midwest and even farther than that," Papa added.

"If you're concerned with acquiring a fleet of fishing schooners, don't be. We have access to those, too," James Jr. said.

"Of course you do. You people have access to everything."

Between a whirling dervish of statistics and interest rates, including a fabricated crisis involving the local demand for an oyster cannery, Cash gave in and finally signed a stack of documents to end the madness. In doing so, he became part-owner of a business he knew nothing about.

"Don't worry, son. We'll walk you through it," James Jr. said.

No one spoke on the short ride back to their house. After James Jr. dropped Addy and Cash off, he stood in the driveway and waited for Addy to finish talking to her father.

"What the fuck just happened, Addy?"

"Not sure I understand your question. You were there with me."

"I survived hell. I *actually* survived. I return, and I'm gassed up with beginning our lives together. You know, starting a family," he said, pausing just long enough to light a cigarette. "I get a job . . . a decent, good-paying job . . . at a refinery. Then one Saturday, I'm lassoed into co-owning a cannery. I don't know the first fuckin' thing about running a cannery!" He finished that cigarette, then lit another.

"They only want to look after us, so we'll have a solid future. I remember Judge Walt offering Papa his help as early as the morning after we married. I think they've spent considerable time designing a fair deal." Addy stood in the driveway, irritated at Cash's lack of respect for what had been handed to him. Her red high heels rubbed her toes, and all she could think about was going inside and putting her feet up.

"They do want me to run the cannery independently, right?"

"Yes, that's what I understood. Most fellas would be thrilled with an opportunity like this."

"I'm not saying I'm not grateful. I only wished I hadn't been bulldozed." Cash ran his fingers through his thick dark hair, now peppered with more than a sliver of gray. "You could've mentioned it to me. That's all I'm saying."

"Again, I didn't know. But think about it, Cash. Isn't this better than working at that smelly refinery in Gulfport?"

"You don't think a cannery smells bad, too?" he countered before walking toward the house. "What were you and your father discussing?"

"Nothing important."

"I don't believe you."

"We'll talk later, Cash, when you're not so angry."

"He's getting that dress shop for you, isn't he?" Cash's voice rose, agitated. "So this is the deal? You hand me over to run the damn cannery. Then, you get your goddamn dress shop. Who *are* you?"

"I don't appreciate your attitude, Cash. I've done nothing to deserve this hatefulness."

"You're correct! You've done absolutely nothing. You didn't get pregnant on that night nearly two years ago, and you're still not pregnant after I've been back for months. What is *wrong* with you?"

Their argument attracted attention from several concerned neighbors huddled across the street at the end of a widower's driveway.

"I don't know, baby. I don't know," Addy said, reaching for her husband, attempting to soothe his feelings. "We'll just keep practicing?"

Cash grabbed Addy by the elbow and shoved her into the side door with no glance over his shoulder to see who might have been watching, horrified.

Later that evening, after Addy had fallen asleep, Cash slipped out of bed. He closed the bedroom door, then wandered along the cottage's narrow hallway. Before picking up the telephone tucked in the phone niche, he listened for any sounds from the bedroom.

Cash dialed a New Orleans phone number and prayed that Esty would pick up.

"Hello," Esty answered on the second ring, her voice cautious, expectant.

"Thank God it's you," Cash said.

"It's good to hear your voice," she said. "Is everything okay?"

Cash babbled, cupping his left hand near his mouth, emptying his heart into the receiver, hoping against all odds that a solution rested on the receiving line. "No, nothing is okay. You were right, Esty. Addy's got a rough spot, where her skin feels bumpy, not smooth . . . where you said it might be." Cash whispered as his voice threatened to disappear entirely. "I'm not crazy. I know it wasn't there before . . ."

"Tell me what to do," Esty interrupted.

"Start asking questions. Somebody knows something. Addy didn't do this alone.

Suzanne

Gulf Coast, August 2013

A new day, a fresh start. Suzanne wakes up and craves a freshly brewed cup of java. Naturally, though, she doesn't expect Max to surprise her with a Starbucks double cappuccino—not after their vicious argument last night that culminated with Remé panicking and calling 911.

Suzanne steps inside the cold-stoned shower and embraces the pulsating hot water spigots. Though reluctant to end her morning spa-like experience, Suzanne steps out because her phone hasn't stopped vibrating.

It's Jack.

"Morning, love. Can you guess my day's highlight? Watching a breathtaking sunrise in the east from my yacht in Pass Harbor. Okay to swing by? I've got coffee to share."

Suzanne laughs. "Why are you asking permission? You've likely seeped through the porch walls and are seated downstairs at the kitchen island. Staring at a cup of coffee you can't drink."

"But I'm not. Trying to play fair."

"Come on up." She has enough time to brush her hair, slip into shorts, and grab a fresh t-shirt. Within a couple of minutes, Jack appears at the door.

"When did you hang a three-moon sign over the threshold?"

Jack's skin is unusually translucent today. It reminds her of the oddly clear-skinned iguanas she'd spotted in Mexico, with visible veins. "Hurry, come inside," she says, fearing the sun's relentless rays will harm him. Then wonders if Jack even qualifies for a sunburn.

Do angels burn?

Jack points above the door's threshold to a three-dimensional hand-carved sign with a full moon in the center and two crescents flanking each side. "I'm impressed you had time to hang a talisman. Since you moved in so quickly."

Suzanne's face blanches when she steps onto the porch and looks up. "Jack, I've never seen this. I'm surprised Max didn't spot it and pitch it out." He hands her a hot cappuccino topped with whipped cream and sprinkled with cinnamon. "Thank you for the coffee."

"So, if you didn't hang it, who did?" Jack asks, darting through the rooms on the first floor. Suzanne stands in one place and awaits his return.

"Calpurnia, I suspect. She shows up with a cauldron of spells and house cleansings, no matter what I say, when she feels the call to react." The coffee is scalding, so she only manages tiny sips.

"One of those cultural hoodoo things, I guess, that conjurers insist upon," Jack says.

"Watching us muddle through life must be so amusing for you." Suzanne sits on one of the new bar stools and admires her surroundings. "I can't imagine the option to come and go at will . . ."

"Can't you? Imagine that?" Jack questions. He returns to the kitchen, now propped atop the island. "Giving my proposal some thought, are you?"

Suzanne ignores the comment, instead asking him about the Lafountain's sacred ground in the Pass. "The more I learn about spells and their power, the more I want to know about specific locations that can work in my favor."

"Why consult me? Why not talk to Calpurnia? She's been around about as long as I have," Jack says.

Every damn day I find out something I didn't know. That I surely needed to know.

"I'm asking you because you're here right before me," she says. "Is our sacred ground nearby?"

"Yes, within walking distance."

"Then let's go," Suzanne says.

"Not before you listen to what I have to say, as my time is running out."

Jack describes the Lafountain's consecrated property as originating hundreds of years ago at the end of Market Street, right along the shoreline. Her second great-great-grandmother, Louisa, was born of Choctaw and French blood, on Shelley Plantation in Bay St. Louis, and as a child, she quickly learned the custom of performing sacred ceremonies held there on a series of enormous shell mounds.

"A fertile location for casting spells. Less than a half-mile from here."

Jack nods. He's growing uncomfortable with direct sunlight slicing through him, so he glides to the sofa and nestles in the shade with one fluid movement.

"I'm furious with Madelaine for keeping us estranged from the family. I know so little about my ancestors . . . who they were before they died and became trapped ghosts. It's inexcusable, Jack."

Sitting erect, hands crossed over one knee, Jack says, "You will get no argument from me, love. I discouraged the disconnect, but by the time she'd given birth to Farrah, she couldn't handle the chaos of your people. And that's when I stepped in and stayed for a few decades."

"Dear God, wait one damn minute. You're not telling me Farrah's my sister? How? Why didn't I know? This changes everything." Jack watches as Suzanne wanders the first floor's perimeter, talking to herself, wrestling to piece together the spotty details of her childhood.

As Jack begins to filter away, there's little time to press for answers.

She returns to the living area and joins Jack on the sofa. "How close are we . . . were we . . . in age?"

"You're six years apart." Jack's voice is weakening, so much that Suzanne can barely hear it.

"Do we . . . did we . . . share the same father?"

"I honestly don't know. I can't say for certain that Madelaine knew. Look, before you judge Mother too harshly, you need to remember . . . wait, you wouldn't know about that . . ."

Facts are tumbling into place. Max killed Addy's granddaughter, my sister, by accident or purposefully. So, naturally, Addy's ghost demands revenge—a must-have to gain eternal peace. And what better individual to execute this mandate? Me, of course, her surviving granddaughter, her first granddaughter.

At last, Suzanne connects a year-long stay at her father and stepmother's house when Madelaine was too ill to parent her. And a concerted thrust for her to spend more and more time there.

"One final question, Jack. Who raised Farrah? Because I didn't grow up with her."

Jack's battle with the sunlight is at the point of defeat, so he rushes his words. "Jay and Sophie Lamar—Esty and Cash's *only* son and daughter-in-law.

Now nearly half of his visage is completely erased, so Jack forges ahead. "You're running out of time, and I need you to listen: First, you're dealing with a psycho. At the very least, Max is a sociopath and more probably a psychopath, so you are in harm's way. Second, love, you're a legacy who must fulfill your destiny." The angel lets his words filter through Suzanne before whispering, "You're the chosen one, chosen to open the portal."

"I've no recollection of applying for that task . . ." she answers defensively.

"Stay focused, love. You don't determine the cross-over time. The ghost does. She'll go when she's ready. She only needs a legacy to open the portal with a spell, not to set the departure time."

As she watches Jack disintegrate, Suzanne leans forward and reaches for his hand, a touch he may or may not feel. "Will you go? Be tempted to cross over?"

Now, Suzanne only hears Jack's thinning voice, for he is no longer visible. "That's why I'm unavailable to assist you. No reason to tempt fate. Rely upon those who've gone before you, Suzanne. Nothing beats ancestral magic at a time like this. It's there . . . waiting for you to awaken it."

Not long after Jack disappears, Suzanne panics over the lack of time to prepare herself for when her ghost demands a cross-over spell to be cast. First, before rituals can proceed, she must cast a protective veil throughout the new house. She locates her well-stocked Longaberger spell basket filled with crystals, tarot cards, oils, and herbs, including angelica root, black mustard seeds, chamomile, ginger, rosemary, and mint.

A jar of black salt is already prepared. Seven-day white, blue, black, and red candles line the lowest shelf in the main pantry, and votives fill several containers.

She begins at the first entrance, at the top of two flights of stairs. It's Friday, so Suzanne lights a blue candle and concentrates on projecting a peaceful, tranquil vibe. She imagines the entire house being swept into a protective shield of azure blue light. After placing a votive at their home's entrance, she works the remainder of the room, lighting blue candles, setting them on windowsills and lining door thresholds. She works through the entire house, repeatedly chanting, "Keep the energy within these walls positive and peaceful. Let no evil enter here."

Again. And again.

Spells are effective when you believe they'll work. Just as Suzanne finishes working in the last bedroom upstairs, she hears a door slam below. Max yells, "Fire! You've set the house on fire, Suzy."

"Stop being so melodramatic, Max," she yells, walking downstairs to double-check, holding the sizeable blue candle in her right hand, still lit.

The votives lining the threshold of the French doors only moments ago are now toppled, their sparks threatening to catch hold of the sofa's back side. She runs to the bedroom and grabs the bed's duvet, hoping against hope to prevent a blaze.

Max stomps the remaining embers before screaming, "Goddamn it, this is a new house, woman. Stop mucking things up with candles and shit." Out of breath, she leans back against a wall.

What can be worse than a disrupted spell?

"I'd never have started if I'd known you would return so soon."

Suzanne retrieves the small candles and sets them on the island to finish cooling along with the blue candle she's still holding. *Maybe. Maybe the spell will take if this candle stays lit.*

She watches Max scrub a few blackened scuffs on the cedar flooring with his fingernails. "I'll get someone to see about this later today. Hopefully the flooring won't need to be replaced." Then, when Suzanne hears Maureen's voice, she has little hope of revisiting the spell.

"It smells horrible in here, Max. What happened?"

"Suzanne nearly blew the place up. Less than a month after I gave her keys to the house."

Enough. I've had enough.

Suzanne rounds the corner of the hallway to cut Maureen off before she wanders beyond the living room. "Be honest, Max. You're the one who kicked the votives by the door, and the rest is history," she says.

"Kicked over burning candles in your new house? I'm not even going to ask," Maureen says. "I won't be long, Suzanne. Just need your husband's signature on a couple of documents."

"What are you signing today?" Suzanne asks.

We'll keep playing this game until the truth is out.

"Nothing that concerns you, Suzy. This is business."

Maureen slips him one page after another, pointing to the tiny boxes that require Max's initials. She hears Maureen mutter something under her breath but cannot identify what they're discussing.

Annoyed, Suzanne pushes forward. "Maybe you can explain something, Maureen, since Max seems to struggle with answering certain financial questions. Why is my investment fund dwindling? The market's not volatile right now, is it?"

"Good Lord, no. I don't know a thing about your account." Suzanne catches Maureen's side-eye glance to Max, cluing her to pursue.

"Well, then, Max. Here's a good time for me to mention that I don't want Maureen managing my money. So, stop immediately."

"Leave Mo out of this. We'll talk after she leaves," he says. Suzanne calmly reaches for her conjuring basket as the two continue ignoring her. "Do not start with this shit again, Suzanne!" Max shuffles the remaining papers to sign. "You're behaving childishly. We've got deadlines, and your interference is annoying."

As she calmly begins to pull a collection of saints candles from the bottom of the basket, Suzanne is relieved to see Calpurnia drift slowly across the expanse of the wrap-around porch. Her spirit guide's well-planned appearance may very well thrust Max over the edge, negating the need for any final doses of nightshade.

Before Suzanne reaches Calpurnia to open the door, Max steps in her direction, as though he intends to physically prevent her from letting Calpurnia enter.

"What are you doing, Max? We've a guest waiting at the door."

Max matches her movement when Suzanne steps to the right, then to the left. His face reddened, his finger pointing, he yells, "I've had enough of you women's mumbo jumbo. It bloody stops now, or you're no longer living in this house."

"I don't traffick with your sort, Max," Calpurnia speaks in a leveled, controlled tone after opening the door. "How stupid are you? You've two witnesses to your threats." She raises her right hand. Max misunderstands the gesture and prepares to retaliate. "Abiit autem malum esse homini." Calpurnia speaks Latin confidently, her head tilted reverently. And again, "Abiit autem malum esse homini," as she steps toward Max.

"Do not vex me, woman. I'm leaving." Ignoring Maureen and the unsigned documents, he runs down the front stairs, jumps in his truck, and recklessly drives away.

Shaken by what she has seen, Maureen scurries to exit by the rear staircase. Then she's intercepted by Jack's voice.

"Think you can leave? Avoid the chaos you helped create?" Then, an unearthly chuckle. Maureen hears the question but can't locate its origin. She rushes to the porch's edge but sees no one when she looks over the railing. As she races down the stairs, Maureen inexplicably trips and lands flat on her face, her upper torso awkwardly extended across the second landing. The documents tucked under her arm take flight with a wind's vortex that originates from nowhere.

Calpurnia tries to calm Suzanne. Hugging her tightly, she says. "It won't be much longer, love."

"His energy is beyond negative . . . I was in the middle of a spell . . ."

"And it should be fine," Calpurnia reassures. "Do you hear a woman crying? Is his assistant still here?"

"I've no idea."

Flustered by another confrontation with Max and her interrupted protection spell, Suzanne sits on the ottoman in the room's center and gazes across the Sound's sparkling water toward the end of the private pier Max constructed for them. She'd never imagined living a hellish nightmare. Right here in paradise.

"I'll go check on her. Can you imagine dealing with him without folk magic?"

Calpurnia helps Maureen gather the scattered papers and sends her on her way. No one notices one lone document tucked under a palm's frond.

Suzanne senses a rapid shift in the atmosphere. A familiar patchouli scent, dipped in musk and May rose, draws her into the great room, where she stands nearly at attention. At first, the air is close and humid, as though tightly wound. Suzanne lowers her breathing level and eases back onto a white loveseat when she feels dizzy.

As the room's temperature dramatically drops, Suzanne directs her attention to the darkest corner. Mesmerized, Suzanne squints as a woman's partial silhouette slowly becomes visible through a misty gray haze. First, she notices its outrageous red patent-leather heels, reflecting more shine power than Dorothy of Oz's glamourous pumps. Then the phantom's festive red and white polka-dot dress appears, poofy with netting for a lively night of dancing.

It speaks: "*Nearly time, my dear.*"

"When?" Suzanne whispers.

"*Soon. Find Madelaine. Finish with Max.*"

Suzanne imagines that she asks, confused, about what finding Madelaine *actually* means. The ghost, attired in a vibrant 1940s party dress and dripping in Mademoiselle Chanel No. 1's May-rose scent, shares a desperate attachment to Madelaine. So it only makes sense that its identity is the trapped ghost of her maternal grandmother—Adelaide Lafountain Lamar. But why is the phantom so confused over the whereabouts of her daughter's spirit?

I don't think I can do it. I cannot cast my first cross-over spell if it means I lose Madelaine again.

38

Max

Gulf Coast, August 2013

As the morning sun spills in from the east, Max leans against the upholstered headboard and watches Suzanne sleep. Peacefully. He adjusts the brand-new white duvet he bought yesterday, covering her shoulders. Regrets gather at his throat—some due to his miscalculations, others inherited. Yet Max refuses to give them a voice, burying them deep.

I wish I'd loved you past your violet-blue eyes and soft auburn hair. Your mellowed curves, your warm sweet spots . . . respected your gift to manage your worlds instead of belittling them. And disparaging you. I hate myself. Hate that I've become a monster, a thief.

Suzanne, by far, is the most quixotic woman he has ever loved. Max steals a couple more minutes before leaving to finalize his exit strategy. Few options remain for a murderer whose time is up—there's simply no way Max can stay in the States. His middle name is *Destruction*, and his victims are all gunning for their pound of flesh.

Max posts a note on the refrigerator's door. "Meeting the

movers on Davis: last load."

It's a lie.

The couple's remaining furnishings and electronics will be delivered to the beach house later today. Based on John's advice to steer clear, he'll be a no-show for his local court date. Max glances at the time on the car's dashboard and parks near Shaggy's at the edge of Pass Harbor. He's looking forward to one last stroll along the main fishing dock facing the Sound. If any passers-by recognize his truck, they'll assume he's seated on Shaggy's deck, waiting for the bartender to release the colorful shutters and open for business. It wouldn't be unusual: Max starting his day sipping a bourbon 'n branch while watching the shrimp trawlers in the Sound.

He leans on the dock's railing and imagines casting a line. When was the last time he spent an entire day fishing? Ten years ago? With Jacob.

So many regrets.

Max is no navigation expert, though he has spent considerable time on friends' yachts. Somewhat flummoxed by the entire catalog of boating language, he's desperate for maritime advice. One small problem: Max has backed himself into such a tight corner that he can't risk calling a friend. So he waits in the harbor and watches.

When Max sees a captain step onto his boat's bow, then take hold of a massive rope line, he walks in the direction of a Sunseeker 68 Sports Yacht.

"This beauty . . . is it yours?" Max cringes at his voice, sounding entirely off his game.

"Yes, indeed, lady's all mine. Seventy feet of pure joy and handles herself beautifully at 36 knots." Dressed in sailing whites, the man smiles at Max, his unusually light skin glistening oddly in the sunlight. "She'll give you one helluva ride."

"Do you book charters?" Max asks, though he doubts the yachtsman has a financial need to shuttle people from one place to the next.

"Not anymore," the man replies, adjusting his blue and white cap, looking for relief from the harsh morning sun. "I outgrew that foolishness on a smaller yacht. No, this lady is solely mine." Max stares, hoping that the mariner might change his mind if he stands there long enough, albeit awkwardly.

"Might you consider leasing? For one single excursion? I can pay you a ridiculous amount of money." Max wants to fast-forward this inquiry, partly because he's disturbed as he watches the man's face. With sunrays aimed directly at the captain's back, aspects of the man's face appear to be disintegrating.

"Look, what's this about? Who sent you?" The yachtsman quickly tires of Max's impertinent stare and rapid-fire questions.

"Nobody. Why do you ask?"

The seaman ignores the question. "Where are you going?" he asks.

"Bahamas. Bimini Island, if possible."

"How soon?"

"Now . . . tonight . . . As soon as possible," Max answers. "Do you know anyone willing to take on a charter? At least partway. Maybe to Florida?"

"You're up to something real shady, aren't you?"

"Don't see that's your concern," Max answers.

"If you want to be on the water until your destination, book an excursion to Destin out of Gulfport. Another to Miami. Then grab a charter aboard a 116 Sunseeker to Grand Bimini, a great spot to disappear. If you need . . . well, that sort of thing."

"My situation is urgent."

"Give me your phone. I'll add the digits for a couple of dudes who charter out of Gulfport Harbor," the man offers.

"Thanks. I'm Max. Your name?"

"Captain Jack Reynolds, here. Nice to meet you," he says. Max can't shake the feeling that they've met one another. "I hope you find your pot at the rainbow's end."

That's one way of looking at freedom.

Max glances at the time on his phone and assumes John's fight against a bench warrant is likely lost. He behaves like a man desperate to disappear as he races to Gulfport's port, fifteen minutes away. He talks with a few men, including the fellow who runs twice-daily shuttles to Ship Island, where the blue-green waters of the Gulf of Mexico welcome swimmers and beachcombers. Then, with a wad of cash, Max hires one of the men Jack recommended and quickly books a custom trip. While he waits for a signal that the journey is mapped, Max sits in the shade of a refurbished lighthouse—another sign that Hurricane Katrina came and went, destroying Gulfport's original.

Suzanne calls for the fifteenth time, so he answers.

"Max," she yells. "Where are you?"

"Errands. Lots to do to get our stuff moved to the beach house." He rubs his throbbing right temple.

"Bullshit. John is livid because you skipped court."

"I'll be back in a few minutes, Suzanne. And try to explain as much as I can." Max watches the neon blue light above the charter company's office switch on—a sign that his trip is charted, and payment is required.

"Home as in the beach house or home on Davis Avenue?" Suzanne is breathless with her endless inquiries.

"*Home*, Suzy. Sweet Jesus."

Silence.

"Max, please call John. You've put him in an impossible situation." The edge in her voice—the one that clips the end of her sentences—that edge of annoyance, as if she cannot be bothered with managing trite details. *I won't miss that.*

"Gotta go. Stay. Give the movers a chance to arrive." Max returns to the charter's office.

"Not one bit of this makes any sense," Suzanne says. Then, Max hears dead air.

It's an impressive skill . . . knowing when to disconnect a call without warning. Damn, I love a woman who knows when to hang up.

Max signs the paperwork and settles with a cash payment that the yacht owner tries to refuse, preferring a credit card. But Max smooths away his reluctance by doubling the deposit. Because the yacht won't be ready until 8 p.m., he has time on his hands. He considers calling in a shrimp po-boy order at his favorite seaside pub but notices ten text messages from Maureen.

Goddamnit, Mo.

The tenth message reads: "Transfer slip is MIA. Can't move funds. Help."

A slew of messages precedes this one, including: "Check the beach house. There was a wind that day."

Damn it, Mo. What happened after I left? You had one assignment. One.

Max foregoes lunch and speeds onto Beach Boulevard, determined to prevent the threads of his three-year plan from unraveling. He parks underneath the house, then sprints up the stairs, moving every piece of furniture on the porch in search of one 8.5-by-11 piece of paper. Before he steps into the house, Max smells burnt sage wafting up from the beach.

He looks down. "Who's there?" he demands. Though there's no response, he spots a reddish-brown crunchy substance scattered along the house's sandy perimeter. He tries entering but can't seem to cross the threshold. Finally, Max screams, "Suzy!"

She suddenly appears from the bedroom suite, wearing an exquisite caftan with her hair twisted in a messy bun. She's wearing a geometric blue Lapis necklace around her neck, with a hand-carved cross choker in the center. Again, she holds a ceramic bowl of burning sage sticks, fanning its smoke with a brush.

Who are you, woman?

"For the last time, Suzanne Martin, explain yourself. Didn't we just rehash this madness?" Max stomps his feet like a child and, in doing so, grinds the red-brown substance on his shoe soles into the porch's cedar flooring. His temper threatens to explode.

Suzanne's voice is calm. "I could ask you the same question, Max."

"What have you done to yourself? To my house?"

She fires back. "What have you done with my money?"

"Clean up this mess, please." Max's tone changes dramatically. "I need to discuss a couple of things with you. Here's a plan: Let's have a nice dinner tonight. Say around 6 p.m.?"

"Why not talk now? Step inside."

With amusement, Suzanne watches Max's unsuccessful attempts to step across the threshold now that an enormous circle of red ground clay, designed to ward off evil intentions, is visible around the home's perimeter and at each door's opening. After yesterday's fiasco, Calpurnia left a medium-sized wooden box at the bottom of the stairs with a prophetic message: "Mimi Jeanne's magic within. Open when you're ready."

Max's anger explodes. "This shit needs to be done by the time I get back. Open some goddamn windows and let some fresh air in." Max senses a shadow of movement in the far back corner of the living area as he turns to go. But after a double take, he sees nothing askew.

"Problem, Max?"

"Who's here?" Max asks.

"Nobody. Just you and me," she says.

"You're lying."

"No, Max. No one else is here." She doesn't tell her husband that he just missed a priest's Bless 5, which required placing crosses at all four corners of the house, leaving one in the middle.

Since driving is too risky, Max chooses to walk along the shoreline and sit at the water's edge. From a distance, he watches John's car come and go from the house. Then, a police car with flashing blues pulls under the house, leaving quickly.

Hours later, Max rides the elevator to the first floor, no longer trusting the stairs, and finds Suzanne making dinner, acting as though everything's perfectly normal. When she sees Max walk in, she arranges the place settings on the porch's teak table.

"Thank you for returning my wife," he says, kissing her cheek. Better to pretend all's well.

"I cleaned a little. And left some things in place."

After scanning the kitchen, he needs help understanding her reference. Suzanne pours a glass of wine while Max heaps more Maker's Mark than usual into his crystal highball glass—the bottle of bourbon infused with the last of the nightshade.

It's sticky and humid on the porch despite the air conditioning flowing through the French doors and the ceiling fans oscillating at full speed. It's too early to enjoy a shrimp étouffée dinner. A tossed salad would've been more appropriate since neither one has an appetite.

Awkwardness cloaks them like a salty-wet beach towel doused with sand. Max chews his peppered shrimp quickly and gets right to the point.

"I'm missing a bank voucher, Suzanne. Have you seen it, or anything that resembles an official transfer slip?"

Suzanne looks beyond the porch's railing and across the Sound's waters. She slowly sips her wine. "No, I haven't seen a bank voucher, Max," she says. "But I have decided it's time for you to return the money you've stolen from my investment account. If not, you'll face more charges than you're currently battling. Like embezzlement."

Max stops eating, short of choking. He stands, then slams the table against the porch railing, clearing it in one sweeping movement, perhaps to prove that he's still in charge, despite Suzanne's sage stalks, hoodoo spells, and grounded red clay. He tumbles down the back stairway before throwing up repeatedly, then passes out in the sand.

Much later, he wakes to Remé standing over him, screaming for Suzanne to call 911. Max recalls her refusal to do so.

He doesn't remember the malevolent spirit that immobilized him, but surely hears its guttural voice now. "*Not enough conjure. Too little nightshade, love.*"

"I'm okay, Remé. Don't have time for the medics. Just give me a ride," Max says.

Remé helps Max ease into his car. As Remé shifts gears, Max asks, "One last favor, my friend. Drop me off at Gulfport's harbor?"

"I've been expecting this," Remé says. "Kinda surprised it has taken you this long to leave."

Max lowers the passenger window of his business partner's sedan to drink in the sea air, praying that his nausea will settle before he boards the yacht. "I'm not coming back. You know that, right? And I can't tell you where I'm going."

"I know everything, Max."

"Take care of Jacob. Please keep him in the business. And see that he gets my truck. Okay?"

"The less information we exchange, the better," Remé says. He hands Max an overstuffed manila-colored business envelope. "This is from John and me." Max is visibly confused. After everything he has dragged his best friend and his attorney through in the past five years, he is shocked when Remé says, "Just don't spend it all in one spot."

With that, Max barely slips from Remé's car before it speeds away. As he approaches the slip where *Popeye's Olive*, a seventy-three-foot beauty, is anchored, he sees its captain and small crew awaiting his arrival.

"Ready, Mr. Max?"

"Hell, yeah."

"We'll get you to Destin. You'll board the next vessel there to Ft. Lauderdale. After that, you're on your own. We don't want to know what you do next."

"Thank you. I've a generous tip for you and the crew. For

getting things organized so quickly," Max says.

"Then we're off." Shortly after the captain disappears, Max hears the rev of the yacht's motor. There's a short reverse movement, a bit of a turn, slight acceleration, back to barely an idle, increased speed, and finally open water.

Max doesn't look back.

He accepts a champagne cocktail offered by a sexy brunette. She must have been below deck when the others greeted him earlier. "Will you join me in a toast?" She agrees, and they raise their glasses to the horizon as Max admires the storm clouds moving in and imagines a new life free of the encumbrances of the law. He believes the only thing standing between him and his freedom toward the east is the intercoastal waterway and the enormous Gulf of Mexico.

He fails to notice a strange west wind stirring up dramatic bursts of energy from behind the yacht. Concocted by a bolstering of angry trapped ghosts—and fueled by justice. Together they serve one purpose and one purpose only.

To escort Max straight to Hell.

39

Addy

Gulf Coast, September 1947

The phone rang early on Thursday morning. Papa called to report that a reconnaissance plane based at Keesler had spotted a hurricane off the coast of Florida. Its target? The Mississippi Gulf Coast. It had to be official, since Biloxi's hurricane flag had been hoisted since midnight.

After Addy set the receiver back in its cradle, the phone rang again. Eddy, Cash's right-hand man, called for the second time and demanded to speak to him. Half-a-dozen oyster shuckers had failed to report for the morning shift—a crisis, since multiple orders had to be processed for shipping before the railroad lines shut down for safety. Cash immediately called Papa and James Jr. for help.

"Protect our investment, son. I'll meet you there in a few minutes. We'll shuck oysters until the trains pull out, if need be," Papa said.

Addy signaled Cash that she wanted to speak to her grandfather.

Wound up and out of breath, she asked, "Shouldn't we

worry about yours and Mimi's place, Papa? Instead of what's happening at the cannery this morning?"

"We've weathered our share of storms, Addy, both here and in Louisiana. The house in the Pass is far enough back on the bluff that you needn't worry. And the seawall will protect against a surge. I've got a man here latching the hurricane shutters, and Ida's helping Mimi fill the bathtubs with water."

Cash's quick exit left no time for a second cup of coffee.

"I think Mimi needs to go to New Orleans, Papa. Why is she still here?"

"Jeanne's got a mind of her own, Addy. Like you. When they finish saving water, she'll head to the church to organize a shelter. If you want to tell her otherwise, go right ahead. But it's not going to be me."

Who are you kidding, Papa? Mimi's stirring things up in her potter's shed, likely plotting a hex on the hurricane.

Addy paused, giving Papa a chance to say more. "By the way, Dotty has her husband's car today, so we're moving a few things to the dress shop. Before the storm hits."

Papa reminded Addy they'd be on their own since all hands were needed at the cannery to finalize oyster orders. "You sure this is a good plan, young lady?" Increased static on the phone line made it difficult to hear her grandfather speak. ". . . fifty-mile-an-hour winds forecast by mid-afternoon."

"Papa, please don't lecture me. I want to hang my sign from the window facing Market Street. It'll have to do until the permanent lighted one is delivered." When he didn't reply, she hurried her explanation. "We'll haul the fabric bolts upstairs first. Then, the dress forms. You know, things we can handle ourselves."

"I wish I could convince you otherwise, but that seems pointless. Hurry along, then. But when you're finished, stop by the cannery . . . need all the assistance we can muster. If those rail cars roll out without our orders, we're in a heap of trouble."

The breakfast dishes were dried and stacked when Dotty honked from the driveway. Addy grabbed her latest sketch pad and set of charcoal pencils, held together with a tightened rubber band and a black satin ribbon. Then returned to the hallway to pick up the sign. Dotty helped her load the dress forms.

"Hey, honey," she said as Addy slid onto the front seat. "Are you too excited for words?"

"Can you believe it? Our move-in day is finally here. What did your husband say?" Addy asked.

"He walked to the BX early, what with the storm coming, so I didn't have a chance to remind him, but I made sure to grab the car keys."

Addy turned to examine the material bolts piled in the back seat. "All these are yours?"

"Yes, indeed. I've been secretly collecting remnants from Madison's and ordering extra bolts," she laughed. "Plenty to fashion a dozen cocktail dresses."

It was a short drive—short enough to walk if they hadn't been hauling a carload and battling windy weather. Dotty found a great parking spot right at the bank building's side entrance on the most trafficked street in the Pass.

"You do have the key, right?" Dotty asked.

"Of course, silly. Grab as much as you can carry."

A man walking toward Pass Harbor stopped just shy of Dotty's Mercury sedan, his fedora tipped against the bristling breeze. He smiled, watching the women struggle to keep the material from flapping off the bolts as the wind strengthened.

"You ladies aware a hurricane's approaching?" Had Addy been less distracted with her day's plan, she might have noticed the man's air of familiarity. And his bizarre buoyancy, drifting against the wind gusts.

"Yes. But we've been counting down to our move-in day for so long . . . didn't want to let it pass without hauling a few things into our new dress shop," Addy announced. Anxious to step into the bank building, she nodded a go-ahead signal to Dotty.

"Surely not everything, I hope," the man continued. "Not on a day like today."

"No, just enough," Addy said. "So we can meet with our clients after the storm passes."

"I'd offer to help . . . tell you what. I've got some business down at the cannery, but when I'm finished, I'll lend a hand on my way back if you gals are still at it." He held the door for Dotty, hauling another load in from the car.

"Thank you so much," Addy said, shaking hands with him. "I'm Addy, Addy Lamar."

"Jack Reynolds, insurance sales," he said. "Pleased to meet you, Addy. Say, you're not Mrs. Jeanne Lafountain's granddaughter, are you?"

"Yes, sir. I surely am."

"I should've known, what with the violet color of your eyes. Enjoy your day, ladies. And be careful," he added. Jack tipped his hat and walked toward the wharf.

They made several trips to the second floor, not bothering to wait for the elevator that Dotty described as slower than molasses. It wasn't until they struggled to carry the dress forms up two flights of stairs that they regretted not waiting for some assistance. Then, Addy peered from the large bay window that faced the Mississippi Sound and gasped. The skies had darkened considerably in the past thirty minutes. Waves crashed against the marina's piers higher than she'd ever seen. She turned to gauge her friend's reaction.

"I've never seen the Sound look this furious," she said. "I can't see one single barrier island at all."

Across the entire breadth of the waters leading to the Gulf, as far as visibility would allow, the waves continued to swell in strength and height. Still, Addy maintained a foothold in the shop, refusing to leave. She had spun this dress-shop dream of hers far too long. And paid an incalculable price for doing so.

She cringed, thinking of how shrewd she'd been, selling out Cash—forsaking their infant as payment in full and folding to her grandfather's threats.

Had the lies been worth it? Her indeterminate loss?

Dotty suggested setting up a display of dress materials—from brocade and tulle to imported French silk and Southern polka-dot cotton—against the backdrop of the walled shelving. Why not? They'd come this far, with no idea when they'd return or how long it would take to restore power once the storm passed.

They placed two designs on the dress forms: a silver ball gown with hand-stitched sequins and a tea-length cocktail dress in mauve satin. Dotty placed a glittery pair of stilettos, pointing them outward at an attractive angle under the satin dress. Addy balanced her sign in the window, facing outward—*Adelaide's Couture Designs*.

"Will we ever be ready to open? There's so much more we need, Dotty. Trifold mirrors, your sewing machines, an entry table, more seating for our clients, and a screen for fittings. Maybe a small parlor with a bar where husbands can wait?" But one more glance out the front windows was sufficient to discourage them from lingering. If the water's rage were any indication, they'd stayed long past the best time to go.

"Where do you want me to drop you off?" Dotty asked.

"The cannery. Everyone's shucking oysters, so Cash and Papa won't miss today's rail run before the lines shut down."

"You need my help?"

"Goodness no, Dotty, I don't dare ask you for another thing. You've been a gem, honey. I don't know what I'd do without you." Addy scooched closer to Dotty on the front seat and hugged her friend goodbye. "What am I talking about? I can't thank you enough."

Dotty squeezed Addy's hand tightly. "You know I love you, dear friend."

"Sometimes I think you're the only person who understands

me. And accepts me for *me*."

"Don't be silly, girl. Cash would die for you," Dotty said, already looking in the rearview mirror, gauging the best way to back out of the parking bay. "He loves you so."

Addy said a quick goodbye, then ran along the pier to the cannery's main wharf, watching the live oaks along Beach Boulevard sway with the wind despite their impressive 500-year fortitude. This hurricane would be no match, she thought. They'd survive this storm as they'd survived others.

Cash saw her enter the steaming area and yelled, "Addy, take off your damn high heels and put on an apron." Addy ignored him and grabbed a clean apron before stepping into a covered building that rattled with the wind's roar. She kept her beloved shiny red heels in place, because she loved the crunching sound of ground oyster shells as she approached a shucking table.

Finally, the conveyer belt started to move, piled with oysters straight from the steamer. Addy quickly went to work, grabbing shells with her left hand and shucking with her right, careful to avoid puncturing through the meat. She kept a steady pace, throwing the meat into a bin headed for the washing belt and pitching the emptied shells aside: her head down, her thoughts focused, her hands flying. When she finally took a breath to examine her surroundings, she saw Esty scurrying along the walkway connecting the main office to the canning department.

Shouldn't my sister be in New Orleans? Maybe Mama Charlotte had sent Esty to pick up Mimi and take her back to New Orleans, a safer location until the Gulf Coast storm passed.

Addy didn't stop shucking, though she was furious that Esty was in the Pass and hadn't bothered to come by the house. Hadn't offered to help her and Dotty move supplies into the dress shop. After a few moments, Addy recognized her husband's voice arguing loudly with another man: Jack, the same man she'd just met outside Market Street who'd offered to help. Just then, Papa walked up to check on her progress.

"Papa, do you know that man?"

"Which man?"

"That man over there. The one who is talking with Cash." When she turned to point, no one was there. "Sorry, they've stepped away. I met him earlier today."

"Do you remember his name?" Papa asked.

"Jack, somebody." Addy concentrated on resuming her shucking speed, not looking up at Papa.

"Mimi knows a fellow named Jack, a family friend. But I've no idea if he sells insurance. He comes around whenever she gets a notion about a thing or two." Papa untied his apron and hung it on a hook near the washing area.

"I'll ask Cash later. Seems like a nice man, so I can't imagine Cash yelling at him."

"It's business, Addy. It's always business. Don't think anything of it." Papa looked exhausted. He'd been overseeing the cannery's fermentation process for hours. "I'm leaving, love, and suggest you do the same," he said, scrubbing his hands and forearms. "Cash will be here until the last container of oysters is loaded on the train. Should I swing back around after I pick up Mimi?"

"I'm staying, Papa. It's an emergency, isn't it?" Addy nodded in the direction of the last of the diligent shuckers who hadn't moved for hours, some sitting on their benches, others leaning against the tables. "I'll finish the next bin, then find Cash."

"Won't you reconsider?"

"No, I want to do this. It's my turn to help my husband. He's done a lot for me."

"Has he?"

Ignoring Papa's inference, Addy asked if he'd run into Esty.

"No, why do you ask?"

"She's here."

"That makes no sense, Addy. She wouldn't drive over from

New Orleans in this weather. We'll see you back at the house. Plan to ride out the storm with us. Tomorrow's another day." Papa kissed the top of his beloved granddaughter's head before leaving.

"Yes, of course."

"See 'ya later, love."

"I love you, Papa," Addy shouted behind her grandfather's back as he walked away. Between the racket of the metal roof and the roar of the wind, he appeared not to hear her.

Within the hour, Cash began sending workers home as the weather conditions deteriorated. He and Eddy raced through their routine to board up and batten down. By then, it occurred to Addy that her shucking efforts were futile. The race against time now prioritized protecting the cannery against the hurricane. She was the last person to leave the shucking room after scrubbing in the wash bin, using the last of the Ivory soap. Addy closed the heavy doors behind her and threw the latch.

On the way to her husband's office, she heard Cash reassure a few of his fishermen, whom she suspected were terrified of losing their schooners. Though she imagined Papa had arranged for the cannery's fishing boats to be moved to the higher ground designated for such earlier in the day, this last group of oystermen may not have been included in that gesture.

Exhausted, Addy stretched out on a couch in the back of Cash's office, situated there for nights that ran late and turned into early mornings. Before she started to drift off, Addy heard the horn of the last train of the day and smiled, knowing the cannery had met the deadline. Soon people from all over the world would receive oysters harvested, cleaned, and canned from one of the richest reefs in the country.

She dozed off and on. Then woke to the sound of the wooden door jostling. *Did the door lock? I must be dreaming.* Addy dismissed her thoughts and quickly fell asleep.

An hour later, the intense battering of the angry Gulf's

waters against the cannery's walls woke her with a start. Terrified, Addy realized she had been left behind. It was dark as death inside Cash's office. When she jumped up to flip the light switch, she found the electricity already knocked out. Feeling her way to the office door, she screamed when she realized it was locked.

Who locked Cash's door? Without checking to see if anyone was inside his office?

Addy pounded on the door with her fist and yelled as hard as she could manage. Since the crashing waves against the cannery's walls were deafening, there was no way for anyone to hear her cries for help. Tears formed at the edge of her eyes despite her best efforts to remain optimistic.

If I don't find a way out of here, I'll surely be swept away!

She remembered a small window in the corner of Cash's office that looked over the shuckers' workbenches. She yanked the curtains back and struggled to open it. Naturally, this window was locked, too. Addy whirled around, searching for a heavy item, and found a fleur-de-lis paperweight on Cash's desk. She flung it as hard as she could against the glass, shattering it into a million pieces. Addy dragged a chair to the window and climbed through, landing on a ledge that the cannery's previous owner had designed to spy on workers. She remembered a rail ladder nearby. Addy carefully inched her way to the ladder in the dark, then stepped on each rung until she reached the shucking room. Back where she'd started hours ago.

"Cash? Papa?" she called, knowing her pleas were fruitless. *Wait, Papa already left. But that doesn't explain why Cash would leave without checking on me.* "Why am I the only one left here?"

Only the wind answered with another deafening howl.

Addy figured if she made her way to the pier, she might be able to grab ahold of the handrails for support and claw her way back up to the boulevard, even if it meant crawling on her hands and knees and grasping onto the planking for support.

Bereft. Heartbroken. Addy could not fathom one single reason Cash would leave her to die. Alone.

Unless. Unless he knows.

The wind gusts had increased so dramatically in the past few hours that walking the pier was impossible. Had the hurricane's direction turned quicker than anticipated? Addy fought to center herself against the power of the squalls and held tightly to the railing to resist slipping into the Gulf's raging waters. Then, when the tip of one of her heels stuck between the grooves of wood along the pier, she fell hard. Flat on her face.

Out of nowhere, Jack, the man she had met only hours before, reached for her hand to help her stand. Instead, Addy trusted the railing to help support her, but when her body weight leaned against it, a horrible cracking sound erupted.

When Addy lost her balance as the railing split, she tumbled into the cold, harsh water. As she struggled to reach the surface for air, she spotted a fishing net still attached to one of the moorings and grabbed onto it, thinking she could swim back to the pier and climb up. Jack miraculously appeared again and moved the net closer to her reach. Addy's efforts to hold on were lost when the inside wall of a fifteen-foot wave careened upon the entire cannery's wharf. She was swallowed in the swell.

Her final thoughts were peaceful as she drifted into the raging Gulf water that had merged into the Sound. She saw her sweet baby, Madelaine, and prayed for the family who'd adopted her. There Jack was again, beckoning her farther out to sea. When Addy's spirit lifted, it came with a jolt, allowing her to view the end of her life through the eyes of Papa standing dangerously close to the seawall, and Mimi, horrified, as she ran from the car. Both desperately screamed her name.

Drifting. Until the final vision of her earthbound life appeared: Esty stood near the entrance of Pass Harbor. She looked so pretty, like she'd just come from Mass, wearing a lilac dress and the amethyst bracelet Mimi had given Addy on the day she and Cash married. Despite the horrific wind gusts, her sister held on tightly to a toddler, a little girl dressed in pink. And Cash? He embraced Esty and the toddler, trying his best to shield them from the horror of watching Addy's body drift out to sea.

She felt no hatred. Within a heartbeat, Addy violently became one of Hurricane George's fifty-one casualties in 1947. After the hurricane passed and recovery efforts were underway, the *Tarpon-Beacon* would list Adelaide Lafountain Lamar's name among the other Gulf Coast residents who did not survive.

Soon, the drifting stopped. But Addy's angel didn't disappear. Jack lingered because it was his divine duty. But mainly because no one should be alone in death.

Clearly, I did not intend to die today.

40

Suzanne

Gulf Coast, August 2013

A gentle rain shower cuts the day's heat at twilight on a quiet Tuesday in late August. Suzanne admires the waning strokes of high tide, leaving hundreds of oyster shells in its wake. From her perch against the railing of the beach home's lone widow's peak, she emanates an omniscient poise—imagining the women who'd waited centuries ago for their beloveds to return from the sea. Descending the circular stairs to the second floor, she senses a desperate plea rising from Addy's ghost. In her mind, Suzanne hears "*Madelaine . . . where's my Madelaine?*"

Suzanne cannot fathom why her mother's spirit is lost to Addy.

I'm neither a ghost, spirit, nor angel, and even I communicate with both of you.

Though Suzanne missed the opportunity to know and love her grandmother, she now recognizes her heart. She realizes that Addy's residual energy has always been guiding her, encouraging her, though she didn't fully understand its genesis. Finally, Suzanne can acknowledge Addy's deep-seated love and nudges of reassurance that she craved from Madelaine. Yet found absent.

Just in time to let her beloved go . . .

Now that Max is dealt with, Suzanne anticipates that Addy's ghost will choose the coming hours to make contact and insist upon the spell that will free her. But there's a problem no one could have anticipated: If Addy realizes that her daughter, Madelaine, has *not* permanently crossed—is it conceivable that she may choose not to go?

Sitting on the front porch, Suzanne watches a row of white rockers, lined up, facing the horizon. Nothing yet. No sign of an anxious ghost tapping her toes. No sign of others gathering for a reunion. She closes her eyes as the whoosh and whip of the coastal winds surround her—a sure sign that a Spirit World event, anticipated for decades, is imminent. If a developing tropical system stirring up the Gulf of Mexico materializes, it would complicate Addy's cross-over and ironically mirror the tragedy of her life's end.

Suzanne knows the family saga—the story of their wealthy heiress connected to Chanel's perfumery family, who suddenly married a fighter-bomber pilot near the end of World War II, throwing the Lafountains into a tailspin. An occurrence no amount of spellcasting could alter.

And what she has learned from Jack fills in the gaps: Addy, forced to give up her baby for adoption, sealing much of Madelaine's life struggle. Louisa, born on Shelley Plantation near Bay St. Louis, her birth kept secret for years because of her Choctaw heritage. Mimi Jeanne, an enchantress before her time, compelled to accept the limitations of conjure. Finally, Madelaine, conceived in a hideous, violent act, hindering any hope of a contentment-filled future.

Though Addy relied upon her clairvoyance, she rejected Mimi's offers to develop her inherited spellcasting abilities.

What if Addy had embraced her preternatural gifts? Would she have survived?

Within these anticipatory moments, Suzanne recognizes that she is more like her grandmother than ever imagined. Though she loved Madelaine, Suzanne viewed her mother's penchant for rootwork as a rigid wedge. Suzanne's desires were simple: She'd spent a lifetime yearning for a copasetic mother-daughter friendship.

An antique white rocker begins to slowly move, though the coastal breeze is long gone. An icy chill starts at the tips of Suzanne's toes and climbs to her torso, filling her veins with excitement. Suzanne smiles when the classic fragrance of Mademoiselle Chanel No. 1 overwhelms the atmosphere. Her patience is rewarded as the faint illumination of a young woman's silhouette appears, then dissipates in seconds.

Holding her breath, Suzanne inhales sharply and wills Addy's ghost to stay. Pressure builds in her right ear, producing a shrill ringing sound that signals what will follow. When Suzanne closes her eyes and begins rocking, she feels an intense outpouring of love that's so overwhelming, she would have given anything in her life to have experienced it firsthand. It's as if Suzanne's experiencing an entire lifetime of love, wrapped up in a few parting moments.

"Hello," Suzanne whispers. "I've been expecting you."

The rocking continues—off rhythm. Suzanne rushes to voice unimaginable words.

"I think of you often, Mimi Addy. I'd have called you that after *your* grandmother if you'd lived. I get it. I now understand that you've always been at my side . . . So . . . it's hard to let go." As tears threaten, Suzanne powers through to speak her final words. "But not before I thank you for loving me. And protecting me when I'd no idea that I needed it."

The rocking slows. Suzanne balances her focus. She's ready to prepare for the spell, but must ask one final question—one that's troubled her for months.

Why did Max have to be punished? So you'd be free to go? Since you hold him responsible for Farrah's death . . . and because she and I are both your granddaughters . . . it's all related to the line of enchantresses, right?

Suzanne listens intently, but there's no response. How can there be one? A Spirit World's plane of accountability is inconceivable. Vastly different from the manner issues are dealt with in the mortal world, which ineptly relies upon the laws of the land to bring about justice.

"I can only hope that I haven't nearly killed a man for no damn good reason," she whispers.

Suzanne alerts Calpurnia, who's meditating in a dune of sea oats nearby. She sends a text: "It's nearly time." Then grabs Mimi's tattered spell box, used yesterday to cleanse the house, tucked behind a planter near the French doors.

It's spell-ready, filled with a lighter, gold pointer, white candles, and fresh pink and dried red rose petals. Also, ground black salt. Suzanne double-checks a small notecard printed in Latin. She doesn't want to fail at the only task her maternal grandmother ever asked of her.

Then a rocker begins a frenetic movement. Suzanne panics, for Addy's ghost is agitated. "Tell me . . . how to calm you."

The ghost whimpers—"*Wait. Wait. Wait.*"

The outdoor temperature drops by at least thirty, maybe forty degrees. Bimini sprints back and forth across the porch from one side to another, barking loudly, until he finally lays by Suzanne's feet. He sighs. He whimpers. His ears perk up, on high alert to react and protect.

Then another rocker, opposite where Addy appeared earlier, begins its slow, methodical motion. Suzanne gasps. Just in time, she hears rapid footsteps on the staircase. Suzanne calls out, "We're on the porch."

Calpurnia arrives in full celebratory attire, wearing a red and brown silk caftan with an orange and yellow turban atop her head. "We?" she asks, smiling broadly.

"I know it's confusing, but I'm certain another spirit is joining us. Could it be Madelaine?" Suzanne stands and greets Calpurnia with a hug. "I'm so thankful you're here. I'm only prepared to cast one spell . . . could more be necessary? I didn't expect this—honestly, I didn't know what to expect."

The second rocker abruptly stops.

Is that you, Madelaine?

"Come sit with me, Cal, so we don't frighten either one away," Suzanne says.

"That's rich, Suzanne, very rich. You, guiding me."

"No disrespect. But since I've never cast a cross-over spell . . . don't want a single thing to go wrong." Suzanne reaches for the fringed shawl she keeps in a basket between rockers as the temperature continues to dive. "Mimi Addy's energy is so powerful tonight, Cal. I'm certain she's ready to go. But this other one, the one that just joined us, doesn't feel the same way. And without a reveal, how do I know?"

"Yes, you do."

"Need permission to go, love?" Calpurnia asks casually. As though inquiring about the price of a cocktail at her favorite coastal pub.

The rocker hosting the unidentified spirit starts and stops again.

Suzanne yearns for Jack's reassuring presence, his peace and guidance. *What if I miss a step or repeat too many layers of the incantation? Or mispronounce the Latin? I cannot mess this up, or Addy's trapped here forever. With me entangled in an endless cycle of hauntings by discontented ghosts.*

Calpurnia provides a calming effect and explains, "You're blessed with a full blood moon tonight. Any trapped phantom desirous of crossing over, any spirit who has come and gone many times, will distinguish *you* as the chosen gatekeeper. You possess the skeleton key, my dear. Understand this—more than one entity *will* locate the portal once you've opened it."

Suzanne listens for ghosts who hover and spirits that linger.

"The Earth's preparing alongside us. Even the jellyfish along the shoreline are quivering with anticipation. Have you noticed?" Calpurnia asks.

When Suzanne stands and looks to the east, she's overwhelmed by nature's response—amazed by the accumulation of life as brown, pink, and white pelicans gather in untold numbers on the sandbars, seemingly stretched to the horizon after the first low tide. Seagulls saturate the sky, while lest terns perch amidst the dunes, all chirping in perfect pitch, applauding the moment at hand: A trapped and troubled soul will soon reach her nirvana.

But it's the hundreds of jellyfish, edging the shoreline for as far as the eye can see, that capture Suzanne's heart with their sparkle and magnetic glow, pulsating a pathway to the next world. She trusts the Spirit World to take up where she leaves off and lead Addy home to eternal peace.

They wait for the phantom's signal. Suzanne turns to Calpurnia and says, "I have so many questions. But there're limits to what a ghost can explain. Maybe you know . . . *why me*?"

Calpurnia shakes her head in disbelief. "Lovey, you are Addy's legacy. You fulfill what she could not. She abhorred folk magic, hoodoo, conjure, whatever they labeled it then. Mimi's encouragement was insufficient. It was enough for her to deal with her clairvoyance. Sound familiar?"

"Did she have a fair shake? Seems like so many things got in the way." It's nearly impossible for her to imagine the pain Addy experienced, the pain of so many loved ones letting her down. "I hope that she felt joy." Suzanne stops tapping her fingertips on the arms of the rocking chair. "No point in denying my role in all of this."

"Too late for that, love. You're already practicing."

"Only a few spells," Suzanne lies.

"Takes only one." Calpurnia continues, "After decades of failing to accept her death, Addy's prepared to cross. She can experience safe passage because of you, Suzanne. You hold the key to her portal of peace. It's time."

As gusts of wind increase and encircle them, a light, feathery touch on Suzanne's right shoulder alerts her to listen.

"Joining Addy."

Suzanne's heart pounds.

"Mother?"

In an instant, Madelaine's spirit is revealed in all her 1960s glory, dressed in bell-bottom jeans, a macramé headband, a knit-ribbed t-shirt, and aviator glasses. One platform shoe keeps her rocker moving in rhythm.

Overcome with emotion, Suzanne whispers, "I don't think I can do this if both of you are leaving me."

In unison, the spirit voices of both her mother and grandmother speak: "*Yes. You. Can.*"

Gusts of residual ghost energy whirl uncontrollably on the porch, pitching the rockers forward. Although the power switch is off, a row of ceiling fans rotates faster than ever. Planters brimming with blossoms crash to the floor, scattering blossoms, dirt, and roots.

It's impossible for Suzanne to mentally decipher their words, with vocal bursts firing simultaneously from Addy's ghost and Madelaine's spirit. It's a frenetic scene as Bimini senses the chaos about to be unleashed.

Suzanne lowers her head, covers her ears. "If there's something to interpret here, Cal, I'll leave it to you."

"Guilt," Calpurnia offers. "If I had to guess. They're letting it go."

"That makes sense. And whether or not it's true, it makes me feel better."

"Come now, time to open the portal."

When their bare feet step onto the sand, Suzanne watches rows and rows of sea oats sway furiously, as far as the eye can see, infused with energy and expectation. She's reminded again that this moment is unprecedented. Usually, following high tide, the water of the Mississippi Sound is docile and still. But that's not the scenario tonight.

Suzanne walks several hundred steps to ensure she's standing on or near the Lafountain's sacred ground. As the sea breeze picks up, the waves intensify. Suzanne retrieves the gold pointer from Mimi's roughly carved wooden box. Distanced far enough from the wave action, she draws the pentagram in the sand, ensuring three points at the top, then two at the bottom. She then follows the marking with the charcoal salt. Suzanne places rose petals along the drawn lines before closing the circle. White candles at the pentacle's five points miraculously remain lit despite the wind gusts. Suzanne raises her arms to the heavens and calls on air, fire, water, earth, and spirit for energy and assistance.

At first, Suzanne chants slowly, then much quicker and louder as the wind increases: "Spiritus reditus in pace, spiritus reditus in pace, spiritus reditus in pace, spiritus reditus in pace . . ."

Calpurnia observes from the dunes nearby, admiring Suzanne's renaissance—from a nubile spellcaster to a full-fledge enchantress, qualified to execute one of the most compelling hoodoo spells ever crafted.

Suzanne faces the direction of the water, her arms extended. Her embrace includes the magnitude of a blood-red moon, now providing a well-lit pathway for trapped ghosts and lingering spirits. "Go in peace, my Addy. Max will never, ever hurt anyone again."

When the jellyfish glisten with unearthly energy, a magical symphony of the Earth's energy boosts an enormous wind gale above Suzanne, then slams through her mid-section so forcibly that she ends the spell face-down in the sand, her breath momentarily taken.

Addy's journey into the afterlife takes place less than a mile from where a tidal wave swept her into the Gulf's angry waters sixty-six years ago to the date. In the indomitable fashion expected of Adelaide Lafountain Lamar, her crossing is as quixotic as her life. Yes, even her death.

Realizing the completeness of what has occurred, Suzanne kneels in the sand, her tears both joyful and sad. Once a trapped ghost enters the ether—there's no turning back.

Calpurnia, nearly hidden by a six-foot sand dune, yells when she realizes one final step remains. "Stand up, Suzanne. Now! Time to close the spell. Do you see what's happening?" she shouts.

A spirit wind whips up the energy of a thousand trapped ghosts, now soaring out to sea, lifted with the anomalous development of a raging riptide at 2 a.m. Within moments, a massive star far to the east flashes brightly as waves crash along the shore, nearly drenching them both.

"If you don't close the spell," Calpurnia insists, hurrying to Suzanne's side. "This madness can last for hours. The deed is done. Time to end it."

"I'm waiting for Madelaine's spirit to cross. I didn't say her name during the spell. Did she leave? I don't want to close it until my mother crosses. If that's what she chooses."

"Her spirit has drifted back and forth for years, making an appearance, then disappearing when necessary. Your mother's spirit has never been trapped, Suzanne. She chose at her death to come and go. To be near you."

Suzanne respectfully listens, retraces her steps, and retrieves the candles that have lost their flames. She gathers what's left of the rose petals and buries a handful deep in the sand to seal the spell. After brushing away the lines of the pentagram, she announces to the west, south, east, and north, "We are done. With no harm to none."

I'd never have resisted conjure for so long if I'd only known the power of what awaited me.

Suzanne lights the logs already arranged in the firepit. She and Calpurnia collapse in the Adirondack chairs to await the sunrise. Still damp from the giant waves crashing on the shore, they huddle underneath quilts, for a chill lingers though it's nearly September. As the glimmer of a fresh new day encroaches, joy and contentment infuse Suzanne's being. "I feel it. Addy's finally at peace," she says.

While she drifts toward a twilight sleep, Suzanne imagines a spirit placing an elegant heirloom bracelet atop the right arm of her chair. But she floats into a deeper sleep when she hears a newborn's wailing cry—in the distance.

Epilogue

After the Cross-Over

Suzanne's cell rings, jarring her. She doesn't remember having her phone with her last night. Perhaps Calpurnia placed it on her chair before slipping away in the pre-dawn hour. It's Maureen. When she moves to answer it, something on the chair's armrest tumbles into the sand.

Annoyed, she answers, "Yes?"

"Is Max with you? I've been trying to reach him for hours."

"No, I haven't seen him since he stormed out of the house. Yesterday." Suzanne scoots forward in the deep-seated chair and surveys the area. It looks like a tropical storm blew through the west end of the beach—flattened dunes, uprooted sea oats, scattered dried seaweed, bits of oyster shells, and overturned patio furniture.

"Do you know what's happening with him?" Maureen asks, her voice thin and shaky.

"Honey, I wouldn't know where to begin. But if I *do* hear from your boss . . ." She considers hanging up, then changes her mind. "Some advice? Consider him gone for good."

"That's rude of you," Maureen says. "Given my present circumstances."

"You're speaking in riddles . . ."

"No, ma'am. I'm speaking clearly. I'm in Mexico, waiting for Max, just like we planned. But it's been days since we last spoke. And I'm thinking . . . yeah . . . I've been played."

This woman's got some nerve.

Suzanne twists around in her chair to locate what fell into the sand seconds ago.

Between breathless sobs, Maureen stutters, "But I need to do . . . the right thing."

"Take a breath," Suzanne says.

"Under Max's orders, I've been siphoning your investment fund for months," Maureen blurts her confession, confirming Suzanne's suspicions.

"You do realize, of course, that I'm fully aware of this. I've already contacted my attorney to begin proceedings against you."

"No . . . no, don't do that. Please. About an hour ago, I transferred the money back into your account, including the interest Max earned."

What a grand gesture. How about the truth?

Suzanne believes Max and Maureen were forced to terminate their original plan to drain the only account Max could access when a forged withdrawal notice got swept up in a wind gust. Probably prompted by Jack, since he was at the beach house that day. Calpurnia found it nearly glued against the trunk of a palm tree after cleansing the house for the umpteenth time. She burned it during sage smudging.

Click—the call disconnects. Suzanne stands, and when she steps away from the Adirondack chair, she sees a gorgeous African amethyst bracelet glistening in the sunlight. When she brushes the sand from its marcasite detail, she realizes it's the same bracelet she noticed in Max's bedroom.

Suzanne places the bracelet on her wrist and calls Calpurnia, who, naturally, doesn't answer. Seeking a further explanation, she wonders if Jack's at Shaggy's, so she walks along the shoreline to the pub, admiring the sailboats drifting in the Sound.

She spots Jack waving from his favorite corner on the upper deck, smartly tucked under an umbrella tilted against the sun. It appears Jack is visible to others today, because a waitress is fawning over him.

"Your face is glowing, love. Good news to share?" He raises two fingers toward the bar, signaling for another round. "You look like a different person."

She considers her sixteen-month journey, culminating successfully in the past few hours. "I feel reborn," she says. "Mimi Addy crossed, of that I'm certain. And thank God for Calpurnia, who reminded me to close the spell before things got out of hand."

Two Blue Moons arrive at the table, orange slices included.

"And Max appears to be long gone," she says. She smiles, then sips her beer.

"I knew you'd be fabulous. Why wouldn't you? After all, you're a Lafountain." He looks at his phone and notices a news alert on the Associated Press app. "Seems a yacht explosion off the coast of Ft. Lauderdale early this morning created a mess. Says here that the Coast Guard is continuing its search, but divers hold little hope of locating survivors."

"Hmm . . . wonder where the yacht was headed?" Suzanne's eyes roll as she looks across the Sound toward the east.

"Best report I've had all day," Jack says. "Deserves a toast, don't you think?"

"Absolutely." Suzanne taps her tall, chilled glass against Jack's, who pretends to sip.

"Here's to eternal love," he says. "Beginning in this world, and . . ."

"Continuing into the next," Suzanne completes his thought.

She couldn't have crafted a better segue to ask Jack a couple of questions.

"I need answers. About Madelaine."

"Looks like you've already found one," Jack says, pointing to the bracelet.

"It's hers?"

Jack nods. "It became Madelaine's. But I distinctly remember the day Jeanne presented Addy with the bracelet for additional protection. On her wedding day."

Suzanne sips her beer, assimilating more information about her family that knows no end.

"Whom do you believe left it behind? As often as Madelaine now reveals herself to me, it seems her spirit could have . . . should have . . . already passed it on. Any idea?"

"I don't know." Jack squints hard at the sun shifting higher in the sky. "We don't always see the whole picture, love. After Addy died in Hurricane George, that wretched storm of '47 that stirred up from nowhere, everything changed. Esty had already located Madelaine and started adoption proceedings after learning her sister's marriage had been annulled. She dropped out of college to raise the child. Sadly, no one felt it prudent to share this information with Addy."

"Good God," she says. "Was her papa okay with this?"

"Certainly not. James Sr. disowned her from inheriting one single dime from the Lafountain estate. She and Cash struggled for years . . ."

"Stop. Right now," Suzanne interrupts. "What do you mean, Esty and Cash?"

"Sorry, guess I left that out. They married shortly after Addy's death. Anyway, they struggled to raise Madelaine because she proved to be a handful. Even as a teen, she was expelled from boarding schools that Mimi paid for because she refused to give up folk magick. Madelaine gave birth to you, love, while still in college."

Suzanne's heart fills with sadness for her mother. Despite

their conflicted relationship, hearing the details of her mother's early struggle to make sense of her life is devastating.

"Why do you think she was so troubled?"

Jack's countenance appears to weaken as a blue aura materializes, first around his face, then spreading to his arms and his hands. He pauses before answering. "Often, a hopeless cycle begins when a child's conceived amidst the throes of violence. Perhaps Madelaine's only purpose was to bring you into the world—so *you* could fulfill a prophecy that she could only imagine."

Her eyes brimming with tears, Suzanne nods and slowly smiles.

"Since my clock is ticking, love, 'least for this go around, there's probably one more thing I need to mention . . ."

She squeezes the last bit of orange juice into her beer glass and listens.

"After Farrah's birth, Madelaine signed adoption papers entitling Jay and Sophie Lamar to raise Farrah. I always assumed that Esty pressured her to do that. Afterward, Madelaine became estranged from everyone. She spent a lifetime carrying the cross of Addy's vengeance."

What a mess. If only Addy hadn't been forced to give up Madelaine.

Generations later, the resounding impact of such a pivotal decision ordered by the Lafountain patriarch, who chose money and prestige over his family's future contentment and safety, still packs a devastating punch.

"Man, I get it. Talk about sins of the father," Suzanne says. "Madelaine, me . . . Addy, Mimi Jeanne, Louisa, even Farrah, and God knows who else: We're all attached for eternity. And, naturally, that includes you, Jack."

He grimaces at the sun. "Quite a club you've joined, dear—our connection in death—perhaps more potent than the one shared in life."

"Is it possible that Madelaine contributed more to honor her legacy . . . in death, compared to when she was alive? By looking after the ghosts of Farrah and Grace?"

Jack doesn't answer. He's far too concerned with his disintegrating countenance to respond.

When an achingly familiar scent of patchouli and jasmine drifts by, Suzanne gasps as a strand of Madelaine's burnt-umber hair tickles her cheek. She brushes it away quickly, believing her imagination is getting the best of her. But when she hears the awkward sound of platform heels pounding the wooden-planked deck, along with a forlorn infant's wail, Suzanne chokes on her drink.

Madelaine didn't cross over. Does Grace remain here, too?

Reaching for Jack, although she knows her touch will melt through him, she asks, "Why?"

"Love. It's that simple, my beloved enchantress. It's your grandmother's final gesture of gratitude—in case you need assistance along your journey. Madelaine's spirit will come and go, for that remains her choice. But Addy's crossing is final. And so is Farrah's."

"And baby Grace?"

"She's coming with me. For now. Farrah's waiting."

As tears well in her eyes, Suzanne says, "Thank you, Jack, for everything. One more toast before you go?"

"To love," Jack whispers, as he gently places Louisa's marcasite wedding ring in the palm of Suzanne's left hand.

Then, Jack filters away.

Jeanne Lafountain's Spell Book

August 1944

5 a.m.

Didn't sleep last night. Or the night before. I sit here in my shed, trying to gather a spell. To protect Addy. Guide her and keep her from further harm, now only hours away from reciting her wedding vows.

There's no conjure strong enough. No magick to keep her safe from the evil of her rapist.

I blame myself. For not demanding that she stay home that night . . . Addy . . . so close to her summer's end. So excited to return to Newcomb with graduation around the corner.

What's worse than all of this? Not standing up *to* my husband, James. Not standing up *for* my granddaughter. Not heeding Addy's despair.

I am a coward, Addy. And so very ashamed that I let you down.

All I can offer you now is Louisa's amethyst bracelet, hewn by her Choctaw father when he was forced to hide in plain sight. Crafted to keep your great-grandmother's secret safe from prying eyes and judgmental cotton planters.

May it shield you along your journey, Addy. You must promise to pass it along to *your* daughter when you are blessed with one.

And may all the Lafountain enchantresses who follow embrace its powers.

END

About Atmosphere Press

Founded in 2015, Atmosphere Press was built on the principles of Honesty, Transparency, Professionalism, Kindness, and Making Your Book Awesome. As an ethical and author-friendly hybrid press, we stay true to that founding mission today.

If you're a reader, enter our giveaway for a free book here:

SCAN TO ENTER
BOOK GIVEAWAY

If you're a writer, submit your manuscript for consideration here:

SCAN TO SUBMIT
MANUSCRIPT

And always feel free to visit Atmosphere Press and our authors online at atmospherepress.com. See you there soon!

About the Author

Photo credit: Bloom Photography

Deborah Trahan is a writer, educator, and author of the novel *A Southern Enchantress*. She is a lifelong beach lover, now living her dream only steps from the Gulf Coast's crystal-white sand, where her tropical garden provides joy and inspiration. When she's not plotting new ideas for her next writing project, Deborah relaxes on her garden swing suspended from a huge live oak tree with her husband, sipping her favorite blueberry wine cultivated and aged in Mississippi. Her golden retriever, Bimini, who enjoys several cameo appearances in her debut novel, is often by her side.